The U

MJ White is the pseudonym of bestselling author Miranda Dickinson, author of twelve books, including six Sunday Times bestsellers. Her books have been translated into ten languages, selling over a million copies worldwide. A long time lover of crime fiction, the Cora Lael Mysteries is her debut crime series. She is a singer-songwriter, host of weekly Facebook Live show, Fab Night In Chatty Thing.

Also by MJ White

A Cora Lael Mystery

The Secret Voices
The Silent Child
Leave No Trace
The Deadly Echoes
The Unspoken Truth

MJ WHITE

THE
UNSPOKEN
TRUTH

hera

First published in the United Kingdom in 2024 by

Hera Books
Unit 9 (Canelo), 5th Floor
Cargo Works, 1-2 Hatfields
London SE1 9PG
United Kingdom

A CIP catalogue record for this book is available from the British Library.

Print ISBN 978 1 80436 711 7
Ebook ISBN 978 1 80436 710 0

This book is a work of fiction. Names, characters, businesses, organizations, places and events are either the product of the author's imagination or are used fictitiously. Any resemblance to actual persons, living or dead, events or locales is entirely coincidental.

Look for more great books at www.herabooks.com

Printed and bound in Great Britain by Clays Ltd, Elcograf S.p.A.

1

For those who feel invisible,

And those who speak up against hate.

This story is for you.

Nay, if I turn mine eyes upon myself,
I find myself a traitor with the rest

King Richard III, Act IV, Scene I
William Shakespeare

Prologue

Transcript of text conversation, Evidence no: CN/097/SSCID

Bad news.

I heard.

Can we appeal?

Unlikely. Too many resources given to it already.

But if she talks?

She won't.

How do you know? Press will be sniffing round, throwing cash. She'll take it.

They hate her. They always have. Stop worrying.

What if she sues?

What with? She lost everything when she was sent down.

But if someone thinks she has a case they could persuade her.

Nobody wants her back. Nobody's going to give a shit about her side of the story.

I need to see you. Tonight?

No. Too soon.

When then?

I'll call you.

When, babe? I miss you.

Don't start. Give it a week. I'll call you. Don't text me again till I call you, okay?

Okay. But if you don't call, I'm going to come to yours.

I'll call.

You'd better.

[Conversation ends]

ONE

SHONA

It's bright in London this afternoon. The sun hurts my eyes as we emerge onto the ancient stone steps. Funny, I've seen this location so many times on news reports over the years that it feels like I've been here before. But it's alien, too, with the sun and the camera flashes and the crush of bodies jostling to get to me.

'Shame!' someone yells from behind the crowd.

'Murderer!' another screams.

I'm free. But will I ever be free of them?

Alan, my barrister, raises his hand and the press vultures hush. A sea of mobile phones and microphones swells towards us.

'Justice has been served today,' he states, his deep voice clear above their clamour.

It's the voice I've heard for the last three days, as I've watched the Appeal Court consider my case. Strong, velvet-soft, insistent. A voice I've put my faith in. He told me he sings opera in his spare time. I can imagine him taking centre-stage, silencing everyone. Like he is now, today's stage a world away from the one he sings on.

'My client has protested her innocence from the outset, maintaining her dignity through the long years of her wrongful imprisonment. The verdict today proves what Ms Pickton, her family and her community have known all along: that she was innocent of the crime of which she was convicted. Today, a serious miscarriage of justice has been righted. I would like to thank Mrs Justice Margaret Greene for her careful, wise and steady consideration of Ms Pickton's appeal, and both legal teams in the case for their fair and respectful dealings that led to this significant verdict.'

Before we went into court, I'd asked him if I should say something, if we won. But Alan suggested he should do it for me. Now I'm standing before the swathes of unsmiling journalists, the jeers and shouts of the protestors continuing beyond them, I'm glad he's talking for both of us. It doesn't matter that we won – that I won't be returning to prison after nine years of hell. They still think I'm guilty. They convicted me in their newspapers long before the courts ever did, and they won't change their minds now. I know their sort. The games they play. They'll write their stories with doubt in the tail, a last-line sting leaving readers with a lie.

'I have a prepared statement to read on behalf of my client.' Alan opens the folded sheet of paper with a flourish, as the cameras click and flash like quickening heartbeats. 'For the nine years of my wrongful imprisonment, I've maintained my innocence. I should never have served a second of it. I should have been believed...'

Their phones and mics are trained on my legal counsel, but their eyes remain on me. On the steps of the famous law courts, I feel exposed.

'...Now, thanks to today's decision by the Court of Appeal, I can finally start to rebuild my life. I would like to thank my legal counsel, Mr Alan Gilles, KC, and his team, who have worked tirelessly and never stopped believing in me. I hope that lessons have been learned from my case, and that these will inform future investigations carried out by South Suffolk Police. Thank you to my family, my community and those who have fought so long for my sentence to be quashed.'

My words sound different in his voice. Good, just different. He's added some of his own, as we agreed, shifting things around, adding depth and authority in that velvet tone of his, to make sure nothing I say can be twisted.

4

Except it will be, won't it?

I force my eyes to meet theirs. I won't look away for a moment.

I didn't kill Cassandra Norton.

I wasn't even on the street where she died.

But I know who was.

And if they come for me, I'll be ready.

TWO

CORA

'Morning, Doc.'

'Morning, Joss.'

'Lovely day for it.'

'It is indeed. Anyone else here yet?'

'Nope.' The bearded man smiled as he opened the large steel gate. 'You're the first. In you come.'

'Cheers.'

Dr Cora Lael smiled and raised her hand in thanks to Joss Lovell as she drove onto the St Columba Street site. Parking in her usual spot by the mobile building that served as a gatehouse, a reception and an office, she got out and opened the boot of her car, reaching in to fetch a large plastic box.

'Let me get that,' Joss called, jogging across from the gate he'd just locked.

'It's fine, honestly.'

'Fine it might be, but I do the lifting around here.' He shot her a wink as he swung the box out of the boot as if it was empty, not packed to the brim with teaching materials, paper and books. 'You should know that by now. It's easier to just let me get on with it.'

In the four weeks Cora had been working with Joss Lovell, she had learned three things: one, that he was hardly ever without a smile; two, that he usually got his own way, whether by charm or cunning or a mixture of both; and three, he was true to his word, no matter what.

The HappyKid Project was a voluntary initiative, co-founded by her boss – and friend – Dr Tris Noakes, and Joss Lovell, outreach lead for the Suffolk Gypsy and Traveller Communities. While its current operation was barely a month old, it had been meticulously curated over several years between South Suffolk Local Education Authority's Educational Psychology Unit and two settled gypsy and traveller sites in Ipswich and Felixstowe.

The project aimed to provide educational and personal wellbeing support to the children on the sites, maintaining continuity when problems arose that might otherwise have kept them from school. When the green light was eventually given, Cora had been one of the first to volunteer, keen to broaden the help available to local children from her professional standpoint, and knowing what it meant to Tris from her personal one. Two teams of volunteer teachers had just been recruited to swell the ranks and the services offered, plus a group of SENCO support workers.

It had been hard fought for and hard won, a fact not lost on Cora and evident in the attitude and stance of both Tris and Joss.

Stiff resistance from some factions in the local council had delayed the project for over a year from its planned start date. They argued that it would divert funding away from children in mainstream education, supposedly short-changing them while boosting the interests of a far smaller community. Cora suspected it had more to do with a tiny but vocal group of councillors whose right-wing leanings had become more pronounced in recent months, no doubt brought to the surface by the prospect of imminent council elections. Even more of a reason to make it a success, Tris had argued – to show that local education authority units would not bow to discriminatory – or political – pressure.

Whatever the politics surrounding it, the project itself was what drew Cora – the chance for greater outreach to learn how best to tailor services that met not only the needs of children within gypsy and traveller communities, but also the traditions and beliefs held by their families.

She followed Joss across the site to a small grey portacabin that served as the classroom. It had been donated to the project by a local haulage firm, its owner the grandson of a Roma woman who had been involved in the establishment of the permanent site just outside Felixstowe, twenty years ago. Inside, it had been painted a sunshine yellow, with orange and red seats around pale blue tables. Cora always felt as if she was walking into a sunset over the sea when she came here. One side of the space had squashy bright orange floor cushions and yellow beanbags – a gift from the St Just WI, orchestrated by Cora's mother, Sheila.

'The kiddies need somewhere cosy and bright to sit,' Sheila had told her friends in the group when she'd presented her idea to them. 'Sunny seats for happy kids.'

Cora smiled now as she helped Joss unpack the box and set out its contents across the tables. It heartened her that Sheila had reclaimed her voice and her drive, lost for several years in the wake of Cora's father's death. The cosy seating area was testament to her mum's renewed hope and life – and the perfect setting for wellbeing chats with the kids who attended the project sessions. In the four weeks she had volunteered here, Cora had experienced several significant conversations with the children, the relaxed and happy environment fostering trust and bravery that a grey, faceless space might not have inspired.

'How many are we expecting today?' she asked Joss, storing the empty box behind a fabric screen that also served as an exhibition area for the children's work.

'Twelve, I hope. Should be a good one.' He smiled. 'Word's spreading.'

'That's good to know,' Cora replied. 'Now we're finally up and running we need to make sure we're delivering what we promised.'

Joss chuckled. 'You sound like Dr Tris now.'

Cora shrugged. 'Occupational hazard when I work with him every day.'

'What is?' The cheery smile of Dr Tris Noakes, director of the Educational Psychology Team, met them as Cora and Joss turned.

'That I'm sounding like you.'

Tris feigned horror at this. 'Bloody hell, that's a scary thought. Joss, if she starts banging on incessantly about architecture or baked goods, send for help!'

'No fear of that,' Cora replied, with a grin. 'Although my mum did send these.' She pulled a large Tupperware box packed with homemade rocky road bars from her bag, a gift from Sheila Lael delivered yesterday after Sunday lunch at a country pub.

The director's face lit up like a kid in a sweet shop. 'I love your mum, did I say?'

Joss peered into the box and whistled as Tris removed the lid. 'I think I might love your mum, too.'

'Mitts off, you two,' Cora laughed. 'They're for the children.'

'Maybe nobody will turn up today after all.' Joss shared a conspiratorial grin with Tris, giving Cora a glimpse of the cheeky schoolkids they had once been together. 'And if that happens, we can console ourselves with *these*…'

'You're both impossible.' Cora laughed when Tris and Joss bowed to her. 'Who else are we expecting today?'

'Merryn from the SENCO team and Sam from the teachers. They'll be on the project tables, so if you can man the wellbeing area, I'll step in where needed.'

'Great.'

Ten minutes later, Merryn Hayle and Sam Fitzpatrick joined them as the first of the children began to arrive. Joss welcomed the kids at the door, while Sam manned a craft table making pom-pom animals and Merryn led a reading comprehension exercise. Two young sisters, Maire and Trinity, headed straight for Cora, keen to show her their latest Kandi bead bracelets. Last week, they had revealed their favourite craft, making brightly coloured plastic bead bracelets peppered with names and messages, to trade with their friends.

'I traded this one with my cousin,' Maire said, pushing up her jumper sleeve to reveal a blue, white and gold beaded bracelet at the head of a group of five. It bore the phrase *ALWAYS 4 EVA*. 'And this one I made this morning.'

U MATTER was spelled out between red and yellow beads, a bee charm hanging from one side.

I'm not to worry – a whisper of the young girl's voice sounded from the happy beads. *Ma said so.*

Cora betrayed none of what she'd heard in the steady smile she wore, but she noted the flutter of nerves that leapt in her stomach as the young girl's thought-voice repeated.

Her unique ability to sense emotional echoes from objects had characterised her life since she was sixteen; what had once 'othered' her in friendship groups she had now explored and harnessed in recent years. She had become a police consultant expert alongside her day job and was learning to push the boundaries of the audible fingerprints she sensed from objects, building three-dimensional soundscapes around them in her mind that revealed so much more than simply emotional thought.

Here, as part of her work for The HappyKid Project, her ability provided useful insight into the young lives of the children she met. Through the items they brought to show her and their belongings, she had access to all manner of thoughts – concerns and triumphs, questions and dreams. It gave her a connection to their lives that none of her colleagues could easily access – a privilege she didn't take lightly.

The flurry of nerves appeared again, and Cora noted the word that summoned them with each repeat of the whispered voice: *worry*. As she'd pressed into her ability, physical manifestations of the emotional echoes had begun to accompany the hidden voices. It helped Cora gauge the strength of emotion beyond that of the volume level of the audible voices, even if the visceral experience was often unpleasant. She had long learned to accept that discomfort was a necessary companion of her insight.

U R STRONG – read the next bracelet, the white letter beads surrounded by lines of alternate pink and lilac.

It'll blow over – insisted Maire's thought-voice.

'I like this one,' Cora said. 'That's a great message, too.'

'Pink and purple are my favourites,' Maire beamed, her smile free of any outward sign of concern.

'I like the green and black,' Trinity added. 'Like Elphaba in *Wicked*.'

The conversation shifted to colours and music and Cora allowed it to flow uninterrupted. At this stage, the emotional echoes were nothing more than markers for her – to be noted and moved on from. Building strong relationships with physical conversations was far more important here than anything she could sense.

As the girls chattered on, Cora glanced across the packed classroom towards Joss and Tris, who were engaged in deep conversation by the door. Concern creased Tris' brow as he listened to his friend, the two men keeping their voices low beneath the industrious hum of the room.

'Dr Cora?'

Trinity was smiling when Cora looked back. 'Is he your boyfriend?'

'Who?'

'Dr Tris?'

Flushing a little at the unexpected question, Cora laughed. 'No, he's my boss.'

'Maybe she likes Joss instead,' Maire exclaimed, eyes twinkling at the thought of scandal.

'Maybe she'll marry them both,' Trinity added, Cora's feigned gasp of shock causing the sisters to collapse in giggles on the floor cushions.

Laughing, Cora shook her head at them as their mirth continued, earning her a quizzical look from Tris across the room, which she returned with a helpless shrug.

Sudden shouts from beyond the windows of the classroom caused everyone to look up, the conversation and laughter snatched from the room. Joss raised a hand to gesture for calm, then nodded at Tris, who followed him outside.

Cora, Merryn and Sam exchanged glances, quickly returning to their young charges to reassure them. But the children kept their eyes on the door, all smiles stolen.

Then came a bang, dense and heavy against the side of the portacabin. A shattering of glass followed as the door flew open, revealing a panicked Tris.

'Everyone out!' he yelled. 'Quickly, follow me!'

Dazed, Cora took the hands of the sisters and hurried outside after the other children and teachers.

They emerged into thick billows of acrid, grey smoke as more shattering glass and loud shouts erupted around them.

'Get the kids to safety!' Joss yelled over his shoulder as he and a group of men raced towards the source of the smoke.

'What's happening?' Trinity wailed, grasping Cora's hand as they ran towards the back of the site.

'Don't worry,' Cora replied, her own shock channelled into determination to spirit the children away from the commotion. 'Let's follow Tris.'

Shouts filled the air, both actual and emotional, as panic swept across the rows of mobile homes and vans. Cora muted as many of the hidden voices as she could, but the sheer force of fear rushing at her made navigating the noise impossible.

'Over here!' A young woman in the distance waved from the entrance to a squat, steel shipping container.

Cora, Merryn, Sam and the children raced towards it. As they hurried inside, Tris drew alongside Cora.

'What's happening?'

'People at the gate,' Tris managed through ragged breaths. 'One of the vans is on fire.' He pulled his phone from his back pocket. 'I'm calling the police. Stay with the kids.'

Before Cora could protest, he ran back towards the smoke and noise.

'Inside,' the young woman urged, slamming the steel door shut after them.

Within the dimly lit metal space the terrified sobs of the children echoed and swelled, the hidden voices of their fear fuelling Cora's own horror. Forcing the noise away, she joined the teachers as they huddled together with the children.

Who had attacked the site, in broad daylight, with no warning?

And why?

THREE

MINSHULL

'*Shit…*'

DS Rob Minshull grabbed his jacket and a set of pool car keys as he and DC Dave Wheeler sprinted out of the CID office.

'I *told* you this would happen,' Wheeler panted. 'Not even twenty-four hours she's been out and it's started already.'

'We don't know it's connected,' Minshull returned, slamming through the double doors at the end of the corridor and descending the stone steps two at a time. Wheeler's footsteps echoed close behind as they headed to the fire escape that led to South Suffolk Police HQ's car park.

'Bollocks is it not,' Wheeler scoffed, squinting as the bright sunlight beyond the fire door temporarily dazzled him. 'I said if she came home, they'd be after her.'

'But she isn't even there, Dave. Protection found her a flat in the town. She wasn't likely to return to the site, even though the community invited her home.'

'With respect, Sarge, it doesn't matter. Bastards like that don't need the truth; they throw their missiles first and ask questions *never*.'

Snapping the seatbelt of the dusty pool car across his body and starting the engine, Minshull wished he didn't agree. Since the news had broken of Shona Pickton's Appeal Court victory, he'd been dreading recriminations from the tiny, vocal minority dominating the press coverage of the case.

While it shouldn't be true, the cruel fact was that Shona had been a target long before a court of law convicted her of the murder of Cassandra Norton, nine years ago. The moment a link was uncovered between her and the local settled gypsy and traveller community, her fate was sealed. The press, keen to vilify the community at every opportunity, had taken great delight in painting Shona Pickton as a villain, tainting the case with their vicious, bigoted opinions. Since the first suggestion of an appeal, thirteen months ago, resentment and fury had been steadily building, both online and in local paper opinion pieces; an incendiary mix that could only lead to one outcome.

Incendiary in literal terms, it transpired.

The call had come in twenty minutes ago: first responders on the scene reporting one caravan completely gutted by fire, and neighbouring buildings and vehicles damaged by bricks thrown onto the St Columba Street site. The fire service was already in attendance, but the residents of the permanent traveller site on the edge of Felixstowe were reeling. The thugs responsible for the attack were long gone; a blessing, all things considered. But that didn't mean the people living there were safe.

Minshull was grateful for small mercies where he could find them. But what caused the panic now coursing through him as he sped through Ipswich, was the source of the call.

Dr Tris Noakes.

Dr Cora Lael's superior and colleague – who had become a friend of Minshull's in the few years he'd known Cora. If Tris was there, Cora might be too. And while Minshull knew his concern should be for everyone on the site, the prospect of his close friend being in danger terrified him.

He vaguely recalled Cora talking about the voluntary project she and Tris had helped set up at St Columba Street. She'd been full of it during one of their regular Sunday morning runs along the promenade in Felixstowe, buzzing about the project finally receiving the green light after months of delays and organisational red tape. She'd glowed with it – which was partly responsible for Minshull's patchy recollections of the details. It had been so much fun to watch his friend sparkling with excitement that her words had passed him by.

Was Cora there today? He couldn't remember her naming specific days for the project sessions. What if she was hurt, or the children in her care injured?

A fire engine and a first responder vehicle flanked the entrance to the site, alongside two patrol cars and a police support van, their lights blazing. Given recent resource problems that had beset the rural force, Minshull found it heartening that so many of his emergency services colleagues had been able to respond quickly to this.

But any relief he might have felt vanished when he saw the state of Cora's car, parked near the reception building nearest the front gate. Although far enough from the smouldering remains of the caravan, it had been in range for the missiles thrown from the gate. Its side and rear windows were smashed, while angry dents had been punched into the length of its bodywork.

Wheeler tensed alongside him as they passed under the police tape and headed onto the site, stepping carefully over shards of broken glass and brick fragments. A uniformed PC talking to a tall, bearded man raised a hand when she saw Minshull and Wheeler approaching.

'Here they are now. Morning, Sarge, Constable.' PC Steph Lanehan's brief smile was as grim as Minshull felt. 'This is Mr Joss Lovell, senior project worker on the site.'

Minshull nodded his acknowledgement, reciprocated by the man. 'How are you doing, sir?'

'Not the best,' Joss Lovell replied, his tone flat, his eyes bearing the tell-tale stare Minshull had witnessed in shock victims before.

'I can imagine. Anyone hurt?'

'Not that we can see.'

'That's good to know, at least.'

'Is it? It could have been worse, but what we had was bad enough. And it won't be the end...'

Watching the team of firefighters dousing the burned remains of the caravan, Minshull wished he could summon

16

better words to comfort people in situations like this. Dave Wheeler was a past master at it, always armed with the right things to say. Minshull, conversely, stuck to what he knew best: questions and facts. 'Who else was in the vicinity of the attack?'

'Seven families in their homes, twelve kids in the classroom back there.' Joss jabbed a finger over his shoulder. 'Plus the volunteers of the project, who don't live onsite.'

'And the owner of the caravan?'

'That one's been empty a while. It had been offered to a friend, but they never took us up on it.'

Minshull nodded. The potential for disaster hung heavy over them, like the smoke that stung their eyes and caught in their throats. 'Where is everyone else?'

'I've gathered them together at the back of the site. The paramedics are checking them over and my aunties are doling out tea.' Joss led the way without being asked, Minshull and Wheeler trailing in his wake.

Minshull had passed the St Columba Street site many times on his drive into Felixstowe to meet Cora, but this was the first time he'd set foot within its boundaries. It was larger than it appeared from the gates – a blessing, probably, given this morning's attack. The static caravans and mobile homes were arranged in neat rows, some with seating and planters outside as makeshift gardens. Windchimes and brightly coloured windmills caught the smoke-filled breeze, plastic strip curtains billowing from open doorways and wary dogs eyeing the detectives as they walked past.

'Have you received any threats recently?' Minshull asked. 'Anyone with a grudge against you, or who might want to cause you trouble?'

'People who hate us, you mean? Take your pick.'

It was a daft question, of course. As Minshull struggled to formulate a decent reply, Lovell took pity on him.

'We've had no trouble for a couple of years. It's been quiet, to be honest, which is unusual. I thought we'd more or less reached a truce locally. As much as we ever can.'

'I understand.'

'I appreciate you trying to. But let's not split hairs, DS Minshull. You know who's responsible as much as I do. The bastards behind their keyboards and the wannabe dictators hiding in the council chambers.'

'And the Court of Appeal?'

Joss snorted. 'It's nothing to do with us.'

'Has Ms Pickton made contact with anyone on this site?'

'You'll have to ask them.'

'But you've heard nothing personally?'

'No. And I don't expect to.'

'You don't think she'll come here?'

'With respect, that's a bloody stupid question. Look at what they did! Would *you* risk coming here after that?'

'Well, no, I...'

'Shona Pickton lived here years ago, before she joined her ma in a housing project in town. The community offered her the use of the van for her return, but it was clear from the outset that wouldn't be appropriate. Your lot arranged accommodation for her instead. I don't know how the bastard journalists got wind of our offer – or if they even knew at all. It makes no difference, anyway; they were always going to come gunning for us, weren't they? Whether we had her here or not. Easy target, we are. The root of all evil, according to them. And nobody ever gives a shit about countering their vile lies.'

Minshull saw it then, as plain as the homes around him: the weariness that cloaked the young man like a sea-sodden overcoat, far too heavy for his frame. The expectation of trouble from bitter experience, the fear of it coming to steal anything positive the community could achieve.

He couldn't imagine the toll that would take on you, day after day.

As the son of a detective, the worst he'd ever had to deal with was mockery from his schoolfriends. *Copper's kid... Piglet... What's your dad going to do? Arrest us?...* As a detective himself, Minshull was used to encountering hostility from certain factions of the general public. It came with the job, more so now that public trust in the police had been so eroded. But at the end of the day, he could leave it at work, his life beyond his job unaffected. What would it be like if those problems and prejudices followed you home, refusing to leave?

'We'll do everything we can to find those responsible,' he said.

The young man's eyes narrowed. 'You'll forgive me if I wait to believe you.'

Minshull conceded. Under the current circumstances he couldn't blame Joss for reserving judgement until the police delivered. The jury was out until tangible progress could be made.

And it *would* be made, Minshull promised himself.

The Cassandra Norton case was another matter entirely – one he knew would likely end up on his desk. His superior, DI Joel Anderson, had already alluded to it this morning, the shock of the attack on the St Columba Street site bringing the issue suddenly front and centre. South Suffolk Police would have to reopen the murder investigation that had wrongfully sent Shona Pickton to prison. It was unavoidable: the murderer must still be at large. With nine years having passed since the crime was committed – affording the perpetrator almost a decade of distance between themselves and police – how could Minshull hope to find the person responsible?

Minshull, Wheeler and Lovell turned a corner and the small group of adults and children came into view. Some of the children were visibly distressed, huddled together with siblings and friends, while the adults stood guard around them. At the centre of the group were Cora Lael and Tris Noakes, crouched between the children, listening to them.

Cora raised her head and met Minshull's stare with a thin-lipped smile of her own. Minshull's own relief to see her unharmed was tempered by concern that she was there at all, but he kept his personal response in check as Tris stood to greet him.

'Good to see you, DS Minshull, DC Wheeler,' Tris said, ever the oil on fractious water.

'How are you holding up?'

'Everyone is shaken, understandably. But it could have been so much worse.'

Joss glanced between the two men. 'You know each other?'

'We go way back,' Tris interjected, saving Minshull from an awkward answer. 'Rob is a good man to have on our side. Dave, too.'

Wheeler raised a hand in thanks. 'How are the kiddies? Is there anything we can do to help them?'

The project officer's frown softened at Wheeler's request. Wheeler had that effect on people. The universal 'dad' of the team, blessed with a heart of gold.

'They'll be good. Thanks.'

'I'm going to liaise with our colleagues in the fire service and work out the best way to secure the site,' Minshull said, the practicalities of the job far safer ground for him. 'I'm also going to request a patrol to remain here at least overnight tonight. It might take a while to get it happening, but the fire crews are likely to be here for the next few hours at least, so you won't be alone.'

'Will you be taking evidence?' Tris asked.

'The support officers are picking up what they can. They'll be able to do a more thorough sweep once the fire is dampened down.' He turned to Joss. 'Are you and the residents happy for that?'

'Happier than we normally are to see you.' The barest hint of a smile smoothed the barb of his reply.

As Wheeler moved towards the group, Cora left the children and joined Minshull.

'How are you?' he asked.

'Better than my car.'

'I saw. Sorry. Need a lift home?'

'No, thanks. Tris is going to drive us back later.'

'It's no trouble, honestly. We'll be done in an hour or so.'

'I'm needed here.'

'But there's not much you can do, surely? You should be at home…'

'This is our project and we're here for the children. They need our support.'

'Maybe the community should handle it from now…?'

'Thanks for your concern, but we'll work on it together. We'll be fine.'

Minshull watched her return to the children, her physical move a death knell to further discussion. It took him a moment to process. Then, smarting, he turned to Wheeler.

'We need to organise statements. And DI Anderson should be briefed with the latest developments.'

Wheeler's grim expression encapsulated all of Minshull's sentiment.

FOUR

ANDERSON

It was the shitshow he'd seen coming. But that made it no easier to face.

DI Joel Anderson did his best to keep his irritation at bay, for the sake of his team. Not their fault that this had come to a head so soon after the Appeal Court ruling. Not his, either. Only his superior, DCI Sue Taylor, should have known better. Many times, but specifically last week, she'd dismissed his concerns on the subject outright.

It won't be an issue, Joel. The conviction is secure.

Bollocks to that.

He bristled again at the memory. He'd afforded her grace to manage the impending storm, going to see her in private to raise the issue instead of taking it higher. Some thanks he got for that. She could just never admit she was wrong, could she? Bloody imperious, arrogant individual! Convinced her own case was watertight, despite the holes rapidly appearing as the Appeal Court hearing picked it open.

Anderson, on the other hand, had been only too aware of what lay ahead if the appeal landed in Shona Pickton's favour.

The attack on the St Columba Street site was a shock, though, even to him.

He'd expected vitriol from the right-wing press, especially those who had taken such delight in accusing the entire gypsy and traveller community of the Cassandra Norton murder. Pages of incendiary insinuation in the lead-up to the appeal, followed by the inevitable '*Woke British Justice System Panders to Gypsies*' headlines the moment the verdict was given. Grossly unfair, racist finger-pointing at a marginalised community denied the right to speak back.

But he hadn't expected actual violence to beat the journalists to the charge.

There were kids on that site, for crying out loud. Young families. Bairns. Something the sick bastards with their missiles and incendiary devices didn't care about. Already, he took it as a personal affront that anyone would think their actions were justified.

Not on his patch.

Not on his watch.

'But weren't you the SIO when Shona Pickton was arrested, Guv?' DC Kate Bennett's question dragged Anderson back to the CID office. It was only then that he realised he'd been subconsciously glaring out of the window at the rooftops of Ipswich stretching away from Police HQ.

'Not my circus, Kate.' The one point of solace in all this. His problem it might become, but he hadn't sent Shona Pickton down for a murder she didn't commit. That was all DCI Taylor's doing.

Bennett's confusion betrayed her assumption. Not that Anderson thought any less of her for it. Everyone who hadn't been at South Suffolk Police HQ when the Cassandra Norton murder investigation took place would assume the same thing – that Anderson had been in charge then, as he was now.

'I don't understand, Guv. When Sue Taylor became DCI, you became DI. Didn't you?'

'I did. But I spent six months as Acting DI, which you know as well as I do meant I was the bottle-washer and not the landlord. Nobody saw Rob's father's sudden retirement coming – least of all him. So DCI Taylor was promoted from DI in CID and I was fast-tracked to DI. But she didn't want me as Senior Investigating Officer, so she insisted on taking charge of the case.'

Taylor's loud protestations that Anderson lacked the necessary mettle to lead such a high-profile investigation had stung at the time. That the case had come back to bite her on the bum now was a bonus Anderson intended to enjoy.

Largely because his own assessment of the original case had been proved correct.

He would never admit it to anyone in the CID team, but Anderson had always doubted Shona Pickton's conviction. The newly appointed DCI Taylor and the high-ups reeling from DCI John Minshull's sudden departure were too keen to see a swift conclusion to the investigation, while Anderson, with his lowly Acting DI status, was never given the opportunity to voice his concern.

By rights, Sue Taylor should have had nothing to do with the active investigation, but the team were emerging from a decade of John Minshull's iron grip on operations, his insistence of maintaining control from the DI's office rather than the better-appointed space on the upper floor blurring the line of command. A precedent had been set – one that would prove difficult to challenge.

As Acting DI, Anderson had been forced to watch as Sue Taylor followed the example of her predecessor, a stubborn cuckoo in the CID nest, refusing to be ousted. The memory of that – and of the way Taylor had dined out on the success of the investigation for years afterwards – made the latest development far sweeter than it should have been.

'We'll have to reopen the case now, won't we?' Bennett's tone was cautious.

Anderson hefted a sigh as he checked his watch. 'I think it's a priority, given what's happened this morning. That's what I'm going to recommend. Whether I'm heard is anyone's guess.' He offered Bennett a grim smile. 'I may be some time in this meeting. Pray for my mortal soul, eh?'

–

His superior was stony-faced and silent when Anderson entered the meeting room. Superintendent Ian Martlesham rose from his seat to greet him, a surprisingly warm handshake throwing Anderson momentarily off guard. That the Super was here at all hinted at the seriousness of what lay ahead. Might he be the ally Anderson needed for the reopened investigation?

'Good to see you, Joel,' Martlesham barked. 'Would that it were under better circumstances.'

'Would that indeed, Sir.'

'Right, take a seat and we'll get started.'

'Sir.'

Anderson resisted the urge to glance at his immediate superior as he did so. He didn't need to see Taylor's face to know her response. Barely contained fury steamed from the DCI, her rigid posture and bitten-back silence louder than a scream.

'I know you will have heard the news regarding Shona Pickton's successful appeal. I understand the Crown has no interest in pursuing a counter motion. It is, as we suspected, a significant event for South Suffolk Constabulary. We are, and will continue to be, under scrutiny of the highest degree. So, we must act.'

'Sir.'

Martlesham gave a long sigh. 'In short, we need to put this right. Immediately.'

Taylor's knuckles whitened in her lap.

Martlesham's eyes slid to her. 'Your thoughts, DCI Taylor?'

'Whatever you think best, Sir.'

Anderson could have imagined it, but he swore he saw a tiny flicker at the corner of Martlesham's mouth.

'And yours, DI Anderson?'

'I agree, Sir. You should also be aware that this morning the St Columba Street settled traveller site in Felixstowe was attacked. Bricks and bottles thrown, a caravan set on fire. We strongly believe it's linked to the Appeal Court verdict.'

Martlesham stared out from under lowered brows. 'Linked?'

'Yes, Sir. Shona Pickton lived there for some time a few years prior to the events that led to her arrest. There had been some press speculation she might return to the community upon her release.'

'That is worrying. All the more reason to act.'

His pointed glance at DCI Taylor was stubbornly ignored. Martlesham returned the weight of his stare to Anderson.

'We'll reopen the case, as a priority. Immediately. I am requesting that all necessary resources be diverted to do this. Joel, let me know what you need in terms of manpower. I know DC Les Evans is back to work this week – a blessing for you all, I imagine. But I'm happy to request uniformed officers to be seconded to swell your ranks. You'll need help to re-examine all the statements and evidence from the original investigation.'

Taylor's body tensed at the last two words.

Anderson offered Martlesham his brightest smile. 'I appreciate that, Sir.'

'Excellent. Sue, anything else you want to add?'

'No, Sir.'

'I trust you will give DI Anderson and his team your full co-operation?'

'Of course.' Her reply was delivered through gritted teeth. Anderson wished he could have been a fly on the wall during the meeting between Sue Taylor and Ian Martlesham prior to his arrival. Oh, to see her being torn to shreds by her commanding officer! Anderson could only imagine the sparks that had flown...

'Good. I'm also going to request an independent party to oversee proceedings.'

Anderson hadn't anticipated that. Neither, it transpired, had Taylor.

'Is that necessary?' Taylor was staring now, her carefully held mask slipping.

'Yes, it's *necessary*, DCI Taylor. A serious miscarriage of justice has occurred. Our response will be scrutinised microscopically by the press and the public.'

'We did our job...'

'You sent an innocent woman to prison.'

'Shona Pickton was far from innocent...'

'The Court of Appeal disagrees.'

'I believed she was guilty.'

'You got it *wrong*.' Martlesham's sharp reply cut the air. 'And now we must do everything in our power to rectify that mistake.'

'But...' Taylor's words were silenced by her superior's raised eyebrow. 'Sir.'

He observed her for an uncomfortable moment before turning his attention to Anderson. 'I've requested two officers from the Special Investigations Team to oversee the reinvestigation. We're still working on logistics, but my hope is they'll arrive before the end of the week.'

'Sir.'

Typical, Anderson mused. Five months managing a chronically understaffed CID team and now he wouldn't be able to move for extra bodies in the office. Funny how quickly resources could be summoned by the high-ups in a public relations crisis.

'That's all. Thank you both. Joel, if you could brief your team immediately, please? I've arranged for the evidence files to be delivered to CID this afternoon. You will have an email from the records team, detailing the size of the consignment. When you receive it, let me know your estimate for extra manpower required and I'll authorise it by return.'

'Sir. Thank you, Sir.'

Anderson's pulse crashed at his temples as he strode back towards the stairs that led to the CID office. It was a ton of work he hadn't budgeted time for, but the reopening of the Cassandra Norton case now eclipsed all else. His heart was heavy with the news he carried for his team. They had barely recovered from a multiple murder case two months before. And now this?

They knew it was coming already, of course. But that made it no easier to impose upon them.

'Joel – wait!'

Anderson's spine bristled. He stopped by the door to the stairwell, but didn't look back.

Let her come here and say it to my face.

Taylor was red-cheeked and a little out of breath when she reached him. 'It's a mistake,' she hissed, any semblance of control abandoned now. 'The whole thing's a pack of lies.'

'It's a priority, Ma'am.'

'You worked on the investigation. You know we got the right person.'

'With respect, Ma'am, I was merely Acting DI at the time. It wasn't my place to have an opinion.'

She smarted at that, as he knew she would. 'You were as much a part of the investigation as the rest of us. And I don't recall you disagreeing with any of it.'

'I'm disagreeing now. As DI.'

'You will support me and your fellow officers…'

'I will do my job.' He let his words take full effect, gratified by the flap of his superior's mouth as shock stole her reply. 'Cassandra Norton's killer is still at large, and I intend to change that.'

'DI Anderson, I am still in charge.'

Anderson's smile was charged with pity. 'Of course, Ma'am. And I know you'll lead us by example. Now, if you'll forgive me, I have a briefing to organise.'

She was still staring after him when the door closed in his wake.

FIVE

MINSHULL

'Well, look what the cat dragged in.'

DC Les Evans grimaced as the CID team rose from their desks to greet him. 'Okay, whatever.'

'Lovely to have you back, matey,' DC Dave Wheeler smiled. 'We got your desk all ready for you.'

He stood back to reveal the balloon-and-streamer-wrapped desk, Evans' groan causing a swell of laughter from his colleagues.

'And we thought we'd give you a week off from cakes,' DC Kate Bennett replied with a smile, as she presented him with a large, iced cake – a jokey reference to the number of times Evans had 'cakes' called on him, a penance imposed by colleagues for being in trouble or not pulling his weight.

'A whole week off, Kate? Must be my lucky day.'

Evans received it all with dour good humour, the pronounced care with which he moved between the team a telling reminder of the injuries he was still recovering from.

Minshull watched from the edge of the room, surprised when a rogue knot of emotion appeared in his throat. The team had endured so much in the DC's absence and still hadn't really addressed the shock of their colleague falling victim to a vicious attack. His empty desk had been a stark reminder of everything they'd all lost.

Every police officer carried the spectre of loss with them, whether they admitted it or not. Everyone knew they could be one shout away from never coming home – a fact all hoped would never be anything more than a necessary devil on their shoulder. Minshull had lost colleagues when he was in Uniform. The shock of almost losing Les Evans had been a blow he never expected. The DC had been a dubious member of the team for years, the butt of many jokes and the maker of more, never more than two steps away from crossing the line and a source of near-constant irritation for his superiors. But his sudden, brutal removal from the team had revealed how vital a part of it he was – and reminded every detective in South Suffolk CID just how fragile the line was between life and death in the job.

'Sorry your desk is so tidy,' DC Drew Ellis quipped, his colleagues' laughter an instant reward. 'I expect you'll sort that quickly.'

'You know me, Drew.' Evans' voiced cracked just a little. His colleagues averted their eyes. 'And I see Dave's provided me with coffee, just the way I don't like it.'

'Cheers.' Wheeler shook his head, his wide smile absolving Evans' rudeness.

'Appreciate it,' Evans mumbled, sitting at his desk.

'Okay, now our missing limb is back, let's get on,' Minshull said. 'We'll have a briefing in five minutes, please.'

'Let's have it now.' Anderson strode into the office, pausing to clap a hand on Evans' shoulder with a smile. 'We have a new investigation that requires our immediate attention.'

Minshull watched his superior carefully as the team wheeled their desk chairs to the centre of the room. There was a fierce sense of purpose in Anderson that Minshull instantly recognised. The DI had his teeth into something – and considering he'd been summoned to a meeting with DCI Taylor and the Super, with the shock of the attack on the St Columba Street site still reverberating, Minshull would lay easy odds on what it was.

'Do you want to brief us first, Guv?' he asked, glancing at the list of notes he suspected he would no longer need to share.

'Aye, thanks.' Anderson's nod spoke a thousand words.

Minshull returned it with one of his own and held up his hand for quiet. 'Okay, everyone, settle down, please. Guv, you have the floor.'

'Cheers, Rob.' Anderson hefted a sigh designed to be seen by the team. 'No prizes for guessing what I'm about to say. The Super has requested we reopen the Cassandra Norton case, with immediate effect. The new investigation has been given the operational name of Phoenix. We'll have at least two independent investigators joining us to oversee our work and I've been promised extra bodies to assist us.' He grimaced. 'Yes, I know. Months and months with no extra help and now we'll be tripping over officers.'

Minshull and the team responded with bitter laughter. Everyone was still recovering from the workload they'd carried in DC Evans' absence, while their requests for extra assistance went ignored. The predictability of their superiors' response now made it worse.

'I won't sugar-coat this: it'll be a bastard of a job. Every piece of evidence must be gone over, every original statement checked. We have to identify the key players from last time and find people who slipped through the cracks. We'll need to talk to Ms Pickton, too, if she'll allow it. We're starting with a nine-year disadvantage, and a potential murderer still at large. But we have to get it right this time.'

The look he shared with Wheeler was telling. What had they both witnessed in this office, nine years ago? Minshull made a note to talk to Wheeler once Anderson was back at his desk.

He remembered the case, of course, albeit from afar.

He'd been in Uniform when Shona Pickton was arrested and charged with the murder of the former Miss Suffolk. It had been the first high-profile case Minshull had witnessed, and he still recalled the buzz around the station as the search for Cassandra Norton's killer dominated their work. He'd done door-to-door inquiries in the street where the twenty-two-year-old was found with a fractured skull, lying in a pool of her own blood. The coroner ruled that she had suffered a blow to her chest that caused her to fall, incurring the catastrophic skull injury when she hit her head on the way down.

The evidence against Shona Pickton had appeared to convince the original investigation – and the twelve members of the jury unanimously – that she had killed Cassandra Norton, and a threatening note in her handwriting, found in the victim's home, persuaded them that the killing had been premeditated.

Anderson slowly and meticulously detailed the key pieces of evidence, adding them without comment to a list on the large whiteboard beside Minshull's desk.

'Here's what the original investigation found. A taxi driver startled the young woman's assailant at the scene, who ran when he left his taxi to confront them. His description proved key for identifying and arresting Shona Pickton. She was described as having a light build, blonde hair tied back in a short pony-tail, wearing a black hooded sweatshirt, jogging trousers and trainers. A sighting by a woman sitting outside a pub a street away, minutes before the attack, placed Shona in the vicinity. This was followed by an anonymous tip-off from a neighbour, who claimed to have seen her running back to her apartment in a highly emotional state, wearing clothes that matched the description of the assailant's attire given by the taxi driver. Following the tip-off, Ms Pickton was arrested at her apartment, where officers discovered a black hoodie and trousers stashed at the bottom of her wardrobe. The trainers were never recovered, but the accusation was made that Ms Pickton discarded them due to what would likely have been considerable bloodstaining.'

Minshull studied the expressions of the CID team as they listened to Anderson. Bennett was already wearing a frown, Ellis making rapid notes beside her. Wheeler's notebook page remained empty on his lap as he carefully observed Anderson. Evans squinted at the list, his own summation of it unclear.

'In interview, Ms Pickton couldn't explain why she had been seen near the murder scene, why she had returned home so clearly distressed, or why, an hour later, she had left her home wearing different clothes,' Anderson continued. 'She claimed to have been nowhere near the crime scene, but when pressed for information couldn't account for her movements on the night in question, nor her considerable distress. She mentioned one person who could vouch for her – a former boyfriend – but when questioned he denied any knowledge of seeing her on the day of Cassandra's death.'

'It seems sketchy, Guv,' Bennett said, as Ellis looked up from his note-taking.

She had a point.

Anderson gave a weary shrug. 'It was. Until a search of Cassandra Norton's home uncovered the letter.'

He stuck a photograph to the whiteboard. A single sheet of paper, typed, with a line of spidery handwriting and a signature at the end.

'The letter warns Ms Norton to "*keep away from him*". It suggests that Ms Norton may come to harm if she does not comply. This line here—' he indicated the single line of handwritten words, '—is what ultimately convinced CPS to authorise a charge.' He peered closer and read: '…"*Let it go, or you'll die*"…'

The team didn't respond, staring at the letter.

'The handwriting and signature were confirmed as Ms Pickton's. She denied ever writing it. But that, together with the two eyewitness statements placing her at or close by the scene and the discarded clothing found in her home was deemed strong enough evidence to indicate guilt and premeditation. She was subsequently charged with murder. Despite pleading "not guilty" from the outset and maintaining this throughout the court proceedings, she was found guilty by unanimous verdict and sentenced to twenty-two years in prison.'

Minshull hadn't seen Shona Pickton, apart from a glimpse of her as she was brought into Police HQ, when Minshull and his uniformed colleagues were tasked with creating a human barrier to the gaggle of press photographers and journalists jostling for a view of the suspect. She'd looked terrified as she was hustled inside.

How must it have felt for her, innocent of the charges she faced, having her frantic denials ignored and dismissed by the investigation?

Had Anderson thought her guilty, then? And if not, had he tried to speak up? There was no hint of either as he stuck a photo of Shona Pickton to the board, the image made famous by the barrage of press articles from the time and resurrected recently in the coverage of the appeal hearing.

'Is the letter why the Appeal Court acquitted her?' Ellis asked, his pen momentarily paused from studious note-taking.

'Partly.' Anderson's stony expression betrayed nothing. 'Ms Pickton's representative argued that with so few words in Ms Pickton's handwriting it was impossible to rule out that some or all of the message had been forged. But there were other issues, too: searches of the victim's home being haphazard and poorly controlled, the margin for error being considerable and the widespread press coverage prejudicing the jury in their decision-making.'

'So, could someone have planted the letter?' Bennett was frowning as she chewed the end of her pen.

'That's one thing we have to ascertain,' Anderson replied, his tone already resigned to the task ahead. 'One of many. Which is why we'll be watched on this one from the start.' Anderson gave a long glance at the image of the young woman before he turned back to the CID team. 'And it goes without saying that leave is out of the question until we have a result.' He received the groans with grim apology. 'I know, I'm sorry. Believe me, I'm not over the moon about it, either. But we need to get our heads down and pull together. Rob, what do we have from the incident this morning?'

Minshull accepted the baton and moved to the whiteboard. 'The St Columba Street permanent gypsy and traveller site near Felixstowe was attacked this morning. A caravan was set alight – thankfully with no casualties – and the site was pelted with bricks and missiles. Vehicles damaged, glass everywhere, residents terrified, as you can imagine.'

'Is it connected to Cassandra Norton, Sarge?' Bennett asked.

'I think we should work on that theory, Kate. *The Daily Call* ran a story on its website shortly after the verdict this morning, stating that Shona Pickton would return to the site as a member of the gypsy and traveller community. The report claimed she had been given a caravan at St Columba Street as a homecoming gift from the community.'

'Was it true?'

Minshull sent Ellis a despairing look. 'It was *The Daily Call*, Drew. What do you think?'

'Sorry, Sarge.'

Minshull relented. 'No, you're right to ask. According to the residents I spoke to, Ms Pickton was initially offered the caravan subsequently damaged in the attack as a home in the event of her release, months ago. But this was quickly ruled out by both her legal counsel and our colleagues in police protection. Any of whom could have told the journalist this, had they been afforded the opportunity. Ms Pickton did live on the site for several years before Cassandra Norton's murder, but moved out to a housing project in Felixstowe to care for her mother there. Again, that information would have been easy to come by. My guess is the journalist thought they'd got lucky and ran the story without checking.'

'Why don't they bother with facts any more?' Ellis asked.

'Facts get in the way of a good story, don't they?' Evans replied. 'Lazy bastards, the lot of them.'

'Dr Lael was on site when the attack took place,' Wheeler added. 'Working with a bunch of kids.'

The news rippled through the team. Cora's contribution as a police consultant had become a vital part of their work, her involvement with their last major investigation cementing her place both professionally and personally among the team. Evans, too, returning to the fold after serious injury, had much to thank the psychologist for.

'Is she okay?' Evans asked, a deep frown furrowing his brow, creasing the angry red scar that now resided there.

'A bit shaken, as you can imagine,' Minshull replied. 'Her car was trashed in the attack. She and Dr Noakes were leading an outreach project session with a group of children from the site. It's a blessing the building they were in wasn't nearer the entrance.'

'The kids were terrified, poor littlies.' Wheeler's cheeks flushed. 'Trouble is now, they're sitting ducks, aren't they? Any knuckle-dragging idiot with a brick or a broken bottle could go back there. And the patrol we requested for the front gates only has clearance for twelve hours.'

'I'll request longer,' Anderson confirmed. 'Seeing as the Super's in a giving mood.'

'Please, Guv. If one paper has used that line, you know the rest will follow. It was what they latched onto last time. No chance they'll pass up the opportunity to troll it out again.'

'Consider it done.'

'Cheers, Guv. So, plan of action for us?'

'Start to look back. The evidence boxes have been sent for and should appear this afternoon. The Super is going to arrange extra bodies for us when I can work out how many we'll need. In the meantime, we look for anything and everything we can find connected to the original investigation. News coverage, reports, articles. Shona Pickton's two aunts established a website campaigning for her release, continued after their passing by a small group of supporters, so there should be a lot of information on there, too. As soon as the evidence files arrive, we'll assign them to everyone.'

'We'll inform Cassandra Norton's family immediately,' Minshull said. 'Should we contact Ms Pickton?'

Anderson considered Minshull's question. 'I think we contact her in the first instance to inform her we're reopening the case. I suspect she'll want nothing to do with us – and, frankly, I wouldn't blame her. But we owe her the opportunity to be heard.'

'Do you want me to do that, Guv?'

'Contact her solicitor, please, Rob. He'll be able to advise.' Anderson surveyed the CID team. 'As soon as we have names of original witnesses and those who gave us statements, we'll start face-to-face interviews. I'll need everyone on those – with the exception of Les.'

'It'd be good for me to go out, Guv,' Evans protested.

'You're to remain on light duties until further notice,' Anderson returned.

'No change there, then,' Ellis quipped, his gentle mockery a welcome moment of lightness as the team considered the weight of the task ahead.

'Great to be back,' Evans muttered.

'Aw, come on, Les, admit it: you've missed us.'

'Oh yeah. Like a hole in the head.'

Minshull risked a smile. 'Good to be back to normal. Okay, everyone. Let's get started.'

SIX

CORA

The car was a write-off; its bodywork too damaged by bricks and smoke to be salvageable. It was what Cora had suspected, but it made the news no easier to receive.

Replacing it would be a headache she didn't need. Purchasing a new car was out of the question, which left only previously owned cars available to her. With an ability like hers, a second-hand vehicle brought its own unique set of issues, namely the voice echoes from previous owners. The audible fingerprints she could sense, pressed into the very fabric of seats, belts, doorhandles, footwells and glove compartments; the ghosts of unseen frustrations, conversations and thoughts playing on repeat in the unique soundscape of the car's interior that would likely accompany her on every journey until they finally faded away.

With public transport between Felixstowe and Ipswich being time-consuming and constraining, Tris had kindly offered to car share for the immediate future. Cora was glad of this, even though the prospect of being so beholden to him sat uneasily within her. She much preferred being responsible for her own travel; the time spent alone on journeys an opportunity to decompress from the demands of her job and the effort of navigating the unseen soundscapes of everywhere she went.

It couldn't be helped, though. The challenges raised by the attack on the St Columba Street site, combined with the demands of her job, made car-hunting a luxury she couldn't entertain. Until the situation lessened, she would have to be content remaining a passenger.

Besides, there were more pressing problems to deal with.

'Out of the question,' Tris Noakes barked at his desk.

His uncharacteristic anger caused Cora and her two psychologist colleagues to look up from their files in the adjoining office.

'I know exactly what your *concern* is, Councillor Moss, and frankly I don't care. It has taken years to get this project off the ground and I'm not about to let an inconsequential vocal minority on the council dictate its future.'

Dr Alannah Hope looked at Cora in surprise, the silver ring in her right eyebrow catching the light of the office spotlights. '*What?*' she mouthed. Cora replied with a helpless shrug. Their colleague, Dr Ollie Rowan, followed suit.

'You heard me, sir. *A minority*. None of whom have paid us the slightest notice until today…' Through the open door to his office, Cora saw the thud of Tris' fist on his desk, the resulting shockwave causing a tumble of papers from his overflowing in-tray. 'I've no doubt I'll hear more from you on the subject. So be it.'

The slam of the phone receiver returning to its cradle was accompanied by his loud groan of frustration.

Ollie was first to the door. The longest-serving member of the team, there was little he hadn't witnessed here. He'd served under Tris' predecessor and knew the rocky landscape of council operations well.

'Bastards being bastards, boss?'

'I just… I shouldn't be surprised, but it beggars belief.' The strain was evident in every word. 'I mean, *shit*, Ol, do they think we can't see through them?'

Cora and Alannah rose from their desks to join their colleagues.

'How bad is it?' Cora asked, already guessing the answer.

'The pointy-white-hat brigade wants the project shut down. Immediately. They're threatening to challenge our right to operate HappyKid on both sites. On *health and safety* grounds.'

The air was punched from the space as the psychologist team responded with uniform dismay.

'Who's saying that?'

Tris raised weary eyes to Cora. 'Stephen Moss. Julianne Gilbert. Roy Alsingham. Imogen De la Hay.'

Alannah snorted. 'The Four Harbingers of the Apocalypse.'

'The very same.'

Cora observed Tris, nerves balling within her. 'They can't stop it, can they? We had full council support.'

'Officially they can't touch us. But they can cause enough noise and obstruction to disrupt our work. That's their *modus operandi*, isn't it? Make themselves appear more powerful than they are so they gain support. And if they talk to the press...' Tris kicked his chair back from his desk as he stood, pacing the cramped space beyond it. 'If they link it with the racist crap resurfacing over Shona Pickton it could be catastrophic.'

'What can we do, Tris?' Ollie asked, concern and purpose warming his question.

'We need to decide where we stand. And nail our colours there.' He stopped pacing and looked at his team. 'Cora, this is your call as much as mine or theirs or anyone else's. I can't ask you to continue, unless...'

'I'm in,' Cora replied.

'But your car...'

'It's just a car. Those kids don't get the choice to walk away. So, I don't want it, either.'

She had considered little else since she and Tris had returned from the St Columba Street site. Rob Minshull's well-meaning attempt to persuade her to leave had fired her resolve to remain.

'And if they insist we stop?'

'Then I'll go as an independent volunteer. The children need us – more than ever now, given the trauma they've experienced this morning. Merryn and Sam were saying the same thing back at St Columba Street. We haven't worked so hard to establish HappyKid just to abandon everything now.'

'Extra bodies here, too,' Alannah offered, Ollie nodding in agreement beside her. 'Bonus points for annoying the council thugs.'

Tris Noakes observed his small team with a swell of pride. 'Thank you. They're calling a meeting later today, so we'd best prepare ourselves. I'll call Joss and bring him up to speed. He'll be expecting it, I reckon, but I know what it'll mean to him to have us all on board.' His worry-darkened eyes moved to Cora. 'And Rob? If the police ask us to stay away?'

'They can only advise us. We have every right to maintain visits to the site.' Cora lifted her chin, determination in her stance. 'Leave DS Minshull to me.'

–

Within an hour, news coverage of the attack on the St Columba Street site had powered ahead from local interest story to national headlines. Cora could imagine gaggles of journalists rubbing their hands with glee at the opportunity to link Shona Pickton's exoneration with the violence.

LOCAL RESIDENTS DEMAND ACTION AFTER TRAVELLER VIOLENCE

'WE DON'T WANT THEM HERE':

TENSIONS EXPLODE AS SHONA PICKTON RETURNS

FELIXSTOWE BRACED FOR GYPSY SITE BACKLASH

The increasingly lurid headlines rolled across news sites, a poison-penned parade of hate and prejudice gathering momentum with each passing hour. Cora observed it with a heavy sense of foreboding. It was utterly unfair; an onerous and tenuous link between the wrongfully imprisoned woman and the community so often victim to misinformation and mistrust.

By three p.m. she had seen enough. Excusing herself from the office, she grabbed her coat from the rack by the door and headed outside. She needed air and space, neither of which were in sufficient supply in her workplace.

The offices of the South Suffolk LEA Educational Psychology Unit were situated just off Landseer Road, not far from the Port of Ipswich, on a small trading estate. A car park edged with low bushes and a strip of lawn lay in front of the three squat red brick buildings. As green space went, it was diminutive. But when Cora needed respite from the pressures of her job, it offered vital sanctuary.

It was cold this afternoon, a chill November wind blowing in unhindered from the nearby marina. Cora pulled her handknitted circle scarf closer to her chill-stung cheeks, the soft yellow alpaca wool soothing to her skin. Like the bright beanbags and floor cushions at The HappyKid Project, her scarf had been a gift from the ladies of the St Just WI. Her mum, who had yet to be seduced by the delights of knitting, had asked two friends at her weekly group to craft a scarf and gloves for Cora.

'Because I worry,' she'd insisted, when she'd presented her daughter with the warm woollen treasures. 'You're always out in all weathers, walking miles by the sea. You need to take better care of you.'

The scarf was new enough to still retain audible echoes of the lovely lady who had created it, although the happy chatter of nonagenarian Enid Maybury was gently fading now, becoming lost between the strands of wool. Cora would miss it when it was gone.

The comfort was at stark odds with the bile and fury that had dominated her observation of the news sites.

As she sat on a bench on the car park periphery, she bristled at the memory of everything she'd witnessed. What gave anyone the right to determine who could and couldn't live somewhere?

Joss had told her how long the gypsy, traveller and Roma communities had been in Suffolk, their legacy stretching back centuries. They were woven into the fabric of the land as much as the county's agricultural and maritime histories – generations of nomadic people intrinsically linked to the story of the county Cora called home. How dare anyone suggest they had no right to call it theirs?

A buzz from her coat pocket brought her back from her thoughts.

ROB calling

She considered letting the call go unanswered to voicemail, but at the last minute changed her mind.

'Hi Rob.'

'I wanted to check how you're doing. And Tris,' he added, almost as an afterthought.

Cora smiled, despite her mood. 'I'm okay. How are you and Dave?'

'Busy. We're reopening the Shona Pickton case.'

It was what Cora had expected, but with the backdrop of the current press frenzy it felt portentous. 'That's going to be a task.'

'Tell me about it. We've just taken delivery of the original case files. The boxes have almost filled one of the meeting rooms.'

'Wow.'

'I know. Late nights and long shifts for the foreseeable.'

There was a pause, and Cora could hear the buffeting of wind with the distant sound of traffic. She imagined Minshull standing at the top of the steps leading from the fire escape at the rear of Police HQ to the staff car park, his favoured place for making calls he didn't want his team to hear. *Great minds think alike*, she mused, letting her gaze travel across the council office car park beyond.

'Look, I was wondering… Some of the evidence we have will be physical items retrieved from Cassandra Norton and found near her body in the street where she was murdered. I know it's been a long time, but do you think you'd be able to sense anything from them?'

Cora frowned. 'Not after nine years.'

'But if they'd been sealed in evidence bags shortly after being collected? I wondered if it might keep the audible fingerprints fresh like… like…'

'Tupperware?' Cora finished for him, amused by his theory. 'I don't think it works like that, Rob.'

'But would you be willing to try?'

His question hung in the frigid air.

It was impossible – wasn't it? The longest Cora had sensed voices on objects after someone had died had been those attached to her late father Bill's belongings in the family home she then shared with Sheila. The final ebb of his thought-voices occurred a little under four weeks after his death – their disappearance almost as crushing to her as his physical passing; a second loss as the echo of his voice passed into silence.

A stab of pain brought tears to her eyes as she considered the possibility of Minshull's request. If she had kept something of Bill Lael's, sealed immediately in the aftermath of his passing, might it have retained his emotional echoes?

In light of that, her answer was clear.

'Yes,' she said, aware of the sudden race of her pulse as the wind picked up pace around her. 'Whatever you need.'

SEVEN

WHEELER

Wheeler had anticipated the evidence files from the original Cassandra Norton investigation might be many.

But not *this* many.

Kate Bennett's glances grew more despondent with each lap as she and Wheeler made the slow, repeated trudge from the delivery van out in the car park, up the stairwell to the second floor and into the rapidly filling meeting room along the corridor from the CID office. Drew Ellis, too.

Wheeler thought of Anderson, suspiciously busy elsewhere when the delivery arrived, and Evans, finally smug behind his desk, excused from carrying the evidence file boxes into Police HQ due to his current 'light duties only' remit. Jammy gits.

At least Rob Minshull had rolled up his sleeves to help. He shared only brief smiles with Wheeler when they passed in the corridor, his brow knotted in thought. Was the physical task an aid to his thought process? He'd been noticeably preoccupied since the team briefing, and Wheeler could only imagine the pressure he was silently heaping on himself.

'Where do you want these, Dave?' Bennett was staring uncertainly at the growing skyscrapers of boxes blocking light from the meeting room's single window, as Wheeler entered with two more.

Wheeler grimaced. 'Anywhere they'll fit.'

'Is it safe to stack them this high? If they topple, it could take someone out.'

'This is the biggest space they could give us. All the other rooms are booked.'

Bennett deposited her boxes on the lowest pile, level with her shoulders. She groaned as she stepped back, rubbing the small of her back. 'It's going to take months to go through these, isn't it?'

'Let's hope not, eh?'

'Do you remember anything about the case?'

Wheeler blew out a whistle. 'I remember the angst, more than anything. Sue Taylor on the warpath, Joel having all the 'acting' pranks played on him while getting no respect from anyone, and the high-ups at all of our throats.'

'People played pranks on Anderson?'

Wheeler grinned at his colleague. How quickly she'd forgotten. It had only been a few years ago that Bennett had been involved in the pranks pulled on Rob Minshull during his probationary period that took him from a detective constable to a detective sergeant. 'Tradition works at all levels, you know.'

'But during a murder investigation?'

Wheeler had to concede it seemed inappropriate. 'It's just what happens, Kate. You need fun and mucking around at times like that.' All the same, Wheeler wondered now if much of the so-called good-natured mickey-taking had been an excuse for Taylor to keep Anderson in check.

Bennett steadied a box that had twisted over the edge of a stack. 'What about the people involved in the case?'

'It's all a bit hazy, to be honest with you. Lots of inter-views with relatives of the victim, friends too, but that was mostly background stuff. There was a bloke Shona Pickton kept insisting could give her an alibi, but when he finally came in for interview he flat-out refused. And Cassandra Norton's brother, who phoned us every day demanding answers. It was relentless – and that was without the packs of journos dashing after us wherever we went.'

'And what about Shona? What was she like?'

Wheeler felt his heart sink. He'd sat in on two interviews with DCI Taylor leading, one near the start of Shona's time in police custody and one near the end. The difference between the two had been stark. From a young woman frantic to be heard, to an emotionally broken person confused over the slightest detail.

'I don't think she knew what hit her. She came in thinking she was assisting us, and Sue Taylor just dismantled her. We thought the realisation of what she'd done was coming home to roost. But now? I don't know.'

'That's the last of them.' Ellis nudged three boxes onto the already crowded meeting room table. He looked fresher than Wheeler felt, the merest hint of pink across his cheekbones the only visible sign of the effort he'd expended.

'How come I'm sweating like the proverbial porker, Drew, and you look like you've had a gentle stroll?'

Ellis grinned. 'Maybe the gym isn't such a huge waste of time after all.'

'Gym, *schmim*,' Wheeler retorted. 'Give me my bike any day.'

'Three words, Dave,' Ellis said, patting his bicep. 'Upper. Body. Strength.'

Wheeler rolled his eyes. 'Ah, get away with you. We don't all want to look like Thor.' His heart warmed as he saw the barely masked compliment land on his younger colleague. Ellis had made it his mission in recent years to transform his once gangly body, and the fruits of his labours were clear to see.

Bennett observed her colleagues with mild amusement. 'Are you two done, or should I leave?'

'What's happening?' Minshull appeared at the door, looking only marginally more tired than Ellis.

Wheeler kicked the sting of envy away. Come the spring he'd be back to cycling to work again and the encroaching swell of his stomach over the waistband of his work trousers would be gone.

'Bit of male bonding, Sarge,' Bennett replied, her grimace amusing Ellis and Wheeler. 'Rescue me?'

'With pleasure,' Minshull laughed. 'There's a long list of records back in the office with your name on them.'

'Sanctuary!' Bennett breathed, as she left the box-stacked room, Ellis close on her heels.

In the doorway, Minshull waited for Wheeler. 'Dave, can I ask you something?'

'Fire away, Sarge.'

'Did you believe Shona Pickton was guilty when she was charged?'

Ah, so that was the reason Minshull had been so preoccupied. Now it was voiced, Wheeler realised he'd been waiting for the question.

'Honestly? I'd like to say no, I never thought her guilty. But back then everything seemed to point to it. Her being seen close by, what she was wearing, what the taxi driver saw, the stuff we found in her wardrobe and then that letter the search found. Her signature, her handwriting on the bottom of it. It seemed to add up. You know how it is, Minsh, when you're in the thick of things. Conclusions are easy to jump to. All the conversations in the office, the briefings, the statements, it all stacked against her.' He wished he could have been more gallant in his reply, but it was the truth.

'And Joel?'

'He kept his head down – not that Sue Taylor ever gave him the chance to speak much. But he was the only one raising questions about it. Wouldn't let it go. Bit like Drew does now when he makes up his mind about something.'

Minshull nodded and they began to walk slowly together back along the corridor.

'Can you have a think and make me a list of everything you remember? Anything – theories discussed, people you saw, gossip out of the office. I know it's a long time ago, but you might remember something the Guv doesn't.'

'Consider it done.' Wheeler glanced at Minshull. 'You think we can do this?'

'I have no idea. But we have a family who still need answers, not to mention a woman wrongfully accused of the crime. If we can find something to appease the two, it'll be a result.'

—

Back at his desk, Wheeler stared at the new blank page in his notebook. He wished he'd kept his notes from the original investigation, but he hadn't the space or the inclination for such an endeavour. One of his former sergeants while in Uniform had religiously kept every notebook he'd ever had in the job, stashing them in boxes in his loft. It was only after his death a few years back that his widow found them – handwritten records of every home visit, every briefing and every case going back thirty years. She'd donated the lot to the Suffolk Constabulary museum, as Wheeler recalled. Probably a vital archive of police history for them.

He could imagine Sana's face if he filled their loft with his personal notebook collection. His wife took a dim enough view of the rusting, well-loved bike graveyard in their garden shed. If he added police notebooks to that, she'd probably leave him.

Grinning at the thought, Wheeler cast his mind back to the CID office of nine years ago.

The shadow of DCI John Minshull's reign had barely lifted back then, the arrival of Sue Taylor as newly installed CID head and Anderson's swift promotion to Acting DI a whirlwind from which the team was still reeling. Wheeler had assumed that Anderson would occupy Minshull Senior's office immediately, but DCI Taylor moved in within days. He still recalled Anderson's silent fury at the neighbouring desk where Bennett now sat. Anderson had hidden it well from his superiors, but they'd worked together long enough for Wheeler to see right through it.

He remembered long conversations over after-work pints, Anderson's bitter consternation at being sidelined so soon in his career. It was clear he and DCI Taylor would never be bosom buddies – and so it proved to be.

How would it be this time, with Sue Taylor on the back foot and Joel in charge?

Something about his memory of Taylor's arrival troubled Wheeler. She had always been driven by the need for recognition, from her colleagues and from the media. But she'd seen the Cassandra Norton case as her professional platform from the outset. There had been no mention of justice, or the need to find Ms Norton's killer for the sake of the dead woman's family. She'd made no mention of her own feelings towards the investigation, as Wheeler had witnessed both Anderson and Rob Minshull do on many occasions. It was as if the details of the case were merely stepping stones to an end goal. As if they were an unnecessary burden of the task at hand...

Then there was the family. Wheeler could only recall dealing with Cassandra's brother, Ryan, but that had been plenty. A self-appointed spokesman for the Norton clan, Ryan Norton had taken it upon himself to police the police. Wheeler was the one who answered calls into CID back then, so he'd dealt with the young man more than anyone else. Every day of the investigation, without fail, Cassandra's brother had called. Demanding answers. Furious when Wheeler calmly explained the details of the investigation must remain within Police HQ. Over and over, day in and day out, the same conversation. It had required every ounce of Wheeler's patience and compassion to maintain calm.

The lad was hurting, of course. Hitting out at anyone in his grief. Wheeler had done his best to reconcile Ryan Norton's actions with the reasons behind them, but the constant barrage wore his compassion thin.

And yet the family liaison officer assigned to the Norton family confided privately that she'd rarely seen Ryan Norton at the house. The mother had been inconsolable, sisters and cousins and extended family rallying around day and night.

But wherever Ryan Norton had made his daily calls to South Suffolk CID from, it wasn't the family home.

Wheeler wrote that down.

There had been a boyfriend, too, although he couldn't recall the name. He hadn't come into Police HQ for interview, but a colleague had visited his home. Wheeler vaguely remembered there had been some question over his whereabouts on the night of the murder, but whether through lack of evidence or the emergence of another line of inquiry, it had been dropped pretty quickly. He thought Anderson and DCI Taylor had clashed over it, but they'd disagreed on so much that Wheeler might be mistaken.

He noted it regardless.

Beyond that, there was little he could remember. As he'd told Bennett, the details had deserted him but the memory of the atmosphere in CID during the case burned brightest. It had choked the life from the team, sapping energy and stealing oxygen, a claustrophobic pressure closing in on all sides. Gone were the jokes that sustained the detectives through their darkest times; suspicion and conspiracy theories usurping them. You didn't forget that kind of feeling in a hurry.

'How's it going?' Minshull was at his desk when Wheeler looked up.

'Sketchy, I'm afraid,' he admitted, holding up his notepad.

'That's more than I remember. Thanks Dave.'

'Want to go through it now, Sarge? I can pop the kettle on?'

Minshull gave a rueful grin. 'Much as I'd like that, I can't. I have to call Shona Pickton's barrister.'

'Ah.'

'Exactly.'

'Reckon he'll hear you out?'

Minshull's hands shoved into his trouser pockets, his shoulders slumping a little. 'He'll take the call. Whether his client will want to talk to us is another matter.'

'I don't envy you that, Sarge.'

'Me either.' Minshull nodded at Wheeler's notebook. 'Keep thinking, yeah? Anything you can remember could really help. Because after that, we'll have to start wading through those evidence boxes.'

His parting shot delivered, he headed for his desk.

Heart heavy at the thought of the task, Wheeler returned to his list.

EIGHT

SHONA

The police want to meet with me.

I bet they do.

Alan said this could happen, and he was right, of course. I haven't watched the news or dared to look online, but he says my case is all over the place. 'Puts the police under scrutiny,' he said yesterday, when he was driving me to my new flat. 'They'll want to be seen to be proactive.'

He says it's up to me whether I want to participate in the new investigation. I can't be tried again for the same crime, so I would be safe to talk to them. But I remember the way they were last time; the way they twisted my words and questioned everything I told them until I didn't know my head from my feet. The way they made me feel.

I've fought all my life for my own space. For my right to be heard. The last nine years I've been denied it. I don't know if I can put myself through it again.

My new place doesn't feel like home. I don't know if it ever will. The few boxes of my stuff seem lost within it already, a pathetic pile in the middle of the living room floor. I haven't even got a cover for my duvet or sheets for my bed, yet. There's so much to sort and I just don't have the energy to think of anything else.

Alan said to wait a while before I make any decisions. The police have informed him that they're reinvestigating, as they are legally required to. Beyond that, they have no power to dictate what I do.

I just keep thinking about the real killer.

And the man who made sure I went to prison.

The police don't know the truth about either of them. What I know could blow the case wide open.

If they believe me.

I don't think I can take the risk of them not.

I need to think about this. Focus on me for a bit. Lie low until the worst of the media stuff blows over. Alan reckons it will, in time. Until then, I'll hold on to what I know.

I can't think about it today.

NINE

MINSHULL

'I'm sorry, DS Minshull.'

'Did you stress to Ms Pickton that she's under no threat of arrest?' Minshull asked, wishing he didn't sound like he was grasping at straws.

'I did.' The barrister observed him from behind the old oak expanse of his desk. 'It wasn't the most comforting assertion, as you can imagine.'

The morning beyond the large window of the barrister's Ipswich office cast a sombre grey-blue light across the expensive carpeted floor towards them. The scent of fresh coffee and paper filled the air, Minshull secretly enjoying the delicious dark brew he'd been given when he'd arrived. He'd slept fitfully last night, following long hours of unpacking evidence files at work, and hadn't had time for breakfast before the start of his morning shift.

The call from Alan Gilles, KC, had been an early morning surprise when Minshull arrived at his desk, the request to meet at the barrister's Ipswich town centre offices fuelling his hopes that Shona Pickton might consent to be interviewed.

All hope of that had been lost, however, minutes after he'd received his excellent coffee.

'I give you my word,' he countered, as if it would ever be enough. As if that might swing the balance in his favour.

'With respect, neither I nor Ms Pickton know the value of that.'

Minshull's toes bunched in his shoes. Of course, the barrister had a point: the police hadn't exactly proved themselves trustworthy towards Shona Pickton. What reason did she have to believe them now? Neither she nor her counsel knew Minshull, or that he considered himself different from his predecessors. He hadn't sent her to prison, but he'd been a cog in the machine that had. And while he hoped policing standards were better now than nine years ago – *his* standards being higher, his pursuit of justice the driving force behind everything he did – he bore the weight of responsibility for her wrongful imprisonment as much as everyone in South Suffolk Police.

'I understand.' Dropping his guard, Minshull appealed to the barrister on his own terms. 'Just, please, tell her I'm going to do everything I can to rectify this.'

Gilles leaned a little towards him. 'Are you speaking officially, or off the record?'

It was potentially dangerous territory – and DCI Taylor would likely skin him alive if she learned of it – but the urge to draw his own line in the sand won over every professional concern.

'Personally. We have a task ahead of us, and nine years' disadvantage on the perpetrator. It's going to be tough. But my team and I won't stop until we uncover the truth. Ms Pickton has every right to stay away, of course. Nobody is going to demand otherwise. I just want her to know – from me – that I will be doing this for her.'

The barrister's surprise brought Minshull up short. He'd said too much, the aftereffects of the attack on the St Columba Street site, Cora's defiance and the hateful news headlines directed at Shona Pickton skewing his judgement. Quickly he stood, keen to leave.

'Right, I should go. You have my direct number, Mr Gilles. Should you wish to discuss any aspect of the reinvestigation, please call me.'

The barrister rose, his handshake genuinely warm. 'I appreciate that, DS Minshull. I'll pass on your message.'

Minshull waited until he was a street away from the well-appointed offices in the centre of Ipswich until he allowed himself to slump. He'd overstepped in there. Allowed his personal response to surface. That wasn't like him. What was it about this investigation that elicited such emotion?

A weak November sun hazed ineffectually through a milk white sky over the town as he walked quickly back to Police HQ. The stationary lines of irritated drivers snagged on the roads he passed confirmed he'd been right to forgo a car for the meeting. Besides, the walk would help him think.

Without Shona Pickton's perspective, the new investigation was stymied before it had properly begun. He would have to rely upon nine-year-old interview notes from her instead, piecing together new lines of inquiry from the imperfect fragments of her testimony. That required time they could ill afford, even with the two extra officers Anderson had requested from Superintendent Martlesham.

The notion of time was a challenge, too. Minshull felt the pressure of a ticking clock, despite the case being nine years old. Beyond his superiors' demands for a swift conclusion, he was all too aware of the dangers bubbling just below the surface. The threat of violence to the gypsy and traveller communities, the fear of reprisals and exploitation of adverse news stories by factions with an axe to grind – an incendiary mix of hate, prejudice and opportunism that could blow at any moment.

He had to act.

And while he knew the possibility of Shona Pickton relenting on her stance was slim, he decided to hold out hope for a reprieve.

Without it, he had no idea how they could succeed…

–

The morning briefing was filled with weary detectives, huddled around mugs of coffee far inferior to the brew Minshull had already enjoyed. Stacks of evidence boxes stood sentry beside every desk, an ominous reminder of the work that the briefing could offer his colleagues only brief respite from.

The whiteboard by Minshull's desk, used in every major investigation as a focal point, had been cleaned since Anderson's initial briefing. A clean slate. A fresh start. It was as much symbolic as practical: *that was before; this is now.*

He offered his team a brief, consolatory smile. 'Before we start, I want to address the current situation with the St Columba Street gypsy and traveller site: Until we find otherwise, we're treating this as a retaliation attack linked with Shona Pickton's recent acquittal. I've asked Sergeant Tim Brinton to put together a Uniform team to investigate it. Superintendent Martlesham has greenlit this, and will be liaising directly with Tim. Anything we find that pertains to that attack will of course be shared as first priority. Clear?'

'Sarge.'

'Yes, Sarge.'

'Okay, good.' Minshull wrote CASSANDRA NORTON at the top of the whiteboard and turned back to the team. 'I want to go over the facts as we know them, concerning the last-known movements and discovery of the body of Cassandra Norton. I know the Guv mentioned some of this before, but I want it fresh in our minds as we start work on it. Everything is up for question, okay? Every detail accepted before, we must consider now as objectively as we can. We'll scrutinise everything, question the validity of every piece of evidence, however small. And if it's found wanting in any way, we'll discard it. So, let's begin.'

He placed a photo of the young woman on the whiteboard. It would be familiar to everyone as the murder and high-profile investigation surrounding the death of the former Miss Suffolk had dominated the news for weeks.

As expected, Minshull witnessed recognition register in every watching face.

Cassandra Norton had been undeniably beautiful: blue eyes, a heart-shaped face, an English rose complexion and a glossy mane of long blonde hair. The press had dined out on skimpily clad photos of her taken during her beauty contest days, satin sashes worn across little more than sequins and shiny lace, long legs made almost endless in the highest heels, and glittering crowns nestled in her perfectly styled hair. *An angel*, they'd breathed, their enthusiasm made grubby by their overeager observations of her body. *A perfect English beauty, robbed of a glittering future*. It had felt seedy at the time, Minshull remembered, the news reports and tabloid headlines leaving him cold.

The contrast with the woman charged with her murder couldn't have been starker. Shona Pickton was slight, her collar-length dyed blonde hair worn in a tight ponytail scraped severely away from her face. The only photographs the press used were of her arriving in court from remand prison, her thin frame disguised by a dark skirt suit and off-white blouse that seemed to have been pulled in to fit. She appeared pale-faced and exhausted, with minimum make-up, giving her a harsh and pinched look. A police arrest photo later leaked out and was given a greyish filter that, when printed, gave her a ghoulish appearance.

Minshull had deliberately not selected one of the media's chosen images of Shona Pickton, instead sourcing a family photo from a campaign website posted by her aunts several years before. A photograph taken on Felixstowe seafront in summer, long before the name Cassandra Norton ever encroached upon her life. In it she was smiling, her face transformed by bright sunlight and a lack of concern, her hair loose and soft, with seasalt-sculpted curls dancing around her face. Would the original verdict – and public opinion – have been different, Minshull wondered, if media outlets had chosen to show this picture instead?

'Here's what we know,' he continued, a handful of photos in hand. 'According to statements, Cassandra Norton, aged twenty-two, left the family home at 35 Seaton Road around five thirty p.m. on Thursday 16th April, 2015. She drove a red-and-white Mini – the last car journey she would make that night.

She returned to her flat here, at 18D Leopold Road, some-time after that. Her boyfriend, Nicholas Wright, stated that he arrived at her flat around seven p.m. They had a drink together and all seemed fine. But then they got into an argument, and she asked Wright to leave. According to him, he left the property at around eight fifteen p.m. and drove back home. Cassandra told him she was due to meet a friend, but didn't state who she was meeting or where.'

Minshull pinned a map of Felixstowe onto the board, with Leopold Road marked in red pen. He then took a blue pen and circled another point, a few streets away.

'Fast forward to just after nine p.m., here, in Orwell Road, outside Trinity Methodist Church, now known as *Felixstowe Methodist Church @ Trinity*. Mr Huzaifa Beshaira, a taxi driver, had just dropped off a fare in Victoria Street, here…' He marked a street running adjacent to the church. '…and was heading back to the taxi rank when he saw a figure lying on the pavement near the entrance of the church. Dave, have you got that Google Maps photo I asked for?'

'Yep.' Wheeler left his chair and handed the printed sheet to Minshull.

'Cheers.' Minshull fixed it to the board. 'As you can see, this side of the church, bordering Orwell Road, has these distinctive concrete raised flowerbeds running alongside the building.'

He indicated a collection of concrete planters arranged in runs of squares connected by a low wall, the points of the square beds jutting out diamond-style towards the kerb. On the one nearest the blue-painted church door, Minshull drew a large red circle.

'Mr Beshaira stated that he saw a woman lying slumped on the floor and another figure leaning over her. He stopped his taxi and got out, but the second person ran from the scene. When he went to the woman, he found her unconscious, blood all over this corner of the planter and pooling around her head. He called 999 at nine fifteen p.m., and an ambu-lance was in attendance twenty minutes later. Cassandra Norton was pronounced dead at the scene at nine forty p.m. A post-mortem confirmed significant bruising to her chest, which they surmised was evidence of a blow that caused her to lose her balance. As she fell, she hit the planter, incurring a large fracture to the rear of her skull. It was a catastrophic injury that resulted in a fatal loss of blood.'

'What do we know about the second individual, other than this was presumed to be Shona Pickton?' Bennett asked.

'According to Mr Beshaira's statement, the figure was white, of slight build, with collar-length blonde hair pulled back in a ponytail. He said they were dressed in black – he remembered a sweatshirt that could have been a hoodie and either black skinny jeans or leggings with white trainers. Beyond that he couldn't recall more specific details.'

'Had Cassandra walked from her flat?' Ellis asked, looking at the map. 'It's only a couple of streets away from that church.'

'It was assumed she had,' Minshull replied. 'Certainly her Mini was parked outside her flat in Leopold Road when officers returned there. Which means that she left her house sometime after Mr Wright's departure at eight fifteen and before the discovery of her body by Mr Beshaira at ten past nine.'

'Were her friends interviewed, Sarge?' Bennett asked.

'The ones the investigation could find. But there could be more. That's one thing I want us to be looking out for as we revisit the files.'

'Could one of her friends fit the description of the second individual at the murder scene?'

Minshull nodded at Ellis, impressed by the insight. 'It's possible, especially if the initial investigation failed to identify everyone Cassandra was close to.'

'What about the letter?' Bennett asked. 'The one the Guv told us was found at Cassandra's flat?'

Anderson raised his hand, the image from before held between his fingers. Minshull accepted it, knowing the Appeal Court's verdict had rendered it no longer admissible.

'I'm not adding it here,' he stated, holding the photograph up for the team to see.

'No, Sarge, what I mean is, how did it get into Cassandra Norton's flat? If Shona didn't write it, as she maintained – and the appeal judge ruled it unreliable – who did? And if it was intended to throw Shona Pickton under the bus, who planted it there? And when?'

They were all good questions, for which Minshull had no answers yet.

'Bear it all in mind, Kate, but I don't want the letter to derail our new investigation,' he said, Anderson's stare failing to dissuade him. 'Keep your eyes open for anyone who might have had cause to put Shona Pickton in the frame, but don't let it pull focus from the main task at hand.'

'We could ask the boyfriend about it,' Wheeler offered, the slightest note of urgency in his voice as he rushed to pour oil on dangerously fractious waters. 'See if Cassandra told him about the threat, or if he'd seen it in the house.'

'Or if he planted it.' Evans' typically dry offering was noted from the back row.

'Like I said, we rule nothing out,' Minshull stated, keen to draw a line under the speculation. 'Our primary concern is identifying anyone and anything that the first investigation missed. Then we look for motives. Let's move on, shall we?'

'What about the CCTV evidence, Rob?' Anderson's bark redirected the conversation, to Minshull's relief.

'Good point, Guv.' Minshull stuck a grainy video still on the board. 'We have CCTV stills in the evidence but unfortunately not the video files. They confirm the presence of a person of slight build, wearing black. From the stills it's impossible to determine if this person's shoes are white as the taxi driver noted. But the person's hood is down and light-coloured hair pulled into a tight ponytail is visible.'

'Were any other suspects fitting that description questioned?' Bennett asked.

Anderson and Wheeler exchanged exhausted glances.

'No, Kate.'

'Once Ms Pickton was arrested and the two witness statements had been taken, things moved pretty quickly.'

Minshull felt his colleagues' pain. In the light of what they now knew, the details that had appeared so firm during the original investigation were revealed as frayed and thin. The more the previous case was unpicked, the more it came apart. Watching Ellis and Bennett's reactions to the case was an education.

'That brings us up to date with the basics. Now, before we all start tackling that roomful of evidence down the corridor, I want to focus on details that anyone present during the original investigation can remember. Anything from your side, Dave?'

Wheeler brandished his notes. 'A few bits, Sarge. We suspected the boyfriend for a while – Nicholas Wright. He worked nights as a doorman at Jester's nightclub, and there was some discrepancy in his alibi for the night of the murder. I can't recall what that was, but I can search for it.'

Minshull wrote *NICHOLAS WRIGHT* on the board. 'Okay.'

'And then there was Miss Norton's brother, who wouldn't leave us alone. Ryan Norton. Remember him, Guv?'

Anderson groaned. 'Hard to forget him, Dave.'

'Now Janey March was FLO, as I recall, so I went to chat with her before the boxes arrived. She remembers Ryan staying away from the family home, but the Guv and I both know he called here every day, demanding information.'

'Was he older or younger than Cassandra?' Minshull asked.

'Younger. Couldn't have been more than nineteen or twenty, I reckon.'

'He might not have lived at the home address, even at that age. Maybe he wasn't there because he had a home elsewhere?'

'True. I just remember it standing out that he wasn't around for his family when so many other relatives were, that's all.'

'Probably because he came here to chew your ear off every day for a month,' Anderson chuckled.

'Probably, Guv.'

Minshull made a note towards the bottom of the board. He'd add bits of interest here for the time being. 'Good. Anything else?'

'There was one more thing, Sarge. I sat in on two of the interviews with Ms Pickton. In both, she mentioned a man who could corroborate her story. Her boyfriend, whose house in Montague Road she was seen running away from. She maintained she'd been in such a state that she hadn't known where she'd run to, and that around an hour later, the boyfriend came looking for her in his car, driving her back to her home. But when we brought the bloke in for interview, he refused to say he was with her.'

'Name?'

'Karl Cuskie.'

A cough from Evans summoned Minshull's attention. 'Sound familiar, Les?'

'Yes, Sarge. I'm surprised you don't recognise him.'

'How so?'

Evans stretched his legs out, wincing a little. 'Everyone knows Karl. One of our best informers over the years. Total bastard, mind, but he came up trumps more often than not.'

Minshull glanced at Anderson. 'Do you know him, Guv?'

'I know of him. Haven't used him myself.'

'But it didn't seem odd to you that his name was brought up as an alibi for Shona Pickton? Or suggest her involvement with a known police informer might have been cause for concern?'

Anderson considered the question, his brow furrowed. Minshull knew he might have overstepped the mark, but how come a flag hadn't been raised, even when Cuskie declined to corroborate Shona's story?

'It should have, Rob.' The DI released a long sigh. 'All of us should have seen it. But the juggernaut of the case, the speed with which theories were abandoned – it's not surprising things were missed.'

Minshull shelved his irritation. There would likely be many such occasions as the original evidence was re-examined: he would have to hold his own opinions in check to deal with them. He changed tack. 'Did anyone you know talk to him?'

'Les, clearly.'

'Your pa, too,' Evans offered, the mention of Minshull's father sinking his heart like a dropped stone in the sea. John Minshull would think nothing of consulting a known informer, despite the practice being officially outlawed by their superiors. But since when had protocol and rules ever bothered his father?

'So, Ms Pickton insisted Karl Cuskie could give her an alibi?'

'Exactly.' Wheeler grimaced. 'Because although they'd split up earlier that evening, she said he'd come to find her and they'd reconciled at her house.'

'But he denied that happened?'

'He was adamant he'd never gone looking for her. Said the state she was in he could easily have seen her hurting someone.'

Minshull took this in. Had the breakup, occurring so close to the time of Cassandra Norton's killing, been viewed as a reason for Shona Pickton lashing out? He could imagine the conversations that may have taken place in this office around that theory.

'What if they split up because Cuskie was seeing Cassandra Norton?' Bennett rolled her eyes at the laughter this elicited from Evans and Wheeler. 'What? It's possible.'

'You ever seen Cuskie?' Evans snorted. 'There's a reason he chose to be an informer. Face like his doesn't win any beauty contests. Plus, he would be at least twice Cassandra's age. Unless he had secret millions stashed away, I can't see a former beauty queen falling for him.'

'Shona was young, too.' Clearly, Bennett wasn't to be easily dissuaded. 'And there are many reasons people want to be together. What if Cuskie dumped her for Cassandra and Shona went looking for her?'

'We'll consider it alongside everything else,' Minshull cut in, keen to keep the conversation on track.

'Sarge?' Ellis' hand rose, an endearing habit he'd yet to discard.

'Yes, Drew?'

'Could Cuskie have refused to give Shona an alibi as a form of revenge?'

Minshull frowned. 'What, knowing it would put her in the frame for murder?'

'Yes.'

'I think it's a bit dramatic.'

'But it's possible. I mean, if you were mad at your ex and saw a way to hurt them, that would be one hell of a kick.'

'But she said Cuskie split up with her,' Bennett argued.

'Yeah, but we don't know what she said to him when he did,' Ellis returned. 'What if Shona threatened to tell the people Cuskie had ratted out that he was an informer? Or tell police about the dodgy stuff he was doing? Sending her to a certain prison sentence would ensure his secrets were safe.'

It seemed preposterous, but it was a question they should consider. At this stage, anything and everything was up for consideration.

Minshull added *REVENGE?* underneath Karl Cuskie's name. 'We need to speak to Mr Cuskie again. Any idea how to contact him, Les?'

Evans paled. 'Don't look at me. I haven't spoken to him in years.'

'Ask around for me, please? Someone here will know.'

Begrudgingly, Evans accepted.

'Thanks. Can someone find me contact details for Cassandra Norton's boyfriend, too? See if we have an address on file, check DVLA for driving licence details. Failing those, the nightclub where he worked might know.'

'It closed down in 2020,' Bennett said. 'Shut during the lockdowns and never reopened.'

Minshull nodded. It was far from unique among the businesses in Ipswich. The pandemic had ravaged many of the shops, cafés and entertainment venues in the town, the empty units and faded FOR SALE boards testament to the damage months of lost revenue had caused.

'See if we can find former owners, maybe, Kate? They might be able to shed some light on Nicholas Wright as an employee and tell us where he might be now. Companies House should have historic listings of past owners, so check there.'

'On it, Sarge.'

'Thanks.' Minshull's gaze fell on the stacks of evidence file boxes. 'Okay, let's get cracking with the case files. Make a note of everything you find and alert me to anything that might offer us a line of inquiry. I know it's going to be a ball-ache, but let's just work through it, yeah? Tim Brinton should be sending us our Uniform bods later this morning, so that's something.'

'Any idea who, Sarge?' Ellis asked.

'Not yet. But whoever we get, we'll be glad of them. Thanks everyone.'

As the team returned to their desks, Minshull looked back at the whiteboard. Three names, as yet unfamiliar:

CASSANDRA NORTON.
NICHOLAS WRIGHT.
KARL CUSKIE.

How were they linked, if at all? What circumstances had brought them together? And what twists of fate had bound them with such an horrific outcome?

TEN

Transcript of text conversation, Evidence no: CN/098/SSCID

Reopening the case? WTF?

I said wait a week to contact me.

This can't wait. Why the new case?

Stop worrying. They know nothing.

But if they find new stuff?

They won't.

I need to see you.

I can't. Not yet.

When?

Soon.

You said it would blow over.

It will.

Have you seen the news? Journos everywhere. They're not going to let this drop.

They'll only stay till the next big story breaks. Hang tight, it'll be OK.

I need to see you.

Wait. And don't talk to anyone.

ELEVEN

Afternoon news report, BBC News channel

'Back to Suffolk now, and the unfolding drama surrounding Shona Pickton's successful appeal of her twenty-two-year murder sentence, after serving nine years behind bars. Elodie Watling is in Ipswich for us this morning. Elodie, what's the feeling there?'

'Hi Mike. A heavy shadow hangs over this county today, following the violent scenes witnessed at a gypsy and traveller camp in Felixstowe yesterday, just eleven miles from here. I'm at the headquarters of South Suffolk Police, the constabulary heavily criticised by an Appeal Court judge for its handling of the Cassandra Norton murder investigation, nine years ago. There's been much activity here this morning, many people arriving for what must be crisis meetings as the case is reopened. But the police are remaining tight-lipped following Superintendent Ian Martlesham's press statement yesterday.'

'Do you have any sense of how the reopening of the investigation is being viewed by local people?'

'I went out in Felixstowe yesterday to talk to people in the town. And the overwhelming sentiment is dismay that this case is being revisited. Many remembered the fear following Cassandra Norton's murder, nine years ago. Several still consider Shona Pickton a killer. Overwhelmingly, people didn't want her back in the county – and the violent attack on the St Columba Street traveller site is being viewed as proof that she isn't welcome. One man I spoke to said he doubts Cassandra's killer will ever be found while South Suffolk Police remain in charge of the investigation.'

[Cut to vox pop interview in busy high street]

Man: 'Well, they're useless, in't they? Should be out chasin' stolen tractors, not solvin' murders. That's about all they're good for.'

Reporter: 'You don't think they can handle this investigation?'

Man: 'Of course they can't! They stuffed it up last time, and they'll stuff it up again, just you watch.'

[Cut back to reporter next to Police HQ]

'Calls are growing for a bigger, more experienced force to take over the murder investigation. I've heard a rumour that special observers have been appointed to keep a close eye on detectives here. If that's true, detectives from South Suffolk CID will not have an easy ride this time around. Mike, back to you in the studio.'

'Elodie, thanks. And just a reminder that Holly Carlson will be discussing the Cassandra Norton case and the worrying rise in traveller violence on Real Talk, straight after this news bulletin...'

TWELVE

ANDERSON

'Guv.'

Anderson snapped his laptop shut, the smug face of the news anchor vanishing from view. He offered Wheeler a weak smile.

'Yes, Dave?'

'You do yourself no favours watching that crap.'

Knowing Wheeler had him rumbled, Anderson sagged. 'I know. But they seem to know more about this investigation than we do. How did they find out about the bloody observers?'

'I've no idea. But the *bloody observers* are on their way up, so you'd better get ready.' His cheeky grin did little to soften the news.

'Great. Let's hope they didn't see their arrival being announced to the nation.'

'I'm sure they'll be flattered. Any idea who we're getting?'

'Nope.' Anderson wished he did. Bad enough that DCI Taylor was hounding him at every turn and demanding inform-ation, without an observation team scrutinising his every move as well. He appreciated the gesture from Martlesham, but he could do without further complications to contend with.

'There's one bit of good news to cheer you up, though,' Wheeler offered, watching Anderson's speedy attempt to make his document-strewn desk more presentable.

'Oh?'

'We have an address for Nicholas Wright – Cassandra Norton's boyfriend.'

Anderson stopped tidying. 'Great! Where?'

'Sunderland.'

'Oh.'

'But – *but* – get this: I called him and it turns out he's in Lowestoft right now, visiting his sister. He's coming in for an interview with his solicitor at ten tomorrow morning.'

Any step forward was worth celebrating. And this was a big one. 'Dave, I could kiss you.'

'Please don't.'

'Spoilsport,' Anderson returned with a grin, the knowledge of the development warm within him. At least he'd have something to show the observers on their arrival. That put him in a significantly stronger position than five minutes ago. 'Keep the news of this within the office, okay? Just till we've talked with him tomorrow.'

'Sue Taylor sniffing around again, is she?' Wheeler asked, his wry observation proof that he was more aware of the dynamics in Police HQ than most people would ever give him credit for.

'I'm hoping the Super keeps her occupied for the rest of the day.'

'Miracles can happen, eh, Guv?'

Anderson clapped a hand to his heart. 'I'm a believer, Dave.'

'Guv?' Bennett appeared at the open doorway of Anderson's office. 'The observers have arrived.'

'Excellent.' Anderson braced himself against the flood of nerves, his smile as steady as he could make it. The team would all know, of course, but he didn't have to show them. Straightening his jacket, he strode out into the main CID office.

Minshull was by the door, shaking hands with a smartly dressed man and woman. They had the kind of polish regular coppers never achieved, their outward appearance suggesting the importance of their role. No early mornings and long shifts for them, Anderson mused. No late-night office pizzas or operational minefields, either.

'Ah, Guv, this is DI Joy Tsang and DI Boyd Guthrie,' Minshull said, stepping back, the observers turning as Anderson moved to greet them.

But Anderson was already grinning.

'Good to see you both.'

Guthrie's eyes twinkled over his impressive red beard. 'You too, Joel. Long time, eh?'

'I don't want to think how long.' Aware that Minshull and the team were observing the exchange with bewildered interest, Anderson switched back into his professional persona. 'Please, come to my office. Rob, can you arrange refreshments for our guests?'

'Of course, Guv. Tea? Coffee?'

Tsang requested coffee, Guthrie tea. Anderson declined the offer.

'Excellent. Follow me, please.'

It was only when the observers were safely seated beside Anderson's desk and the door firmly closed that Anderson let his mask slip.

'I can't believe it,' he said, laughing as he exchanged familiar hugs with Guthrie and Tsang. 'When did you both start working in observations?'

'Three years ago,' Tsang replied, her smile a welcome sight after the worries Anderson had battled all night. 'I never thought we'd be observing you, though.'

'Me either, Joy.'

'Better be on your best behaviour, laddie. My wife's a terrier,' Guthrie warned, chuckling as Anderson feigned fear. 'Joking aside, it's good to see you. Even if the circumstances are less than ideal.'

'Indeed.' Anderson resumed his seat, the buzz of seeing old friends tempered by the task they faced together. 'We're all under the cosh, as you can imagine.'

'How's it going?'

'Slow, Joy. Although we've had a development this morning that might prove fortuitous.' A thought occurred to him. 'Does Superintendent Martlesham know you know me?'

'I doubt it. But it won't affect our work,' Guthrie assured him. 'We're merely here to observe, not pick fault or assess you. Besides, it might make our presence here a little easier for you. I imagine you have enough to deal with without worrying about observers.'

Anderson smiled his thanks to the friends he'd known since police training college. It seemed a lifetime ago that they'd shared student accommodation together, the memory of those days still warm. They had reconnected on a training course a few years later and remained in touch ever since. Anderson and his wife Ros had even been invited to Joy and Boyd's wedding, five years ago, when his friends finally admitted what everyone else had long suspected and tied the knot. That they had kept their individual surnames spoke volumes about the pair: consummate professionals at work, their personal lives fiercely protected.

He would be careful not to abuse the link here, but privately Anderson felt a surge of relief. Secret allies in a case beset by silent accusation and thinly veiled suspicion would make all the difference.

Ros would love the news.

His wife had stayed up with him last night, stifling her own yawns as she poured endless cups of chamomile tea and listened to the relentless parade of Anderson's fears blowing through his restless mind.

'It isn't personal, love.'

'It feels like it is.'

'Yes, well, it's going to, isn't it? Your superiors haven't exactly been fair to you in the past. But try and see it as support to help you run a better investigation than Sue Taylor managed.'

Ros' wry humour had helped, also that she understood. She'd ridden every twist and turn of Anderson's police career beside him, witnessed every injustice, railed at every bad decision made against him. Had it not been for her unshakeable faith in him as he'd faced the darkest days of his career, Anderson was certain he would not be here now.

Support, where it could be found, mattered more than anything.

Tsang and Guthrie's smiles cooled into professional courtesy as Minshull arrived with two mugs. As soon as he'd gone, they relaxed again.

'So, how do we do this?' Anderson asked.

'We'll remain in the main office and attend all team briefings,' Tsang explained. 'Do you have a desk for us in there?'

'All ready and waiting.'

'Good. We're to report to Ian Martlesham regularly, so we may occasionally leave for those meetings. When we return, we'll need you or your DS to apprise us of anything that's happened during our absence.'

'Of course. Am I to discuss strategy with you away from the team?'

Guthrie shook his head. 'No need. Most of the time you can forget we're here – unless the kettle's going on.'

Anderson returned Guthrie's grin. 'That's a given, Boyd. Anything else?'

Guthrie and Tsang exchanged glances.

'The only other thing I'd mention is to refer to us by rank and surname in front of the team. They might guess we know each other from what they've just seen, but it's best to maintain formality from here on in.' Tsang smiled. 'When the three of us are meeting in your office, first names are fine.'

'No problem.' Anderson allowed himself to relax, the tug of tiredness at his bones too present to ignore. 'Off the record, I'm so glad you're here. This investigation is likely to be brutal.'

'We have every faith in you,' Guthrie affirmed. 'Now, bring us up to speed on where you are, then we'll get started.'

THIRTEEN

ELLIS

Something weird was going on.

Anderson had been like a Caledonian bear with a migraine first thing, his words short and his temper shorter still. Everyone knew why, though nobody dared say it. Observers meant scrutiny, and scrutiny often meant trouble. What agenda did they have?

But since he'd disappeared into his office with DI Tsang and DI Guthrie, Anderson had become a changed man.

Ellis caught Bennett's quizzical look as the DI showed the observers to their desk. They acted as though Anderson's greeting earlier had been nothing more than a polite welcome, but there was an ease between them at odds with their professional demeanour.

What was going on?

'Drew, any joy on the family statements?' Minshull asked, wandering over to Ellis, a large stack of files in hand.

'Just going through them now, Sarge.'

'Anything yet?'

'A lot from Cassandra's father, Mitchell. He was estranged from the family at the time of her death.'

'Contact details?'

'The number on the statements is unobtainable. But I'm going to do an address search. We should have that on file for contact purposes.'

'Right.' Minshull nodded and Ellis saw his eyes slide to Anderson and the observers before returning to him. 'What does he say in the statements?'

'He insisted her boyfriend was responsible,' Ellis replied. 'He clearly hated the dude. *He treats her like crap. They argue all the time. The last time he threatened to shut her up – you can't tell me that isn't proof he wanted to hurt my girl.* It's pretty intense stuff.'

'How many statements did he give?'

Ellis checked the growing list on his notepad. 'Three. One the day after Cassandra was found, one a week later when he came into the station and one just before Shona Pickton was arrested.'

'Odd. Was a reason given for so many statements?'

'He insisted, apparently.'

'Did he change his statement?'

'That's the thing that doesn't make sense: they're almost identical. You can tell he was getting angrier and more belligerent by the final one, but the details are the same. He didn't trust her boyfriend; he thought she'd been harmed by him.'

'Are there any notes from the investigating officers at the time?'

'Yes – here.' Ellis tapped his pen on a line of his notes. 'Sue – *DCI Taylor* – noted that she tried to dissuade Mitchell Norton from making any more statements after the second one, but he insisted.'

'Why should she dissuade him? He was dealing with the loss of his daughter.'

Ellis had wondered the same thing. 'Reading between the lines, I reckon DCI Taylor thought he was a time-waster.' He knew Minshull would understand the undercurrent of meaning beneath his answer.

She'd made up her mind and he was getting in the way.

Everyone knew Sue Taylor held very definite views, not easily challenged. Her snap decisions were the source of much consternation across Police HQ. Optimistically, it could be attributed to the force of her convictions, her unwillingness to settle for accepted wisdom and her drive for better things. Realistically, it was more to do with protecting her position at all costs.

Likes the sound of her own voice and the feel of her own boots, his mum would say. His mother had only met DCI Taylor once, at a charity function, and disliked her on sight. As Kaye Ellis was near legendary as a judge of character, Ellis knew better than to question her verdict.

DCI Taylor wouldn't welcome the chumminess between Anderson and the two observers, that was certain. However cool they were being about it now, they clearly had some shared history. If they thought the team wouldn't notice it, they were wrong.

Minshull sighed. 'Right. Keep trying to find contact details for Mr Norton, please, and in the meantime carry on with the family statements.'

'Will do, Sarge.'

Ellis waited until Minshull headed for Anderson's office before he leaned across to Bennett at the neighbouring desk. 'How's it going?'

Bennett grimaced. 'Glacial.'

'Who's in your pile?'

'Friends of Cassandra Norton. Which is just as fun as it sounds.'

Ellis stifled a laugh. 'What are they saying?'

'That it was *out of character* for her to be on Orwell Road, alone, at that time on a Thursday night. That she had no enemies and had a perfect life. That whoever murdered her must have done it out of lust or jealousy.'

'That sounds like the picture the press painted of her,' Ellis replied. 'Dave's going through the newspaper coverage from the time and said pretty much the same.'

Wheeler looked up from his stack of files. 'Taking my name in vain, you two?'

'Never, Dave!' Bennett smiled. 'I was just telling Drew about the statements from Cassandra Norton's friends – that she was a perfect woman with a perfect life.'

'That'll explain the newspaper articles that all cited *a friend of Cassandra Norton* for their authority,' Wheeler said, lifting a yellowing copy of *The Daily Call* from the open file on the stack upon his desk. 'Reckon they were all giving interviews to the press?'

'Maybe they cared about their friend,' Evans muttered from somewhere behind the bombsite of his desk. 'No law against that.'

'True, there isn't, Les,' Bennett agreed. 'There's just something about the tone of all their statements. They're so similar I've had to keep checking back to make sure I haven't moved onto someone else's by mistake.'

'A united front?' Ellis suggested.

'Or a careful cover story,' Bennett countered.

'Is there no mention of Nicholas Wright in the friends' statements?'

'I've yet to come across one if there is.'

Ellis considered this. 'Could they have known Wright was domineering and have been trying to protect their friend?'

'Possibly. But if they loved her as much as they claim to, why not bring it all down on his head? Why hide it behind the *perfect girl, perfect life* narrative? It wasn't going to help Cassandra Norton, was it?'

'Perhaps they were scared, too?'

Bennett looked at Wheeler. 'Maybe.'

'Or maybe Mitchell Norton was wrong in his assertions about Wright,' Ellis argued. 'It could just be as simple as that.' He caught DI Tsang watching the conversation from across the CID office. It made him uneasy, being watched like that. He turned his attention squarely back to his desk-neighbours. 'Are you going to try to contact any of the friends?'

'As many as I can,' Bennett replied, the wearying prospect of interviews evident in her expression. 'I'm hoping I can piece together a better picture by hearing their testimonies in person.'

'Good luck with that.'

'I'll need it.'

Glancing at the observers, Ellis lowered his voice to a whisper. 'We all will.'

FOURTEEN

CORA

The Columba Street site that Cora and Tris returned to was like a different place.

Gone was the laughter and constant activity, the outward signs of life. People watched from windows instead of open doorways. Children remained indoors, the only movement outside the caravans and mobile homes the strain of anxious dogs against long chains. Large loops of razor wire had been attached to the front gates, thick sheets of plywood obscuring the view through the bars from the roadside. A police patrol car was parked at the end of the lane leading to the site, the only approach towards it. Tris had told Cora they would remain in place for at least one more day.

But was it enough?

Were any of the changes enough to dissuade further attacks?

Joss met them at the gates, waiting while Tris parked his Land Rover Evoque where Cora's car had been damaged. He greeted them with longer than usual hugs, their presence there more welcome than his careful expression suggested.

'How are you doing, man?' Tris asked, his arm around Joss' shoulders as they walked towards the classroom building.

'Better for seeing you.'

'How are the kids?'

'Scared. Quiet. Withdrawn, some of them. You being here will help.'

'Everyone's agreed to continue,' Cora said, baulking at the large, ugly crater in the plasterwork of the project building, the result of the missile thrown at the classroom. Any further and it could have smashed the window beneath which she and the two girls had been sitting.

She shuddered.

Most of the debris had been cleared, the bloodcurdling screams of the bricks and broken bottles thankfully gone. But hate muttered from the dust at the peripheries of the space, prejudice and rage swept into the patches of grass between the concrete bases of the vans. Bristling against them, Cora reached out with her mind and firmly silenced each one.

The dissenting thought-sounds had no place here.

The project room was clean and bright as ever, but conspicuously empty. There was no session today, only a meeting with Joss, Tris, Cora and a couple of the senior community leaders from the site. Cora had messages to share from Sam and Merryn, who were working in their schools today, together with Alannah and Ollie from the Ed Psych Unit, all keen to affirm their support.

The meeting also gave Cora and Tris a chance to talk freely. It had become abundantly clear that proper conversations could not be conducted at their office; the loud opposition from the four councillors now making itself felt in every sector of local authority control. Someone in the building was feeding overheard information back to the councillors; not everyone in the adjoining offices as sympathetic to The HappyKid Project as Cora and her colleagues had hoped.

As Tris had predicted, the dissenting councillors had already sought to disrupt operations, tabling questions in council chambers deliberately designed to obstruct and obfuscate council business. One thing was certain: they had nailed their colours firmly to the mast and were unlikely to be mollified by anything Tris or Cora said.

It was safer to be here, where their work mattered.

Joss arranged chairs in a circle in the middle of the classroom and Tris moved to greet Geraint Mohan and Avram Ward from the site. When all were seated, Tris began.

'Firstly, I want to say thank you for allowing us back. I realise the past twenty-four hours have been horrendous for you. I appreciate your faith in us.'

'Goes without saying, Tris,' Joss replied, the elders nodding in agreement.

'The children have always been at the very centre of HappyKid and that won't change. We want to be here for you, for the whole community, especially now. But you have the final say, as always. If you want us here, we will be. If you don't, we won't.'

'The kids need you,' Avram said. 'And we need the support.'

'Then you have us.'

Joss frowned. 'What about the councillors shouting us down? Will they let you stay?'

'They can't stop us,' Cora replied, her pulse quickening. 'We're all agreed that we'll continue, even if the council officially removes its support. Everyone is ready to come, extra volunteers, too.'

'Your car...' Joss began, his voice low.

'It's just a car,' Cora repeated, the sentiment the same here as it had been with the team in the office. Tris caught her eye and she added, 'Besides, it means I get to be chauffeured around in his swanky Land Rover for the foreseeable.'

A ripple of amusement around the circle eased the tension in the room. Cora felt it ebb a little, then race back like an insistent tide.

'So, what do you propose we do from here?'

'Good question, Joss,' Tris replied, his smile fading. 'What matters is the children's wellbeing. So we'll start by talking about the attack and working through fears and worries. I propose we run activities as usual, for consistency and to inspire confidence, but our main focus for the immediate future will be dealing with emotional issues and building coping strategies for the children.'

'Might need some of that for us, too,' Geraint added. He laughed along with Tris and Joss, but Cora sensed a serious request disguised by the joke.

'We're here for everyone,' she said. 'Whatever you need.'

While Tris, Geraint and Avram discussed access and plans for future sessions, Joss moved over to Cora.

'Fancy a wander around? Some of the kids want to see you.'

'I'd love to,' Cora agreed.

They left the project building and began a slow navigation of the site. The bitter wind that had characterised the last twenty-four hours had abated at last, the temperature a little warmer than it had been for days. Cora was still glad of her scarf, the constant chatter of its creator now almost inaudible.

The first two vans they passed had their curtains firmly drawn. But when they reached the next home, two eager faces appeared in the front bay window.

Cora smiled and waved, delighted by the children's instant smiles. Joss knocked on the door, calling through the frosted glass to ask permission to enter, but when he opened the door, he was almost knocked off the top step by two small rockets as the children dashed out.

'Steady now,' he laughed. 'Don't floor the Doc!'

Trinity and Maire paid no attention, slamming headlong into Cora's waiting embrace.

'We thought you'd stopped coming.'

'Da said they totalled your car.'

'Did you fight the Nazis to get in?'

'Of course I'm still going to come,' Cora laughed, breathless from the welcome. 'And yes, my car got smashed, no I didn't have to fight anyone to get in, but it takes more than both of those things to stop me.'

'Can we still make stuff? And go to the reading corner?'

'We're going to carry on just like before.' She pulled back to look at the girls. 'How are you two doing?'

'We weren't scared,' Trinity replied, her chin high.

Maire observed her sister incredulously. 'I was.'

'I was, too,' Cora admitted, glancing at Joss for support. 'I think we all were.'

'But you'll make them go away now?' Maire asked, wide blue eyes seeking Cora out. 'Make them stop?'

Her trust shattered Cora's heart. If only it were as easy as wishing trouble away. Despite the unanimous decision of the HappyKid team to continue, Cora was aware of dark clouds gathering over the council. The four councillors kicking up dissention wouldn't be dissuaded by the volunteer team's act of solidarity. Buoyed by the media frenzy, they'd push until the issue wielded power for them.

Leaving Trinity and Maire's home with promises to return in two days' time, Cora and Joss walked on. More children greeted them, some waving from the safety of their vans, others daring to venture outside. With each now familiar face seen, Cora's resolve strengthened.

They reached the strip of field behind the shipping container where they'd taken refuge during the attack, leading to the perimeter fence that marked the back of the site. A dark bank of pine trees lay beyond, their planting so thick that no sunlight was visible between the branches and trunks. Crossing the field towards the fence, they walked in companionable silence.

Cora heard no peripheral voices from Joss, but his body voiced a tale all of its own: worry etched into his brow, tautness across his back and shoulders hinting at unseen burdens he carried, and a nervous flicking of his thumb and forefinger where it hung by his side.

The green space was welcoming and well cared for, even in mid-November. During HappyKid project sessions, the children had mentioned to Cora that they played there often, riding bikes or running around. A space for them to be kids, to dream up incredible adventures, to stretch both their limbs and their imaginations. It was worryingly quiet now. Had any of the children used it since the attack?

They had almost reached the perimeter fence with its ominous forest neighbour when Cora decided to break the silence.

'I was thinking…'

'I wanted to ask you something,' Joss said, suddenly, causing Cora to stop.

'Okay.'

'Before the attack, during one of the sessions, Tris said something… About you.'

'Oh?'

He stopped walking and faced her. 'Tell me if I'm out of line…'

Nerves twisted in the pit of her stomach. 'What did he say?'

Joss gave an uncomfortable cough and shoved his hands into the pockets of his jeans. 'That you hear stuff? *Know* stuff?'

On guard now, Cora said nothing, waiting for more.

'Do you have the Sight?'

It was such an unexpected, archaic phrase that Cora laughed.

Embarrassed, Joss stared at the still verdant grass. 'You don't. I got it wrong. Sorry.'

'No… hang on…' Cora regrouped, shelving her amusement. It was an honest question. She just hadn't anticipated sharing details of her ability with him, here. 'I'm not a psychic, if that's what you mean. I can't *see* things. But I *hear* them.'

His water-blue eyes met hers. 'Hear? What?'

She took a breath. In any other circumstance it would be inappropriate to share details of her ability. Neither Alannah nor Ollie knew at work, and Cora and Tris had taken great care to keep the details of Cora's ability under wraps. But she sensed Joss was asking from a point of experience her colleagues would never have.

'I have emotional synaesthesia. It's very rare and not much is known about it, but in a nutshell, it allows me to hear traces of emotion and subliminal thought surrounding objects that have been handled. I feel emotion, too; like a snapshot of someone's experience at the moment they touched the object.'

'Like an audible memory?'

86

Surprised, Cora smiled. 'Yes, exactly like that. The best way I can describe it is that I can hear audible fingerprints where physical ones have been left.'

'So, you'd hear these fingerprints from items the kids show you?'

'Yes.'

'Only when they're holding them?'

'No – I can sense emotional voices days and even weeks after an object has been touched.'

'What about years?'

It was the second time she'd been asked that in the last two days. Why was that? Cora chose her answer with care. 'I've never tested it that far back. Usually, it's a matter of weeks at best.'

'Right.' Joss nodded, his gaze moving out to the pine forest.

'Is it a problem?' Hesitancy danced in her question.

'No – no, not at all. I was just – interested. That's all.'

'If it helps, I don't listen purposefully to the voices I hear in the project room. I can mute the sound – like turning down the volume on a car radio. I never note what I hear in this kind of a setting. It's an observation, nothing more.'

'What did you hear from the girls?'

'I'm not sure I should…'

'Please? I'm not judging.'

Cora avoided his eye. 'Nothing just now. But on the day of the attack, I could hear concern.'

'Concern? About what?'

'It wasn't specific. Only that the girls had been told not to worry and it would all blow over.' She offered a hopeful smile. 'It could be about anything, though. Everything is full of drama and feels like the end of the world when you're their age.'

'It would blow over…' His voice trailed away into the breeze.

'I don't think it was related to the attack.'

'It could be.' He risked a glance back. 'The night before you came for the HappyKid session we'd discussed Shona Pickton's acquittal. We had a meeting in the project room, all of us. Safe to say we saw trouble coming, even though we knew she wasn't returning here.'

'Did you receive any threats before the attack?'

'No, but we know how this plays out. They blamed our community last time and the media hasn't changed their stance. It's worse now than ever, with their clickbait headlines and the way they pursue easy targets.' He shook his head. 'But that's beside the point. If we carry on the sessions – *when* we carry on – could you tell me if you hear anything?'

A flood of potential risk factors raced into Cora's mind. What if Tris considered it a violation of privacy? Or a professional crossing of the line? They needed to stay united if they were to weather the storm and keep HappyKid running. And while she liked the project leader, did she know Joss well enough yet to entrust him with such information?

'I don't know. Why do you want to know what I hear?'

'Because this community is proud and private. They won't always tell us their real opinion, especially if it goes against the grain of the general consensus. But if I had some insight…' He offered the smallest trace of a smile.

'I'll need to clear it with Tris.'

'Fine by me. And take some time to think it over, if you need to.' His expression softened. 'I didn't mean to drop it on you like that, sorry. I'm just trying to find any advantage I can.'

'I understand,' Cora said. 'I'll think about it.'

FIFTEEN

MINSHULL

'Karl Cuskie, fifty-four. Had several run-ins with the law over the past twenty years but miraculously never served time.'

Minshull eyed Evans, who slumped further in his seat.

'Do we have a contact number or address?'

'Nothing so far, Sarge,' Ellis replied. 'He moves around a lot, apparently.'

'Within Suffolk?'

'Within Ipswich. The six possible addresses we found for him over the last three years all turned out to be previous ones.'

That was very odd indeed. Minshull stared at Cuskie's name on the board. 'Why would anyone want to move around that much?'

'Let's just say our Mr Cuskie likes to be in charge of who can and can't find him,' Ellis said.

Minshull stifled a groan. 'Keep looking, please, Drew.'

'He drinks in The Green Dragon on Silent Street most nights,' Wheeler offered, consulting notes he'd made around Police HQ talking to older colleagues in different departments. 'It's where the old guard drinks. Word is he'll show up there in time for the shift change and have information ready for anyone who buys him enough drinks at the bar.'

Surprised, Minshull turned to Evans. 'Les? That true?'

Evans nodded sullenly. He should have been the one asking colleagues, but Minshull suspected he'd palmed off the responsibility on Wheeler. Although a direct disregard of orders,

Minshull could see why he'd done it. More people were likely to talk to Wheeler, whose good nature inspired conversation and trust, than Evans who had likely pushed his luck with them in the past.

'He's been a regular there for years,' Evans confirmed. 'You knew where to find him if you needed him. He'd wait at the end of the bar like he was holding court. Some of the high-ups had his number, too. I know your dad did, Sarge.'

It was meant as a dig, but this time Minshull was prepared.

'Anyone else?'

'Tim Brinton said his predecessor used him regularly. Reading between the lines, I think Tim might have succumbed a couple of times, too.'

Minshull wished he could be shocked by this news, but it was depressingly predictable. Results mattered in policing – even more so today, with forces under so much public scrutiny and pressure from the top to improve crime figures. Was it any wonder some of his colleagues turned to questionable sources to get results? That several names of officers he'd hoped would know better were on Wheeler's list only increased his disappointment.

Informers were, and should remain, a thing of the past, as far as Minshull was concerned. People who kept themselves unaccountable for their own crimes by providing police with information on other criminals were the lowest of the low in his opinion – and what was to say that they wouldn't be as willing to pass information back to the criminal fraternity regarding the police? How could you trust someone so ready to throw their own friends and associates under the bus for the right pay-out?

'We need to talk to him – *on* the record,' Minshull added, before anyone could suggest he go seeking out a police informer. 'Keep looking for that address, please.'

'Sarge.'

'Yes, Sarge.'

'Thanks. Now, has anyone managed to uncarth Karl Cuskie's original statement or interview notes in our endless navigation of the evidence file mountain?'

'Sarge.' To Minshull's surprise, Evans raised a hand. 'Located the transcript just before the briefing.'

'Good work, Les,' Minshull replied, impressed. 'Don't think I've ever seen you so eager in here before.'

'Probably the medication I'm on,' he returned, a rueful grin masking a compliment accepted. 'Don't worry, it'll wear off, soon.'

'What does he say?'

Evans harumphed with the effort as he repositioned his body to a more upright position. When he produced a pair of reading glasses from a pocket of his crumpled suit trousers, a gentle round of sniggers passed around the detectives. Slowly, Evans slid the glasses up onto the bridge of his nose with a deliberately placed middle finger.

'Er… Cuskie is asked about the night in question: "Did you see Shona Pickton that evening?", to which he replies, "I was at home alone." "All evening?" DCI Taylor asks. "Yes," he replies. "Shona has told us she met you for dinner, then you got into a *violent argument* and she left the house. Is that correct?" Cuskie says, "I don't know why she'd say that." DCI Taylor presses him. "But she *has* said that." Cuskie then says, "She's just mad we broke up last week." "When, last week?" DCI Taylor asks. "Tuesday, I think." Then, later on, he's asked again if he saw Shona Pickton that night. He gets really agitated at this point – the notes record he got angry and started to shout. The last recorded statement from him says, "She's lying to protect herself. Trying to drop me in it. I never saw her that night and she never called me."…'

Minshull's attention snagged on a sentence. 'Back up a mo,' he said. 'Cuskie says Shona was *trying to drop him in it*? In what, exactly?'

Evans shrugged. 'Trying to frame him as an accomplice? Or pin the murder on him instead of her?'

'Or just get him in trouble, as revenge for breaking up?' Ellis offered, with a hint of triumph. 'Like I said earlier, only different.'

Wheeler and Bennett laughed, despite the seriousness of the briefing. Their amusement fractured the tension in the CID office, like cracks traversing ice before the arrival of a thaw.

'What?' Ellis demanded, observing his colleagues' mirth with bewilderment.

'Just like you said, Drew,' Wheeler chuckled, 'only not.'

'That's what I said,' Ellis protested, missing the joke entirely, which only served to make Minshull and Anderson entertain smiles. 'Are you saying you don't think it's a possibility that Cuskie was scared Pickton might throw him under the bus? If he'd dumped her, humiliated her...'

'Or if he'd left her for Cassandra Norton,' Bennett suggested, her own words stealing her smile.

The team looked at Bennett. From their desk beside the whiteboard, DI Tsang and DI Guthrie began to watch, too.

Minshull sensed a weird atmosphere rolling in between the CID team's chairs, like an ominous progression of mist over late autumn fields. 'And that's why he thought Pickton had killed Cassandra? So in the interview he was protecting himself?'

'You have to admit, Sarge, that would be one hell of a motivation, if he thought she might be framing him for Cassandra's murder.'

'You're having a laugh,' Evans scoffed. 'A former beauty queen and a bloke twice her age?'

'Why not?' Bennett returned. 'Wouldn't be the first time...'

'If he had money, maybe. Or power. Neither of which Cuskie has. Trust me, the only thing that scrote has to offer is his gob and the ability to run fast.'

'All the same...'

But Evans was having none of it, his laughter igniting fury in his colleague. 'Bollocks, Kate. Look, I'm not saying Cassandra Norton wouldn't go for an older bloke, but not someone without the means to keep her.'

Bennett glared at him. 'The Dark Ages called: they want your attitude back…'

'Okay, okay,' Minshull stepped in before all-out war occurred, mindful of the two observers currently witnessing this all playing out. 'I'll admit, it sounds unlikely. But we keep it on the table. We've encountered stranger things in investigations before. Les, did Cuskie offer any information regarding Shona knowing Cassandra Norton?'

Packing away his mirth, Evans scrabbled about on his desk to find another open file. The desk was definitely returning to his pre-leave state, a sight both comforting in its familiarity and deeply depressing to be seen by the observers. 'Here… DCI Taylor asks Cuskie if Shona knew Cassandra Norton. "Yes, she did," he says. So the DCI asks, "How well?" "Really well. They even worked together a while back." So, the next thing he's asked is, "Where was that?" But he says he can't remember. Then there's this – which seems an odd question to go to… "Might Shona Pickton have had reason to wish harm on Cassandra Norton?" And Cuskie answers, after a pause: "She hated her. Said she wished her dead." Then the interview ends. No further questions.'

'Why didn't the DCI push it?' Ellis asked, Bennett agreeing. 'That accusation is huge.'

'Is there another interview?' Wheeler suggested.

'Not that I've found.'

The sudden twist jarred Minshull's mind. 'Hang on… wait.' He lifted his hand, as much to give himself a minute to think as to signal for calm. 'Are we suggesting Cuskie believed Pickton had murdered Cassandra Norton, so by refusing to give Shona Pickton an alibi he could ensure he wasn't linked to it?'

Bennett shrugged. 'Maybe he thought, with his track record as an informer, he'd be assumed complicit. I mean, he *was* dodgy and had been for years.'

'He assumed he'd be blamed rather than Pickton?'

'Exactly that.'

Minshull observed his team. 'But he thought her capable of murder.'

'Yes,' Bennett replied. 'Or he wanted us to think that, as revenge, because *she* dumped *him* for having an affair with Cassandra.'

'Sarge,' Wheeler cut in. 'I remember Shona Pickton being interviewed. I was present for two of the four interview rounds. Both times I saw her, she insisted she was no longer in touch with Cassandra Norton.'

'But she said she knew Karl Cuskie?'

'Yes, she confirmed he was her former lover. She was adamant that Cuskie could prove she was nowhere near Orwell Road that night because they had been together.'

A dull ache lodged itself at the centre of Minshull's brow as the conflicting theories were tossed around like small ships caught in a squall. There was only one person who could put the record straight.

The problem now was finding him.

SIXTEEN

BENNETT

Thin, grey morning light limped into the South Suffolk CID office, much like its detective team. Even a surprise delivery of *maritozzi* buns and coffee from DI Anderson's much loved Italian deli in the centre of Ipswich couldn't sustain their spirits for long.

Around every desk the box-spectres of the previous investigation stood sentry, gloomy reminders of the work that remained. Added to this, the frustration caused by thwarted attempts to contact Karl Cuskie, Ryan Norton and Cassandra's estranged father, Mitchell, and the prospect of another long shift in what seemed destined to be an endless investigation, hung heavy on everyone's shoulders.

Bennett groaned as she hefted the next evidence box onto her desk. Everything ached today, not helped by a restless night after her half-hearted attempt to reorganise furniture in her rented house. She'd brought so little from her marital home when her former husband had sold it from beneath her, that her whole life outside of work seemed to consist of flat-pack furniture construction and endless paperwork.

That was another reason for her mood this morning: the *decree nisi* that had been waiting for her on the doormat when she returned home last night. One more step to ridding her life of Russ Bennett for good.

Her overzealous attempts to rearrange her space had been fuelled by the stark, business-like letter from her solicitor. A physical action to purge any memory of her almost-ex from her world. She regretted it now, her aching back's loud protestations with every move a painful addition to her morning's work.

The observers were already at their desk when she'd arrived, and were now working quietly, heads bowed. They seemed friendly enough, but Bennett sensed the carefulness with which her colleagues had worked since their arrival. Ellis was right though: he'd confided in Bennett yesterday, during a lunchtime visit to the canteen, that Anderson's response to them seemed off.

'He's too relaxed,' he had said, between bites of steak baguette. 'I saw how he was before they arrived. We all did. No way he doesn't know them.'

'Does it matter if he does?' Bennett had asked, wishing she had an appetite to match her colleague's. Since the end of her marriage, she'd struggled to find the energy or inclination to eat anything, only succeeding because she knew her body needed fuel. Would the thrill of food ever return? 'It might make life easier for all of us if he's happy.'

Ellis had conceded her point, but it had remained on Bennett's mind ever since.

Whatever the truth, DI Tsang and DI Guthrie seemed destined to be a part of life in CID for the foreseeable future. Whether Bennett or any of her fellow detectives would become accustomed to the strange scrutiny was another matter...

'Sarge, Nicholas Wright is here for his interview,' Ellis said, the desk phone's receiver hooked between his ear and shoulder as he shifted a large pile of evidence files to the edge of his desk.

'Cheers, Drew. Tell Pauline I'm on my way.' Minshull stood and swung his jacket from the back of his chair. 'Kate, fancy coming in with me on this?'

The invitation was like sudden unexpected sunlight on a day of heavy rain.

–

Pauline Wilks, near-legendary Desk Sergeant, offered Bennett and Minshull the grimmest of smiles when they entered Reception.

'Your man's over there,' she said, her voice low, her raised eyebrow the only clue necessary to gauge her opinion. 'Can't miss him. Orange puffer jacket.'

Bennett looked across the row of plastic chairs in the packed waiting area. Sure enough, the tall man in the centre was easy to find, standing out like a well-padded Belisha beacon in a sea of grey and blue. Beside him sat a bored-looking solicitor, as grey in the face as the suit he was wearing, checking his watch.

Minshull moved across to greet them, followed by Bennett.

'Mr Wright, hello. I'm DS Rob Minshull and this is my colleague, DC Kate Bennett.'

Wright stood, his solicitor scrambling to his feet beside him. 'Nick Wright. And this is my solicitor, Keith Madeley.'

'Thanks for coming in,' Minshull said. 'Shall we?'

In Interview Room 2, Bennett watched Cassandra Norton's former boyfriend with interest as he and his solicitor took their seats at the interview desk. He appeared relaxed and in good humour, despite the unscheduled detour from his trip.

'How was the drive down from Lowestoft?' Minshull asked, sorting his notebook and papers.

'Not bad. Bit of traffic, but no major delays.' His accent was neutral, but Bennett detected a slight Suffolk lilt still present.

'That's good. Okay, if you're both happy, we'll get started.' He nodded to Bennett to begin the recording.

After listing the date, time and individuals present, Bennett handed over to Minshull.

'Thanks for your participation today, Mr Wright. The purpose of this interview is to revisit your statement made as part of the first investigation into the death of Cassandra Norton, nine years ago. As you know, the investigation has been reopened and, as a result, we are talking to everyone who gave statements before. I have your original statement here, and a copy for you.' He slid a copy across the desk towards them.

Bennett noted the coolness with which Nicholas Wright scanned his words. Keith Madeley looked on impassively, then clicked his ballpoint pen to take slow, unhurried notes.

'Do you recognise that document as the statement you made and signed, nine years ago?'

'Yes.'

'Okay, thanks. I'll recap some of the main points in that statement first and then I have a couple of supplementary questions for you.'

Wright nodded.

'You say in your statement that you saw Cassandra Norton on the evening of Thursday 16th April, 2015.'

'Yes.'

'And that was around seven p.m.'

'Around that time.'

'Where did you see Ms Norton?'

'At her flat. She rented a one-bedroom apartment on Leopold Road.'

'In Felixstowe?'

'Yes.'

'And how did Ms Norton seem to you?'

Wright shrugged. 'Just – normal.'

'What was normal for Ms Norton?'

'She had things on her mind, but she wasn't overly stressed about them. I saw her for an hour. We had a drink and talked about a job she'd been doing for a friend.'

'What was the job?'

'Deliveries.'

'Of what?'

'She didn't go into details.'

'Was that a new job?'

'That one was, yes.'

'What other work did Ms Norton do?'

Wright sniffed. 'Modelling. Promotion work. She had a load of jobs after winning the beauty contest. Car shows, trade shows, bridal catwalk stuff. It varied, but she was always busy.'

'Thank you.' Minshull made a note and scanned his marked copy of the statement. 'Then you said that you argued and she told you to leave?'

'That's right.'

'What time was this?'

'About eight fifteen p.m. She was staring at me from the window as I drove off.'

'Right.' Minshull tapped the page of his notebook with his pen. 'Can you tell us what you argued about?'

Wright blinked. Bennett saw him swallow hard. 'I can't remember. We argued a lot when we were together.'

'Was it about her new job? Or the promotion work?'

'I don't... I don't think so, no. It was probably a power struggle. It usually was. Cass believed the hype about her – the Miss Suffolk thing and all the sleazy sods who came out of the woodwork promising her the earth, so long as she was wearing a bikini.' He gave a grunt of disgust, and Bennett could only imagine how he'd reacted to his girlfriend's modelling work. 'She liked getting her own way and when her mind was set, nobody could dissuade her.'

'Were you worried about her new job?' Minshull asked.

'I could have been. Sorry, I don't really remember. Nine years is a long time.'

Not if you loved someone, Bennett thought. She still remembered the last argument she'd had with her dad as he was getting into his car, less than an hour before a speeding HGV crossed the central barrier on the A14, killing him instantly. They'd fought all her life, and she would never describe them as close, especially not when she joined the police. But her final, furious words to her father were thorns that pierced her heart whenever she thought of him.

If you hate me so much, maybe you shouldn't come back...

Swallowing hard at the razor-sharp recollection, she watched Minshull's slow, deliberate note-taking, wondering if Wright's answer had raised a question mark as it had for her.

Rob Minshull was always a closed book during interviews. But that was little different to his demeanour in the CID office. He liked to keep his cards close, his emotions in check. Recent years as a DS had softened him somewhat – and there had been exceptions where Bennett had glimpsed his true feelings – but his strength lay in what he withheld. In an interview situation, even one like this, it gave him an edge.

'Do you know what she was doing for the rest of the evening?'

'She said she was meeting a friend.'

'At what time?'

'She didn't say.'

'Did she mention the friend's name?'

A pause. 'No.'

Minshull caught it like an eager dog with a stick. 'Are you sure?'

'I said before.' Wright tapped the copy of his 2015 statement. 'Look, here. *She said she was meeting a friend but didn't say which one.*' He sent Minshull a smug smile.

'Did she say where they were meeting? Were they going out for food or drinks?'

'No.'

'Do you think she was meeting her friend in Orwell Road?'

Bennett saw Wright's expression fall.

'Because that's where she was found, wasn't it? On the pavement in front of Trinity Methodist Church.'

Wright's gaze dropped to the desk. 'She… she didn't say.'

'We realise this must be painful,' Bennett said, a gentle nudge to Minshull to remember compassion in his questioning. 'But it helps us to know any reason Cassandra might have had to be in that area of town at that time.'

'Cass made it very clear that questions weren't welcome,' Wright replied, an edge to his voice. 'I accused her of seeing someone else. That's when she told me to leave.'

The admission took Minshull by surprise. There had been no mention of this in Wright's original statement. Why was he sharing it now?

'Who did you think she might be seeing?'

Wright bristled. 'There was some bloke called Karl sniffing around her. She told me it was nothing, but I think they were screwing each other. I haven't been able to get that out of my mind.'

'Did she mention his surname?'

'No, just his first name. *Karl with a K*. Like it made him special.'

Bennett's ears pricked up. 'Karl Cuskie?' she asked, glancing at Minshull to make sure he didn't mind her uninvited intervention.

'Sounds right.'

Bennett had floated the theory in the CID office, but the sudden possibility of Cassandra Norton and Karl Cuskie actually being in a relationship was still shocking. Why was Cassandra potentially mixed up with a man like him? From what Bennett had learned of the police informer – and his photo on file – he didn't seem the kind of man a beauty queen might choose for a partner. As shallow an observation as that was, really, what were the chances? And why hadn't this been mentioned in Wright's first interview? Was the *Karl* that Wright suspected his girlfriend of infidelity with the same police informer currently avoiding their inquiries? And why was this only coming to light now? Might the information have changed the course of the original investigation if it had been revealed nine years ago?

'You say he was *sniffing around her*,' Minshull began, and Bennett wondered if his mind was whirring as fast as hers. 'In what way?'

'Said he wanted to support her modelling career, or some bullshit. Sponsorship. There was a local business he was involved with, and he'd promised her paid gigs representing them at events. She denied being involved with him, of course. Told me

I was insane for even thinking it. But there was an excitement when she mentioned his name that I never heard when she talked about me.'

Minshull turned the page on Wright's original statement, his eyes scanning the lines of text. 'But you didn't mention this here.'

Wright avoided eye contact.

'Can I ask why?'

'I was in shock. Losing her, I mean. It didn't seem important in the light of her death. Thing is, I was paranoid back then. Stunning girlfriend on my arm, turning heads wherever she went, with people looking at us wondering what the hell she was doing with a guy like me. I saw every bloke Cass talked to as a potential threat. I'm not proud of how I was back then. Nine years is a long time to think better of things.'

Minshull let his gaze linger on Wright for a moment longer than was comfortable. Then he looked down at the printed statement on the interview desk. 'Do you wish to add this to your statement now?'

Wright nodded, glancing at his solicitor, who did the same. 'Also, I want it on record that this Karl bloke was the one who'd got her the delivery job. I didn't like Cass having so much to be grateful to him for – I reckoned it was proof of him worming his way into her life, until he could push me out of it.' He gave a long sigh. 'I was a bastard to her about that. I've regretted it for years.'

Minshull glanced at Bennett, who accepted the invitation to take over while the DS made notes.

'Is there anyone else you can remember who may have wished Cass harm? Anyone she might have mentioned to you, or shared a grievance about?'

'She never mentioned any other names. Although she kept talking about *the new crowd* she was hanging out with. She said they were more fun than her old friends, did more exciting stuff.'

'Like what?'

'She never said. I just remember the way she lit up when she was talking about them. Like they mattered to her. Like they gave her something I couldn't.' He stared directly at Bennett, a look that chilled her bones. 'I *hated* that.'

It was all Bennett could do to return to her notes without shivering.

'Okay. Just one more question. In your statement you say that you were at home with your mother on the evening that Cassandra was killed. But notes from later in the case mention that your mother was away visiting friends in Thetford and didn't return until the following Monday.'

'You spoke to my mum?' Wright's pointed look at his solicitor registered a direct hit.

'My colleagues did,' Minshull replied, coolly. 'As I'm sure you can appreciate, in a murder investigation every fact has to be double-checked.'

Wright blinked. 'I'm sorry... I...'

To Bennett's surprise, Nicholas Wright suddenly broke down. She and Minshull watched in stunned silence as the man sobbed, accepting a handkerchief from his startled solicitor.

'Mr Wright, do you need a moment?' Minshull asked, his question noticeably softer than before.

Wright shook his head, gasping for air as he covered his eyes with the handkerchief. After several minutes, he fixed his reddened eyes on Minshull and Bennett.

'Forgive me. Mum passed away just over a year ago. The thought that I...' Emotion stole his words. He reached for his cup of water, drinking in ugly gulps until it was empty. 'I need to retract that claim.'

'That you were with your mum?'

'Yes.'

'Okay. I'll ask again: where were you between eight forty-five p.m. and nine ten p.m. on the evening of Thursday 16th April, 2015?'

Wright cleared his throat, his words unsteady when they followed. 'I was at a poker game. Nobody knew. Least of all Mum… She hated gambling. It took my dad, you see. He lost everything – the house, all the furniture, all their savings. In the end he couldn't cope and… they found him in a field, miles away.'

'I'm sorry to hear that.' Bennett heard real compassion in Minshull's voice when he said it.

Wright brought the handkerchief to his mouth for a moment, his eyes squeezing shut. 'It would have broken her heart if she'd known where I was.'

'Who were you playing poker with?' Bennett asked, keen to maintain the momentum of this sudden turn of events despite the desperately sad story Wright was recounting.

'Charlie Motson, a few guys from the pub, Phil Sheehy, and Jake Kilburn.'

The final name hit like a bolt from the blue.

Bennett was all too aware of that name. Everybody in Police HQ was.

Jake Kilburn – the alleged head of a large local crime syndicate. A businessman with his finger in many pies, which all conveniently disappeared the moment anyone looked too closely or asked awkward questions. An upstanding member of the community, if you believed the generous and frequent references to his charity work in the *Suffolk Herald*: a man you didn't ever want to be on the wrong side of if you heard the rumours around his alleged extra-curricular activities.

'How did you come to be invited?' Minshull asked, knowing as well as Bennett did that nobody ended up associating with Jake Kilburn by chance. You had to be vetted and checked before you could hope to be invited.

'I did some business with Mr Kilburn, years ago.'

'What kind of business?'

'I installed a computer system for his office and upgraded all the tech for him and his associates. Back then I was working freelance, and it was the biggest contract I'd scored. He was impressed and didn't forget me.'

He said this with unconcealed pride. Bennett couldn't think of much worse than Jake Kilburn *not forgetting* you.

Minshull frowned. 'In your first statement you said your occupation was a nightclub bouncer.'

Wright's eyes widened just a little. Bennett noted it as she studied his reaction.

'That's right, I did… Thing is, I was doing freelance tech stuff during the day. For friends, acquaintances… Building up my business.'

'But you didn't mention it as a profession?'

'No.'

'Can I ask why?'

'Well… um… because it was…' Wright blinked quickly, mind clearly sifting several acceptable responses. 'Cash in hand.'

Now it made sense. No tax paid, no questions asked. Not the thing to mention in an official police statement if you didn't want to risk the ire of HMRC.

'And now?'

The man opposite Bennett and Minshull blanched. 'Now it's my business. Legally. And as far as tax is concerned.' A glance at his solicitor was rewarded by a slow nod.

'I see. And where did this poker game take place?'

'At a club Mr Kilburn worked from occasionally. It isn't there now.'

'Address?'

'It was at the bottom of Bent Hill, just up from the junction with Undercliff Road West.'

Minshull looked up from his notes. 'Was this a private club?'

'Very private. Only people Mr Kilburn invited could go in.' Again, the same note of pride sounded in Wright's reply.

'And how long were you there?'

'Until two, three o'clock in the morning?' Wright's smile faded. 'I lost nearly a grand.'

'Did Cassandra make any attempt to contact you?'

'No.'

'Did you try to contact her?'

'No. She'd made it clear I wasn't welcome. It was always best to let her calm down after a row, leave the ball in her court for her to get back in touch. The first I heard about what had happened to her was next day, when one of your lot came to my house.'

'Okay.' Minshull looked at Bennett. 'I think that's everything.'

Bennett nodded back.

'Is there anything else you'd like to tell us, Mr Wright?'

Wright's solicitor tapped his notes, his client glancing down and back.

'I need to state for the record that my relationship with Jake Kilburn was purely personal,' he said, his words robotic and unlike the usual form of his speech. 'Apart from the computer system installation at the beginning of our association, which was done on the recommendation of a mutual friend. It's important to me that you understand that.'

–

'Was it my imagination,' asked Bennett as she and Minshull were heading back to the CID office, 'or did he seem more upset about the money he lost in the poker game than the girlfriend who was murdered the same night?'

'I thought that, too.'

'And all that stuff he failed to mention the first time. If he thought Cassandra was having an affair with Karl, why not mention him as a potential route of inquiry?'

Minshull shook his head. 'Are we really believing that a beautiful, twenty-two-year-old woman was having an illicit affair with Karl Cuskie?'

'I know I said it was possible, but the thought of it being real...' Bennett risked a smile. 'He was with Shona Pickton, though. She was in her twenties, too.'

She felt the sting of condemnation immediately. How easy had it been for Bennett to accept the validity of Karl and Shona, yet be so aghast at the potential of Karl being with Cassandra? Hadn't that been the image the media pushed of Shona, that she had little worth compared with Cassandra?

'We keep it all on the table,' Minshull replied – and Bennett wondered if he felt chastised by it, too. 'Certainly, it raises questions for Cuskie – if we ever manage to bring him in. If he was having an affair with Cassandra, is that why he refused to give Shona an alibi? Would refusing to comply keep his secret safe?'

'Maybe Shona didn't know.'

'Or maybe that's why Cuskie ended things with Shona.'

'To be with Cassandra?'

Bennett slowed her pace, her thoughts everywhere at once. 'I can't see it, Sarge. I think it was Wright's jealous mind talking. Did you see how his face changed when he said he hated Cassandra's association with Karl? It gave me the shivers.'

'I saw that. Not really sure what to make of him, to be honest. If Cassandra Norton's father's fears were real, Nicholas Wright was a potential threat to her. Did he paint himself as a victim to take him out of the frame for her murder? There was definitely something odd about his replies.'

'They were empty,' Bennett agreed, passing through the door at the entrance to their floor as Minshull held it open for her. 'Emotionless. Apart from when we mentioned his mum.'

'That's it, exactly.'

'But it changed when he spoke about Jake Kilburn, eh?'

Minshull shared her surprise. 'Who would have had Suffolk's Godfather on our bingo card for that interview?'

'Total curveball,' Bennett agreed, a new thought presenting itself. 'Could they be linked?'

Minshull stopped in the corridor, feet away from the entrance to CID. 'In what way?'

'What if Wright's association with Jake Kilburn wasn't as cosy as he'd like us to think? What if he owed too much money?'

'Meaning what, Cassandra was collateral damage?'

Spoken aloud, it seemed to lose all credibility. Bennett raised her eyes to the flickering strip lights above. 'You're right. It's a daft idea.'

'Not daft, just – *imaginative*.' Minshull's kind smile was a balm to Bennett's embarrassment. 'I reckon if Jake Kilburn wanted to hurt Nicholas Wright he'd go straight to the source. From the rumours I've heard about him, he doesn't play games.'

Bennett had to concede the point. She'd had little direct contact with Kilburn over her years in CID, but she'd seen plenty of examples of the damage he could allegedly do. *Allegedly* because the 'businessman' was a master at avoiding any association with evidence that might incriminate him, and always surrounded by the best lawyers money could buy.

The very mention of his name in the otherwise routine interview, while nothing more than an interesting anomaly, was nevertheless unsettling.

Bennett's heart plummeted when she returned to her desk. The two evidence boxes she had inspected and catalogued prior to attending Nicholas Wright's interview had been cleared – and three more had taken their place. Beside her, Ellis was hunched over a stack of open files, while beyond him Wheeler's desk appeared to be vanishing under the sea of Post-Its that constituted his note-taking system.

It was never-ending, and they had only just begun.

Elsewhere in the CID office, another source of frustration had raised itself. The name Karl Cuskie was causing headaches, as each new lead pursued for finding him proved fruitless. Despite Wheeler's best efforts to talk to colleagues and Evans' grudging attempts to do the same, it seemed that nobody had seen or talked to the man for at least twelve months.

'Anything?' Minshull asked, arriving at Bennett's desk, two hours later.

'Not much, Sarge, sorry. Although I do have this—' She handed over a slip of paper she had been waiting for the right moment to deliver. An address for Mitchell Norton, Cassandra's estranged father, correct as of two months ago, along with a phone number.

Minshull brightened. 'Great work. I'll ask DI Anderson to call him.'

'Cheers, Sarge. Has the Uniform team had any joy looking for the people who attacked St Columba Street?'

'Some leads,' Minshull said. 'It's going to take time to find them.'

'If we find them at all,' Ellis chimed in, holding up his hand when he saw Minshull's frown. 'Sorry, Sarge. It's just you know how it goes with mob stuff.'

'I do. And I also know Tim Brinton and his team are determined to find them. So have a little faith, Drew.'

'Sarge. Sorry, Sarge.'

Bennett watched her colleague redden and duck his head back to the stack of files before him. Poor Ellis. He was only saying what everyone on the team feared. Organised thugs tended to be better organised these days. And what worried Bennett more was the power behind the mob. The attack on the site was no opportunistic, knee-jerk reaction. Someone somewhere intended it to cause maximum distress and attract the attention of the press. Even if Tim Brinton's team identified the site attackers, would they unearth the original instigators?

But right now, finding anyone connected with the investigations would be a start.

'What's going to happen with Karl Cuskie?' Bennett asked, her train of thought voiced. 'If we can't find him, do we rule him out?'

'Not an option, given what Nicholas Wright told us,' Minshull replied, the weight of it already evident in the pronounced shadow beneath his eyes. 'If he was involved with Cassandra Norton – and then refused to give an alibi for Shona Pickton – it has huge implications for the case.'

'Cuskie involved with Cassandra?' Wheeler's head appeared above his computer screen. 'You don't mean…?'

'Believe it or not, Dave.'

Wheeler's grimace expressed everything Bennett was feeling.

'If he was and he knows you've found out, he'll go to ground.' Evans' voice sounded from behind a stack of evidence file boxes. 'No way you'll find the bastard then.'

Minshull's expression set like granite, as if he'd seen the way ahead and was determined to pursue it. 'We'll find him. No matter what.'

SEVENTEEN

MINSHULL

He shouldn't be here.

But even as Minshull turned left into the small street, he was resolved to see this through.

What other option was there?

They'd contacted everyone who knew Karl Cuskie. Pursued every address they'd unearthed, discarded countless dead-end lines of inquiry. And nothing. No sign of the man. According to Wheeler, the most recent contact any officer from South Suffolk Police had had with Karl Cuskie was over a year ago.

Had he gone to ground? Had he seen Shona Pickton's acquittal on the horizon and made himself scarce? Or, as Les Evans had intimated, had he realised his affair with the murdered woman would be uncovered?

Minshull wasn't naïve enough to think the police informer had ceased his dodgy operations. That stretched the realms of possibility beyond any reasonable limit. People like Cuskie knew what they were good at. It had brought him money and likely freedom from conviction enough times to make it still worth the risk.

Was he dead?

It was a valid consideration. If he'd chosen the wrong person to tangle with, or shared information that upset someone sufficiently, he could well have been 'disappeared'. In truth, it had been a while since the known criminal fraternity had purposefully *lost* someone. That Mafia-style tactic was mostly the stuff of legend (and occasionally the domain of the neighbouring Essex gangs).

Ellis had found no death notices listed in any of the *Suffolk Herald* obituary sections from the date of the last investigation until the present day. But obits were only useful if you had someone in your life willing to post one. Judging by the snippets of information Wheeler had collected from various colleagues in Police HQ, Cuskie seemed unlikely to have anyone still loyal to him who fit that description.

As he walked along the oddly named Silent Street, Minshull had to admit he was intrigued. While many of his colleagues would swear they never used police informers, Minshull suspected he was in the minority as someone who had never encountered one. He had a single grainy photo to refer to, found in police records from fifteen years ago.

And a location within the pub to head for.

The Green Dragon did not at first appear to be a pub at all, its plaster portico and Georgian windows identical to the few offices that neighboured it. Only a small, scratched CAMRA sticker in the lower pane of the window nearest the heavy black front door indicated its true identity. Minshull checked the street for any eager onlookers, but it was empty. Satisfied he was alone, he pushed open the door.

Many of the historic pubs in the county Minshull had visited wore their history with a healthy dose of pub chain uniformity. Beams and low ceilings overlooked carefully curated thrift shop tat – old clothbound books, wooden tennis rackets, replica railway station signs and the like. Pub meals all served on achingly hip slate platters with modern music blaring from decidedly non-historic speakers…

Not this pub.

Walking inside The Green Dragon was like being transported back in time. There had been the concession of a clean-swept stone flagged floor where once sawdust would have been scattered, and LED spotlights concealed behind its sloping beams, but the bar, the beer pulls and even some of the bottles gathering dust beneath the optics appeared to have been there for a couple of hundred years.

No radio or jolly playlist here; only the burr of low conversation and the clink of glass. Bull's-eye glass-panelled wooden screens separated some of the seating booths, where figures hunched over their pints. The floor was slightly sticky, the scent of beer strong. An open fire in a cast-iron grate and hearth crackled and spit, flanked by two weather-beaten red-brown leather wing-backed armchairs, one occupied by a man with a newspaper crossword, the other empty, its scratched seat fraying at the seams.

Minshull half-expected the room to fall silent on his entry, like he'd seen in the Western films he would watch with his sister Ellie and brothers Joe and Ben as kids on Saturday mornings with their grandmother. But nobody acknowledged his presence.

So much for being the justice-fighting newcomer of his boyhood dreams...

He swallowed the urge to laugh as he approached the bar, where a diminutive woman of uncertain years with spiky red hair and an impressive collection of tattoos was restocking glasses. As he neared her, his gaze drifted to the left, following the contour of the dark patinaed wood.

There, sitting on a high wooden stool, was a man. Older, with less hair and more of a paunch now, but unmistakably the man in the photo Minshull carried in his pocket.

It was too easy. But the confirmation of the theory that had dragged him here in spite of his own better judgement was enough. A lead. One that Anderson would probably have his hide for...

'What'll you have?' asked the lady behind the bar.

'Pint of Silver Adder, please,' Minshull replied with a smile, reaching for his wallet. 'And whatever our friend at the end of the bar is having.'

The landlady raised an eyebrow.

'He'll have a double whisky,' she stated, flatly. 'He always does.'

The man at the end of the bar didn't even look up.

Minshull was careful to keep his eyes on the drinks prepared before him, the picture of calm despite the frantic duck-paddle of his nerves below the surface. What was he doing here? Was he even doing it correctly? If his father could see him now, he'd never live it down. John Minshull would think all of his corrupt prayers for his fiercely principled son had been answered.

He paid and moved slowly towards his quarry.

'I believe this is yours,' he said, his voice low, sliding the glass of amber liquid along the bar.

Karl Cuskie glanced out of the corner of his eye and gave a loud sniff. 'Very kind.'

Minshull acknowledged this with a nod, lifting his own glass to his lips for an unhurried sip of ale. He kept his eyes focused on the dusty bottles on the counter below the optics, and said nothing.

'Let him lead, if you find him,' Wheeler had confided, as he was leaving CID earlier. He was careful not to reveal his own opinion, but clearly had Minshull sussed, after a frustrating day of dead ends in the search for Cuskie. 'He can clam up if you're too eager. He likes to be in control. Makes him feel important.'

Sure enough, Cuskie followed Wheeler's advice to the letter, every move designed to discern who held the balance of power. Minshull let the muted sounds of the pub surround him, soothing his nerves. If Cuskie wanted him to wait beyond the end of his pint, so be it.

The minutes passed, the level of ale slowly descending down Minshull's pint glass. When it was almost gone, Cuskie relented.

'Figured it was a matter of time before one of you came.'

'You're not easy to find.'

Cuskie gave a snort of amusement. 'Not too keen on hide and seek, me. Like to make myself scarce.'

'And yet, I found you.'

He conceded the point. 'So you did. What do you want, then?'

'Just to talk.'

'No offence, mate, but I in't looking for that kind of date.' Watery blue eyes slid to observe Minshull, retreating back beneath bushy grey eyebrows when he saw his joke fail to have an effect. 'Fair enough. So talk.'

'Not here. I need you to come to the station.'

'No fear!'

The landlady looked up from her tray of dishwasher-sparkling glasses.

Cuskie held up his hand in apology, lowering his voice back behind a whisper. 'Never going to happen.'

'We're revisiting every statement,' Minshull replied. 'I just need you to confirm what you told police before.' *And the rest*, he added to himself. *So much more than you think we know.*

'I'm confirming it now, here.'

'That won't work…'

'S'all I got for you, mate. I said my piece nine years ago. No need to say it again.'

Minshull changed tack. 'Shona Pickton might disagree.'

Another snort, this one riddled with derision. 'And I care because…?'

'Because you loved her once.'

A beat. Minshull retreated, taking a slow sip of his pint. Cuskie's hand had frozen halfway to his whisky glass.

'How… who told you that?' It was a trip; his previous insistence that he hadn't known Shona well, gone in an instant.

'Just a guess,' Minshull replied, with a shrug. 'But you did. Maybe that's why you didn't vouch for her. Why you split up with her, the night Cassandra Norton died. Maybe she got too close.'

'Shut up!'

'Or maybe you couldn't stand her being with anyone else after you, so you threw her under the bus. Or you had secrets of your own to hide...'

'You know *jack shit*...'

'Maybe.' Minshull finished his pint. 'I just think, if it was me, and I'd had nine years to think about a decision I made that caused someone else needless pain, I might want to put the record straight. Or, if I wanted to make sure my name was kept out of new theories in the reinvestigation, I might jump at the chance to be ruled out early.'

Cuskie said nothing, his hand gripping the whisky glass.

Minshull lifted the empty pint glass, inspecting the cream lace ghosts gliding sadly down to the dregs. 'Great pint, that. You should try one.' Placing it on the bar, he nodded his thanks to the landlady and began to walk away.

'When?'

Cuskie's question met Minshull a few steps from the door. Slowly, Minshull turned back, his breath kept steady despite the thunder of his heart.

'I'll be in my office from eight a.m. tomorrow.'

'Not tomorrow.'

'Well, I'll be there, same time, the day after.'

Cuskie sucked air through his gritted teeth. 'Fine. But I'm not changing what I said.'

Across the flagstones of the pub floor, the two men observed one another. In the brief unspoken understanding the moment facilitated, Minshull thought he caught a fleeting shadow of remorse.

His task complete, he left The Green Dragon.

It was done.

Now all he had to do was wait.

EIGHTEEN

Transcript of text conversation, Evidence no: CN/163/SSCID

Plod came sniffing around. Earlier.

Where?

Green Dragon.

But you said nothing?

… (typing)

You said NOTHING?

I might have talked to him.

What the hell?

What could I have done? The bloke jumped me. Bought me
a drink.

You could have said no.

I couldn't help it.

You could have NOT BEEN THERE.

I've got to make a living. You don't pay my bills, do you? And
it was just a drink.

Not just a bloody drink if you spoke to him! Idiot!

Calm down. He just wanted a chat.

About what?

What do you think?

What did you say?

Nothing! Just that I stood by what I said before, so no point changing it.

He wanted you to change it?

I said I wouldn't. Relax. I'll lay low for a while. But you owe me.

NINETEEN

MINSHULL

Being in possession of information that could shift both the mood and the momentum of his team was a powerful motivator. Buzzing following his conversation with Karl Cuskie, Minshull arrived for work three quarters of an hour early the next morning, surprising DC Pete York, the night detective, who was just finishing his shift.

And more good news awaited him. Drafted into the gargantuan task of tackling the evidence boxes, York had unearthed another eyewitness statement.

A man working in a chip shop just off Orwell Road reported that he had seen Cassandra Norton pass the window in the company of a young man, around 8:50 p.m. They were laughing as they walked, leading the eyewitness to think they were a couple. The young man was around the same height as Cassandra, wearing a dark top and jeans.

'This is brilliant, Pete,' Minshull said, skimming the lines of the statement.

'It was filed in an odd place though,' York observed. 'With lists of calls received after a national appeal for information. The usual cranks, you know. People from hundreds of miles away, people spouting their own odd-bod theories, supposed psychics swearing Cassandra Norton was talking to them from beyond the grave. The full idiot parade.'

Minshull surveyed the other contents of the box. 'Why was it in there? It's evidence that suggests someone other than Shona

Pickton could have been at the scene, twenty minutes before Cassandra Norton was found fatally wounded.'

'Exactly, Minsh.' York lifted his glasses to rub his eyes, the toll of the overnight shift evident as he neared its dying minutes. 'Listen, I've been around the block more than once in my career and I've seen most things. This smacks of someone not wanting it to be seen alongside the main statements.'

Minshull stared back. 'You think the misfiling was deliberate?'

York shrugged. 'I think it's *convenient*. Included in the general body of evidence but failed to be brought to bear in the main case for prosecution? Seems dodgy to me.'

'It could have been missed? Filed in a hurry?'

'Something so potentially vital to the case? Nah, mate. That doesn't happen by chance.'

York's comment stayed with Minshull all morning, as he continued his methodical search of the evidence files. Many aspects of the original investigation concerned him. The speed with which Shona Pickton had been deemed prime suspect; the eyewitness descriptions that didn't entirely match but were relied upon to support the case; the pressing ahead with the threatening letter found in Cassandra Norton's apartment as key evidence, despite Shona Pickton's constant denials that she'd sent it; and the complete lack of dissenting voices or alternative theories reflected in the records kept.

No wonder the Appeal Court had found in Ms Pickton's favour. The case against her was a shameful catalogue of inconsistencies.

But there was more: an itch he couldn't quite reach.

Could Shona Pickton have been deliberately framed for murder?

It seemed preposterous, but the possibility refused to be explained into silence. He should talk to Anderson about it, but therein lay a whole new set of issues. Anderson might have been an Acting DI at the time – and Minshull well knew how toothless an acting position could feel – but he was still part of the investigation team. He would have been party to daily briefings, theories discussed in the CID office, lines of inquiry followed... He would have seen the mounting case against Shona Pickton, noted the speed with which she was considered prime suspect and witnessed the summary dismissal of other potential suspects.

Why didn't he speak up?

Could he have been part of the plan?

Minshull kept a covert watch on his superior as Anderson passed in and out of the main CID office. The DI appeared to be in unusually good spirits, given the enormity of the task at hand. That in itself raised a flag. Was it just the prospect of taking his superior officer down a peg or two that was fuelling his good mood? Or did he consider himself exempt from the criticism and repercussions currently faced by DCI Taylor over the failings of the initial investigation?

By one p.m., Minshull could put it off no longer.

Steeling himself, he picked up the misfiled witness statement and headed for Anderson's office.

'DS Minshull, a word.'

The barked command met him just as he raised his hand to knock on Anderson's door. It wasn't a request from one of his team. And it wasn't a question.

Turning slowly, internally lobbing select obscenities at the furious figure of DCI Taylor, who was standing just inside the main CID office, Minshull offered her a gracious smile. 'Of course, Ma'am.'

'Not here. In my office.' She stared pointedly at him, oblivious to the unwitting audience gathered around the desks.

Or maybe, for their benefit.

Minshull remained standing, chin high, stuffing his annoyance behind cool compliance. DCI Taylor might want to exert power in front of his team, but he wouldn't give her the satisfaction of scurrying at her command.

'I need Rob here.' Summoned by the commotion, Anderson appeared in the doorway of his office.

'In *my* office, DS Minshull,' Taylor repeated, blanking Anderson. '*Now*.'

Minshull could feel the bristling resentment of the team around him on his behalf as he left the statement on his desk, a stultifying atmosphere rising around him like oppressive summer heat before a storm. He didn't meet their eyes. He didn't need to. With Anderson's seething rage at his back, he followed Taylor out of the office.

She said nothing in the corridor, the brisk strike of her heels a jarring, determined sound. Minshull followed a pace behind, his steps steady, a quarter beat after hers. The journey up the stairs to the floor above was meant to evoke fear, to make him sweat, but he remained cool and controlled. Whatever Sue Taylor was about to throw at him, he would be ready for it.

'Close the door.'

Minshull did so, arriving at her desk.

'Don't sit.'

He stood firm, his back rod-straight, his head held high.

Taylor made a show of taking her seat, the desk chair significantly better appointed than Anderson's or Minshull's would ever be. All well-worn tricks designed to shrink the confidence of the person opposite. All unlikely to have any effect on Minshull.

The thought of the newly discovered witness statement fired his resolve, the knowledge of it – and what it implied for the flawed investigation DCI Taylor had presided over – was all the power he needed to face her down.

'I am disappointed in you,' she began.

'Ma'am?'

'Of all the detectives in CID, I would have expected more integrity, more discernment from you. Especially when you come from such esteemed stock...'

The urge to laugh arrived hand-in-hand with the need to kick something. Sue Taylor had worked as a DS and then a DI under Minshull's father, so how she could trot out such hackneyed deference for his well-known corruption beggared belief. John Minshull was the antithesis of everything Minshull wanted to be as a detective – his questionable morals, loose definition of justice, and constant grappling for power a complete anathema to his son.

'Forgive me, Ma'am, but what is this regarding?'

'I think you know exactly what.' Taylor's hawk-like stare pinned him to the spot, a hunter preparing to strike. 'Tell me, DS Minshull, why you thought it appropriate behaviour to seek out and converse with a known police informant?'

The penny dropped. Minshull battled to keep his expression neutral. 'Ma'am?'

'Did you think it wouldn't get back to me? That I wouldn't find out?'

How the hell *had* she found out? 'With respect, Ma'am...'

'*With respect*, DS Minshull, you know the official policy on soliciting information from informers. That practice was outlawed for good reason. *I* outlawed it. It's a relic of the previous governance of CID and has no place in modern policing.'

Not so deferential to his father, after all, Minshull mused, nerves fluttering despite his best efforts to contain them. But if Taylor thought her snide reference to John Minshull would deal him a blow, she was wrong.

'I'm well aware of the official policy, Ma'am,' he replied, eyes locked with hers now. 'But Mr Cuskie gave official statements during the original Cassandra Norton investigation. And we had found no way to contact him, despite our best efforts. I was merely...'

'Karl Cuskie has no relevance to the re-investigation,' Taylor snapped.

'He was named by Ms Pickton as a potential alibi. His statement refusing the alibi was instrumental in her being charged with murder.' Minshull didn't mention the accusation Nicholas

Wright had made. Taylor didn't need to know that yet. He would ask the question when Cuskie came in tomorrow. If he came in…

The colour rose in Taylor's cheeks as her indignation increased. 'Do you know how it would look if a journalist got wind of your seedy little chat? At a time when we are under intense scrutiny? Do you have the slightest idea of how potentially damning that would appear?'

'We've been instructed to revisit all individuals who gave signed statements regarding the original case…' Minshull began.

'Not Karl Cuskie! He's not to be trusted. He has form…'

'Every statement has to be revisited. The Super requested it…'

'*I* am in charge of CID, DS Minshull. *I* decide…'

'With respect, Ma'am, we're all under the charge of Superintendent Martlesham on this case.' Before Taylor could reply, Minshull added, 'And in light of the observers he appointed being present in CID, it is of utmost importance that we follow his orders to the letter.'

The observers. The final kick.

Stung, Taylor glared back. 'Your meeting wasn't official.'

'I saw an opportunity, Ma'am, and I took it. We had exhausted all other avenues to contact Mr Cuskie, time that could have been spent tracking down Cassandra Norton's killer. I acted on the information I had…'

'You went behind my back!' Taylor withdrew a little, her voice shaking with the effort to control it when she continued. 'Behind the backs of your *immediate superior* and the Super and I. It is unconscionable behaviour.'

'It was necessary. And it worked. He's agreed to come in tomorrow to resubmit his statement.'

DCI Taylor's mouth dropped open. 'What?'

'Tomorrow, Ma'am. Just after eight a.m.'

'Well, I…'

'So, if that's all, Ma'am? We have a considerable workload today, as I'm sure you're aware.'

'Go, then. But I *will* be informed of every new interview made as part of this investigation from now on.'

'I'm sure DI Anderson will keep you up to date, Ma'am,' Minshull risked, fury powering through him.

'Out! Get out of my sight!'

–

Minshull thundered down the steps from the third floor, the full weight of consequence finally registering. How had DCI Taylor discovered his meeting with Karl Cuskie? Had one of the other drinkers in The Green Dragon reported it? Minshull had assumed the older men guarding their pints were too old to still be serving if they were coppers. But could the old guard still have connections to use when it suited them? Was Taylor more closely linked to the old guard than her very public pledges to root them out might suggest?

All he'd told Anderson and the team when they arrived that morning had been that one of the contacts for Karl Cuskie had borne fruit, leading to the meeting arranged for tomorrow. What would Anderson say when he learned exactly how he'd contacted the police informer?

And how could he broach the subject of the potentially shelved witness statement now?

Reaching the second floor corridor, Minshull wrestled his fast-escaping thoughts back under control. He needed to breathe and think. He needed to...

'Care to tell me the reason for that pantomime?'

Anderson was leaning against the wall, a few doors down from the CID office.

Minshull ground to a halt. 'Guv...'

'Because, entertaining though it was to see our esteemed DCI with her knickers in a twist, I didn't appreciate being blanked in my own department in your name.'

'I'm sorry, Guv. If I can explain...'

'Oh you'll explain all right.' Anderson strode towards him like a Caledonian warrior about to strike. 'But not here.'

Paling, Minshull fell into brisk step with his superior as Anderson led him back towards the corridor. 'Where are we going?'

'Out of earshot,' Anderson growled.

TWENTY

ANDERSON

It was freezing outside. Anderson chastised himself for not bringing a coat. He hadn't exactly been thinking of appropriate attire when he left the CID office to await Minshull's return.

The fact he was even cold spoke volumes. Despite him now living longer in England than he ever had in Scotland, he felt a traitor to the land of his birth. Cold weather should be in his blood, along with a healthy dislike of the English and a taste for *uisge beatha*, the water of life. What a soft *sassenach* he'd become.

But his fury at DCI Taylor had eclipsed all other considerations and impulses. How dare she march into his department and remove his second-in-command, without even a glance in his direction?

They had left the car park of Police HQ and were now out on the streets of Ipswich. Anderson hadn't planned a route, either – the urge to put distance between them and their workplace the only motivation for their departure.

As a means of getting Minshull out of Police HQ it had been effective. As a well-planned operation it was haphazard in the extreme. Anderson finally relented, coming to a halt.

'Okay, that's far enough.'

They had stopped beside the low stone wall of an old church, hidden away in the labyrinth of back streets. Anderson filled his aching lungs with stingingly cold air and faced his colleague.

'Am I to know what that was about, or am I due another embarrassing interruption from our noble DCI?'

Minshull slumped against the wall. 'I went looking for Karl Cuskie.'

What was that supposed to mean?

Oh. *Shit*, no…

Facing his DS, Anderson folded his rapidly goose-pimpling arms across his chest.

'You went to The Green Dragon.'

'None of the addresses we found were right. The phone numbers unobtainable. Dead ends at every turn. We were wasting too much time trying to find him when the answer was *right there*…'

'So you decided to bypass official protocol, explicit orders from our superiors and your own usually sound judgement to go and seek out an informer?' Anderson cut across him.

Minshull couldn't look him in the eye. 'Guv.'

At least there was this. Minshull would be personally beating himself up over his actions, however much he might have hidden the fact in the face of DCI Taylor's criticism. Would Anderson have made the same call, given the lack of progress and the pressing of time? He knew the answer to that, and it wasn't pretty.

'Good,' he said, rewarded by the look of pure shock from Minshull.

'Sorry?'

'You saw an opportunity and you took it. Let's face it: we've had precious little forward motion so far. It was imperative we found Cuskie and you did.'

'I don't know how she found out, Guv. I swear I was careful.'

Oh poor dear trusting boy! Anderson observed Minshull with a mix of wistfulness and pity, his own days of such wide-eyed innocence regrettably far behind him. 'Mate, it's a pub where retired cops drink. You chose the worst place to be discreet.'

'*Crap.*'

'Yep.'

'But he's coming in tomorrow.'

'You sure of that?'

'As sure as I can be,' Minshull replied. 'Which is more certain than I could have been before I went looking for him.'

'Not much of a comfort, but it'll have to do.' Anderson leant against the church wall, really wishing he had the warmth of his coat pockets to bury his hands in. 'Don't sweat it, kid.'

A snort from Minshull caused Anderson's head to turn. 'Did you just channel James Cagney?'

'I'm so bloody cold, it's possible.' Anderson checked his watch. 'Look, Tutti's isn't far from here. It's warm and it has the best coffee in Ipswich. And if anyone asks where we went, it was to fetch much needed *maritozzi* buns for our hardworking team.'

'You're going to *spend money*, Guv?' Minshull returned, the joke warming after the confrontation. 'Should we alert the authorities?'

'Consider it an indication of my commitment to your well-being,' Anderson growled back, enjoying the lightness. 'And don't ever question my motives again.'

'Noted,' Minshull grinned, but his smile instantly disappeared. 'Except... I have to ask you something.'

'Can you ask me *in* the deli?'

'*Guv...*'

'Fine. But let's walk before we freeze.'

Minshull was quiet for the first two streets they walked along, the knot of his brows concerning. He was never slow in speaking his mind – a characteristic Anderson was both irritated by and grudgingly relied upon.

'Out with it, then,' he demanded, when the waiting became too much.

Minshull stopped walking.

'Did you know about the other eyewitness?'

'What?'

'The guy in the chip shop, who saw Cassandra Norton walking past with a young man, around eight fifty p.m.?'

Was this a trick question?

'I don't know what you're talking about…'

'You were there, Guv, in the office, when all that shit was being discussed.'

'Aye, I was. But I was also out chasing statements from family and friends and strangers convinced they'd seen her.'

'That statement could've changed everything. You have to see that.'

'See what? You're not making any sense. Have you found something in the evidence files? And if so, why wasn't I informed immediately?' The sudden change in Minshull unnerved him, the switch from jokes to in-your-face challenge.

'I need to trust you, Guv!'

All of Anderson's words left him. He stared at Minshull, open-mouthed.

Minshull appeared stung by his own outburst. What *the hell* was going on?

'We're dealing with evidence from a case that already looks unfit for purpose. It's a mess, Guv. And the worst thing is, you were there, as DI…'

'*Acting* DI…' Anderson corrected. But it was an empty retaliation.

'You had authority. You must have seen that statement.'

'Rob, I did no such thing.'

Minshull looked up – and to Anderson's horror he saw fear in the eyes of his colleague. 'Did you bury it, Guv? To strengthen the case against Shona Pickton and get a result?'

Anderson could only stare back.

'Because including a statement placing a young male with the victim, so close to the time of her murder, could rule out Shona Pickton, right? He had blond hair and was wearing dark clothes – not a hoodie and tracksuit bottoms like other people saw, but the two witness statements the police case relied upon didn't quite match, either. Is that why it was shelved with the post-appeal crank callers?'

Blood pumped at Anderson's temples, tension pulling his fingers into tight fists at his side.

'Is that where you found it?'

'Is that where you *left* it?'

It was a standoff now: both men staring each other down, oblivious to the passing traffic and furtive glances of passers-by.

'I've never heard of that statement.'

'How did you miss it? You were a team…'

'We were a bunch of dogsbodies jumping to Sue Taylor's drum,' Anderson spat back. 'I had no more authority in there than the youngest DC, and probably less than that. Having *Acting* in your job title just means you get grief from everyone, above and below you, as well you know.'

Minshull wasn't pacified, his stare searching Anderson out. 'I've tried rationalising it, Guv. But all I can see is DCI Taylor scrutinising everything we do, as if reopening the case is a personal insult; you and Dave doing all you can to distance yourself from any of the initial investigation, expressing doubts today but failing to act upon them back then; and now this important statement shoved in a box with phone statements that was clearly never pursued. Then DCI Taylor's reaction over Karl Cuskie this morning, and now *this*…'

'This?'

'Dragging me out of HQ to berate me in the street.'

'I am not bloody berating you, Minshull! Believe me, you would know if I was.'

'Did you shelve the statement? Or do you know who did?'

'I told you, *no*. I don't recall a chip shop worker ever contacting us.'

Minshull's breath came in short, sharp bursts, the frozen ghost of his exhales rising into the winter afternoon air. 'I need to trust you,' he said again, the fight fast fleeing from his voice.

'You can.'

'So, if it wasn't you who filed the statement there, or Dave, I think someone else wanted that evidence buried. Someone who had a vested interest in charging Ms Pickton for murder. Someone inside the building.'

All of a sudden, it all became horribly clear. The insinuation. The obvious suspects, further up the chain of command. But why would they want to pin a murder on someone who might not have even been there when Cassandra Norton was attacked?

'We have no proof,' he murmured, his thoughts betraying his best judgement with each imagined machination. DCI Taylor? Or someone above her? One of the top floor bods with a point to prove to the journalists currently baying for blood on the front steps of Police HQ? It was a dangerous theory – and yet its threads and twists came together in Anderson's head far too easily.

'We have a statement incorrectly filed,' Minshull pressed on. 'And a senior officer clearly rattled that their investigation is being picked apart.'

'But the Super...'

'The Super has only been in his position for five years. Before that he was at another force. Maybe he suspects foul play...'

'No. Impossible. Martlesham is an idealist, he thinks the best of everyone. There's no way he'd suspect DCI Taylor of working against him.'

'What do you believe, Guv?' The question was arrow-sharp, expertly aimed.

'I believe we need evidence.' Even as he replied, Anderson loathed every word. 'A body of evidence, Rob, not hearsay and conjecture. We don't accuse senior officers without a damn-near watertight case. And I need to see the statement.'

'Of course.' Minshull hesitated. 'I want to believe you, Guv. I don't think you'd tamper with evidence – I don't believe that's your style. But I don't know what you'd do under that kind of pressure and scrutiny.'

Anderson swallowed the bitter confession. There had been a time, years before, after the murder of a young local boy, that he himself didn't know what he was capable of. When his career had hung in the balance and his grasp of reality had been worryingly weak. Minshull knew some of what had happened in the aftermath – and how an investigation they led together had tested Anderson to almost breaking point again. It was no wonder his DS was asking the question now.

'I wouldn't hide evidence,' he replied, willing Minshull to believe him. 'Or try to influence a charging decision. You have my word on that, Rob, for what it's worth. And I will provide you with as much supporting evidence for my part in the first investigation as I can.'

Minshull gave a slight nod. 'I appreciate that, Guv.'

'Okay.' Winded by the exchange, Anderson pulled back. 'We need a strategy to look into this. And we have to be careful. If what you think is correct, the forces that derailed the original investigation may well be watching, ready to do it again. And this time they may go to greater lengths to prevent the truth from becoming known. So, we speak only between ourselves – and this goes no further – until we have what we need to escalate it. Agreed?'

'Yes, Guv.'

'Okay.' Relieved they were at least united by the unexpected turn of events, Anderson risked sending a grim smile, relieved when it was returned. 'Are we good?'

'We're good. I had to ask, Guv.'

'I know. And I'm glad you did. Now, let's go to Tutti's. I don't know about you but I'm freezing, hungry and I bloody need caffeine.'

'Sounds like a plan.'

Chilled from more than the air temperature, Anderson began to walk once more, Minshull falling into step beside him.

TWENTY-ONE

Transcript of 999 emergency call received by Suffolk Ambulance Service 8:50 a.m.

Ambulance, is the patient breathing?

– No... I think he's dead... There's blood everywhere... I think he's been shot.

Where are you now?

– Maidstone Road in Felixstowe. I'm at his house, 105.

And you think he's been shot?

– Yes. I can't believe it. I just saw his front door open and popped round to check he was okay and I found him like this...

Can you see where he's been injured?

– In his head... Right at the front...

Can you find a pulse for me?

– No. No, I can't. There's nothing I can do for him...

Just take hold of the patient's wrist and see if you can find a pulse for me.

– I don't want to move him.

You don't have to move him, okay? Just press your fingers on the inside of his wrist.

– I can't feel anything. He's so cold... oh... Shit, no...[sobbing] No...

What's happening?

– *[sobbing increases] The back of his head... It – it isn't there...*

Okay, sweetheart, try to stay calm. You're doing great. An ambulance is on its way now. Stay on the line with me and someone will be with you as soon as they can.

– *Hurry, please! There's so much blood...*

TWENTY-TWO

WHEELER

'Tenner says he's a no-show.'

Wheeler groaned, but he couldn't hide his grin. He'd never been much of a fan of office sweepstakes, especially those initiated and presided over by his colleague. But the very mention of one today meant only one thing: DC Les Evans was back.

He'd been quiet upon his return to the CID office after months on sick leave, not helped by the new Cassandra Norton murder investigation and the crushing workload. Wheeler had worried that this diminished version of Evans might be permanent, but this morning's announcement signalled a welcome return to form.

'Fifteen says he will,' Wheeler returned, chuckling when he saw the eye-roll from his colleague.

'Fifteen? Pushing the boat out, aren't you, Dave?'

'Christmas is coming next month. Got to look after the pennies,' Wheeler said.

'*Fifteen*,' Les huffed, marking it on his pad. 'Kate?'

Bennett didn't even look up from her screen. 'Not doing it.'

'Oh come on!'

'Nope. Too busy.'

'Drew's doing it.'

Ellis turned in the small kitchen area, tea towel and half-dried mug in hand. 'Am I?'

'Yes, you are,' Evans smirked. 'Because I know you can't resist a flutter. And also, with Kate out of the running, your chances of winning have dramatically improved.'

'Good point. Tenner says he'll show.'

'See, Kate? Nice to see *some* competitive spirit in here.'

Bennett muttered something under her breath.

'What was that?' Evans asked, placing a hand to his ear. 'Didn't quite catch it.'

'I said *Okay, Grandad*,' Bennett shot back. 'Twenty says he doesn't.'

'And she's *in*!' Evans announced, noting Bennett's bet. 'Now it's a competition!' He grinned at a now despondent Ellis standing by the sink. 'Tough break, Drew. Still, you win the moral victory for staying true to your impulses. Unlike *some...*'

'Causing trouble are you, Les?' Minshull asked, walking back into CID from his badly concealed pacing of the corridor. Clearly the sight of Evans back to his old questionable self was as gratifying for him as for the rest of the team, but Wheeler knew the pressure of the forthcoming interview would be heavy on Minshull's shoulders.

Nothing had been said officially about how Karl Cuskie had suddenly been located, or why he'd agreed to revisit his statement, other than that a last-ditch attempt to try one of the long list of potential phone numbers had suddenly, unexpectedly, produced a result. Wheeler wasn't buying that for a second. Not that he'd say so to Minshull – or to Anderson, who had been similarly circumspect about it.

Minshull must have visited The Green Dragon. It was the only possible explanation.

Wheeler watched his colleague now, all forced humour and smiles in front of his team. He couldn't blame him, of course. Had he been in Minshull's position and then been handed such a piece of information, he would have gone looking, too. It had worked, hadn't it? *Any port in a storm*, his father always used to say.

Karl Cuskie was proof that chasing a tip-off could pay dividends.

But at what price?

Wheeler caught Minshull's eye and saw the mask slip again.

It didn't help that Cuskie was already ten minutes late. Or that Minshull had been in the office an hour earlier than anyone else and had been pacing pretty much ever since. Already it felt like they were setting themselves up for a fall.

Wheeler had only given into Evans' attempts to drag him into the sweepstake to honour the return of his colleague. But he'd voted against his instinct. He'd lose his money, of course: the loss a strategic one. Because if Wheeler put his money where his gut told him it should be, Minshull would know he agreed with Evans.

Cuskie wasn't coming.

Wheeler knew it with every atom of his being.

Ten minutes became twenty, edging past half an hour and heading towards the start of the next. With every ten minutes over the agreed meeting time, Minshull's pacing became more pronounced; Evans' jokes landed less gracefully, and laughter in the CID office began to ebb away to self-conscious silence.

When Sergeant Tim Brinton from the uniformed division suddenly walked in, the eyes of every detective left their screens as one. Minshull froze in the centre of the room.

'DS Minshull, may I have a word?'

'Of course, Tim.'

Brinton's polished boots danced a little on the tired and patched CID office carpet. 'In private, Sarge?'

They strode out into the corridor and the door of the office cut their trailing voices with a soft *shhchukk* of the hydraulic closure mechanism.

Bennett glanced at Wheeler, who shrugged. Ellis and Evans stared at the door, brows furrowed.

Bad news had a tension all of its own. A shape, an intrusive rush that went before it. Wheeler didn't hold with atmospheres and signs as portents of doom, but bad news was an exception. He'd witnessed enough of the stuff to sense its approach. It was the thing you dreaded: the ever-present shadow waiting to be noticed. Every officer had a sixth sense for it, whether plain clothed or uniformed. The longer you did the job, the sooner you recognised it; and the more you feared its unheralded intrusion.

Five minutes.

That was all it took for Brinton to deliver his message, leaving Minshull to return alone to CID, ashen-faced.

'Sarge?' Wheeler asked, the moment Minshull reappeared. It was both an instinctive act and a way to open the floor for whatever news the DS now possessed.

'Everyone, listen please. Control received a call from our ambulance service colleagues twenty minutes ago. Karl Cuskie was found at his latest address just before nine o'clock this morning, in the hallway of his house. He had been shot dead.'

A rush of sound and reaction from the team crashed towards Minshull. He stared hollowly back.

'Shot, Minsh?' Wheeler repeated, his slip to Minshull's informal nickname a casualty of the deep concern he felt towards him.

'Single bullet wound to the forehead. Fatal injuries to the brain and rear of his skull. Instant death, according to paramedics.'

'An execution,' Ellis stated.

The room seemed to drop several degrees in response.

'An execution,' Minshull repeated. 'I need to tell the Guv. Dave, we should get down there, if you're up for it?'

'Always, Sarge,' Wheeler affirmed, his reply overlapping Minshull's request.

Minshull gave a vague nod and started to move, then turned back. 'So – uh – you and Kate win, Les.'

'Sarge…' Bennett began, horrified.

'It's not important,' Evans mumbled, eyes fixed on his desk.

Minshull dismissed their protestations with a wave of his hand. 'Forget it, both. Five minutes, Dave?'

'Okay Sarge…' Wheeler's reply faded as Minshull entered Anderson's office and softly closed the door.

–

The drive to Karl Cuskie's rented terrace was stung by sharp silence. All of Wheeler's tried-and-tested conversation starters failed him, leaving him to focus grimly on the road ahead.

Minshull sat like a rock in the passenger seat, the only movement to indicate he hadn't entirely become stone an occasional slow blink and the rapid beat of his right thumb on the locked screen of his phone.

He was in no fit state to view the body of the man he'd invited to Police HQ, but Wheeler knew that fact was unlikely to deter him. Minshull had ignored Wheeler's suggestion that Anderson go in his stead, just as Wheeler knew he would.

Did he blame himself? Wheeler suspected he might. The timing of Cuskie's murder was at best a terrible coincidence, at worst the unthinkable.

Even now, passing fields and small villages en route to Felixstowe, Wheeler couldn't get his head around it all.

Karl Cuskie murdered? By whom? And why?

Had word of his chat with Minshull reached the ears of the wrong person? Had someone with a vested interest in Cuskie's ongoing silence intervened to ensure it was permanent? Could someone who blamed Cuskie for Shona Pickton's arrest and incarceration have sought him out to exact revenge?

Had Shona taken matters into her own hands after years of forced silence?

Or had the same killer who stole Cassandra Norton's life in 2015 returned to steal Cuskie's?

They entered Felixstowe and drove to Maidstone Road, to the address where Cuskie had been found. A large section of the road was cordoned off with police tape and guarded at each end by grim-faced uniformed officers. Finding a place to park, Wheeler killed the engine and turned to his silent colleague.

'Are you good to go, Minsh? Because if you need a moment...'

'I'm fine,' Minshull replied, snapping to attention and exiting the car.

Wheeler blew out his frustration as he watched Minshull stalk off towards the police cordon. It was going to be a bastard of a day.

'You take on too much,' his wife, Sana, had said last night, after he'd reeled off a list of every colleague he felt personally responsible for, when they should have just been enjoying dinner.

'It's not a crime to worry about my friends,' Wheeler had returned.

'It might well be if you're losing sleep over it and stressing to the point of making yourself ill.'

'I'm not stressed.'

'Oh sure. Tell me, how many days have you had headaches for now? Five? Ten?'

'That's not the job, it's because I've not been out on the bike...'

'Would you listen to yourself? You don't get paid enough to take on everyone else's burdens as well as your own. I'm worried about you, D. You're putting all of this on your shoulders, and something will have to give...'

Something *was* giving, Wheeler grumbled to himself now, as he left the CID pool car and jogged painfully after Minshull. His back had been playing up for a week, his shoulders so knotted they felt like stiff macrame ropes under his skin. And the headache that had been in place for well over a week showed no signs of abating, either.

So Sana was right. But what good did that do him?

The people he cared about needed someone in their corner. If he didn't do it, who the hell would?

Minshull was already showing his warrant card to the uniformed officer at the police tape cordon when Wheeler limped up to them.

'Number 105, in that run of terraces just up there, Sarge.'

'Cheers, Vi.'

'Not gonna lie, Sarge, it's a bad one.'

Minshull grimaced. 'Aren't they all?' He ducked under the tape and began striding towards the address, Wheeler scurrying to keep up.

'Sarge – *Sarge...*' Wheeler reached level with Minshull and placed a tentative hand on his arm. The gesture worked, Minshull slowing a little. 'Take a breath before you go in.'

'I'm fine...'

'You're not. You know you're not.'

Minshull stared ahead at the white-suited SOCO team officers heading into the crime scene. 'I went to see him.'

'I know you did.' When Minshull stared at Wheeler, he shrugged. 'I guessed. Wasn't the hardest fact to work out.'

'I had to do something. We need his testimony... *Needed...*'

'You can't beat yourself up about it, Minsh. Blokes like Cuskie live their whole lives one step away from crossing the wrong party.'

'But if this was retaliation...'

'Then we find out who did it, just like we'll find out who murdered Cassandra. Are you sure you want to go in there?'

Minshull hesitated for a moment, then nodded. 'Yes, I'm sure. But I'm glad you're with me, mate.'

That was all Wheeler needed to know.

TWENTY-THREE

MINSHULL

Dave Wheeler was right: he was blaming himself.

Yesterday he had been so smug, so proud of his own cleverness in visiting Karl Cuskie. Feeling like he'd scored an advantage, anticipating the surprise and congratulations of his colleagues. Cuskie would be brought to the centre of the new investigation, and, if he was more forthcoming with the truth now that Shona Pickton had been acquitted, he might provide a new perspective that his first statement had lacked.

He was a new perspective all right.

A silent, bloodied mess of a new perspective that could well derail the case.

Cuskie's body lay supine on the deeply stained hall carpet, where his neighbour had discovered it this morning. The neighbour was at home next door now, being comforted by family. It would be Minshull and Wheeler's next port of call when they had finished at the crime scene. SOCOs filled the narrow space, painstakingly recording every detail of the body's placement, injury, blood spatter and surroundings, moving in a slow, respectful, well-practised ballet around the victim.

Murder scenes had a starkness to them, a contradictory mix of stillness and activity, silence and carefully whispered conversation. Minshull found it both chilling and calming in equal measure. A reverence for the victim, coupled with an unspoken determination to establish justice for their death.

Checking his blue shoe covers were in place and accepting a mask and pair of gloves from Wheeler, Minshull forced his eyes along the hall to take in as much detail as he could.

'You make those look good, DS Minshull.' A familiar boom of a voice sounded beside him, eliciting a smile before Minshull even raised his eyes.

'Why thank you, Brian. You don't look so bad yourself.'

Brian Hinds, chief SOCO, chuckled. 'Blue latex is all the rage for us this year.'

Minshull's nerves settled a little. Working for a small rural force such as South Suffolk had its advantages, not least that the pool of people you encountered in the course of your job was reassuringly small. He'd attended many crime scenes in the company of Hinds and his team, and their presence here was more than a comfort.

'So, how's it looking?' he asked, reluctantly returning to the task at hand.

Hinds glanced back at his team and the body in the hall. 'Victim's injuries are concurrent with significant head trauma caused by a single gunshot applied to the frontal bone of the skull. It's a precise wound. Something I wouldn't expect to see in a victim of an unplanned attack.'

'An execution?' Minshull suggested, relaying Ellis' words from earlier.

Hinds raised one bushy eyebrow. 'Bit Hollywood as descriptions go. But deliberate? Most likely. Deadly? Instantaneous. Skilled? I would say so. Duty pathologist will be able to confirm this in far greater detail.'

'When are we expecting them?'

'Any moment.' Hinds glanced over Minshull's shoulder, a generous smile illuminating his eyes over the top of his face mask. 'Or now, in fact.'

'Now what?'

The familiar voice caused Minshull and Wheeler to look back to the street. The dark kohl-lined eyes of pathologist Dr Rachael Amara crinkled into a smile over her mask.

'How's that for timing, eh?' she asked, the mischief in her tone a bright contrast to the horrors only feet away. She splayed out her fingers, wiggling them theatrically like a stage magician. 'One might even say *spooky*. If you summon me, I will come!'

'We always had you pegged as a mystical mage, Dr A,' Hinds chuckled.

'And you were correct, Brian,' Dr Amara stated. 'It's why I spend so much time hanging around the deceased. The *stories* they tell me you wouldn't believe...'

Minshull remembered the first time he had encountered the enigmatic pathologist, back before he progressed from DC to a DS. The rumours about her were rife and she had a reputation for scaring new recruits silly. Minshull had been terrified about meeting her the first time, but found her to be a complete original – fiercely intelligent, unashamedly strange, with a sense of humour so dry it rivalled the Atacama Desert for aridity. Given the nature of her specialism, maybe her unique quirks made navigating the endlessly dark and sad territory of her job easier, Minshull mused. Coping strategies for the endless parade of injustice, anger and death were as unique and personal in the force as each officer's fingerprints. You found your armour and you wore it every day.

The sight of Dr Amara today was welcome as always. Between her and Hinds, Minshull was confident answers would be found and evidence located. He needed certainty today – or as close to it as he could get.

He stood back against the faded wallpaper of the hall to allow the pathologist to pass, watching the SOCO team part reverently as she reached Cuskie's side and crouched beside his body.

'Hello, love,' she said, barely a whisper close to Cuskie's face. 'Let's find out all we can for you, eh?'

Wheeler glanced at Minshull. No matter how many times they had witnessed this, the sight of the gentle, respectful greeting Dr Amara offered to the bodies she inspected never ceased to be striking.

As the pathologist began her inspections, Hinds made his way over to Minshull, gesturing for them to go back outside. Minshull was glad of the invitation and led the retreat, waiting for Hinds and Wheeler by the SOCO van parked next to the kerb. The three men lowered their masks, the frosty November air sweet after the stench of the hallway.

'Nasty one,' Hinds said, leaning against the side of the van. 'I hear he was an informer?'

'Apparently so.' Minshull gave a grim smile. 'He was supposed to be coming in to revisit his statement for the Cassandra Norton murder case this morning.' His gaze strayed back up the front path of the Edwardian terraced house to the scene inside. 'Not much chance of that happening now.'

'I've heard the name,' Hinds admitted. 'Karl Cuskie. A couple of my team started out in Uniform before retraining as SOCOs. When they were new recruits, their senior officer used to visit Cuskie regularly. Archie in there was quite shocked to see him today.'

'He's been doing his thing for years,' Wheeler cut in. 'I never met the guy, but plenty at Police HQ did.'

Hinds folded his arms across his white paper overalls. 'Well, whoever dispatched him knew what they were doing. Do you think it's related to him coming to see you?'

It was a valid question and asked with no hint of malice, but it registered at Minshull's core like a sharp kick.

'I want to believe it isn't,' he said, 'but the timing...'

All three men grimaced in unison.

He could dress it up any way he wanted: the likelihood of someone murdering Cuskie by chance on the day he may have changed his statement to police was negligible. Word must have got back to whoever had a vested interest in Cuskie's silence, and they'd ordered a hit.

A gangland-style killing seemed preposterous in the pleasant surroundings of a popular Suffolk coastal town. But it had to be a possibility. Because why else would someone want Cuskie dead? If police knew him as an informer, Minshull would lay odds on Suffolk's criminal fraternity acknowledging him as such, too. Considering all the people Cuskie had ratted out to police over the years – apparently with no consequences to himself – what had tipped the balance against him this time?

It had to be connected to Cassandra Norton.

But how?

'Any word from the chap who found him?' Wheeler asked, his question calling Minshull back from his thoughts.

'The next-door neighbour? Saw him briefly, when I arrived. He's at home now, in a bit of a state, poor sod. The only reason he went round was because he was collecting his bin from the street and noticed Cuskie's front door wide open. There's a liaison officer with him, if you wanted to pop in?' Seeing Minshull's glance at Cuskie's house, Hinds continued. 'We'll be a while here, Rob. Until we've recorded the scene and Dr Amara's done her in-situ observations there's really not much you and Dave can do.'

'Brian's right,' Wheeler encouraged. 'We might as well make the most of the opportunity while we wait.'

–

Gareth Hartman was a broken man. Sandwiched between his brother, Graham, and best friend, Ann, he stared with unblinking eyes at a point beyond Minshull's shoulder, as if the spectre of his murdered neighbour was hovering there.

PC Charlie Ross pushed a fresh mug of tea into Hartman's pale, shaking hands. 'There you go, sweetheart,' she soothed.

'Thanks...' Hartman's reply shuddered to nothing.

Minshull kept his question respectful and low. 'Mr Hartman, I know this is hard, but can you tell me what you remember from this morning?'

Hartman swallowed hard. 'I went to get the bins... I bring Karl's in if he hasn't done it. Sometimes he does it for me. Just a thing we do, you know? A neighbourly gesture. I'd taken mine in and was coming back for his when...' A sob strangled his words, the gentle hands of his brother and best friend instantly squeezing his arms in response. 'I'm okay, thanks... I got his bin and wheeled it around – and that's when I saw his front door. At first I thought he might be on his way out to say hello, you know? Like he does sometimes. Bit of a natter, chat about the footie, the usual bollocks. But he didn't appear. And the door was properly open. I thought he might have had a break-in. We've had some in the street this year. So, I went up to check...'

'You did the right thing, Ga,' his best friend said, kissing his shoulder. 'You shouldn't have had to see that.'

'And you called 999 as soon as you saw him?' Minshull asked, as gently as he could.

'Soon as I saw the blood...'

'Did you hear anything, earlier this morning, or last night? Raised voices, cars arriving or leaving in a hurry, anything that might indicate a confrontation?'

'That's the thing: I don't remember. But I've had trouble sleeping lately so I got these new earplugs. Couldn't hear a hurricane once they're in.'

'And did you notice anything unusual in the street this morning, besides Mr Cuskie's open door?'

'No. Just the bin lorry coming up and the yob over the road giving them grief because he said they were late.'

'When was that?'

'Just after eight, I think.'

'The bin crew didn't see anything?' Wheeler asked.

'That's what I don't get,' Hartman said, staring at Wheeler as if he'd read his mind. 'Noisy bastards wake everyone up with their crashing about, but they didn't see the door open or... or what was inside...' He stuffed a tissue against his mouth.

How long had Cuskie lain beyond his open front door? Until Dr Amara could inspect the body they wouldn't know for certain. How many people had passed the crime scene since Cuskie was killed?

'What about in the last few days? Have you seen any people or cars outside Mr Cuskie's home?'

'No more than usual,' Hartman replied with a sniff. 'Karl gets a lot of visitors. People coming and going at all hours.'

'Anyone in particular? Or anyone you've seen a few times?'

Hartman considered Minshull's question. 'There's a bloke, older, comes most weeks. He never stays long and he never says hello if I'm out the front. Tall, he is, built like a freight train. Bald head with one of those Peaky Blinders caps perched on the top – it's too small for his head so I always think it looks comical. Nothing funny about him, though. Looks like he'd snap your neck as soon as breathing.'

Minshull made notes, while Wheeler took over. 'Did you see him yesterday?'

'I didn't. Sorry.'

'Okay. Anyone else?'

'Couple of women. They'd stay longer, but that wasn't surprising. Karl always seemed like one for the ladies. Though what they saw in the ugly sod, heaven only knows.'

'This is really helpful, Mr Hartman, thank you,' Minshull said, standing up. 'If we need to ask you any further questions, are we okay to come back?'

'Any time,' Hartman replied. He attempted to rise from the sofa, ignoring the protestations of his companions, but Minshull intervened.

'We'll see ourselves out. Thank you for your help.' He nodded to the liaison officer, who wordlessly followed Minshull and Wheeler out to the door.

'If he remembers anything else, I'll let you know,' Ross said, her voice low beneath the conversation happening back down the hall.

'Cheers, Charlie.' Minshull smiled. 'How long will you stay with him?'

'Until I'm called back,' Ross replied. 'By the way, Mr Hartman mentioned that several houses in the street have doorbell cameras. Salespeople came here a couple of months ago after the break-ins and quite a few of the neighbours signed up. He seemed to think Karl Cuskie had one, too.'

Minshull brightened immediately. 'Brilliant! I'll get a door-to-door arranged in the street and see what we can find. With any luck we'll catch sight of Cuskie's visitors. Hope it goes okay in there.'

'I'm just making tea and conversation,' Ross returned. 'Rather my job than yours.'

Walking back out to the street, Minshull and Wheeler returned to the side of the SOCO van to await entry into Karl Cuskie's house.

'Reckon the cameras will have picked anyone up?' Wheeler asked, pulling a half-unrolled packet of Extra Strong Mints from his coat pocket and offering one to Minshull.

'The houses are closely built, lots of good streetlighting – I'd say we have as good a chance as anywhere in town,' Minshull replied, the mint on his tongue making the cold air feel even icier in his lungs.

A buzz from his jacket pocket sent his gloved hand in to retrieve his mobile phone. He lifted it to view the caller.

CORA calling

'Problem?' Wheeler asked, seeing Minshull's expression.

'No. Cora has a meeting today with some council leaders who object to her and Tris still running the project at St Columba Street. I asked her to let me know how it went.'

Wheeler's eyes narrowed. '*You* object to her and Tris being there. Shouldn't you have been at the meeting?'

It was as much of a dig as Wheeler was ever likely to give, but it still hit home. 'I don't object to… I'm not like *them*.'

'I never said you were.'

'Those councillors want an excuse to victimise people. You've seen them mouthing off in the *Suffolk Herald* any chance they get. I think the project is great. I just…'

'…Don't want Cora there?' Wheeler finished, knowingly.

'Or Tris. Or any of the team. Not while the threat remains.'

'And what about those poor kiddies, eh? They don't get the choice of staying away.'

'You sound like Cora.'

'Yes, well, she speaks sense, too.' Wheeler scuffed the toe of his work shoe against the kerbstone. 'Believe me, I know there are people wanting anyone different to get out of Suffolk. Sana and me have had it for years. The boys, too. Look a bit different and you're instantly a threat to some idiots around here. Grinds my gears, it does.'

Wheeler didn't often talk of the issues he and his wife had faced, but Minshull knew them well enough. 'I know. Sorry, Dave. I just worry about her.'

'Her privilege to have a choice, Minsh. She's using it for good.' He nodded at the screen. 'Are you going to answer that?'

Minshull considered it, then pocketed his phone. 'I'll call her when we're done here.'

'Make sure you do,' Wheeler replied, his opinion impossible to hide. 'Soon as you can. The doc needs our support – yours more than anyone's.'

Minshull stuffed away his annoyance as he watched their colleagues working around Karl Cuskie's body.

TWENTY-FOUR

CORA

'It's gone to voicemail.'

'Leave him a message.'

'And say what, exactly?' Cora stared helplessly at Tris Noakes. She'd hoped Minshull might answer, but a message was too much to consider in the face of – *this*.

'That we've been attacked,' Tris stated, an audible tremor in his voice betraying the shock now laying siege to the whole team.

Every shard of glass at their feet hissed hatred. Every mark of garish red paint daubed to form huge letters across the entrance to the Educational Psychology Department seethed accusation.

SCUM...

You have no place here...

Go and live with them if you love them so much...

Every pane of glass in the entrance lobby had been smashed, dog faeces smeared across the frames and forced into the letterbox, the letters on the sign leading to the offices scratched off and replaced with badly spelled slurs Cora wouldn't even deign to acknowledge.

It was a blessing that none of the team or their charges had been by the entrance when the attack had taken place. But even that seemed calculated – at the exact time that Cora, Tris and the team were in a heated debate with the objecting councillors, thugs sympathetic to their cause were attacking their building. The councillors had called the meeting in the conference room at the adjoining building, away from their well-appointed offices in Ipswich, a highly unusual request by all accounts. Had that been deliberate? Cora couldn't rule it out. Not that councillors Stephen Moss, Julianne Gilbert, Roy Alsingham and Imogen De la Hay would ever accept responsibility, of course. People like them never got their hands dirty.

It was only because Tris had locked the front door as a last-minute thought while the meeting was in progress that the vandals had been prevented from entering the building.

Cora didn't want to think what might have happened if they had.

The sound of hurried heels across the car park made Cora and Tris turn. But when they saw the owner, both of them resolutely stared back at the damaged frontage of their building.

'I... just... heard,' Councillor Imogen De la Hay rushed as she reached them. 'Bloody hell. I mean *bloody hell*. And we were all in the next building! If they'd decided to storm it... With us inside... I mean, it doesn't bear thinking about!'

'We should count ourselves lucky for that,' Tris returned, every word doused in deep sarcasm.

'We should, Dr Noakes. Are you and your team okay?'

'Not really, Imogen.'

De la Hay exacted a theatrically heavy sigh, her suspiciously taut features refusing to show any outward sign of emotion. She possessed the kind of medically assisted facial sculpture that meant she wore a permanent half-smile, regardless of whether she was amused or not.

In this case, Cora suspected the former. This would play into her hands beautifully.

'Well, as I and my colleagues said in the meeting, before we were *shouted down*, if you antagonise public opinion you cause all manner of unpleasant repercussions. Endangering not just your team but us visiting councillors, too. We can't ignore this. Mark my words, nobody will be safe from these attacks if we don't take firm action immediately.'

'Funny how it happened while we were away from our building,' Cora stated, her eyes firmly set on the ugly graffiti and smashed windows, so that she could be talking to anyone. 'When there was nobody here to be injured.'

'I fail to see what's funny about that,' De la Hay retorted. 'Of course, next time you might not be so lucky.'

'Is that a threat, Councillor?' Tris turned to her.

'Of course not!'

'Because it sounds like one to me.'

'I'm merely pointing out that unless you withdraw from that *gypsy camp*, the strength of local feeling is only likely to get worse.'

'You mean the St Columba Street permanent gypsy and traveller site?' Cora corrected.

'I know exactly what I mean, Dr Lael. I came to offer moral support. I didn't come to be verbally abused and accused of collusion.'

'Moral support, is it? Not an opportunity to gloat?'

'I don't appreciate your tone, Dr Noakes. I merely came to help.'

'Help? Right. So, when Alannah and Ollie return with the brooms and bin bags and buckets of water we need to remove that *racist, derogatory slur* daubed across our building, you'll be ready to help us?'

Imogen De la Hay didn't reply, her thickly applied foundation registering the slightest change of shade.

'Don't worry, Councillor, Alannah's bringing rubber gloves, too. I know how much you dislike getting your hands dirty.'

'Don't think this will be easily forgotten, Dr Noakes,' De la Hay spat back, a crack in her professional demeanour revealing the ugliness behind it. 'If you continue pandering to *those people*, this will only get worse.'

Tris stood his ground, a small rise of one eyebrow the ultimate wordless put-down. 'Thank you for your concern, Mrs De la Hay,' he replied, coolly. 'But acts like this only strengthen our resolve. If whoever did this thought they could deter us, they *seriously* underestimated my team and me.'

Incensed, but robbed of any suitable reply, the councillor turned on her heels and furiously click-clacked away across the car park.

'Impossible woman!' Tris kicked a shard of broken glass, sending it skittering across the block paving.

Out! Out! Out! it hissed, as it skidded away.

Firmly muting its thought-voice in her mind, Cora placed a gentle hand on her colleague's arm.

'Don't, Tris. She isn't worth it.'

'I thought it was odd they called a meeting here today,' he bit back. 'They never come here. I should have known what they were planning...'

'We have no proof they were involved,' Cora replied, hating the fact. Of course there would be no proof. That was how they would have wanted it. 'You didn't back down, just like you didn't in the meeting. They underestimated us and our determination to keep going. You should be proud of that.'

'I was... I am. But that was a direct threat just now – we both heard it.'

'I agree. But they want us to claim that so they can accuse us of overreacting. They may be clever enough to keep their noses clean, but they aren't clever enough to change their approach. We've seen it countless times before. You know how it works.'

'So, what do we do?'

How could she answer that when the attack – and what it implied for the future of The HappyKid Project – had taken them all by surprise? Cora retreated to the comfort of her psychology studies. 'We cross the transaction. They try to engage us negatively, so we deny them the drama they need to perpetuate their campaign.'

'By changing the narrative?'

'Exactly. We carry on and we don't succumb to the tempta-tion to battle them. We've already won because we have the wellbeing of the kids at the project at the heart of everything we do. That has to be our focus.'

Tris raised his eyes to the overcast sky. 'You're right. Sorry. She just infuriates me.'

'You and half the council.' Cora looked back at the damage. 'But whatever we do, we need to tell the police.'

'I'll call 999. But you should call Rob back. Leave a message this time.'

'He can't do anything. He'll be in the thick of interviews for the reopened Cassandra Norton case. Whoever did this is long gone, that's how they planned it.'

'But he needs to know.'

Cora knew Tris was right, but she was reluctant to make the call. Minshull had made his opinion clear on Cora continuing her HappyKid work – would he use the attack to prove his point? 'I will. It's just...'

'*Call* him. He'll be concerned. And the people who did this may well have been responsible for the St Columba Street attack.' Tris folded his arms, his expression signalling he understood far more than she liked. 'You know I'm right.'

Knowing she was defeated, Cora walked a few paces away and called Minshull again. Relief washed over her as his voicemail connected.

'Rob, it's Cora. Our building was attacked while we were in a meeting. Nobody's hurt, but they smashed the entrance and painted offensive slurs across the windows. Tris is reporting it to Control. I just... I just wanted you to know.' She watched Tris raise his hand to welcome Dr Alannah Hope and Dr Ollie Rowan as they headed over with cleaning supplies. Needing to say more, but not sure quite what, she added, 'I'm fine. We're fine. The whole team is clearing up now. Call me when you can, okay?'

A knot of unease formed in her stomach as she rejoined her team.

'Right, who's doing the sweeping and who's grabbing a sponge?' Ollie asked, holding a brush in one hand and a large yellow sponge in the other. 'If you're really good, you can choose what colour rubber gloves you wear, too. We have blue, black, yellow and a rather fetching pink.'

Ollie's over-the-top attempt to inject humour into the situation worked; the comical sight of his manic grin and enthusiastic display of cleaning accessories eliciting smiles from the team as they set to work.

Tris and Alannah swept up the debris, depositing them in neat piles that hissed and swore behind Cora's back. Meanwhile, she and Ollie opted for washing the red painted letters away, Cora focusing on both the visible paint and its invisible monologue spitting its hate and fury.

The physical act of washing the windows, doors and brickwork of the entrance brought with it the ultimately satisfying audible act of slowly, deliberately and completely dissolving the hidden voices. With each journey of the sponge across the damage, Cora felt her power growing over the sounds only she could hear, until they were almost inaudible, replaced by gentle bursts of birdsong coming from the trees surrounding the car park.

Soon, others came to join the clean-up effort, alerted to the attack as word spread through the local council buildings. People Cora had only seen across meeting tables at interdepartmental gatherings stood shoulder to shoulder with her and her colleagues, a general buzz of spirited conversation masking fierce defiance.

Although nobody said it, Cora heard their determination in every section cleaned, every pile of debris bagged and removed.

Not in my name…

This is disgusting…

We can't let this happen again…

It was immensely humbling, this quiet act of solidarity. It soothed the verbal bruises left by the four councillors' harsh words in the earlier meeting, and De la Hay's thinly veiled threats after it. Cora saw the effect such support had on Tris, Alannah and Ollie; her own spirits lifted for the first time that day.

And with it came a renewed sense of resolve: that the forces behind this attack could not be allowed to spread their fear and hatred unchecked. That if a fight was what they sought, a fight would be what they'd get.

By the time the clean-up was complete, handshakes and back-slaps exchanged, and the LEA teams dispersed back to their own departments, Cora's resolve was set like immovable rock.

Nobody was going to stop her keeping The HappyKid Project alive.

TWENTY-FIVE

ANDERSON

The poor bloke who'd discovered Karl Cuskie's body had done them a favour – *twice*.

His mention of the doorbell–cam salesperson's successful trip to Maidstone Road had proved impressively fruitful: ten houses in the road had cameras installed, including three close by on the same side of the road as Cuskie's home and two opposite it, plus several in the approach from both sides.

Together, they would build as clear a picture as possible of visitors to and from Cuskie's house on the night he died.

It was more than Anderson could have dared to hope for, and all he could do not to hug every member of his team as each detective studied the footage. On every screen in the CID office, shadowy figures and monochrome cars passed by, the videos freezing from time to time as the team stopped, time-checked and enlarged sections of film to capture every detail.

If Cuskie's killer had visited the house within the twenty-four-hour window currently being studied on screen, they would be on camera.

And Anderson needed that information urgently. Had the same person who killed Cassandra Norton killed Cuskie? Did they know he was due to visit Police HQ? Had he been silenced because he knew who they were?

The knowledge of that, combined with the misfiled eyewitness statement, set Anderson's nerves on edge. Did whoever deliberately buried the chip shop owner's statement have an agenda to misdirect the investigation? Or, worse, was someone in the force back then taking orders from outside? And had that person or persons acted to silence Cuskie now?

Question was, who stood to lose the most if Cuskie revisited his statement?

Observing the current occupants of the CID office, Anderson thought back to the original team who carried out the initial murder investigation, picturing them in the seats now occupied by Bennett and Ellis.

Back then, there had been two other DCs along with Wheeler. DC Geoff Westerbrook and DC Mickey Johns.

Geoff Westerbrook was in his late fifties and the sort of detective who kept his head down. He didn't do small talk and Anderson knew very little of his home life. Shortly after the Cassandra Norton investigation was completed, he took early retirement and moved to South Wales – replaced in CID by Les Evans.

Mickey Johns couldn't have been more different. Where Westerbrook was the stoic, silent presence in the corner of the office, Johns was the voice raised over everything. The joker, the opinion-giver; the one with a million theories to share and fingers in every pie. Had his loud protestations of wanting justice for Cassandra Norton masked a darker purpose?

Anderson could well imagine Johns visiting The Green Dragon after a shift and sharing a pint and not-so-subtle conversation with Karl Cuskie. He was on his third marriage by the time he applied for a transfer to West Midlands Police; the last Anderson heard of him was that he'd started an affair with a colleague in his new posting within weeks of arriving.

Had Mickey Johns hidden the evidence? He'd certainly crowed the loudest when Shona Pickton received her life sentence for murder. Bought rounds of drinks after work and made toasts with repulsive racist slurs Anderson wished he hadn't heard.

Cuskie's neighbour had reported a regular visitor. *Tall, he is, built like a freight train. Bald head with one of those Peaky Blinders caps perched on the top.* Anderson's memory of Johns was a tall, broad man, his thinning hair a source of significant embarrassment to him. Could he be bald today? Might he be back in Suffolk, visiting Cuskie to keep him in line?

Or could he be working for someone else instead of the police now? Someone on whose orders he'd misfiled the eyewitness statement to strengthen the case against Shona Pickton?

Was that possible?

Had Johns intended to frame Shona Pickton from the beginning, or had her proximity to the murder scene been a fortuitous serendipity? And could he have got wind of Cuskie's planned visit to CID now? Mickey was many things, but a murderer? It seemed preposterous, but Anderson made himself consider the possibility. Until they could unearth the truth, everyone was a suspect...

'Guv!'

All heads lifted around the room.

Heart in his mouth, Anderson hurried over to Bennett's desk. 'What do you have, Kate?'

'A visitor. Eleven fifty-six p.m.'

Anderson rounded the desk and stared at the frozen image. All of his theories vanished instantly.

'A woman?'

'I think so, Guv.'

The figure was blurred a little in the pool of light cast by the streetlight beside Karl Cuskie's house, but a mid-length ponytail of blonde hair could clearly be seen over the turned-up collar of a long, dark fitted coat, as the figure made her way past.

'Which camera is this?'

'Number 103.'

'Cuskie's other next-door neighbour.'

'Correct.'

The range of the camera meant that the figure was out of shot before Cuskie's gate, but on a quiet night when not many

161

passers-by had been spotted yet, Anderson was encouraged by the sighting.

'Right. Which house number is directly opposite Cuskie's house?'

Wheeler checked the street plan. 'Number seventy-two.'

Crossing everything, Anderson glanced up at his team. 'Please tell me the owner of number seventy-two is the proud purchaser of a video doorbell?'

'Here, Guv.' Evans raised his hand, sending a rueful grin to Ellis when he realised he'd stolen the younger DC's habit.

Anderson was flying now, his pulse racing.

'Check your footage for between eleven fifty-four p.m. and eleven fifty-eight p.m., just in case the timestamps are out of sync. Everyone, do the same. We're looking for a person, possibly female, with mid-length blonde hair tied in a ponytail, dressed in a long dark coat.'

The frantic clicks of computer mice ensued around him, the sense of a chase firing the atmosphere in the CID office.

'Number ninety-three at eleven fifty-five p.m.,' Bennett called.

'Eleven fifty-seven p.m. at number ninety-seven,' Ellis announced.

'Les?'

'Fast-forwarding now…' Evans scanned the sped-up footage until a click from his mouse caused him to stare at his screen. 'Here! Eleven fifty-seven p.m. by this timestamp.'

Anderson was at his desk in two strides.

There she was.

Light hair in a ponytail over a long, dark coat. The glimpse of a skirt hem beneath, then high heeled mid-calf boots. The figure opening the gate and walking up to Karl Cuskie's front door…

Anderson held his breath as the woman raised her hand to ring the doorbell.

Look back, he urged her. *Just once.*

The woman's back remained turned towards the doorbell camera. It made sense, of course. The street beyond was empty, many of the surrounding houses in darkness. She could carry on with no fear of being seen from the street.

Who was she? Girlfriend? Lover? Associate of one of the shady operatives Cuskie was said to report to? Anderson peered closer to the screen, the details visible providing no further clues.

The front door began to open, light within registering as a line of bright white in the grainy footage.

And then, the woman glanced back over her shoulder.

The features were unmistakable.

Irrefutable.

And yet, completely incomprehensible.

Shock registered in a long expletive from Evans, followed by a wave of incredulities and obscenities as the rest of the team crowded around his desk.

But Joel Anderson said nothing, his mouth dry, his words gone.

Minshull arrived at his side, following the shocked gazes of his colleagues to Evans' monitor screen.

'*Bloody hell…*'

The woman's face was in full view in the freeze-frame, the streetlamp spotlight leaving no uncertainty. As Evans zoomed in on the figure, it only became clearer.

'Guv?'

Anderson stood as still as the woman on the screen, but beneath his stone exterior an incandescent fury tore through him. Rage that he'd been blindsided. That he'd been judged and sidelined by Karl Cuskie's late-night visitor; made to feel years of guilt and shame for things he'd never done by this person who was clearly shameless and guilty as hell.

DCI Sue Taylor's face remained frozen, enlarged to full size on Evans' screen. Her identity beyond doubt: the evidence visible on more screens than she could ever hope to hide.

'Call the Super,' Anderson's voice growled from somewhere far away from the rest of his body. '*Now!*'

TWENTY-SIX

MINSHULL

The next hour was a blur.

The shaken CID team continued their search of footage from the time of DCI Taylor's arrival to the moment the neighbour found the body next day. At 12:16 a.m., she exited the house, leaving the front door open, and hurried down the road in the direction of the mini roundabout and junction with Seaton Road. There were no other people in the area until the camera at number 72 picked up Gareth Hartman across the road collecting his wheelie bin outside his house at number 107 and discovering Cuskie's open door at number 105 – and what lay beyond – at 8:55 a.m.

The video footage confirmed the suspicion no-one in the CID team wanted to believe: that nobody had visited Karl Cuskie since DCI Sue Taylor knocked on his door, stayed for twenty minutes and then ran away.

The evidence was damning. The consequences brisk.

Superintendent Martlesham ordered an immediate arrest warrant, insisting that he accompany Anderson and Minshull to take DCI Taylor into custody. While they awaited his arrival, Anderson briefed his stunned CID team.

'I don't know what to think,' he admitted. 'We just have to follow the Super's orders to the letter.'

Minshull couldn't blame his candidness. He was in shock, as they all were, navigating a course unfamiliar to all – unthinkable until moments before. The arrest of a senior officer, at her place of work, in full view of her colleagues. Not even Les Evans could have laid odds on that one.

'It should go without saying, but I'm saying it anyway – *none* of this gets outside the office. Not even a hint of it. Tell nobody until the arrest is made. We can't risk DCI Taylor being tipped off.'

'Guv.'

'Yes, Guv.'

'Of course, Guv.'

Minshull stepped in. 'No emails or texts or friendly phone conversations, either,' Minshull added. 'Even with significant others or friends outside the force. We have to keep this under wraps until the DCI is safely in custody. Understood?'

The team mumbled their agreement.

'Good. As soon as the Super arrives, we'll go. Dave, can you call Tim Brinton and ask for a couple of his officers to accompany us, please?'

'You think things might get nasty, Sarge?' Wheeler asked.

'I don't think she'll start fighting her way out,' Minshull replied. 'But we need to acknowledge the seriousness of this. It's a signal to everyone in the building that nobody is above the law.'

'What shall we do, Sarge?' Ellis asked.

'Double-check the footage from yesterday morning until Mr Hartman's appearance just before nine a.m. today. Liaise with each other to draw up as comprehensive a timeline of events as possible. If we can get some sense of a coherent time frame with corresponding captures, we'll have something strong to build on.'

As Bennett, Ellis and Evans returned to their screens – and Wheeler, for want of something to keep his mind busy, made coffee for them all – Minshull and Anderson retreated to the privacy of Anderson's office.

'*Shit*, Rob,' Anderson breathed, leaning against the newly closed door.

Minshull stared helplessly back. 'I know, Guv.'

'Why? That's what I want to know.'

'It could be a coincidence...' Minshull stopped himself, rubbing his eyes. 'No. It can't be, can it? She had me over the coals about meeting Cuskie in The Green Dragon. She *knew* he'd agreed to come in.'

'So, she went there to dissuade him...'

'Or silence him? Are we believing that?'

'Stuffed if I know.' Anderson dropped into his chair, eyes fixed on a point beyond the opposite wall of the office.

Where were his thoughts taking him?

Minshull knew the many years of conflict between Sue Taylor and Joel Anderson had taken their toll on his superior. She'd been instrumental in the professional side-lining sanctioned on Anderson after a missing child case became a murder inquiry; the psychological toll on the DI almost ending his career. In the months where the CID team had been without DC Les Evans, DCI Taylor had repeatedly refused to provide temporary cover, even when a quadruple murder case tested the team to their limits.

One thing was certain, however – a fact that surprised Minshull more than anything – Anderson was taking no pleasure in the potential downfall of his immediate superior. Minshull had assumed he would; that Anderson would be celebrating his antagonist's imminent demise.

Nothing could be further from the truth. Anderson seemed utterly deflated, exhausted by the sudden turn of events.

'I'm trying to work out why...' he said, at last.

'Do you think she knew Cuskie nine years ago?' It was the question that had bothered Minshull since the doorbell camera footage had been discovered.

The expression Anderson wore suggested Minshull hadn't been alone in wondering this. 'Before the case?'

'Les reckons Cuskie was an informer long before. DCI Taylor was here then, lower in rank for sure, but what's to say she didn't use Cuskie like so many others did?'

'Nothing,' Anderson conceded. 'I never used the man, but I was never in Sue's circle of friends. Not like you lot in here, all chummy camaraderie and slaying the competition in Sunday night pub quizzes. There was only Dave and me who did that, back home in St Just. Your dad frowned upon it. If it didn't happen in The Green Dragon with the other coppers, he didn't approve.'

That didn't surprise Minshull. Retired DCI John Minshull viewed every second as prime bargaining time. Even on family holidays, when he, Ben, Joe and Ellie were kids, their father would insist on such a packed itinerary of non-negotiable activities that it was always a relief to go back to school. No wonder John Minshull had been threatened by the genuine friendship between his two DCs. Their lack of agenda must have been a stubborn thorn in his side.

'What if she did know him before the murder? Shona Pickton insisting that Cuskie could provide proof she didn't kill Cassandra must have thrown a spanner in the works of their association.'

'So – what? Sue tried to discredit Pickton's argument?'

Minshull shrugged, his mind alive with potential links. 'If Cuskie refused to give Pickton the alibi it would close that line of inquiry. And Sue's association with him would be safely hidden from scrutiny.'

'That's true enough. Is it possible she asked Cuskie to refuse? To keep their association secret?'

'It's conceivable she could have visited him at home – or called him – before the team contacted him to ask for his statement.'

'Or maybe Cuskie was determined to throw his ex-girlfriend to the wolves. To prove his loyalty to Sue?'

'And in return she hid evidence that would have cast doubt on Shona Pickton's guilt...' Suddenly aware of the direction he was careering in, Minshull slammed the brakes on his speeding thoughts. He forced himself to pace the office in the hope of gaining perspective. 'No, hang on – wait. We have no evidence of any of this, Guv. She could have met him for the first time during the Cassandra Norton investigation and struck up an acquaintance afterwards. She wasn't the only copper to talk to Karl Cuskie...'

'But why would she visit him at his home last night? At midnight? When she knew Cuskie was due to speak to us today?'

The detectives lapsed into troubled silence.

'We have to be sure, Guv,' Minshull warned, his voice heavy with the weight of responsibility. 'We can't take this to the Super unless we have solid evidence to back it up.'

Anderson sagged a little. 'You're right. I just can't get my head around it. She was the last person to see Cuskie alive and then...'

'I know. What do we do?'

'We wait. See what action is taken, and what Sue says in her defence. If it looks like any of it might tally with our theories, we raise it then. Agreed?'

It felt wrong. But then, all of it did.

'Agreed, Guv,' Minshull replied, hating the untethered limbo of it all. He watched Anderson gather himself together and stand up, a look of unspoken allyship passing between them as he did so.

'Right. Let's get out there. The Super will be with us soon.'

The atmosphere in the main CID office was muted, the elation of a break so early in the investigation of Cuskie's death clashing shoulders with the shock of his final visitor's identity. At least in this they were united, although it gave them no advantage. They understood, as Minshull and Anderson did. There was no need to say it. Perhaps in the end it would make a difference. Or just bring a point of connection.

Ellis stood as they entered. 'Guv, Sarge, we've just had a call from Control. Someone attacked the offices of South Suffolk LEA...'

Minshull's heart went into freefall. 'Dr Lael...'

The missed call from earlier. The voicemail message still awaiting his attention...

'The team are all fine,' Ellis rushed, keen to assure Minshull. 'Just physical damage to the exterior of the Ed Psych Department building. Painted slurs across the entrance, broken glass panes and bricks thrown. The door was locked, thankfully, so they couldn't get inside.'

'We need to get people out there...' Minshull began, but Anderson cut across him.

'Do we have anyone at the scene?'

'One uniformed patrol on its way, Guv. Sergeant Brinton had another on standby and a paramedic car ready to attend. But Cora – Dr Lael – said nobody was hurt and they'd cleaned up most of the mess.'

It provided little comfort to Minshull, already furious with his lack of action earlier. Had Cora called him from the building while the attack was taking place? Had she sought his assistance before calling it in?

Why hadn't he answered?

'What did they paint on the building?' he asked, his mind forging links he hoped wouldn't hold.

'*SCUM*,' Ellis repeated, all apology for the word he had to utter. 'And other slogans about the gypsy and traveller community I'm not going to repeat.'

Minshull groaned. He hadn't wanted it to be connected, but what else could it have been? Why else would anyone have laid siege to an unassuming local education authority office building that most people weren't even aware was there?

'Guv, I need to talk to Cora,' he appealed to Anderson, who suddenly straightened to attention. Minshull turned in time to see Superintendent Martlesham striding in, flanked by two uniformed officers he didn't recognise.

'Sir,' Anderson said, acknowledging Martlesham's arrival as around the office the team stood to their feet.

'Apologies for the delay. I had to ensure everything was prepared for the arrest.' Martlesham observed the CID team with grave respect. 'Excellent work, everyone. I realise the resulting situation from your discovery is uncomfortable for all. It is likely to remain that way for quite some time. But nobody is above the law. I cannot allow any of my officers to step across the line.'

Bennett, Evans, Wheeler and Ellis murmured their agreement.

'Thank you, all. At ease.' Martlesham returned his stare to Anderson. 'Who will be accompanying us, Joel?'

'DS Minshull and DC Wheeler, Sir.'

Martlesham nodded. 'Very well. And are your team fully briefed on work for while we are gone?'

'I was just doing that when you arrived, Sir.'

'Excellent. Carry on.' Martlesham moved across the office to engage Tsang and Guthrie in careful, low discussion.

'Right, continue to pull together all the sightings and timestamps we have for Maidstone Road,' Anderson instructed. 'We need as comprehensive a timeline as possible. When that's complete, go back another twenty-four hours in the video footage. See if anyone else visits – or if Mr Cuskie's final visitor appears again.'

The team responded with grim smiles.

Anderson turned to Minshull, his hand briefly resting on the DS's arm. 'Cora will be fine. You're needed here.'

Reluctantly, Minshull nodded.

'Ready when you are, Sir,' Anderson called across the office.

Martlesham returned to Anderson and Minshull, as Wheeler joined them. He took a deep breath that belied the presence of nerves behind the steely exterior – a glimpse of the gravity of the task they now faced.

'Good. Let's get this over with.'

TWENTY-SEVEN

WHEELER

He'd seen this before, from the other side. Unceremoniously escorted by unsmiling colleagues, the shock of accusation reverberating as the curious glances of everyone he passed made an ugly spectacle of him. How easily work friends could judge. How quickly the worst could be believed. The fear of the gossip in your wake, twisting and growing and spreading around Police HQ like choking tendrils of poison ivy, insinuation polluting your name and your reputation…

Walking beside Minshull, Wheeler reprimanded himself.

This isn't your battle. They were mistaken about you.

When Minshull had asked him to accompany the arrest party now making its swift, solemn progress to the third floor, Wheeler had accepted without question. Rob needed the support, as did Joel. He didn't want them to go alone.

He hadn't expected it to rake up rubbish from before.

It had been almost a year since Wheeler had been wrongly accused of leaking information from the CID office, but like many of the darkest moments of his police career, he'd buried it deep within himself to be dealt with later. Except, as Wheeler and all his police colleagues knew, it was never dealt with. Just left to fester and decay in the vain hope that it would disappear.

He wasn't over the experience. Would he ever be?

He'd soldiered on, battling hard to return to the way things had been before. But no amount of jokes cracked, hot drinks for his colleagues made, or willingness to go above and beyond at work could bring back the shattered trust in his police family and the system that governed them.

Sue Taylor wouldn't know what hit her.

He glanced at the stony expressions of Minshull and Anderson. They had made up their minds, just as Wheeler's arresting officers had, although the only thing the video footage that had caused his arrest had proved was that he liked to cycle into work far earlier than any of his CID colleagues in the summer. The video evidence for DCI Taylor placed her as the last person present at the scene of a cold-blooded murder.

But the CID team had seen no indication of a weapon, only Taylor's arrival and hurried departure twenty minutes later.

How would she account for those minutes spent inside 105 Maidstone Road?

And would the arresting officers believe what she told them?

They had reached the third floor and filed wordlessly down the unremarkable blue carpeted corridor towards DCI Taylor's office. Doors opened as they passed, officers and staff shrinking back in surprise at the sight of the arrest party. How quickly before word of it spread to the lower two floors of the building, to the various police teams, support staff and assembled workers?

Wheeler grimaced. He knew the answer only too well: knowing this place, about the time it would take the arrest party to enter Taylor's office.

Not enough time to alert Taylor to her awaiting fate.

The DCI stood to attention as soon as she saw Martlesham, her shock and fast-following fury impossible to disguise as she faced the Superintendent and the officers.

'Sir. What is this?'

'Detective Chief Inspector Taylor, you are under arrest for the suspected murder of Karl Cuskie...'

'What?'

'You do not have to say anything...'

'No! Stop!'

'…But, it may harm your defence if…'

'This is preposterous! I have no intention of letting you…'

'…*if* you do not mention when questioned something which you later rely on in court…'

Martlesham didn't flinch at Taylor's protests as he completed the caution. Wheeler joined Minshull, Anderson and their uniformed colleagues in silent support of the Superintendent. Eyes forward, backs straight, an immovable shield of blue. But where his colleagues stared directly at Taylor, Wheeler focused determinedly on a point just above her head.

Guilty or not, he wouldn't contribute to the accusatory stares of an arrest party that still haunted him today. All would be proved or disproved in the interview room. Everything here was just theatre.

'Do you understand?' Martlesham asked, reaching the end of the caution.

'Yes, Sir,' Taylor replied, her argument silenced, a noticeable quiver in her voice. Had anger or fear put it there?

'Leave your desk and accompany us now.'

By the time they entered the corridor, word had clearly spread. Police colleagues sternly observed the steady procession of the arrest party from open office doors. Martlesham led the charge, followed by Taylor, flanked by the two uniformed officers, with Anderson, Minshull and Wheeler forming the rear guard. Wheeler was aware of every pair of eyes upon them, every opinion held at bay behind their silent vigil. He knew that as soon as those office doors closed, speculation would travel like wildfire.

Taylor said nothing as they descended the stairs to the custody suite on the ground floor, an uncharacteristic stance that put Wheeler on edge. She met the eyes of every officer they passed, as if defying them to pass judgement on her. But from his vantage position behind the DCI, Wheeler witnessed the hands clasped so tightly behind her back that the pressure stole the blood from her knuckles.

Sergeant Lyn Vickery at the custody suite desk impassively read Taylor the allegations, as the arrest party looked on. Her personal dislike of the DCI was no secret, but she kept it admirably at bay.

How many colleagues would do the same? And how many would be crowing at the DCI's perceived fall from grace?

Only when Taylor was taken to a cell, awaiting the arrival of her solicitor, did Martlesham officially release Wheeler, Anderson, Minshull and the two uniformed officers from their duty. A strange emptiness hung over them all as they parted ways, the uniformed officers returning to their department while Minshull, Wheeler and Anderson headed for the fire exit that led to Police HQ's car park.

Nobody had agreed to go there beforehand and there had been no conversation between the detectives while they were engaged in their duty. It was a mutual destination, agreed upon without words.

Pushing open the fire exit door, Anderson was first outside. The wind was bitter here, Wheeler instantly longing for the relative warmth of the CID office. Minshull joined them with hands punched deep into his suit trouser pockets, shoulders raised to brace against the cold. The concrete platform beyond the fire escape doors led to a ramp down to the car park tarmac, but the top of it had become a favoured meeting point. After the experience of arresting a superior officer, Wheeler needed the reassurance of a familiar location to soothe the sting.

'So, how do you reckon it went?' Anderson asked, leaning against the steel handrail at the top of the platform. Wheeler couldn't fathom Anderson's mood from his question.

'I think we made a point,' replied Minshull. 'And she's on the back foot now for sure. Let's just hope we don't have to wait too long to start interviews.'

'It was bloody horrible,' Wheeler stated, shock registering in his body as his private thoughts found a voice.

'Dave?'

Why had he let that happen? Why couldn't he have just played along?

'Forget I said it...' he rushed, panic flooding his body.

'But you did,' Anderson pressed, frowning at his colleague and friend.

Wheeler avoided their stares. 'I shouldn't have... I wasn't going to say anything because... well, it doesn't matter why. But I don't want to do that again in a hurry.'

'You think we made a mistake?' Minshull asked. It was a genuine question, the surprise clear in his tone.

'No, of course not,' Wheeler retorted, thoroughly rattled now. 'It's her on the video, no question. But all that *arresting party* drama? Pointless showboating crap. Nobody else needed to see it...'

'You heard the Super. It was done to send a message to anyone else in the building that officers committing crimes would not be tolerated.'

'Oh, they saw that, all right. And it gave them the perfect opportunity to spread their own gossip about it. It'll be all over HQ now.'

'Well, *good*, I say,' Anderson replied. 'The plan worked.'

'It didn't work for DCI Taylor, did it?' Wheeler shot back, cold fingers balling into fists at his side. 'Threw her to the lions, more like. I'm all for shows of strength, Joel, but that was milked to its last drop.'

Minshull stared at Wheeler. 'What's your problem, Dave? We all saw that footage... DCI Taylor has to answer for her actions, just like any of us.'

'Oh, and parading her through the corridors like a warning shot to keep everyone in line was the kindest way to do it?' Wheeler felt indignation bloom within his chest, burning through his veins.

'Why are you defending her?' Minshull returned.

'I'm not defending her...'

'It looks that way to me.'

'Rob – hold on,' Anderson warned. But Minshull wasn't done.

'If you had reservations about her arrest…'

'No! I said I didn't! It needed to happen and it has now.'

'So what's the issue?'

'Nothing. I just don't agree *that* spectacle was the right way to do it.'

Minshull rounded on him, his own frustrations leaking out. 'Oh, you don't? Nice of you to tell us before we invited you, Dave.'

'I'm telling you now! And I didn't exactly have a choice about being part of it, did I? It did nothing for the investigation. It made us look like power-hungry idiots, the five of us shuffling down the corridor like the wannabe FBI.'

'It was a show of strength. Like the Super wanted.'

'It was ridiculous. And unnecessary. And I didn't like it, Sarge. Not one bloody bit.'

'Why on earth not?'

'Because I know how it feels to be a floorshow in this building!'

It emerged as a visceral shout, the ragged edges of it vibrating around the car park. And the point where Wheeler would laugh it off, claim he wasn't feeling great and shelve it quickly, never arrived.

Minshull and Anderson stared back.

'…So stop asking me how I feel about it,' Wheeler finished, too stung now to care what he'd said. They had never talked about the impact of Wheeler's false arrest, and he'd certainly never offered it, resolving that his own thoughts, feelings and emotions on the subject were nobody else's business.

'Dave, I didn't think…' Anderson began.

'Of course you didn't, Joel. Because it was all okay in the end, right? Only I will *never* be okay with the memory of how that made me feel. It's one thing to uphold good conduct and show consequences for rule-breaking. But that wasn't consequences in action. It was a bloody power trip.'

He'd said too much. Revealed stuff he'd sworn he'd never share. Heat rose up his neck, pinching his skin, his stomach tying itself in knots. 'With your permission, I'll go now, Guv. I'm not needed for the interviews am I?'

'No, Dave… But wait…'

Wheeler was already backing towards the fire door. 'Then I'll be on my way.'

Bewildered and betrayed by his own response, Wheeler hurried away, leaving Minshull and Anderson staring after him in shock.

TWENTY-EIGHT

'Felixstowe is not a place used to hitting national headlines. And yet this evening, for the second time in a week, this Suffolk town is braced for a fresh onslaught of media attention. It follows the grim discovery this morning of the body of a man in his late fifties, murdered in his home.

'Karl Cuskie was well known in Maidstone Road, the quiet Felixstowe street where he had lived for almost a year. Neighbours say he was good-natured, a friendly face, someone who always said hello. He lived alone but was sociable, friends visiting his modest terraced home regularly. While it's not known if he had family living nearby, it seems by all accounts that he was someone who felt at home in this community.

'Which is why, this evening, the town that welcomed Karl Cuskie is in shock. Maidstone Road is still cordoned off, with police forensic teams working at the scene since early this morning.

'Little is yet known of how Mr Cuskie died, but South Suffolk Police have confirmed in the last hour that they are treating his death as murder.

'Following the dramatic events of last week regarding the release and acquittal of Shona Pickton for the murder of Cassandra Norton, nine years ago – and the violent attack on a traveller camp on the fringes of the town in the wake of it – this new case has given Felixstowe residents fresh cause to fear for their own safety. We'll bring you more on this developing story as it happens...'

TWENTY-NINE

SHONA

I just saw the news.

I can't move.

I came home from doing a food shop at the supermarket – the first time I've felt safe to do one since I got here – and it was the first thing I saw when I put on the TV. I'm sitting on the edge of the sofa in my rented place, still wearing my coat, the shopping bags abandoned in the kitchen.

And I can't move.

What if they think I killed him?

Because I said it, didn't I? I said the first thing I'd do if I ever got out was find Karl and make him change his mind. To make amends for what he did to me. He put me in prison because he refused to speak up for me. I wanted to know why. I wanted him to tell me why to my face.

Word gets out, doesn't it? Even from prison.

I said all kinds of stuff about Karl when I was in there, before there was ever a hope of an appeal. I was angry with him for such a long time. That sort of information is collateral when you're in there. If you can alter your sentence by ratting out someone else, you do it.

What if someone trying to cut a deal remembers what I told them?

I'm trying to think of who I mentioned finding Karl to just before I came out of prison, and since I got home. I didn't try to hide the fact I wanted to see him. I wanted to meet him, face to face, and ask him to tell the police what really happened. He knows who killed her, and he knows why. He knows more than anyone and he could sort this.

Could have sorted it.

But he can't, can he? He's dead. And somebody's going to think it was me.

Why did I tell people I was going to find him? Why couldn't I keep my stupid mouth shut?

Because the truth is, I did him a favour, not telling the police everything I know about Cassandra Norton. I could have thrown it all out in the open to save my own skin. But I'd promised him – even though he didn't give me the alibi I needed – because I didn't want him ending up the way Cassandra did. I served years of my life in prison to protect that bastard. The least he could have done was speak for me now.

But it's too late.

They got to him before I could. And people like that don't rest when only one person is out of their way. They won't stop until the truth is buried for good, and everyone who dares to cross them are buried with it.

Do they know I know? About everything that's gone on?

And if they shut Karl up to stop him talking, will they come for me next?

I start to get up, but there's a sound from the door that makes me freeze in fear.

I look around, holding my breath, waiting for a knock, or a kick. In the stinging silence that follows, my mind goes into overdrive. How do I get out? The window in the bedroom opens wide enough, but there's a two-storey drop with concrete waiting at the bottom. Would I make it down there alive if I jumped?

I don't know how long I wait: only that the news bulletin ends, and some loud, brash quiz show comes on.

I need to know there isn't someone still there. Contingencies form in the panic of my mind…

If I crawl from the sofa to the open living room door, I can peer around the doorframe down the short hallway to the front door without being seen through the frosted glass panel. If someone's there, I'll see their outline in the glass.

I feel sick as I drop to my knees, edging across the floor towards the door. My heartbeat is so loud in my head I fear the whole neighbourhood will hear it. Even the friction of my knees against the rough carpet is far too loud. Held breath making my lungs burn, I flatten my back against the wall, peering slowly around the architrave.

Sunlight pours through the door panels, the etched decoration in the panes sending shards of early afternoon rainbows dancing across the laminated hall flooring towards me.

The light is unbroken. Nothing to stop it.

I would see the shadow of someone if they were waiting for me.

Mouth dry, I swallow, willing my pulse to slow.

I drop my gaze – and that's when I see it. A white envelope, lying on the doormat.

The letterbox flap. That's what the noise was.

I clamp a hand to my mouth to muffle a sudden burst of nervous laughter, my stomach churning in reply. It's okay. I'm safe. Nobody knows I'm here. Just junk mail like the last three days have brought, addressed to people who lived here before.

Still, I check the door panels one more time before I rise to a stoop, crossing the hall floor to retrieve the envelope before scurrying back to the safety of the sofa.

As the garishly lit quiz show chatters away to itself, I turn over the envelope. It's blank on the front. It'll be one pushed through every letterbox by local posties, no doubt full of adverts and useless crap.

I open it anyway, the relief of its mundanity something I need to savour.

But the single sheet of paper I pull out stops my breath.

I'M WATCHING YOU. SAY NOTHING.
SPEAK AND SOMEONE DIES.

No…

Not again…

I thought I was safe here, that I wouldn't be found.

That they wouldn't find me.

Bile rises in my throat. I force it down.

Because this isn't the first time I've seen this message. Or this handwriting. These letters have haunted me for years.

I thought getting out would make them stop. They found me at the first place I was supposed to stay. That's why Alan arranged for this place for me. But they *know* where I am, even though Alan promised me nobody would find me here. And now Karl's dead, even though I've said nothing.

They know where I am. They're watching me. And if I say anything, someone will die. *I* could die…

I can't tell Alan, not now Karl's dead.

But there is one person I can call. An old friend who offered to help. I didn't think I needed it when they offered a few days ago. But I need it now.

Hands trembling, I reach for my phone.

THIRTY

CORA

The mood in the Educational Psychology Team office had been low since the attack. Cora and her colleagues worked through their regular caseloads, a grim determination set between them.

Gone was the jovial chat and light-hearted banter. Gone too, the music Ollie often played in the afternoon, as the self-appointed music supervisor of the department. On days where no clients were coming into the office, he would regularly curate a playlist of uplifting songs to entertain his colleagues and ease the slow passing of long work afternoons.

There was no soundtrack to their work today. Instead, a prickled silence surrounded them as they worked.

But Cora heard more.

The notes of concern rising from the wastepaper baskets beneath each desk. The thinly concealed anger from empty mugs waiting to be washed. The fear from dropped papers and Post-Its, shivering its way into Cora's consciousness.

Muting each hidden voice felt both necessary to proceed and disrespectful to her colleagues. Hearing their inner thoughts and battles was a privilege and should be treated as such. But as the hours following the attack passed, Cora found she needed silence; the thoughts of her colleagues and friends carefully pushed away to allow her to function.

She'd passed the message on to Police HQ that the team were all fine and the damage to the building superficial and easy to repair. But Minshull was yet to call. Four uniformed officers had arrived to inspect the scene and record the damage, but they left with no mention of the DS. Did Rob even know yet?

Of course, she'd seen the news and understood why Minshull might have been delayed in replying to her message. Another body. *Murder*, according to the eager reporter in the lunchtime news bulletin, whose breathless delivery of the word seemed gleeful and wrong.

Did journalists get a thrill from reporting from crime scenes? Without the burden of trying to work out why someone had been killed, or who had ended their lives, was the process a mere game to them?

Cora recalled Minshull talking once about this in his own job.

'The rush of discovering a new crime is intoxicating,' he'd admitted. 'But it's always tempered by concerns for the well-being of people caught up in it. You don't want there to be lies and loss and all the crap that people go through as a result. But each detail is a part of a puzzle that calls to you, despite everything.'

'How do you deal with that?' Cora had asked him.

Minshull's answer was starkly honest. 'You don't. You try not to look too closely at your response and just get on with the job. People don't want police officers to be navel-gazers. They want us to solve crimes.'

Was that what Cora did with the young children and teen-agers she worked with in the course of her job? Each of them brought issues that caused them emotional hurt and personal challenge. Each of them came to the Ed Psych Team wanting answers and solutions. Cora had identified and worked with issues that no child should ever have to live with, and each case had felt like a personal victory when she'd found solu-tions and strategies that helped the client. But did the prospect of someone else's pain thrill her in the first instance, as the discovery of a body or the report of a crime might thrill Minshull?

The thought sat uneasily upon her as she worked through her caseload.

An hour later, a friendly face appeared level with the edge of her desk.

'How goes it, Dr Lael?'

Tris had crouched his tall frame down so that he could peer up at Cora. It was amusing to see the tall man thus positioned; funnier still, the comically self-satisfied grin he wore for having done it.

'It's *going*. You appear to have shrunk, Dr Noakes.' Cora gave him a rueful grin, loving the lightness her boss could bring to the darkest situation. Tris was one of life's true optimists, a ray of sunshine no matter what. The darker the adversity around him, the brighter he shone.

The fun was tempered with concern, of course, as it always was. Cora saw his efforts to lift the spirits of the team increase in direct proportion to how much he was worried about them.

'Like a frantic, inoffensive jack-in-a-box,' Alannah often called him. 'The greater the pressure he's under, the higher he bounces up to prove he can.'

It was an accurate, if slightly off-the-wall description, and made Cora smile. If only everyone facing adversity had a determinedly bouncy ally like Tris Noakes...

'Did you hear the news from Felixstowe?' he asked.

Cora nodded. 'No prizes for guessing why Rob hasn't called.'

Tris grimaced. 'A reopened murder investigation, the attack on St Columba Street and now a brand new murder case to run altogether? I'd be amazed if the poor chap's still vertical by the end of the day.' He picked up a pencil from the old jam jar on Cora's desk and began to fiddle with it. 'I just had a call from the chief executive. He's asking us to reconsider HappyKid...'

'No.'

'That's what I said. I told him if we abandoned it now we'd be seen as soft targets by any berk wanting to tell us what to do.

And we'd be letting down an already marginalised and much-maligned group in our remit, which would make us look like we never cared about them in the first place. I suggested his constituents might see that as a weakness on his part...'

'Did that work?'

The sigh Tris unleashed fluttered the edges of the case files on Cora's desk. 'Your guess is as good as mine. But he hasn't demanded we stop yet, so we have to take that as a good sign.'

He flicked the edge of the pencil, sending it rolling across the desk towards Cora.

Bloody politicians, it said in his voice.

It was his favourite trick, fuelled by a childlike fascination with Cora's ability. It should have worn thin by now, but the implied belief and trust it revealed meant more to Cora than she would ever tell him.

She laughed and caught the pencil before it toppled off the desk. 'Good to know I'm still amusing you.'

'Always.' He blessed her with a smile she knew her mum would be instantly charmed by, and checked his watch. 'Joss is due in any minute. We'll get the team together in the family room when he arrives. I want to try to keep our conversation as private as possible, away from prying eyes and ears. Okay?'

'Fine by me,' Cora replied. She had been wondering how the project leader had been, following news of this morning's attack. His position was unenviable as the link between their team and the community The HappyKid Project served, fielding issues and fire-fighting on both sides. That kind of constant pressure must be tough to process.

'Great.' Tris jumped to his feet. 'Give me a shout when he gets here?'

'No problem.'

'Thanks.' He made as if to walk to his office, then reversed his steps. 'Oh, and he said he wanted a word with you after we've finished the meeting. Hope that's okay?'

'Sure.' Memories of the unexpected conversation they'd had back at the St Columba Street site returned. Could Joss have more questions about Cora's ability?

The possibility didn't fill her with dread, as it once would have done. Cora had explained her emotional synaesthesia enough times in recent years to understand when questions about it came primarily from a point of curiosity, not fear. Accepting this was part and parcel of her personal quest to investigate the full capabilities of her unique mind. The more she discovered, the more she could explain it – both to herself and to others.

Half an hour later, Joss Lovell hurried into the office. The burden on him was noticeably greater, as Cora had expected. He spoke quickly, as if scared the words might escape him if he didn't express them fast enough, his dark eyes darting beneath dark brows, seeking reassurance from everyone.

'How is it at St Columba Street?' Tris asked as they gathered around the table in the family room.

'Much as it was. I'm afraid they know about the attack here.'

Around the small, brightly decorated family room, the team sagged as one. It was inevitable, given the intense media interest surrounding Shona Pickton and the rise in violence towards the gypsy and traveller community following her acquittal. But the prospect of further worry heaped upon an already beleaguered community hung heavily on the team.

'We're fine,' Tris said firmly. 'Takes more than a bunch of paint-wielding thugs to stop us.'

'Good to know, my friend. Even so, we need to be careful,' Joss replied. 'We're being watched – everyone is aware of it. There's a fine line between defiance and antagonism.'

'I understand that. So, how do you want to proceed?'

'I've been giving it a lot of thought. I really appreciate you all standing with us. The community does, too.' Joss looked around the room, acknowledging every member of the team. His eyes lingered for a moment longer on Cora, a slight nod of acknowledgement in her direction before he looked back at the team a hint of what might come after this meeting. 'But I think we forget the next session and look to restart next week. Take a few days while the storm rages. Regroup. Prepare.'

'Agreed.' Tris affirmed. 'In the meantime, we'll liaise with you and the other volunteers to create a temporary programme that can both deal with issues immediately resulting from the situation, and provide respite for the children to give them some space from it.'

Cora watched her colleagues as the meeting continued, impressed by their shared drive to make the project even more specific to the needs of the St Columba Street community than it had previously been. Might the added pressure of mounting criticism and attack actually lead to a better, stronger project? If it did, it would be the ultimate irony for those who were hell-bent on destroying it.

That alone was worth striving for.

When their discussions were done, the team began to file back to the office. Tris caught Cora's eye. 'I believe you two have things to talk about. I'll leave you to it.' Accepting a hand-clasped handshake from Joss, he left the family room, closing the door quietly behind him.

Joss gave a self-conscious laugh and returned to one of the sofas. 'I see he told you already.'

'He said you wanted to talk to me.' Cora perched on the arm of an armchair, nerves bubbling within her. 'How can I help?'

Away from the rest of the team, Joss was quieter, less certain of himself. His thumb rubbed across the sixteen-spoked Roma Chakra wheel tattoo on the back of his left hand as he looked up at Cora. 'I want to ask you a favour, Doc.'

'Of course.'

'It isn't about what we spoke of last time.' His brows knotted. 'Well, it *is*. Just not the listening at the site.'

Not certain she understood, Cora waited for more.

When she didn't reply, Joss cleared his throat and spoke again. 'It isn't for me. It's for a friend. An old friend… But I need to protect them, so I can't tell you who they are.'

A chill passed across Cora's skin. Instinctively, she folded her arms across her body. 'I don't understand, Joss.'

'I know.' His thumb paused above the centre of the wheel tattoo. 'I'm sorry. I just want to know – in your professional capacity – could you help?'

'As a psychologist?'

'Yes.'

'I could offer some advice, maybe. But it's hard to say how much help I could be without knowing specifics.'

'I realise that. I wouldn't ask if I didn't think you could help.'

'Have you talked to Tris about this?' Cora asked, her mind a-whirr with questions yet to find answers. 'Because he's my boss and anything I do should go past him…'

'No,' he stated firmly. 'I'm asking as a favour for a friend. Nothing official. Nothing that can be documented.'

It felt too vague a request, the potential for a breach of professional standards too great. And yet there was an urgency to Lovell's request. A sense of trust in Cora that she hadn't expected.

'I'm sorry, Joss. I don't think I can…'

'She's desperate!' he rushed, his hand immediately raised in apology. 'Forgive me, Cora. I didn't mean to shout.'

'She?'

'My friend. My good friend. She's scared and she's alone and she thinks someone wants to kill her.'

'She should go to the police.'

'She can't. I can explain everything if you meet her. You have the Sight and…'

'I told you, it's not the same thing.'

What was Joss asking her? He knew nothing of her association with the police, but Cora couldn't escape it. She was part of them now, bound to her police colleagues like the family she'd often heard Minshull and the team refer to the Force. If Joss Lovell's friend was being threatened, the police should know.

'I know. I'm making such a mess of this, forgive me...' He rested his forearms on his knees, his palms flat towards Cora in an open request. 'She can't go to the police. I can't tell you why, but when you meet her, you'll understand. I think you can help her. With your gift. She'll trust you, I know she will. And... And I don't know who else to ask.'

His earnestness made Cora pause, the desperation of his request registering as a tension in the centre of her chest. 'I don't know...' she began, uncertainty infiltrating her words.

'Would you just agree to meet her? And if you can't help or it won't work you can walk away, I promise. Please, Cora.'

She should refuse. This was neither her remit nor her responsibility. But a woman was scared for her life. Could Cora in all conscience refuse such a desperate request?

'I'll meet her,' she said, the rush of relief from Joss almost stealing her own breath. 'But I can't promise to be able to help.'

'You don't have to. Meeting her is enough.' He stood, offering his hand. When Cora accepted, his other hand clasped over it. 'Thank you.'

Cora nodded her acceptance as his hands fell away. 'Will you bring her here?'

'No,' Joss said. 'I'll arrange somewhere. As soon as it's sorted, I'll drive you there – if you trust me?'

'I trust you, Joss. But I have one condition.'

Lovell's eyes narrowed a little. 'Name it.'

'Tris has to know. I can't go with you without him knowing why.'

The project leader observed her for a moment, a muscle dancing in his jaw as he considered this. Cora stood her ground. For her own safety and for the sake of her friendship with Tris, this had to be the condition upon which the meeting rested. If Joss respected that, she was prepared to go – even though the situation felt precarious.

Joss gave a long, slow exhale as he looked at Cora. 'Fine. I'll talk to him before I leave.'

'Thank you. When do you want us to meet?'

'In a day or so. I'll call you.'

Agreement reached – and a thousand possibilities crowding Cora's mind – she led the way back to the office.

Had she stumbled upon a new test for her skills? Or made a costly mistake?

THIRTY-ONE

MINSHULL

'I don't appreciate being dragged in here like a common criminal. In full sight of everyone! It's an insult: to me, to my rank and to my spotless record of service, the likes of which you couldn't even hope to aspire to. Make no mistake about it, I intend to throw the book at each and every one of you responsible for this deep injustice...'

Minshull took a long, slow breath. 'Your name, Ma'am? For the recording?'

DCI Taylor bristled, the pointed look from her legal representative doing little to appease her. 'Detective Chief Inspector Susan Mary Taylor.'

'Thank you. Investigating officers DI Joel Anderson and DS Rob Minshull present. The time is five thirteen p.m.'

He straightened his folder on the interview desk, taking his time to settle, a well-established meditation that anchored his mind to the task ahead, affording him a moment to breathe before the verbal battle commenced. Beside him, Anderson sat rod-straight, stony faced. He wouldn't speak yet, as they had agreed beforehand while they were waiting for Taylor to meet with her solicitor, Gemma Bissett.

'Okay, let's begin. Where were you yesterday evening, between the hours of eleven p.m. and twelve thirty a.m.?'

'I was at home.'

'And where is home, DCI Taylor?'

Taylor stated her address, folding her hands on the desk in front of her.

'Can anyone corroborate that?'

'No. I was alone.'

'And you didn't leave the house at all? Go out to get food? Or visit someone?'

'No.'

'Thank you. I'm going to ask you again, because we have reason to believe that you did, indeed, leave your home not long before midnight, returning in the early hours.'

Taylor said nothing.

'So, the hours of eleven p.m. and twelve thirty a.m. last night. Please think carefully before you answer.'

Bissett looked up from her notes, watching her client.

The DCI eyeballed Minshull.

'I went out. But not for long. Just to fetch some snacks from the twenty-four-hour Tesco.' She gave a slightly brittle cough. 'I – I haven't been sleeping well. For months, actually. Pressures of the job and an old back injury I incurred in my CID days. Most nights I'll watch films into the early hours until I fall asleep.'

'What snacks did you buy?'

'I fail to see why that's important.'

Minshull met her stare. 'Just curious. If I eat late at night I get terrible heartburn.'

'I drink milk,' she spat, every syllable a micro-aggression. 'It helps.'

'Good tip, thanks.' Resisting the urge to smile, Minshull continued. 'Can you tell me how you know Karl Cuskie?'

'Who?'

'Karl Cuskie.'

'He's an acquaintance.'

'Do you know him professionally?'

'No.'

'Personally, then?'

Taylor shifted a little. 'Yes.'

'And how long would you say you've known Mr Cuskie?'

'A few years.'

'How did you meet?'

'I forget.'

'But you met him several years ago and remained in touch?'

'Yes.'

'When was the last time you saw Mr Cuskie?'

Taylor muttered something.

'For the recording please?'

'A few days ago.'

Minshull took time to write this down despite knowing, as well as Taylor did, that it was an absolute lie. When he'd imagined this interview, he thought she would opt immediately for either a prepared statement or 'no comment' replies. But her indignance at the nature of her arrest was palpable in the room, leaking into every gesture, expression and reply.

'How would you describe your relationship with Mr Cuskie?' When Taylor didn't respond, Minshull pressed on. 'Would you say you were close?'

'No.'

'But he's a friend?'

'Yes – I told you.'

'Were you and Mr Cuskie ever romantically involved?'

'What is that supposed to mean? Oh, because I'm a woman and he's a man it must mean we've had sex?'

Bissett looked up from her notes. 'It's an odd question, Detective Sergeant.'

It really wasn't. Why the sudden outburst, the defensiveness? Minshull pushed his irritation down and replied as calmly as he could. 'I'm just trying to establish the nature of the relationship between DCI Taylor and Karl Cuskie.'

'I *said* we're acquaintances,' Taylor snapped back.

Minshull regrouped. 'How often would you say you saw him?'

'Occasionally.'

'Where did you typically meet?'

'Several places. The pub. Sometimes in the town.'

'At your house? At his?'

'Like I said, we were just acquaintances.'

'With respect, Ma'am, you haven't answered my question.'

Taylor slumped a little. 'Occasionally.'

'At yours? At his?'

'Sometimes at his. Rarely at mine.'

'Thank you. So, thinking back to the last time you saw Mr Cuskie. Was that at the pub? Somewhere in town? Or at one of your homes?'

'I… I can't remember.'

'At his house?'

'Possibly.'

It was enough of an admission to move on. Minshull opened his folder and produced print-outs of the doorbell camera footage from the house across the road from Karl Cuskie's home. 'I'd like you to take a look at these, please.'

He handed one each to Taylor and her solicitor, waiting while they inspected them. Taylor's shoulders tensed immediately. The image in the stills was as clear as it had been in the footage, the benefit of the streetlight evident in the level of detail visible.

'Do you recognise the person in that picture?'

Lips tightly shut, Taylor nodded.

'For the recording, please?'

'Yes.'

'Who do you see in that photograph?'

'It's me.'

'That's a still from a doorbell camera video at 97 Maidstone Road, directly opposite number 105, which is the home of Karl Cuskie. This was taken last night, around eleven fifty-seven p.m.' He looked at Anderson, who had been a silently seething observer to the unfolding discussion. 'Do you want to show the footage, Guv?'

Anderson gave a thin smile as he produced a laptop, the footage cued to show Taylor and Bissett.

'The stills you've already seen come from this first clip,' Anderson said, tapping the keyboard to start the playback. 'So at eleven fifty-seven p.m. you approach number 105 from the street and go to the front door. The door opens and you go inside.' He looked up. 'Do you remember this, DCI Taylor?'

Taylor kept her eyes on the black-and-white footage and said nothing.

'Okay, let's see the second video.' Anderson selected the clip and set it to play. 'This was captured by the same doorbell camera at twelve sixteen a.m.' The video played on, showing Taylor running away from the house, the front door clearly left open behind her. 'Can you tell me why you left in such a hurry?'

The DCI stared blankly at the image.

'Did you argue? Did Mr Cuskie ask you to leave?'

'I… I was late. I realised the time and I…'

'Late for what?'

'I wasn't… *It* was late and I had work next day, so…'

Anderson paused the video. 'Mr Cuskie was found dead in the hall of his home this morning, just before nine a.m. The front door was open – as it is here. My team and I have studied footage from the doorbell cameras in Maidstone Road from twelve hours before this sequence up until Karl's neighbour discovers his body.' He fixed Taylor with a look – and Minshull felt the warm air become still in the interview room. 'The last person to see Karl Cuskie alive was you.'

His pointed silence was long enough to allow the weight of the accusation to register with Taylor and her solicitor.

'Tell us what happened,' Minshull urged, when Anderson nodded at him to continue. 'Why did you go to see Karl Cuskie? Why did you only stay for twenty minutes? And why did you run away, leaving his front door wide open?'

DCI Taylor's eyes slid from Minshull to Anderson. She straightened her shoulders and lifted her chin, imperious in her seat.

'No comment.'

THIRTY-TWO

BENNETT

'Absolute bollocks!'

Anderson crashed back into the CID office with a grim-faced Minshull following two paces behind him.

'How'd it go, Guv?' Bennett asked, as Wheeler, Ellis and Evans looked up from their desks.

Bennett sensed the room darken as Anderson stalked the floor.

'She was blatantly lying,' he snarled, counting off Taylor's misdemeanours on the fingers of one hand. 'Said she didn't know him, then said he was an acquaintance. Said she was alone at home last night and then conveniently remembered she'd gone out. And when we presented her with the video evidence, she went straight to *no comment.*'

'How did she react when she saw herself on screen?' Bennett asked. She'd half-expected DCI Taylor to deny the figure captured by the doorbell was her, despite the clarity of the image leaving little room for error.

'It shocked her,' Minshull said, sinking wearily onto his chair. 'But she regrouped.'

'We need to prove the nature of the relationship between her and Cuskie,' Anderson said. 'I need anything we can get from her mobile phone, her laptop and the computer terminal in her office. We need phone records – times, dates, names, text messages sent… Anything and everything we have that can connect her to him.'

'Guv, Forensics collected Cuskie's phone at the scene,' Ellis informed him.

'Good. Call them and see if we can get someone from Tech to look at it ASAP.'

'On it, Guv.'

'Dave, when you were asking around about Cuskie, did anyone hint that the DCI was one of the officers who knew him?'

Wheeler gave a shrug. 'Nothing specific. But there were a lot of half-mentions of names that were retracted pretty quickly when they realised why we needed to know. She could have been one of those.'

It was an uncharacteristically flat reply from Wheeler, Bennett thought. Usually he was the first to offer suggestions and solutions. But he'd been strange since he'd returned from the arrest party. Quiet, refusing to be drawn on any of the details. He'd remained hunched at his desk ever since, with none of his usual joviality. Had he fallen out with Minshull or Anderson?

'Okay, thanks. Keep your ear to the ground for us, please? Gossip is likely to be rife now she's been arrested, so something may come up.'

'Sarge.'

Bennett caught an extended look between Minshull and Wheeler before Minshull returned his attention to the rest of the team. What on earth was that about?

'Actually, can I have everyone's attention for a minute?'

Anderson stopped pacing. Evans and Ellis looked on. Even Wheeler laid his pen down and temporarily abandoned the frantic notes he'd been taking since his return.

'Cheers. The situation as it currently stands is that we now have three active investigations running concurrently. The St Columba Street attack, which we're still monitoring even though the Uniform team are doing the legwork; the reopened Cassandra Norton case and, as of now, we are treating

Karl Cuskie's death as murder. We need to know anyone and everyone who might have wished him harm. I realise that's likely to be an extensive list... But the Cassandra Norton murder case is also a priority. We need to be going through those damn boxes and revisiting as many of the original statements as possible. It's possible Karl Cuskie's murder might unlock new evidence from the people who spoke to police before...'

'Sarge.' Bennett raised her hand. Since the discovery of Cuskie's body this morning and the arrest of DCI Taylor, one question had been itching at her.

'Yes, Kate?'

'Could the two murders be related?'

Silence met her question. When no reply came, the urge to elaborate overwhelmed her reasons to wait.

'I mean, Cuskie was a key witness in the Cassandra Norton murder. He'd just broken up with Shona Pickton, who was then arrested for the murder. And DCI Taylor was SIO on that original case, the driving force behind Pickton being sent down for it. Now Pickton's out and exonerated, the case is reopened and Karl Cuskie, who'd just agreed to come and see us, winds up dead?'

Minshull laid down his notebook. 'You think someone silenced Cuskie because he knew who murdered Cassandra Norton?'

Bennett shrugged, the intense scrutiny of her colleagues heavy around her. 'I just think the timing is interesting.'

Minshull and Anderson exchanged glances. 'Guv?'

'It's possible,' Anderson confirmed, looking to Tsang and Guthrie for their response. When they agreed, Anderson walked over to the whiteboard, writing DCI Taylor's name next to Karl Cuskie's. Then he drew a red dotted line connecting them with a question mark over it.

'Could Shona Pickton have killed Karl Cuskie?' Ellis piped up beside Bennett.

Anderson tapped his chin with the lid of the whiteboard pen. 'Why?'

'Because he refused her an alibi.' Ellis spread his hands wide. 'If I'd done nine years in jail because someone wouldn't tell the truth, I'd want revenge, too.'

'Would you want it enough to kill them?' Minshull asked.

'Well, no… But…'

'I don't buy it.'

Minshull's attention swung to the desk next to Wheeler's. 'Les?'

'She'd only just got her life back, hadn't she?' Evans offered. 'And she'd know we'd come looking for her first. Why give coppers the satisfaction of arresting her again when she'd worked so hard to overturn their last one?'

'Les is right,' Wheeler agreed.

'Bloody hell, Dave, it's a miracle. I'm buying a lottery ticket tonight,' Evans exclaimed with a smirk.

'Okay, don't get carried away.' Wheeler rolled his eyes. 'On *this* you're right. The rest is still up for debate.'

'A-a-and he's back in the room.'

Ignoring the banter, Minshull looked over at Wheeler. 'Explain, Dave?'

'Poor woman got sent down for a murder she didn't commit. Does nothing for her case if the first thing she does when she gets out of prison is bump someone off for real, does it? She's always protested her innocence, all these years. And she'll be terrified of us because she'll assume we'll be out for any opportunity to send her back inside again. That's why she refused to be part of the re-investigation, Sarge. You know that.'

Minshull stood and joined Anderson at the whiteboard. 'So, we're looking for someone else who wanted Cuskie out of the way. Who?'

'Cassandra Norton's killer,' Ellis suggested.

'Someone Cuskie threw under a bus,' Evans said. 'Which, knowing the old bastard, might be a bloody long list.'

'Someone he was working for,' Bennett offered. 'If he'd upset them…?'

'Good points, all,' Minshull replied.

'The DCI.' When Bennett stared at Ellis, he was unapologetic. 'She went to see him, late last night, stayed twenty minutes and fled, leaving his front door open and Cuskie dead.'

'Unless she found him dead,' Wheeler countered.

'And what? Sat with his body for twenty minutes, then got spooked and ran away?'

Bennett had to concede that it didn't make sense. 'We saw the front door open to let the DCI in. If that wasn't Cuskie, who was it?'

'Someone already in his house.'

'How? We've studied the doorbell cam footage for twelve hours before the DCI showed up. Nobody went in the house apart from Taylor.'

'Not from the front.' Wheeler was on the edge of his seat, a new theory bypassing his heavy mood. 'Along that row of terraces, there's a couple of narrow passageways between the houses, running down to King Street behind. Snickets, really, barely wide enough for one person. But if there's one anywhere near Cuskie's house, someone could feasibly approach from King Street and access Cuskie's house across the gardens.'

Suddenly animated, Anderson clicked his fingers at the team. 'Right, someone pull up Google Earth. See if there's one of the passageways anywhere near 105 Maidstone Road.'

Bennett, like her colleagues, began the search. Surprisingly, Evans beat them all to the answer.

'There's one beside Cuskie's neighbour's house at 107,' he called out. 'Might even be a connected alleyway running between the gardens that back onto each other from Maidstone Road on one side and King Street on the other – we'd have to go there to find out, though. Inconclusive from the aerial image.'

'We should send you off on sick leave more often, Les,' Anderson grinned. 'Never known you so keen.'

Evans shrugged off the comment with his trademark dryness. 'You try being stuck in a hospital bed for weeks on end with only an annoying Scottish DI visiting you. It's enough to make anyone want to work.'

'Not just a DI, I heard,' Ellis quipped. 'How is the lovely Maisie?'

Evans reddened. 'She's fine.'

'Okay, we need to see if our trusty doorbell cam salesperson had as much luck in King Street,' Minshull said, dragging the briefing back to some semblance of its intended purpose. 'I'll see if Tim Brinton can send a couple of officers down there to do door-to-doors. We can ask them to check these potential pathways while they're there. Guv?'

Anderson nodded. 'Great. Okay, Kate and Drew, can you chase up DCI Taylor's phone, PC and laptop with Forensics and Tech, please? Dave and Les, carry on with the Cassandra Norton files, if you would.'

A thought struck Bennett. 'What about the gun? Do we even know if DCI Taylor has possession of one?'

'Excellent point, Kate.' Minshull looked at Anderson. 'Do we need to get a warrant to search DCI Taylor's home?'

'I think we should try. I'll call the Super. Then you and I need to plan the next round with our esteemed superior. We'll need to go back in there with a strong game plan.'

'I agree.' Minshull turned to the team. 'Thanks everyone. Let's keep going.'

Bennett watched the DS and DI go into Anderson's office. As soon as the door closed, she turned to Ellis.

'Do you think she did it?'

'I don't know. But...' Ellis abandoned his notes, ducking down behind his screen to whisper back, '...I think her even being at his house shows she knew him better than *just an acquaintance*. And the strip she tore off Minsh yesterday for going to see Cuskie? Totally off-the-chart odd. It isn't like other officers haven't talked to him before. Why go after the Sarge like that, unless she was against Cuskie being brought back to give his statement?'

'Exactly.' Bennett lowered her head, too, until she was inches away from Ellis' face. 'Was she more involved with him than she wanted anyone to know?'

'Or does she know who else he's working for?'

'Like who?'

'I've heard people talking around the building. Cuskie ran errands for some pretty big names in the local crime fraternity.'

Bennett leaned closer. 'Who?'

'I don't know. But I'm going to find out. Fancy heading to the canteen for lunch?'

'No thanks,' Bennett retorted, visions of apologetic salad and trays of claggy hot meals drying to a crisp under heat lamps turning her stomach. 'You might be a dustbin on legs when it comes to food, but I value my guts.'

'Not for actual food,' Ellis retorted. 'For *food for thought…*' His deliberate wink made the penny finally drop.

'Oh. Okay,' Bennett replied, her heartbeat racing with the idea. 'If we can get away, let's do it.'

THIRTY-THREE

MINSHULL

It was going to be a late one.

Without prompt or request, the team had volunteered to stay beyond the end of their shift, each detective's head bowed as they worked. Boxes of evidence crowded each desk, the cardboard towers in the meeting room down the corridor showing no real signs of shrinking, despite the two uniformed officers now stationed there – PC Carla Delacott and PC Liam Hall – working methodically through the files.

Minshull was grateful for all of them, the extent of the double workload only just hitting home. Karl Cuskie's murder had complicated matters beyond all expectation, with half the team now following leads connected to him. Already several police officers had come forward within the building, their statements painting a picture of police association with the informer that extended much further than Minshull had anticipated.

It was depressing, to say the least.

More concerning still were the insinuations that Cuskie had enjoyed an unusual level of favour when it came to his own criminal misdemeanours. Four instances identified so far, over a period spanning twelve years, where charges were dropped – or not made at all – where other offenders would have faced custodial sentences.

For three of those instances, DCI Taylor had presided over charging decisions.

Two of those hadn't even made it as far as Crown Prosecution Service consideration.

If Cuskie had been a first-time offender, a reversal of charge might have been expected. But four?

What hold did Cuskie have over Sue Taylor? Was he in possession of information that might implicate her or damage her career? Or was it something else entirely?

Watching his team working, Minshull tried in vain to make the stubborn threads of the murder case link up.

Why had Taylor insisted she hardly knew Cuskie?

Why wait for CCTV evidence before she admitted their acquaintance?

And if she were innocent of his murder, being the last person recorded as visiting his home, why hadn't she said so?

She had offered no explanation of why she had visited at such a late hour. Or what had happened in the intervening twenty minutes between her arrival and sudden, dramatic exit?

Resorting to a no-comment dialogue when she had already proved her testimony unreliable was a terrible move. She of all people should know that. And, as the evidence began to stack up of her other, earlier misdemeanours regarding Cuskie, what could she hope to gain by refusing to explain their association?

She was furious, of course. For this, Minshull empathised. Being escorted to custody, in full view of your colleagues, was humiliating. Had he been in her position, he would have been incandescent. But was displaying her anger at the manner of her arrest worth more than the threat of a potential murder charge?

He and Anderson were due to interview her again before the end of the evening, with the twenty-four hours they could hold her in custody fast dwindling. The pressure to find admissible evidence to take back to Interview Room 3 was intense and Minshull sensed it, heavy on his shoulders, as he worked to build the strongest case.

He'd wanted to call Cora, but time wouldn't allow. He glanced at his phone on the desk beside his keyboard, where her reply to his hastily sent apologetic text now resided.

I'm fine. Don't worry about me. Hope you find
what you need. Cx

What you need. What they needed was solid, irrefutable evidence. One glance at the unanswered questions in his notes made his heart sink. So many variables, so many theories they couldn't yet prove. At least Cora had faith that he'd find it. He wished he shared her belief in him.

The problem was, all they currently had to add to the existing doorbell camera video evidence were five sworn statements about Cuskie's associates that were tantamount to workplace rumour. A prosecution would tear them to shreds on sight.

The ringing of his desk phone yanked Minshull back from his thoughts. He snatched up the receiver on the second ring.

'DS Minshull.'

'Sarge, it's Lydia Cawley in Tech. There's something you should see.'

–

Five minutes later, Minshull knocked on the scuffed door of the Tech team, a little out of breath from his sprint down to the first floor. When the current investigations were concluded, he really had to get back to his daily running schedule. He'd neglected it lately, the extra workload before DC Evans' return sapping his resolve for a run at the end of his workdays. Cora could already outrun him in the summer when his fitness was up to scratch. If he risked a run with her now, she'd leave him for dust.

A kick of guilt accompanied the thought. He'd asked her to assist him with the nine-year-old Cassandra Norton evidence items days ago, but events since had pushed it back down the list of priorities. When the body was removed from Cuskie's address and Forensics were finished with their investigations, he could maybe ask Cora to inspect the house seeking audible clues. But it would have to wait until they had questioned Taylor. Besides, in the aftermath of the attacks on the St Columba Street site and Cora's workplace, she had enough on her plate.

It felt like distance they didn't need. Necessary, but frustrating.

Pushing the thought away, he smiled as Sergeant Lydia Cawley greeted him at the door.

'Hey, Lyd.'

'Minsh. Come in.'

She ushered him towards a desk near the window. Rain pelted the glass as Minshull took a seat beside the Tech officer, the black winter night beyond making him glad for once to be in the warmth and light of Police HQ.

'What have you found for me?'

'A couple of things. Firstly, this.' She opened a spreadsheet on her monitor, zooming in so that the entries could be better seen. 'This is the call log from DCI Taylor's mobile for the past three weeks. The number in red is Karl Cuskie's mobile number. Some of these are text messages, some calls, some messenger chats, all linked between their two phones.'

Cawley scrolled down the spreadsheet, tapping the screen at every instance of the red phone number. The amount was staggering – more than Minshull had anticipated.

'It's every day,' he said, his eyes tracking the long procession up the screen.

'Sometimes several messages a day,' Cawley agreed. 'Mostly texts and messenger chats. But I'm going to scroll to the entries for yesterday. A couple of texts sent first thing, then a call lasting ten minutes around lunchtime. Two texts received from Cuskie's phone mid-afternoon that appear not to have been replied to. And then this...'

Minshull leaned closer, the date stamp on the entry Cawley indicated with her pen reading 11:23 p.m. A call, lasting seven minutes, thirty-five seconds. Half an hour before Taylor was captured on doorbell cameras arriving at Cuskie's house and going inside.

'She called him before she went there.'

'Exactly.'

'Why so many calls? And not just yesterday but every day for weeks?'

'Must have been a close friendship.' Cawley gave a chuckle. 'I'm always on the phone with my partner but even I don't call her that many times.'

'Partner…' The word grabbed Minshull by the collar. 'Hang on, you've seen records like this many times, Lyd. Would you say that pattern of communication is consistent with two people in some kind of relationship?'

Cawley grimaced. 'Funny you should mention that.'

She opened another window on her screen. As she did so, Minshull saw her cast a careful glance at her colleague, Sergeant Adam Orson, busy at work at his computer on the desk facing hers.

'DCI Taylor hadn't protected any of her messages and her passcode was 1234.' She offered a grim smile. 'That means we were able to access significant portions of text and messenger conversations. It's clear she's deleted earlier ones, but the conversations from the last twenty-four hours were all intact.'

Hardly believing what he was seeing, Minshull scanned the lines of alternating chat between Taylor and Cuskie.

Plod came sniffing around. Earlier.

Where?

Green Dragon.

But you said nothing?

– You said NOTHING?

I might have talked to him.

What the hell?

What could I have done? The bloke jumped me.
Bought me a drink.

You could have said no.

I couldn't help it.

You could have NOT BEEN THERE...

A *plod*. The Green Dragon. Cuskie was telling Taylor about their meeting. The meeting she'd confronted Minshull about the next day. He hadn't understood how Taylor had found out about it: now it was obvious.

It hadn't been passed on by a retired copper, as Anderson had suggested. Or supplied as a tip-off from the landlady behind the bar.

It had come straight from Cuskie himself.

And DCI Taylor had been furious about it.

Had she been scared of their association being uncovered? Was she protecting her own back?

'There's more,' Cawley said, gravely, opening another message log. 'This is from 10:05 p.m. last night.'

The night Taylor visited Cuskie.

The night Cuskie lost his life to a single bullet.

Minshull started to read – and his blood instantly froze.

> I need to see you.

> It's too risky.

> I miss you, babe.

> You said you'd lay low.

> I did. And I am. But nobody's watching us, are they?

> I can't.

> But you want to. Admit it.

> That's not fair. You know I do. If anyone sees us…

> Who's going to see? Come over tonight. You
> don't have to stay.

'What the—?' Minshull hissed, under his breath.

Cawley raised her eyebrows in solidarity.

'How much more of this is there?'

'Plenty. They weren't just friends, Minsh. Far from it. And, given the language between them, my guess is they've been involved for a long time.'

Minshull observed the Tech officer. 'Months?'

Keeping an eye on her colleague, Cawley replied, 'Try years.'

'Years.' Minshull's heart began to thud against his ribcage as a sudden thought blazed into his mind. '*Nine* years?'

Cawley didn't reply. But her tight-lipped smile spoke volumes.

THIRTY-FOUR

ANDERSON

The evidence was damning. The messages available on Taylor's phone revealed a near constant stream of communication between the DCI and the police informer. Shona Pickton's acquittal, Cuskie's concerns that someone may be watching him, Taylor's insistence that he lay low until the heat passed, coupled with frequent assurances that she wanted to be with him – were all discussed in startling detail. Some of Cuskie's pleading with the DCI to meet him strayed into sexting, Taylor sometimes rebuffing his attempts but more often than not encouraged to reply in kind.

Late-night messages, secret exchanges following key meetings while on duty, graphic references made the morning after their clandestine assignations.

Taylor wasn't just acquainted with Karl Cuskie. Or a close friend.

She was his lover.

Anderson felt sick to his stomach that he hadn't seen it, that such blatant, sustained misconduct could have continued, unchecked, for so long.

He sat back in his chair, staring at Minshull who was seated opposite. By the look of his colleague's pale features and haunted expression he could tell his feelings were mirrored.

'So where does this put us?' he asked, at a loss to fathom it for himself.

'I have no idea.'

'Are we suggesting she killed him in a fit of passion? Or because she thought he might reveal their affair?'

'Search me, Guv. But the way they talk about Shona Pickton in those messages makes me wonder...' Minshull baulked, as if sickened by what might follow.

'Go on.'

'Every account we've had so far has suggested that Sue rushed ahead to charge Shona with murder. You've said it yourself, Guv: she was hell-bent on that outcome to the exclusion of all else.'

'She was. What are you saying?'

Minshull paused, as if inspecting his words before he expressed them. 'Cuskie broke up with Shona Pickton on the night of Cassandra Norton's murder. What if DCI Taylor saw an opportunity to remove a love rival?'

'Excuse me?' Anderson couldn't believe what he was hearing. 'Are you suggesting DCI Taylor was responsible for Cassandra Norton's murder?'

'No – but when she saw the witness statement placing Shona near the scene and the coincidence between what Pickton had been wearing and what the taxi driver said the other person at the murder scene was wearing, she saw a way to kill two birds with one stone. A conviction for the murder, and Cuskie's ex-girlfriend permanently out of the picture.'

It was preposterous to consider – but the messages between Cuskie and the DCI suggested otherwise. Cuskie would presumably have been seeing Taylor while he was in his relationship with Shona Pickton – that must have stuck in Taylor's gullet. What better way of ensuring Taylor had him to herself than twenty-two years of separation?

'I can't believe it, Rob.'

'Me either, Guv. But it might explain why the other, contradictory statement was misfiled.'

'Because it challenged the rest of the evidence placing Pickton at the scene?'

Minshull nodded. 'You have to admit, it's convenient.'

Convenient was a strange word for *criminal*, but Anderson couldn't fault the choice. He checked his watch – 7:15 p.m. If they were to present this to the DCI before the end of the day, they needed to act now.

'We should inform the team,' he decided, reasoning that their input would help determine the best course of action. There was no point keeping this from them. Every one of his officers had gone above and beyond to search for evidence for both the reopened case and Karl Cuskie's murder investigation. With the very real possibility of a link between the two cases now evident, they deserved to be made aware.

It was late and they should all have left hours ago. But this was explosive. And it had the potential to blow both investigations apart.

'We should call the Super, too,' Minshull said. 'We need to know how best to proceed.'

'Agreed. It's still not enough to charge Taylor with Cuskie's murder, but it's definitely misconduct regarding the rest.'

'Do we disclose this to her solicitor, Guv?'

At this late hour – and with some hours of custody remaining tomorrow – Anderson was tempted to leave Taylor sweating over the discovery overnight. But his gut told him this might play into Taylor's hands. She must have anticipated the truth coming out, although not in such circumstances. Anderson wouldn't give her the satisfaction of prior warning to prepare a defence.

'We'll be led by the Super on that, but I think for now we hang fire. Let's see what the team think.'

They rose together, walking straight into the main CID office, Anderson braced for the bombshell he was about to drop.

As Minshull gathered the detectives together, Anderson placed a call to Superintendent Martlesham, frustrated when it went to voicemail. His superior's input would have been far preferable, but he couldn't wait for the Super's availability to proceed. Leaving a voicemail requesting Martlesham phone back at his earliest opportunity, Anderson ended the call, looking over as the CID team gathered in the centre of the office.

'Okay, everyone, I'll keep this as brief as I can. Tech gained access to DCI Taylor's phone and the messages they found were... revealing.'

He visibly winced at his choice of word. Anderson winced with him.

Confused, the team looked on.

'There's no easy way to say this, so here it is: the messages found on DCI Taylor's phone suggest that she was in a physical and emotional relationship with Karl Cuskie. That they were involved for a considerable amount of time, possibly as far back as the Cassandra Norton murder investigation.'

Shock shuddered its way around the office. Tsang and Guthrie, seated at their desks, looked on with grim acceptance.

'Tech can retrieve more messages, but from those found on the device already we know several things for certain. One, that they discussed the outcome of Shona Pickton's acquittal in detail; two, that Taylor told Cuskie to lay low; three, that Cuskie informed Taylor of my meeting with him in The Green Dragon; and four, that Taylor accepted Cuskie's invitation to visit him at home, thirty minutes before the footage we have of her arriving in Maidstone Road.'

Minshull paused while the detectives absorbed the news.

'One detail is crucial: that in Cuskie's message to DCI Taylor he made no mention of agreeing to come here to revisit his statement. *I* told her that, when she reprimanded me for meeting him.' He swallowed hard and appeared to stall for a moment, as if a thunderbolt had struck him. 'I can't rule out the possibility that my disclosure of that information may have provided DCI Taylor with the motive to murder Karl Cuskie.'

'No Sarge,' Ellis rushed, joined quickly by his colleagues.

'You couldn't have known.'

'Don't think like that.'

'It isn't your fault, Sarge.'

'I agree,' Anderson added, seeing the effect Minshull's sudden realisation had on the DS. 'You followed protocol. She didn't.'

'Nevertheless,' Minshull continued, 'it's a possibility. So, we follow it up, as we follow up every lead that comes from this new information.'

'Can we charge on the strength of the messages, Sarge?' Wheeler asked.

'Not for murder. Or manslaughter. Misconduct is a different story, as you can imagine, but our priority remains to find the person responsible for Karl Cuskie's death.'

Ellis raised his hand, as he always did. 'Are you presenting this information to the DCI tonight, Sarge?'

Minshull observed the team wearily. 'My gut instinct is to hold fire until the morning. The DCI will remain in the cells overnight and she's going to know we'll be searching her phone and laptop. I reckon that's enough to let her stew about it tonight. It will play to our advantage better than disclosing now.'

'You mean she suspects we'll know but she'll have no proof?' Bennett asked.

'Exactly. Knowing what she's up against means she can prepare before we resume interviews tomorrow. But *not* knowing means there'll be too many possibilities to prepare a case for. She thinks she's outwitted us – but this will unsettle her. That's what we want.'

'I think that's wise,' Anderson agreed. 'In the meantime, we need to be ready. Look for any potential links between Cuskie's death and Cassandra Norton's murder. Is there someone else who might have wanted to silence Cuskie in light of the reopening of the investigation? Or did DCI Taylor fear he was going to reveal their affair and her role in the conviction of Shona Pickton? Do they all have someone else in common that we haven't identified yet?'

'I know it's a needle in a haystack,' Minshull apologised. 'More so, in the light of DCI Taylor's involvement. But tomorrow evening we have to charge or release. We need an advantage, everyone. Find it for us.'

Evans gave a cough. 'Are you meeting with her again tonight?'

Anderson glanced at Minshull, then at DIs Tang and Guthrie. Their unspoken support cemented his decision. 'No. We'll inform her legal representative that we'll recommence interviews at nine a.m. tomorrow. Let DCI Taylor stew in the cells over what we might or might not know.'

Let her worry, he added in his thoughts. About time Sue Taylor found herself on the back foot.

But as the team returned to their searches, Anderson's heart was a rock. What they'd discovered was abhorrent, but it gave them very little headway. They were missing something, he was certain of it.

His eyes rested on the towering stacks of evidence boxes. The answers lay in there. They had to. But would they find them before Sue Taylor was released?

THIRTY-FIVE

CORA

Cora didn't have to wait long for the invitation to arrive.

When she awoke next morning, a little before seven a.m., her phone screen displayed a message from Joss Lovell:

> Hi Cora
> Meeting set for 10 a.m. today. Tris said it's OK.
> I'll pick you up from the office at 9:40 a.m.
> Thanks, Joss.

Nerves played in her stomach as she got ready for the day. What had Joss told his friend about her? What assumptions might have been made? Lovell's understanding of Cora's ability was sketchy at best, respected but not altogether clear. Had he promised his friend assistance Cora would be unable to give?

There was the thought of the journey to meet Joss' friend, too. He hadn't said where they'd meet. It was unlikely to be at the St Columba Street site – beyond that, Cora knew little of Joss Lovell's life, or the places he went when not working. How would she feel, alone with him in his car, driving to who-knew-where?

Cora made coffee in her kitchen and wandered over to the window overlooking Undercliff Road East with its rows of beach huts and the beach beyond. The sea was mercurial silver this morning, stretching out beneath a gunmetal sky. A shiver of cold air snuck through the windows of the 1920s red-brick building, despite the best efforts of the modern secondary glazing installed when it was converted from the former Bartlet Hospital into apartments, years ago. Cora adored the quirkiness of her home, but winters weren't the most comfortable in its draughty corners.

She followed the diagonal progress of raindrops across the glass, her gaze slowly lifting to the sky beyond them. Gulls hung ominously on air currents rising up the hill from the promenade, their seeming inability to move striking a chord within Cora.

Stuck.

That was how she felt. Anchored to some unseen force, unable to find a route forward.

Ahead of her lay two car journeys she'd rather make herself. She missed her car this morning more than any day since its removal from the road. If she could drive herself, instead of sharing cars with Tris and Joss, her mind might have found precious time to properly process where she found herself.

'A rock on your left and a hard place on your right, that's where you are.' It had been her father's favourite saying, his own unique spin on the well-worn phrase. And considering the many years Bill Lael fought battles as a local councillor, he was better placed than most to understand the reality of it. How different he was in his approach to that of the self-serving county councillors currently trying to close the project she loved! Bill Lael would never have stood in the way of something that helped people. But he'd understand exactly where his daughter found herself this morning.

She missed him most days, but today her loss was acute.

He would love that she'd offered to help Joss Lovell's friend in need. Not that it made the prospect of their meeting any easier to consider.

And then there was the issue of Minshull.

Until he got in touch to formally invite her to take part in the investigation, Cora was stuck. She couldn't plan for it, or arrange her work so that an eleventh-hour call from South Suffolk CID wouldn't cause major disruption to Tris and the team. There was also the issue of her lack of transport – yet another element beyond her control. All her life she had relied upon herself, fiercely proud of her own independence. That so much currently rested on the assistance of others challenged her comfort at every turn.

Could Minshull have changed his mind regarding her involvement?

The regular news bulletins suggested the police had their heads down, revisiting every piece of evidence that had been collected for the Cassandra Norton investigation. And now that a new murder had been added to their slate, the pressure to deal with it would be intense. Perhaps Minshull's initial plan to revisit the physical items of evidence had been obliterated by the avalanche of work that had descended upon the team.

But until she heard from him, how could she know?

When she emerged in the park beside her apartment building, Tris was waiting by his car, two large reusable coffee mugs in hand, his breath dancing skywards in the chilled morning air.

'Thought you'd need this,' he called. 'For the day ahead.'

'Thanks.'

'Pleasure,' he replied, as Cora reached him. 'You still okay to go with Joss?'

'Of course.'

'Because if you've changed your mind…'

'I haven't.'

'Or I could go with you, if being on your own with Joss feels inappropriate.' He handed her a cup. 'What I mean is…'

Accepting the coffee, Cora smiled. 'Stop worrying, I'll be fine. Now can we get in the car, please, before we both freeze?'

On the drive into Ipswich, Tris launched into a long, detailed description of an architecture programme he'd seen on television last night. Cora didn't break his flow, content to let him speak. Communication settled him in the way that silence did not. If there was a pause in conversation, Tris would fill it. He relaxed when he was able to vocalise the many thoughts in his mind, where Cora relaxed in the space between words.

Tris talked and Cora listened, both happy to let it be so. The chatter calmed her nerves as much as it appeared to settle his worries.

When they arrived, workmen were already tackling yesterday's damage to the Educational Psychology Department's building – another hopeful sign. The building foreman assured them both that the job was relatively simple, the repairs likely to be complete before the end of the working day.

'Makes you wonder what the point of all the fuss was, eh?' he joked, eliciting determined smiles from the carpenter and the glazier beside him. 'I mean, in a couple of hours it'll be like those bastards never came yesterday. They needn't have bothered.'

Cora appreciated the sentiment, but the implied threat from the attack still remained.

–

Joss Lovell arrived early at 9:35 a.m., chatting to Tris while Cora finished the report she was writing and gathered her things together. He seemed in good spirits and relaxed in conversation, but Cora saw his smile falter in the pauses between. The urgency of the meeting's arrangement and his clear concern for his friend suggested the challenge that lay ahead – setting Cora's senses on alert once more.

Ten minutes later, they were in his car and driving out of Ipswich.

'Where are we meeting your friend?' Cora asked.

'My mate has a place he's said we can use.'

'Where?'

'Not far.'

'And will your friend be there already?'

He nodded. 'I dropped her there before coming to fetch you.'

'Joss, what's this about?'

'You'll find out when we get there.'

'If you give me an idea now, I can make sure I'm ready.'

He cast the briefest glance in her direction before staring back at the road ahead. 'You're ready.'

'That doesn't help me...'

'I know. You just have to trust me on this. She'll explain it best herself.'

The journey took them out into the countryside, dark green under a milk white sky. The further they travelled, the fewer houses and buildings they passed, until they were surrounded by fields and hedgerows, punctuated only by stark lines of wind-bent trees.

Where was the meeting place? Would they be convening in a field?

A remote location. An uncertain destination. Cora forced her eyes on the landscape ahead, willing her pulse to slow.

Finally, a single, dark grey building appeared at the end of a narrow lane edged with skeletal hawthorn bush sentries. Incongruous to its natural surroundings, it appeared to be a steel structure, the kind you would expect to see on an industrial estate rather than in the middle of agricultural land.

At the head of a snaking, rough gravel track, a hand-painted sign on a sheet of chipboard read:

FARMING MUSEUM

'It's a work in progress,' Joss said, as if sensing Cora's confusion. 'My mate Jimmy inherited his dad's collection, and he wants to make it a tourist attraction.'

Cora said nothing, the thought of tourists daring to venture all the way out to this remote location distinctly at odds with its owner's ambition.

They parked next to the building and left the car. Cora followed Joss over the uneven stones towards a roughly painted door, its bright green paint already streaked and faded by the elements. It protested as it opened, a *clack-clack* sound emitting from rusted hinges.

The moment Cora stepped inside, she was aware of sound. Not of discernible voices, but of the echoes left in their wake. A hollow noise, shapeless and without words.

It came from the rows of old machinery and farming implements, rusting hulks of metal arranged in neat lines that filled the entire space. Ploughs, tools, scythes and pitchforks, old tractor attachments and hoppers, farm vehicles and trailers were displayed alongside trestle tables filled with a plethora of smaller metal objects – farming ephemera of generations now past.

The soundscape of the space didn't assault her mind like she'd experienced in second-hand bookshops, for example, where every volume carried the voice of the last person to hold it, or museums where sometimes she'd catch the muted, distant whispers of curators beyond the exhibition case glass. Here, it was the echo of sound layers laid down over years, the audible dents where sound had once resided. It was curious rather than overwhelming – a puzzle inviting her to imagine the shape of what may have once been there.

'You okay?' Joss was watching her closely.

They'd barely crossed the threshold, Cora realised. It must have looked odd to him that she'd stopped so soon after entering the building.

'I'm fine.' She smiled. 'Interesting soundscape in here.'

'Okay.' He blinked as he looked around the space, which to him must have appeared silent. 'Ready?'

'Of course.'

Joss offered a brief smile before he set off between the rows of exhibits towards a small office, situated at the rear of the space. Its single glazed window reflected the collection it served while protecting what was inside from view. With no-one else in sight, it must be where his friend was waiting.

But why the secrecy? Why the remote location?

The moment Cora entered the office, she understood why.

Shona Pickton rose from a faded chair beside a cluttered desk to greet them. She was smaller than she'd appeared on news reports, fragile in real life where in the media she'd been portrayed as strong. Judging by the sight of her now, it was hard to imagine how anyone had considered her capable of sufficient strength to murder Cassandra Norton.

She was dressed entirely in black, further diminishing her appearance; her hair pulled back into a tight ponytail and her eyes framed by a pair of dark-rimmed glasses. When she offered her hand to Cora, her skin was startlingly cold.

'This is Dr Cora Lael,' Joss said. 'Cora, this is Shona.'

'Hello, Shona.'

'Good to meet you, Cora. Joss says you can help me.'

'I hope I can,' Cora replied, uncertain she could. What advice could she offer a woman wrongly imprisoned for nine years?

Joss led them over to a motley collection of seats positioned at one side of the office – a frayed fabric covered footstool, a faded wicker armchair and an old green-and-white striped deckchair. They settled themselves as best they could, but the seating arrangement had them all at different heights. Like the odd location, the unexpected company and the potentially impossible request, it fit the strangeness of the meeting.

Cora immediately found herself in a quandary. Neither Joss nor Shona knew of her work with South Suffolk Police. And while Minshull had yet to officially bring her into the reopened investigation of the murder Shona had wrongfully been convicted of, he had already intimated the possibility of her involvement.

Was it a conflict of interest? If Shona offered details of the original case that might assist Minshull and the CID team now, was Cora duty-bound to share them? Or was that beyond her remit – a remit that currently didn't officially exist in the new investigation?

What should Cora do?

It was too late to refuse to be here. And Minshull's radio silence on the matter of her involvement meant she wasn't spoken for — yet.

And then there were the voices.

From the moment their hands touched, Cora had sensed a tide of whispers around Shona Pickton. Like the strange sound in the main body of the farming museum, they were indistinct, but they carried with them a strong sense of threat — a curling, snaking, shifting wave of fear that registered as a physical sensation at the centre of Cora's throat.

It wasn't the first time a physical manifestation had accompanied the emotion Cora heard in object voices. In fact, the more she used her ability and pushed into its possibilities, the more frequently she experienced physical signs. It was as if the soundscape of the emotional echoes was underscored not only by audible markers but also by sensory and physical indications.

The whispers Cora heard and felt now were all the more acute for the lack of distinct shape — waves, instead of the individual slaps of sound she would more commonly encounter.

Shona was shrouded in them, slowly being crushed by their indiscernible insistence. She sat with her shoulders hunched, her neck contracted into her body, as if shrinking back from the weight of the whispers, her pale features tensed as if in pain.

Plenty had been written about this woman. Plenty assumed and surmised. But nobody had seen or heard what Cora did now.

Was that her remit here? To address the bars of sound that still held Shona Pickton captive? None of what she heard, sensed or felt around this woman could add to the police reinvestigation. None of it would be admissible as evidence. And even considering how far Minshull's understanding of her ability had come over the years, Cora wasn't certain he would ever be able to process what the whispers around Shona meant.

'How can I help?' she asked, her decision made.

'People want me back in prison,' Shona replied, the whispers rising in reply around her. 'They wanted me there in the first place and they're determined to send me back.'

Stunned, Cora struggled to find a reply. What could her ability do to change any of that for Shona? 'Who?' she asked, at last.

'They killed Cassandra. And now they've killed Karl...' Shona's voice broke, the insidious whispers engulfing her words.

'You don't know that,' Joss soothed, but Shona wasn't listening.

'I thought I'd be safe when I got out. But they were waiting, weren't they? And now they've got Karl.'

'I don't know how I can help,' Cora replied, the constriction at the base of her throat caused by the swirling tide of whispered sound making it difficult to breathe.

'I've had letters,' Shona said. 'Somehow, they've found me. I had them over the years in prison. I thought they'd stop when I was released, but at the first place I was meant to be housed they were waiting for me on the doormat. So Alan – my solicitor – arranged for me to go somewhere else. But a letter turned up there, two days ago.' She glanced at Joss, who reached over to rest his hand on her bowed shoulders. 'Joss says you have the Sight. That you know when someone's touched something.'

'I can sense emotional echoes from objects,' Cora explained. 'Like fingerprints of sound.'

The shroud of whispers increased as Shona pulled a plastic zip-lock sandwich bag from a rucksack at her feet. 'I want to know what you can tell me about the person who sent me these.'

Cora accepted the bag. Six letters lay inside, the size and colour of the envelopes identical.

'Have all these been delivered to your new home?'

Shona nodded. 'First one was two days ago, at lunchtime. Another arrived at nine p.m. There was another in my letterbox when I woke at six a.m., then the same pattern yesterday. Morning. Early afternoon. Late night. They say the same thing, in what looks like the same writing: *I'M WATCHING YOU. SAY NOTHING. SPEAK AND SOMEONE DIES.*' She shuddered, the whispers edging tighter around her. 'They're not copies: each one has been handwritten. Somebody is writing them, over and over. And they're watching me. And now Karl is…' Her words cracked and deserted her.

'You think the person who killed Cassandra is the same person who killed Karl Cuskie?' Cora asked, to settle the facts before she set to work.

Shona nodded through tears.

'Why would that link to you?'

'Karl was with her, until the night of the murder,' Joss explained, his deep voice startlingly gentle in the presence of his friend. 'He could have saved Shona from prison if he'd given her an alibi. But he didn't.'

'I always said if I got out, I'd want to talk to him,' Shona sniffed, dabbing at her eyes with the cuffs of her black jumper. 'I couldn't believe he'd sell me out like that. Not unless someone else made him do it.'

'The person who killed Cassandra?'

'I think he was pressured into it, like he was pressured into breaking up with me. I didn't believe his reasons that night any more than I believed he hated me, like he said he did. Karl wasn't a bitter man. He wasn't unkind. He liked to play Jack the Lad, run around with the big boys, but he was always sweet to me. The day I stood in that courtroom, I looked up and saw him in the gallery. He looked like a shell. He couldn't stop looking at me and I swear he was crying when the judge sent me down.'

She picked at her sleeve with thin, anxious fingers. 'We were screwed up in so many ways, both of us, but I don't think he wanted to send me to jail. I don't think he believed I killed her.'

'Did you tell the police this?' Cora realised her mistake the moment she asked her question. 'I'm sorry. I didn't mean—'

Shona waved her apology away. 'It's a fair question. Truth is, I never got the chance. That Taylor woman didn't listen to a word I said. She'd made up her mind before I ever gave my side of the story.'

Taylor. DCI Sue Taylor, nemesis of Joel Anderson and, reading between the lines, the unnamed 'superior officer' who had initially tried to block Cora's appointment as a police expert consultant. She'd never encountered the DCI personally, but from the reaction of Anderson, Minshull and the CID team whenever her name was mentioned, it was clear she wasn't liked.

Cora wished she could share this with Minshull. But what could it add to the reopened investigation, other than underlining the accusation that DCI Taylor and her team had made a grave error in pinning the murder on Shona? That much they knew already – and it did nothing to help them identify and apprehend Cassandra Norton's real killer.

'Did you tell anyone that you wanted to see Karl?'

'Plenty.' The whispers twisted further around Shona as she hung her head. 'I was angry at the start. I wanted answers and I wasn't subtle about it. And word travels inside. You can't keep anything hidden for long – and by the time you realise you should've kept your mouth shut, it's too late.'

'Do you know who's sending the letters?'

'I think so. Or on whose behalf they're being sent.' She looked at Cora, searching her face for signs of hope. 'Can you hear anything from them?'

Joss was watching, too.

In that moment, Cora wished someone was with her who already knew her ability. Tris – or Minshull. She couldn't shake the feeling that the detective should be here, that she shouldn't be looking at the letters, or even talking with Shona, without him present.

But the desperate trust Shona was displaying by sharing the letters with her was impossible to ignore. A woman wronged by so many people – and still being pilloried by large sections of national media – Shona had so much more to lose by being at this meeting than she had to gain. If Cora couldn't help her, who else did she have to turn to? And with Karl Cuskie gone, who else could help?

Cora steadied herself, took a breath and slowly pulled the zip-lock open.

The moment she did, a clear, deep whisper burst out of the plastic. Words filled with threat and urgency; spitting utter disdain and hate:

STAY QUIET!

SAY NOTHING, BITCH!

It was impossible to miss these words. Or the sight of Joss and Shona recoiling as Cora reacted to the emotional echoes attached to the letters. Sharing the experience with two relative strangers was uncomfortable – recent years of working with Minshull and the CID detectives, and Tris in the Ed Psych Department, meant she had forgotten how raw it could feel. It summoned up dark shadows from her formative years, when every person in her life witnessed the effect of her ability, whether she wanted them to see it or not. She had come so far since she'd started to push the boundaries of her ability, but the ghosts of the past were a stark reminder of how vulnerable she could still be.

'What can you hear, Doc?' Joss asked.

'A whispered voice,' Cora replied, zoning in on the hate-filled sound. 'I can't tell whether it's male or female, but it's lower in tone, so an adult rather than a teenager or a child.'

'What is it saying?'

Cora relayed the two phrases that were repeating from the paper held within the plastic.

'Is it the same from all the letters?'

'I think so.' Cora pulled a glove from her coat pocket and carefully lifted out the letters, one at a time. The sound from the bag decreased with each letter removed, but the phrase didn't change, moving instead to the pile on her lap.

'Same words, same voice.'

Closing her eyes, Cora selected one of the letters and focused on the soundscape around it. As she pushed through each layer of sound, she sent her mind out in search of its peripheries – to the air around the voice, looking for clues to background noises and the shape of the air around the repeated words.

She detected a faint echo around the end of each phrase. Then, something else: a low buzz, constant and a single frequency. A light, perhaps? Some kind of electrical appliance? It reminded her of the sound of her fridge, a single-note burr that was so much a part of the familiar sounds of her home that she only ever heard it when she purposefully tuned into it.

Had these notes been written in a kitchen? A larger room, perhaps with a tiled floor, which would account for the distinct reverberation at the end of each repeated phrase?

She felt out further still, to the very edges of the sound-scape, seeking out any identifiable audible markers. But there were none. Carefully retreating through the layers of sound, she finally emerged back in the small office, opening her eyes.

Shona and Joss were staring at her in stunned silence.

'Okay,' she breathed, forcing away age-old fears about what they might think of her now they'd seen her ability in action, 'I can hear the voice and around it a certain amount of reverber-ation. So I think whoever wrote this did so in the same place with every letter. A kitchen, maybe, or a room with a high ceiling and tiled walls or floors.'

'You can tell all that from those?' Joss asked, his question tinged with scepticism.

'From the peripheral soundscape around them,' Cora replied. 'I can sense a three-dimensional audible landscape around the initial voice. It's something I've developed over the last few years. So if I heard an object voice from an item in this room, like this—' she picked up a stapler from the small table beside the messy desk, '—I would first hear the thoughts of whoever picked it up. Then, if I widened the search, I might hear the ticking of that clock on the wall, our breathing, the air enclosed like it is in this small space, the sound constricted between all the things in here. Maybe even the tapping of your foot, Joss, or the jangle of that keyring on your handbag, Shona.'

'Bloody hell,' Shona breathed, shaking her head. 'That's a skill.'

'Not exactly the kind of skill that impresses at parties,' Cora quipped drily, relieved when she saw the joke land with Shona.

'I can imagine.' Her smile faded. 'Is it the same person sending the letters?'

'I think so.'

'Okay.' Casting a careful look at Joss, Shona reached into her handbag again and pulled out a second plastic bag stuffed with many folded sheets of paper. 'Then what about these?'

THIRTY-SIX

CORA

'Are these the letters you received in prison?' Cora asked, taken aback by the amount in the bag.

Shona nodded.

'I asked you if the voices you hear could last years,' Joss said. 'This is why.'

'They started arriving when I was inside.' Shona watched Cora's reaction as she explained. 'From the week I was told I had the right to appeal my conviction. I'd served six years of my sentence then and Alan agreed to take my case on. A day after he visited me to take initial statements to start the appeal process rolling, the first one arrived.'

'How did it get to you?'

'There's a network. You never know about it unless you receive something. The notes would be shoved under my pillow, slipped into my shoes in the bathroom, stuffed into my apron when I was working in the prison kitchen. They found their way to me. And they all said the same thing: *I'M WATCHING YOU. SAY NOTHING. SPEAK AND SOMEONE DIES.*'

'Say nothing to your legal brief?'

'That's what I thought at first, but then they'd arrive on days when Alan hadn't visited me. I binned the first batch, but as the appeal began to go through the stages of consideration, I started keeping them. I told Alan then, and he said to keep as many as I could. I used them as bookmarks, stuffed them into my socks.

I received about one a month until six weeks before I went to the appeal hearing. Then they turned up every other day.'

Joss took the bag from Shona and held it out to Cora. 'Will the voices still be there? After time has passed?'

'I'm not sure.'

It was the truth. Considering what Shona had said about the delivery methods of the letters in prison, it was likely they'd been handled many times in different settings. In Cora's experience, the imprint of emotional sound was finite — it would fade with time and become muddied with sound layers from all who had handled the object. And two years of such constant movement while Shona was collecting and protecting the letters would most likely have obliterated all traces of original sound.

'Please try.' Shona leaned forward, the whispers looping around her body as she did so. 'I want to know.'

Cora knew it was likely to be fruitless. But part of her wanted to know what effect time and use might have on the audible fingerprints left on the stack of notes. If sound remained after three years, might it suggest she could still hear something from Cassandra Norton's belongings, sealed into evidence bags nine years ago?

If Minshull officially asked her to be part of the reopened murder investigation, as he'd intimated before, it could bring answers surrounding Cassandra Norton's death. Maybe testing her ability now would lessen the blow when Minshull discovered she'd met with Shona.

Gingerly, she drew back the zip fastening and focused her mind.

At first, a jumble of muted, shapeless sounds met her — a more vibrant version of the soundscape she'd encountered in the main section of the farm museum. It sounded younger, if that were possible, but beyond the brighter peaks and troughs of noise, nothing much could be made out.

Pushing further out into the fog-shrouded sea of sound, Cora caught the edge of another frequency. Focusing her attention on it, she inched her consciousness nearer, until a shape began to form ahead.

A breath... soft stabs of consonants... the hiss of emphasis...

Cora pressed on in her search, the same sense of threat present now that she'd physically felt from the first set of letters and the constricting whispers that surrounded Shona. Using it as an anchor, she leaned as far into the distant sound-shape as the constraints of her mind would allow.

IF SHE SPEAKS...

The fragment of a phrase arrived in a rush of air, as if being released from confinement. A breathed set of words that once might have been spoken aloud, reduced now to the fraying, faded remnant Cora held in her mind.

There must be more.

There had to be.

It took all her concentration, but she caught a thread of the rest, followed by another and another...

> *IF SHE SPEAKS...*
> *...IT'S OVER.*

What?

Surprised, Cora turned the new words over, as if seeking proof they belonged to the start of the phrase. But the edges aligned, as if they had once been woven from the same fabric.

She wasn't mistaken: this voice was driven not by the power of a threat made, but by the fear of that threat ignored.

But was it the same voice? Or someone else, terrified of Shona speaking out?

Re-emerging in the immediate surroundings of the small office, Cora faced Shona and Joss. 'It's very distorted and damaged,' she said. 'But there's a voice there. Only instead of a threat towards you, it's an internal monologue: *If she speaks... it's over.*'

'It's over?' Joss repeated. 'What does that mean?'

Shona pressed a hand to her stomach, as if she might retch. 'It means I was right. I knew they were involved. I warned her – I said she shouldn't mess with them. But she ignored me, just like she ignored anyone who told her she couldn't have what she wanted.'

'I don't understand,' Cora said, her mind still processing the two successive sound-journeys she'd undertaken.

'They knew I was onto them. They were scared.' She pointed to the first bag of letters. 'But they're not scared now.'

'You know who killed Cassandra?' Joss asked, shocked.

Shona closed her eyes. 'I've always known – I just didn't want to believe it.'

'Who?' Joss demanded.

Shona looked up at him and opened her mouth to reply.

'Wait! No! You have to tell the police,' Cora rushed, the gravity of it all suddenly registering. She couldn't hear this, not when she was a part of the police team. Despite not yet being involved in the investigation, they were her colleagues, under pressure to solve the murder their predecessors had failed to.

Minshull had to hear this, not her. To continue would mean betraying everything she had invested in their working – and personal – relationship.

She stood, backing towards the door of the small office.

'You said you'd help me,' Shona protested, the whispers around her becoming cacophonous. 'You heard what they said!'

'Not like this… I'm sorry.'

'They'll kill me!'

Heart contracting, Cora froze.

'They're not afraid now. They want me to be afraid. They want to silence me – like they silenced Cassandra. Like they've silenced Karl.'

'I work with the police,' Cora rushed in desperation, despite every instinct screaming at her to resist. 'Not on the new investigation – yet. But it could happen.'

Joss' expression grew thunderous. 'You never told me.'

'I never told anyone. Nobody knows except Tris. Not the full extent of it — my ability and the way I use it to help investigations.'

'You're a copper?'

'No. A police expert. They call me in when they think I can help shed light on aspects of a case.'

Shona frowned. 'And they can charge, with the evidence you give them?'

'No. They can't. What I hear wouldn't be admissible in a court of law. But it can help the detectives build a picture, look into things they otherwise might not have, and ask questions that lead to the truth.'

'If I tell you, but not them, and you keep it between us, how would they know?'

Cora ran a hand through her hair, her brow beginning to throb. 'It doesn't matter: *I* would know. I'm sorry. I can't hear this.'

She had done enough — more than she should. Shona had confirmation of her suspicions over the purpose of the letters. Beyond that, it was a matter for her solicitor and the police, if she chose to involve them.

Leaving the office, Cora hurried through the echoing ghost-voices of the museum exhibits and heaved open the door.

In the blank white light of the remote location, she stared out at the dark, misted countryside, stretching out in every direction. She should never have agreed to come here — wherever the hell *here* was.

And now she was stuck in this place until Joss drove her back.

She pulled her phone from her coat pocket, her heart plummeting to the hard, dark stones beneath her feet when she saw the screen register no signal.

'Doc.'

Cora closed her eyes.

The crunch of rough gravel behind her signalled the fast approach of Joss.

'I shouldn't have come,' she began.

'I wouldn't have asked if I'd known.'

'I need to go, please.'

'No.'

He was at her side when she opened her eyes. And he was alone.

'*Please.*'

'What if she doesn't say who it is? What if you work with her until she decides to share it?'

'No...' Cora began, the urge to leave overwhelming.

'Hear me out. Shona doesn't trust anybody. Not before she went inside and absolutely not now. But what you did in there... You changed things. I saw what it meant to her.'

'I can't be involved, Joss. It jeopardises everything, don't you see?'

'Not if she doesn't name names.'

'But if I'm brought onto the case... If my police colleagues ask me... I can't lie to them. I won't.'

'Then don't. Talk to her. Hear what she has to say. And then, for the love of God, help me change her mind.' His hand came to rest on Cora's forearm. 'Because I can't do it by myself. And if her life is in danger...'

'If she mentions anything that could help the new investigation, I have to tell my colleagues in CID.'

Joss observed her as he processed her words. 'I need your help, Doc. I want her to speak out because look what's happening. Those attacks aren't going to stop. Next time it will be worse. Because it always is.'

'I don't know what I can do. I won't withhold evidence.'

'Then help the police find it.'

'Sorry?'

'Lead them to it. If we can persuade Shona to talk to them, great. But if we can't, we find a way to feed them the information.' He let his hand drop. 'I'm scared. And I'm out of ideas. Help us. Please?'

How could she help if she couldn't tell Minshull what was happening? But if Shona chose not to talk to the police, would they ever be able to find the people responsible?

'I need to know why Cassandra was murdered. And how Shona knew her. I need something I can test out as information. If I can do that without lying to the CID team and it succeeds, we'll go from there.'

'Yes. We'll do it!'

'And you need to tell Tris what's going on.'

'Not possible.'

'I'm only here because he agreed to it. He's concerned enough with the attacks and the fallout from Shona's acquittal. Come on, Joss. He's stuck everything on the line to support you. You owe him that much.'

'Fine. I'll talk to him when I return you to the office. Now will you come back inside? Please?'

She should refuse. Demand to be taken back to work. Forget she had ever encountered Shona Pickton, the letters and the whispers of accusation and threat that held the young woman captive.

But the attacks wouldn't end as long as anger and recrimination aimed erroneously at the gypsy and traveller community was allowed to continue. And if someone was hurt – or worse – because Cora hadn't acted when she'd had the opportunity, she couldn't live with herself.

Karl Cuskie was already dead – connected, Shona said, to the murder of Cassandra Norton. Would more deaths follow if police couldn't establish the link?

If helping Shona and hearing what she had to say brought an end to the attacks – if the killer of Cassandra and Karl could be brought to justice, silencing the hate directed at The HappyKid Project and the community it served – she would do it.

Against her better judgement, against everything she'd promised herself about how she would use her ability, Cora followed Joss back into the building.

THIRTY-SEVEN

MINSHULL

They had planned it down to the finest detail. Worked and reworked scenarios and eventualities, identified answers for every conceivable twist and turn. There would be no margin for error, no second pass if mistakes were made.

Minshull and Anderson exchanged nods beside the door of Interview Room 3. They were as ready as they could be.

DCI Taylor and her solicitor, Gemma Bissett, were waiting by the desk inside when the detectives entered. Taylor looked tired, her features pinched by anger. Wearing a pale grey sweatshirt and joggers instead of her usual immaculate uniform, she appeared a much diminished version of herself.

Nevertheless, she observed Minshull and Anderson with utter contempt, eyeballing them as they sat down. Bissett, by contrast, betrayed no emotion and looked as fresh as she had in the first interview yesterday.

Minshull dreaded to think what he looked like.

He'd slept – more than he'd expected to, in fact – crashing a little after nine p.m., and waking with his six a.m. alarm. He'd had coffee and breakfast and was as prepared as possible for what would undoubtedly be a long day ahead. But the task of presenting details of Taylor and Cuskie's affair weighed heavily on him.

Anderson had fared significantly worse.

He'd admitted to staying up until the early hours, debating details of Taylor's misconduct with his long-suffering wife, Ros.

It was clear he viewed the DCI's sustained abuse of power as a personal affront – but given his fractious history working alongside her, it was understandable.

It would be a battle to keep personal recriminations away from the job at hand this morning. Minshull could only trust Anderson's many years of dealing with the innate unfairness of the job to keep his anger in check.

Checking everyone was ready, Minshull began the recording, only for Bissett to raise her hand.

'Before we proceed, my client has a prepared statement she wishes to be read out.'

'Of course,' Minshull replied. That was another ten quid he owed Evans, who had called it last night when details of Taylor's phone messages with Cuskie emerged.

'They'll statement it and think it covers her reasons for visiting him,' he'd said. 'Only it won't cover the rest of her crap, will it?'

One thing was for certain: while having Evans back was a blessing as both a colleague returned and as an extra body for the workload, the resumption of his infamous office sweepstakes was going to hit everyone in the pocket.

Bissett produced a sheet from her notes. 'The statement reads: *"I have known Karl Cuskie for several years and consider him a good friend. He was a personal support to me during my divorce four years ago, knowing both my ex-husband and me, and I value his friendship. Two nights ago, I received a call from Karl to visit him at his home at 105 Maidstone Road, Felixstowe. Both of us are insomniacs, so it was not unusual for us to meet late at night. I took a DVD for us to watch and Karl was going to prepare some snacks.*

"'On arrival at the property, I knocked on the door and it opened. I didn't see who opened it, but I assumed it was Karl. When I entered the hall of the house, I saw him lying on the floor. He had been shot – a single bullet wound to the middle of his forehead. He was dead when I arrived.

"'A man dressed in black with a hood pulled up over a dark blue baseball cap appeared from the living room. I couldn't see his face. He

was yelling at me to get down on the floor. He pointed a handgun at me and told me to stay still. I lay beside Karl's body, expecting to be killed, too. But after a few minutes, I realised I was alone. Seizing my chance, I got up and ran from the house. I didn't shut the door, I just ran as fast as I could. I was terrified the hooded intruder would see me and come after me.

"'I didn't report what happened, as I was concerned that my relationship with Karl Cuskie would be misconstrued. I know he has a history of informing police colleagues but I have never asked him for information of this kind. I regret that I did not immediately raise the alarm, and I recognise that by failing to do so I could have prevented action being taken that night.

"'I did not kill Karl Cuskie. I believe he was killed because he had agreed to assist our CID team with the reopened investigation into the murder of Cassandra Norton in 2015, which I had been made aware of by DS Rob Minshull, earlier that day. This is a true representation of the events of the night in question, offered freely and without duress. I will sign the statement in the presence of my solicitor, DS Minshull and DI Joel Anderson. I will answer no further questions on this matter."…'

'May we have the statement for our records?' Minshull asked.

'You can take a photocopy, but I'll retain the original,' Bissett replied, Taylor offering a superior smile beside her as she signed the statement.

'Okay, thanks.'

It was a necessary delay to the interview, but one that Anderson and Minshull had already anticipated. Anderson left the interview room to photocopy the statement, while Minshull paused the recording. Bissett and Taylor said nothing in the intervening minutes, Minshull calmly taking notes to deny them any chance of eye contact. An uneasy quiet settled between them as the minutes dragged until Anderson's return. Although his outward appearance suggested Minshull was calm, the relief he felt when Anderson reappeared was considerable.

The statement wasn't enough to explain Taylor's presence at Cuskie's house, nor the evidence they had in hand regarding the length and true nature of their relationship. Her mention of an unnamed, unidentified third party at Cuskie's house also required further questioning. Had he gained access to the property using the route the team had suggested, from the road behind and across the rear gardens? Did he leave by the back door?

What irked Minshull more than anything in Taylor's statement was her manner. She'd been combative since her arrest yesterday, some of which was understandable, given the spectacle Superintendent Martlesham had put her at the centre of. But this morning, the harrowing details she'd supplied in her statement were at odds with her demeanour. She didn't act like someone who had lost a close friend – or a lover – experienced the shock of discovering his body and then been forced to endure a terrible ordeal at gunpoint by a hooded stranger.

If Minshull had been forced to lie down beside the murdered corpse of someone he loved, terrified for his own life while in shock and grief for his loss, he doubted he would be coherent today, let alone as imperious as the DCI appeared to be.

She displayed no sign of shock or grief. Only anger, aimed squarely at Minshull and Anderson for placing her in custody. Sue Taylor had never been what anyone would call demonstrative when it came to her emotions. But surely she should be feeling *something* about Cuskie's death?

Anderson showed both the original statement and its copy to Bissett, who then handed them to Taylor to sign. Once this was done, she kept the original and returned the copy to Minshull, who added it to his file. He watched Taylor closely while this business took place. She had relaxed in her seat and was drinking water from the cup she'd been given.

Did she think she'd done enough?

'Thank you for the statement,' Anderson said, his voice steady as he took the lead. 'However, I do wish to clarify some points of it, as you've disclosed new information that you previously withheld.'

'I've instructed my client to refrain from answering, as per the provisions of the statement,' Bissett replied, coolly.

'And you are well within your rights to do so. However, to fully assist us in apprehending the person responsible for Karl Cuskie's death, we need to go over some of the points. I'm sure your client is as eager as we are to bring the right person to justice.'

Taylor's smile tightened.

Bissett indicated for Anderson to proceed with a sweep of her hand.

'Thank you.' He consulted the copy of Taylor's statement. 'You said when you arrived at Mr Cuskie's home you knocked at the door, and when it opened you "*didn't see who opened the door, but assumed it was Karl*", correct?'

'No comment.'

'When you saw Mr Cuskie lying on the floor – your friend, obviously gravely injured – did you try to help him?'

'No comment.'

'Did you try to find a pulse?'

'No comment.'

'Did you attempt to call an ambulance?'

A flicker from Taylor. 'No comment.'

'Your close friend – the person who had supported you not only through your divorce but also as your fellow insomniac, a person you said you often visited late at night – was badly injured. A gunshot to his forehead. His blood everywhere. Did you feel shock? Panic? Did you freeze on the spot?'

'No comment.'

Anderson's eyes never left Taylor's as he tried a different approach. 'Even with your police training, your considerable experience on the job and all of the horrors you've experienced over the years, the sight of Karl lying there, blood pooled beneath what was left of his head, blood and brain matter sprayed across the walls and floor, must have been horrific.'

A faltering blink. 'No… No comment.'

'That level of detail is unnecessary to use here,' Bissett objected. 'My client has already alluded to what she witnessed when she entered Mr Cuskie's property.'

'With the greatest of respect, Ms Bissett, I don't think she has.' His finger ran down the statement, stopping at a section. 'You said, "*I saw Karl Cuskie lying on the floor. He had been shot, a single bullet wound to the middle of his forehead. He was dead when I arrived.*"... How did you know he was dead? Even with his injuries, you had no indication of when he'd been shot. If it had just happened, he might still have been alive. You had an opportunity to report it, to call for assistance. Yet you chose not to. Why was that?'

'No comment.'

'You previously told us Mr Cuskie was an acquaintance. But your statement suggests he was a close friend. The kind of friend you could share personal details with, such as your shared insomnia, and support one another with late-night visits where you would watch a DVD and eat snacks together. Losing a friend like that, someone you no doubt cared so much for, is unthinkable. Is that why you didn't act?'

When Taylor refused to answer, Anderson glanced at Minshull, who pulled two bundles of paper from his folder.

'When you were arrested yesterday, your mobile phone, laptop and iPad were seized. Our colleagues in Tech found these messages on your phone, among others.'

Minshull passed one of the bundles to Taylor and Bissett, observing the DCI's reaction.

When it came, it was a gift.

All of Sue Taylor's carefully crafted control crumbled the moment she recognised the exchanges.

'These are messages between you and Karl Cuskie. This first set goes back approximately four weeks. But the Tech team assures me there are more to be extracted, going back years, in their estimate.'

'Why wasn't I informed of this?' Bissett snapped, her own response telling.

'It was always our intention to discuss it this morning, prepared statements notwithstanding,' Minshull replied. It was only a matter of time before Bissett requested a private consultation with Taylor to discuss the disclosure, but he was determined to read some aloud before that happened, to observe the effect on the DCI.

'… "*Plod came sniffing around. Earlier.* **Where?** *Green Dragon.* **But you said nothing?… You said NOTHING?** *I might have talked to him…*" That was my visit to speak with Karl Cuskie that I informed you about the next day, wasn't it?'

'No comment.'

'Here's another, from page seven of the transcripts. A message conversation between you and Mr Cuskie, thirty minutes before you went to his house and found him dead. "*I need to see you.* **It's too risky.** *I miss you, babe.* **You said you'd lay low.** *I did. And I am. But nobody's watching us, are they?*"…'

'No comment.'

'I request time to brief my client regarding this disclosure.'

Minshull continued, ignoring Bissett, knowing he was pushing his luck. '"**I can't.** *But you want to. Admit it…*"'

'DS Minshull…'

'…"**That's not fair.** *You know I do. If anyone sees us…*"'

'DS Minshull… this interview needs to end…'

'…"*Who's going to see? Come over tonight. You don't have to stay…*"'

'I request a meeting with my client! Immediately!' Bissett's raised voice caused Minshull to finally comply.

Heart slamming hard, he spoke into the recorder. 'Interview suspended at ten fifteen a.m.'

Bissett was on her feet the moment the recording ended. 'I will be lodging a complaint with your superiors regarding your behaviour. The moment I requested a private briefing you should have complied.'

'He knows that,' Taylor hissed. 'That's why he did it.'

She was shushed into compliance by her solicitor as they left the interview room.

As the door closed, Anderson stood, slamming his hand against the wall.

'Bloody hell, Rob, you cut that fine.'

'She had to hear it, Guv. You saw her reaction: she didn't expect us to find that stuff.'

'It was on her phone, for crying out loud! Protected with a password that Perez, my ancient cocker spaniel, could work out. What the hell did she think was going to happen? That we'd be too scared to look at her messages because she's a DCI?'

Minshull leaned against the unforgiving plastic back of his chair, rubbing his aching eyes. 'They were lovers. It's the only explanation. But the *hooded* figure?'

'Convenient, that.'

'Or the truth?'

Anderson sagged. 'We need any CCTV or doorbell cam footage we can get from King Street. See if anyone matching that description can be seen anywhere near the alleyways at any time that evening.'

'No problem. I'll ask Ellis to check with Tim Brinton, see where we're at with collecting it.'

'Good, thanks.' Anderson collected his notepad and papers. 'Might as well get back to the office. Something tells me that Sue and her solicitor will be winding down the clock in their meeting.'

Minshull joined his superior as they left the room. The slightly fresher air of the corridor was welcome, even if the heating was no less aggressive here. The old building's heating systems were very much an all-or-nothing affair, more often than not firing into life on winter's mildest days and faltering the moment the mercury plummeted.

As they walked slowly back up to the second floor, Minshull's thoughts turned to Cora. It seemed an age since he'd asked her to be on standby for the investigation and recent events had prevented him from contacting her. If she'd seen the news, she'd likely know why his call had been delayed. But might she be wondering if her skills were still required?

In truth, Cora was very much required for the reopened murder case – her input could be vital to sift clues from the mountain of previous evidence. And, provided Anderson allowed it, she could be a valuable asset to the eventual search of Karl Cuskie's house. Might she be able to hear echoes of the attack? Or the voice of Cuskie's alleged hooded assailant? Or might she sense only one person standing in the hallway with a gun – the woman Cuskie loved?

Cora was missed, too. Minshull tried to tell himself that he felt it on behalf of the whole CID team, but he missed her presence, both at work and outside of it. He had learned to make sense of his work and home lives through Cora's lens. What he would give to be able to discuss the current investigations with her, to voice his theories away from the pressure and scrutiny of the team and the observers...

'Guv,' he said, when they were a few doors away from the CID office. 'Hang on a minute?'

Anderson looked back. 'Problem?'

'Request?'

'If you're thinking of booking a holiday, I've bad news for you.'

'There goes my hope of a cheeky weekend at Disneyland Paris.' Minshull offered a rueful grin before letting his face fall. 'I think we need Cora, Guv.'

Anderson's eyes narrowed. 'I think *you* need Cora.'

'That's not what I'm saying.'

'Then what are you suggesting?'

Cornered, Minshull hugged his interview folder closer to his chest. 'We need her input. And her assistance. There are historic items that were found with Cassandra Norton, sealed in evidence bags at the time. What if Cora could still hear traces of audible fingerprints from them? And then there's Cuskie's house. Sue Taylor's car. Her phone... Any one of those things could bring information we don't yet have.'

Anderson considered the request. 'We would need to be specific with the tasks we assigned her.'

'Yes, of course.'

'And be very clear about which aspects we'd be seeking supporting information on.'

'Naturally. I think she could give us an edge. Look at how much her insight helped us with the Evernam case. It opened up new avenues we just wouldn't have found easily.'

'I remember.' His superior gave a groan. 'Listen, you don't have to convince me. It's the observers who might prove a stumbling block. They're watching us to ensure best practice. If they disagree with Cora's input...'

'Then you'll have to have a quiet word with them, Guv.' As Anderson's surprise registered, Minshull voiced what everyone in the team had already worked out from the easy interactions between their DI and the two observers. 'Because you know them well, don't you?'

'How did you...?' Anderson spluttered, before admitting defeat. 'Oh *fine*. Yes, they're friends of mine. Have been for years. But the Super can't know, okay? We have precious few advantages in this investigation. Allow me this one?'

'You have it. And the team will agree with me.'

'You're all too bloody good at your jobs, that's the problem.' Wearily, Anderson shook his head. 'Bring Cora in. This afternoon, if possible. She can start on the historic physical evidence from Cassandra Norton. Then as soon as we have Taylor's things cleared for inspection, we'll move her on to them.'

'And Cuskie's house?'

'Maybe. Let's hang fire there, okay? Wait to see if our esteemed DCI decides to add anything to her statement.'

'And DI Tsang and DI Guthrie?'

Anderson observed Minshull wryly. 'Leave them to me.'

THIRTY-EIGHT

SHONA

I said I wouldn't talk to the police. I stand by that.

But Dr Lael is different.

She's not a copper – that's what she said. With her Gift it would be strange for her to be one. But the way she spoke about the detectives she works with? That worried me. She talks about them like I've heard coppers talk about their colleagues. Like that Taylor woman said, over and over again – that she and her team were going to get the result they wanted, with or without my help.

'*You know you're guilty. I know you're guilty. And my team aren't working their backsides off for nothing. I won't let them lose because you don't have the bottle to admit what you did…*'

It didn't matter that the duty solicitor they gave me shouted at her to stop, and threatened her with all kinds of consequences when she didn't. That woman would have had a shouting match with a thunderstorm and expected to win.

I don't know if Dr Lael is as loyal to Taylor as she is to the rest of the team. I can't imagine anyone liking that bitch. But then, I can't imagine why anyone would want to be a copper.

I'll watch what I say about Taylor around the Doc, regardless.

I won't tell her that Taylor was the reason Karl and I broke up that night. That he chose *her* instead of me.

I've wondered for years what would have happened if he hadn't mentioned Sue Taylor to me. If I hadn't found the messages on his phone, all the *I need to see you* and *thank you for our beautiful night* crap. If Karl had just called it off with us, had the balls to admit he didn't love me. I didn't need to know about *her*. I didn't need to know he'd been shagging her all the time he was with me. I would have been hurt, sure, but I wouldn't have run.

Did Taylor know he was with me?

Is that why she pinned the murder on me? To get me out of the way?

And did she really know Karl, like I did? Or the other people he was working for? Or the trouble Cassandra got into because of him?

I won't mention Taylor to Dr Lael. But I'm going to tell her why Cassandra Norton died. Because I'm scared I'm next on the list.

I said I wouldn't trust the police this time.

But Dr Lael is different.

And she might be my only hope of staying alive.

THIRTY-NINE

BENNETT

'*Damn* it!'

DC Kate Bennett didn't bother to find a pencil sharpener, throwing the whole pencil and its broken lead into the bin beside her chair instead.

'Steady on, She-Hulk,' Ellis chuckled. 'Who got you all green and angry this morning?'

'Sod off, Drew,' she snapped, swinging open the top drawer of her desk and snatching up a new pencil. She didn't need his constant jokes, just like she didn't need stupid, sub-standard stationery supplies...

'Watch out, everyone! Kate's got a newly sharpened pencil and she's not afraid to use it!' Ellis announced – because clearly he didn't value his health today.

Bennett knew full well what he was doing: using his ridiculous little-kid humour to chivvy her out of her bad mood. It would work, eventually, too. And that was the most infuriating thing about it.

'Dicing with death again, are you, Drew?' Wheeler asked, leaning between their desks to hand a mug to Bennett. 'Daft beggar'll never learn, will he, Kate? Not till he's been kicked from here to Lowestoft, eh?' He lowered his voice. 'Now sip that slowly. It'll help.'

The fragrant steam rising from the mug tickled Bennett's nose, its scent unmistakable. Chamomile tea. With a spoonful of honey from Wheeler's secret stash.

'Cheers, Dave,' she replied, only managing to maintain a smile until he returned to his desk. The gesture was as sweet as the bringer. A tactic to lighten her mood that *some people* would do well to learn from…

'I'm just trying to make her smile,' Ellis protested, unwisely, given the daggers Bennett sent his way.

'Drew, mate, know when to leave it,' Evans warned him.

'Okay, okay. Sorry I tried.'

Sulking, Ellis went back to the pile of evidence files on his desk. But Bennett was aware of his concerned glances in her direction as she returned to her work.

It wasn't his fault. Or anyone else's. But if she told them why she wanted to kick everyone and everything in sight today, she'd have to tell them the rest. And there was no way she was ready to do that.

Damn bloody DCI Taylor and her bloody affair!

And damn her own response to last night's revelation.

Was she destined to always take mentions of infidelity as personal blows? Why couldn't she compartmentalise that painful part of her life and shove it where it would never be seen again?

It wasn't just the mockery Taylor had blatantly made of the system she enforced so strongly at work. Not just the entitlement to expect not to be found out. It was the audacity, the bare-faced lies. The flaunting of a mask so well-fitting that Taylor believed herself far above reproach.

Like Russ had acted when he'd been found out. As if he was personally wounded by Bennett's objection to him going after what he wanted. And Bennett's family along with him.

Injustice.

She'd felt its sting all her life, from a break-in at her childhood home while she slept upstairs – and the helplessness she felt when the perpetrators were never caught – to countless smaller occurrences she encountered growing up, all of which were outside her control.

Her fury at injustice had driven her to join up as a bright-eyed cadet at the age of nineteen. It had pushed her through the ranks, compelled her to take her detective exam and made her get out of bed every morning ready to fight. If she could kick injustice to the kerb on a daily basis, some semblance of balance might be restored to a world too often weighted in its favour.

She'd been thinking about the family of Cassandra Norton, too: how they were facing their third injustice over her death. First, Shona Pickton's wrongful conviction; next the press raking up old resentments and anger in their daughter's name; and now, watching the reopened murder investigation falling second in priority to a fresh murder case.

Consulting the whiteboard, Bennett realised that nobody from Cassandra's immediate circle had been re-interviewed yet, with the exception of the dead woman's former boyfriend.

According to Anderson, the family's solicitor had conveyed South Suffolk Police's official notice of the reopening of the investigation. Beyond that, what was being done?

Bennett remembered Wheeler mentioning a belligerent brother from the first investigation. Might he have missed the official notification?

Waiting until Ellis and Evans were deep in discussion over Karl Cuskie's known associates, she slipped from her desk and made her way across to Wheeler's.

'Question, Dave,' she said, crouching down beside his desk to avoid being seen.

'Anything for you, girl,' he beamed back.

'When we were talking about what you and the Guv remembered of the first investigation, you mentioned a brother, didn't you?'

Wheeler grimaced. 'Ryan Norton. Bloody nuisance he was. Called us every day of the investigation, demanding details and action. I was sympathetic at first — I mean he'd lost his sister in the worst way and was desperate for answers. But he was relentless. Wouldn't ever accept what I told him, even though I went to pains to explain everything I could. He thought we were lying to him, so every call was an accusation. It wears you down, you know? I don't mind telling you, he did my nut in after four weeks of those calls.'

'Did he give an initial statement?'

'He was one of the first of Cassandra's close circle we spoke to, unsurprisingly. Actually, hang on a mo, I found it yesterday afternoon...' He rummaged through an overflowing stack of papers on his desk, returning triumphant with a pale grey cardboard file. 'Here you go.'

Bennett opened the folder and scanned its first page. 'Odd that he hasn't called yet regarding the new investigation.'

'You know, that was my first thought. Maybe he regretted being so belligerent. I mean, he's older now. Wiser, you'd hope. Nine years is a long time to realise you acted like a tit.'

Bennett hid her smile. Ryan Norton's behaviour must have been trying if it ruffled the feathers of the Nicest Man in CID. 'Has he been contacted yet for re-interview?'

'It was on my list of things to do after tackling this little lot.' Wheeler patted the large stack of files beside him. 'But it's yours, if you fancy it?'

'Would you mind? I'm concerned that we aren't moving the reinvestigation forward quickly enough because of Cuskie's murder.'

Wheeler grinned. 'Be my guest, Kate. Can't say I'd be heart-broken if you got the pleasure of interviewing him instead of me.'

-

It took just over an hour to identify a contact phone number for Ryan Norton. He'd moved house twice in the intervening years – three times, if you counted his move out of the family home, a little under two years after his sister's murder. He'd remained in Felixstowe and now worked as a broker for a local insurance company. It was at their offices on busy Hamilton Road, occupying two floors above a fancy goods gift shop Bennett knew well, that she finally located a contact number and address for him.

She'd seen the name *Hurren Associates* on summer visits to the town with her young twin nieces, both of whom loved to wander around the shop beneath with its shelves of brightly coloured homeware, cards, seaside-themed trinkets and clothing, usually begging for an expensive Jellycat cuddly toy to add to their already extensive collection.

The shop would be filled with Christmas gifts and toys now, Bennett thought, her heart aching again. Not that she'd get the opportunity to take the twins there this year. Iris and Isolde were Russ' sister Megan's daughters. She'd loved being Auntie Kate to the bright-spirited, energetic girls. But that, like so many of the things she'd taken for granted in her life, was behind her now.

Ex-auntie. Ex-sister-in-law. Ex-daughter-in-law. All of these things Bennett had become in the last year, without ever wishing for any of them.

So much lost, in so many ways.

Dismissing her thoughts, she turned to a blank page in her notebook and called the number that the receptionist at Hurren Associates had given her.

The call rang out four times before it was answered.

'Yes?'

'Mr Norton, hello. My name is DC Kate Bennett from South Suffolk CID. I'm working on the reopened investigation into…'

'You took your time.'

'Apologies, Mr Norton. We're revisiting every statement and piece of evidence from the original investigation and, as you can imagine, it's taking a while.'

'And so it bloody well should. Have you any idea of the hell my family's been put through again, since *that woman* got out?

Journalists hanging around, phone calls at all hours of the day and night, notes pushed through the door. My mother's in the late stages of dementia and my stepfather's trying to look after her – he can barely cope with that every day without all this disruption upsetting them both.'

'I'm sorry that's happening to you,' Bennett replied respectfully, not really knowing what else to say. 'My colleagues and I are working all hours and we're committed to finding the person responsible…'

'Yeah, yeah. You'll forgive my cynicism after years of hearing the same meaningless platitudes trolled out.'

As he paused for breath, Bennett rushed in. 'It would help us greatly if you'd consider coming in to revisit your statement.'

Wind snatched from his sails, Ryan Norton was silent for a moment.

'What for?'

'We're re-interviewing as many witnesses as possible, going over everything to see what might have been missed before. It's really important to us that every aspect is checked.'

There was another pause.

'When?'

'At your earliest convenience, sir.'

'Fine. I'm free later today between five p.m. and six thirty p.m.'

Bennett punched the air at her desk. 'That would be great, thank you. Just come to the main entrance of South Suffolk Police HQ in Ipswich. I'll meet you there.'

'I'll bring my solicitor,' Norton stated coldly. 'And I'm not changing a thing.'

The call ended abruptly, Bennett staring in confusion at the phone receiver in her hand.

'Now that's the face of someone who's talked to Ryan Norton for the first time.'

Wheeler was by her desk, another cardboard file in his hand, his wry smile aimed at her.

'He's coming in just after five p.m. He said he's missed you.'

'Nice. So, why the face?'

'He said he *won't be changing a thing* in his statement,' she replied, replacing the phone receiver. 'And then he just hung up.'

'Mm–hmm. Sounds like him. Flounce in, flounce about, flounce out.'

'*Flounce…*' The word amused Bennett more than it should.

'What? That's the word for him! You'll see.' He placed the new file on her desk. 'I found this at the top of the box I just opened. Newspaper articles, clippings, transcripts of news reports, all gathered at the time. I'm pretty sure that was the Guv's idea and DCI Taylor knew nothing of it. She didn't hold with newspaper clippings as evidence unless the journalist who wrote them was a suspect. But Joel did it anyway. It was how we'd learned to do stuff with Minsh's dad – we just carried on when Sue Taylor got the job.'

Bennett opened the folder and inspected the clippings. Some were actual sections from newspapers, but most were scanned or photocopied.

'Dave, these are brilliant,' she breathed.

'You've the Guv to thank for that,' Wheeler replied, beaming from the compliment anyway. 'Talking of which, him and the Sarge'll be back any minute. Best look lively, all of us. I'm guessing they'll not be the happiest of bunnies when they return.'

'Will do.' Bennett caught the fabric of Wheeler's shirt sleeve as he made to leave. 'Thanks. For… you know.'

Wheeler's smile was the picture of kindness. 'Don't you mention it. You're welcome.'

Heart swelling, Bennett returned her attention to the clippings file.

Most of the pieces were from the hours and days immediately following the discovery of Cassandra's body. Harrowing details thinly veiled to comply with guidelines but enough hints at grizzly facts to keep readers flocking back for more. But after the first twenty articles and news reports, earlier features began to emerge.

There was a scan of a two-page centre spread, celebrating Cassandra's Miss Suffolk win, the headline *ISN'T SHE LOVELY?* accompanied by the strapline: LOCAL BEAUTY IS THE TOAST OF THE COUNTY. The photograph was familiar, the image chosen by almost every news outlet to represent the murdered woman. Blonde hair, falling in waves to her shoulders, big blue eyes and generous pink rosebud lips, wearing sky-high heels, a sparkling crystal crown and a silk sash skimming across her lace-effect bikini and perfectly flat stomach.

The article was in a clear plastic pocket, a small wad of smaller clippings behind it. They had been filed together, a snapshot of Cassandra Norton's life between her beauty contest win and her violent death. A supermarket opening, with Cassandra wearing a sharply tailored miniskirt and suit jacket, the obligatory jewelled crown and satin sash slightly at odds with the rest. An interview in the studios at BBC Radio Suffolk, the crown beside her and a pair of headphones in their place. An appearance on the local coverage for Children in Need, cuddling up to Pudsey Bear as they held a large cardboard cheque for twenty-five thousand pounds, donated on behalf of a Suffolk business group.

Something at the bottom of the oversized cheque caught Bennett's eye.

Beneath the signature, the business group name was printed, the letters a little obscured by the yellowing of the paper clipping.

Bennett picked up her mobile phone and selected her camera. Taking as steady a shot as she could, she zoomed in on the text.

After a couple of unsatisfactory attempts, she captured a clear enough image, pinching it on screen to enlarge it as far she could.

She made a note of it and began to flick through the other images.

'Taking selfies are you?' Evans had wandered over and was watching Bennett's progress with unnerving interest. A break from the CID office appeared to have reminded him that other people existed. He'd completed more navigations of his colleagues' desks since his return than in all the time Bennett had worked with him.

'Do you recognise this name?' she asked, selecting more charity event reports and photo clippings from the stack in her hand, laying them out across her desk like a strange game of Solitaire. 'Dunbar Group? It's in all of these articles with Cassandra. Looks like a fundraising outfit. This bloke is in quite a few of the photos, too.'

She picked up a photo of Cassandra, resplendent in an off-the-shoulder velvet evening dress, beside an older man dressed in a well-tailored tuxedo. He had a sweep of white hair and a neatly trimmed cavalier-style beard, and his left arm casually circled Cassandra's waist. Both held glasses of champagne and were smiling for the camera. He looked vaguely familiar, but Bennett couldn't place him.

'Well, well. Friends in very low places,' Evans said, frowning at the image. 'Local well-connected businessman. The epitome of benevolence. The picture of generosity.' He gave a derisory snort. 'Or that's what he wants you to think.'

'Am I missing something, Les?'

'That's Jake Kilburn.'

Bennett stared at the photo. *That* was Jake Kilburn? 'Are you sure?'

While the alleged local crime lord's name had been referred to many times over the years in the CID office, the only image Bennett had ever seen of him was an arrest photo taken thirty years before, when he had been a furious, clean-shaven young man.

'No mistaking that ugly mug. Nasty git in real life. As well as the star of the local business community, old Jake's the local kingpin in the criminal fraternity. Thinks he's the Don Corleone of Suffolk.'

'Hang on,' Bennett said, as Ellis wheeled his chair over to her desk for a closer look. 'I'm sure his name came up in the interview with Nicholas Wright. Cassandra's ex.'

'You have to tell Minsh and the Guv.' Wheeler had joined them now, staring at the mosaic of newspaper clippings spread across Bennett's desk.

'Tell us what?'

The detectives looked up as one.

Minshull and Anderson were standing in the open doorway, stone-faced.

'I think Cassandra Norton knew Jake Kilburn,' Bennett said, her words summoning the DS and DI immediately to her side.

'The clippings…' Anderson shook his head. 'I had Zac Godliman collecting those for me while we were working on the first murder investigation. I can't believe he missed Kilburn in these.'

'Godliman! Now there's a blast from the past,' Wheeler said. 'Poor kid only lasted a year in CID before he walked. Bright as a button, but he couldn't hack it in here.'

Minshull and Bennett exchanged glances. 'Nicholas Wright admitted he was at a poker game with Kilburn the night Cassandra was murdered, Guv.'

Anderson stared back. 'Then it's no coincidence. Kate, Drew, I want you to find me everything you can on these charity functions. Why Cassandra Norton was part of them. How active a role Jake Kilburn played in them all. I need a definite link between these two.'

'Guv.'

'Yes, Guv.'

Anderson picked up the smiling gala photo. In the crook of Kilburn's arm, the former beauty queen beamed back. 'What the hell were you doing with a bastard like him, Cassandra?'

FORTY

CORA

'What the hell?'

'I know,' Cora replied, pacing Tris Noakes' office. 'Joss put me on the spot. And what I heard from those letters…'

'He had no business involving you with this. What was he thinking?'

'He's worried about his friend.'

'His *friend* Shona Pickton, recently acquitted for the murder your police colleagues are reinvestigating?'

Spoken in such stark terms made it sound so much worse. 'I haven't been officially invited to be part of it.'

'*Yet*. But Rob's already asked you to be ready for when they will.'

'I heard the threat in those letters. I think she has a right to be scared. And look at what people are willing to do against anyone connected with her. The attacks, at St Columba Street and here. And Karl Cuskie…'

'And what exactly do you think will happen to you if they discover you're helping her? It's too dangerous, Cora. When you found out who she was you should have called it off.'

'What was I supposed to do? Refuse to help her? Demand Joss drive me back?'

'Yes!' His resolve crumbled in the face of Cora's expression. 'Well, no. You could have delayed it a while at least. Said you couldn't agree until you'd spoken to me.'

'In that place? In the middle of nowhere with no way of getting home by myself?'

'No. I see that.' Tris sat on the edge of his desk. 'It's dangerous. If anyone sees you…'

'We'll be careful.'

'If Rob finds out…'

That was harder to find answers for. Cora had wrestled with the very real possibility of working behind Minshull's back and still hadn't found a way to reconcile herself to it.

'Joss wants us to work together to persuade Shona to help the investigation,' she replied. 'He thinks if she trusts me, I can lead her towards the right decision. If it works like we hope it might, Rob will get Shona's co-operation and be none the wiser about how it happened.'

Tris snorted. 'In what possible scenario do you think Rob Minshull won't find out? And then what? All that trust you've built between you, all the work you've invested outside of the job to reach him, could all be gone. Instantly.'

He was right, of course. Minshull would find out eventually, because Minshull always did. And when he did… Cora didn't want to consider what that might do to their close friendship.

But what she'd heard might just make the difference.

'I *heard* echoes, Tris,' she said, her pulse quickening at the memory of it. 'From the oldest of those notes, that were three years old. *Three years* – I've never sensed any strong residual sound beyond a few weeks before. Only the absence of sound, like when I've visited old houses. Echoes in the space where emotional sound once resided.'

'How clear was the residual sound?' Tris asked, his interest piqued by the new development, as Cora had hoped it would be.

'Defined layers I could peel apart. Hidden sound behind them that was more or less intact. That hasn't happened before – I've just lost all traces of sound at once.'

'Like with your dad?' Tris ducked his head graciously.

'Yes.'

Cora bit her lip against the rush of emotion that always accompanied the memory. Her late father's belongings had become the benchmark for the length of time emotional echoes remained audible to her. His voice had remained strong on his possessions around the family home following his death for two weeks, only starting to fade on the twelfth and thirteenth days until it disappeared altogether. At the time it had been like losing him all over again, the strange comfort Cora had found in the lingering echoes of his voice stolen in a final, cruel kick.

Without realising it until now, she had carried the experience with her to measure all other object voices.

And Shona's letters had finally taken the crown.

'Rob asked me if older echoes were possible to hear. At the time I only had Dad's belongings to go by. Any further back was only a theory. But Shona's letters have shown I can still detect sound from several years ago. What if I can take that to Rob as proof of what's now possible? Of what it could mean for Cassandra Norton's belongings in the evidence files?'

Was she grasping at straws? Would Minshull overlook her meeting with Shona under his radar if it meant she heard something crucial from the items found with Cassandra?

She should have said no when she realised who Joss' friend was. But that decision was far behind her now. What if the ends justified the means?

Tris said nothing, his posture silent-screaming his objection. He was torn, too, Cora knew, hating that he had been dragged into the situation for her sake. His instinct to protect her, his concern for Joss and his innate sense of right and wrong would all be at odds.

As she debated what to say, her mobile phone rang.

Tris raised his head from his hands as Cora saw the caller's name on screen.

ROB calling

Her heart sank. 'It's Rob.'

Tris stood. 'Take it in here, if you like. I need to chat to Ollie anyway.'

Without another word, he slipped from the office, closing the door.

Steeling herself, Cora answered the call.

'Hi Rob.'

'Hey, Cora. Sorry it's been a while. We've been a bit busy as you might have heard.'

'How's it all going?'

The rush of breath before his reply said more than anything that would follow. 'Complicated. Can you come in this afternoon? I know it's late notice, sorry.'

'Tris said it's fine.'

'Excellent. Pass on my thanks, would you?' His voice was ragged at the edges, exhaustion fraying the shape of his words.

'Of course. I'll head over around midday, if that's okay?'

'Perfect. I can bring you up to speed with everything when you get here.' There was a pause, the now-familiar sounds of the CID office playing in the space left by his voice. 'It will be so good to see you.'

Cora considered those words as she tied up the last of her morning's work, her head down to avoid any further discussion with Tris. Minshull's confession was beyond that of friendly chat between colleagues – and that made Cora's chosen course of action seem even more of a betrayal.

Perhaps fate would intervene, leading the CID team to uncover the information Cora might gain from Shona before it ever had to be shared. Maybe they would find something more important, so the success of the investigation no longer hinged on Shona's testimony.

Was it wise to wish for unlikely miracles to absolve her?

–

An hour later, a taxi dropped Cora at the headquarters of South Suffolk Constabulary. Heading inside, she showed her pass to the duty sergeant at the front desk and used the entry code she now knew by heart to make her own way into the building.

It gave her a shiver of thrill to be in charge of her own journey up to the second floor. It was proof of her place here, of her acceptance within the police family. Cora would never have imagined that possible when she'd first visited Police HQ.

Was the acceptance she'd longed for now on the line? Was she entering the heart of South Suffolk Police as a wolf in sheep's clothing?

Shaking off her doubts, she jogged up the stairs and made for the CID office.

Smiles met her as she entered, Dave Wheeler hurrying over to greet her at the door.

'My goodness, Dr Lael, are you a sight for sore eyes!' he exclaimed, ushering her in. 'Come in and save us from our own dodgy company.'

'Speak for yourself, Dave,' Les Evans chuntered, offering Cora a good-natured salute.

'Good to see you back, Les,' she replied, allowing herself to relax into the welcome. The most cynical about her involvement with the team, Evans had much to thank her for. It would never be expressed beyond warm jokes and good-natured humour, but Cora was in no doubt of his gratitude.

'Good to be back,' Evans replied. 'Although with all these damn boxes to get through I'm seriously considering getting another doctor's note.'

'Don't fancy your chances of that,' Ellis returned, raising his hand to Cora. 'Unless *Can't Be Arsed* is a medical condition.'

'If it is, Les could have been signed off for it since the beginning of his career,' Wheeler laughed, along with his colleagues.

Evans feigned offence. 'That's you off my Christmas card list, Dave. Not that you were ever on it in the first place...'

Around the office evidence boxes had been stacked, further enclosing the already limited space. Two people Cora didn't recognise were watching from the usually empty desk next to Minshull's and a uniformed officer was checking off the contents of a file box on the floor beside Kate Bennett's desk. Beneath the laughter and good humour an undercurrent of dogged purposefulness flowed. Frustration and anger bit the air from the stacks of files every detective was working on, weariness whispering back from discarded food wrappers and takeaway drink cups stashed in bins beneath every desk.

Cora hadn't envisioned what a CID office in the grip of a major re-investigation might look like. The reality shook her. She sensed the commitment, the determination and the toll of long hours, saw it etched into the expressions of everyone in the room.

Could she bear to work against all of this?

'Cora, welcome!' Joel Anderson boomed, as he and Minshull emerged from his office. He traversed the office in a few strides, his handshake firm and familiar. 'We'll have the items from the evidence sacks ready for you shortly. Rob, do you want to make a start on briefing Dr Lael while we prepare?'

'Glad to, Guv.' Minshull's smile was a stab to her. 'Let's head down the corridor, okay?'

They left the office together, Minshull leading the way to the smallest of the meeting rooms.

'The main room we use is stuffed with boxes,' he said, indicating an open door ahead. 'We're working our backsides off to get through them, but it looks like we haven't even started.'

Passing the open door, Cora gasped as the cardboard box towers came into view. Another uniformed officer sitting at the box-crowded table offered them a resigned smile.

'You weren't joking,' she said, as she followed Minshull down the corridor. 'How many are there?'

'Too many. Most of it is background stuff collected at the time. But our remit is to go through all of it, to find what was missed.'

The smallest of the three meeting rooms was brightly lit and enthusiastically heated, two features that compensated for the patched carpet and dusty window blinds. Like much of the old building Police HQ occupied, it had seen better days. There had been talk of a brand new, purpose-built space on the edge of the town, but delays and budget cuts in recent years had reduced the possibility to the stuff of whispered legend.

This place had a certain charm, though, in its own faded and dust-filled way. Cora sensed the ghosts of the past settled comfortably amid the tired carpets and well-worn fabric of the building; echoes of conversation and theory held within the flaked plaster of its walls. Unlike the relative newness of her other workplace – bland in its magnolia-and-grey conformity – the character of Police HQ set it apart.

Cora and Minshull sat next to one another at the oval table dominating the room. Only when they were ready to begin did Minshull relax.

'I've missed you,' he smiled. 'I wanted to call, but we had to place a block on all communication out of the building. I didn't feel I could phone you when we'd imposed that on everyone else in the team.'

'I understand. Is that usual, though?' Cora asked, unsure if this was an actual thing or a convenient excuse.

'Not always. But this time it was necessary. There's been a… development none of us saw coming.' His careful choice of words piqued Cora's attention.

'What's happened?'

'DCI Taylor's been arrested.'

Cora stared back. 'What for?'

'She was the last person to see Karl Cuskie alive. CCTV footage from doorbell cameras in the street caught her going to Cuskie's home late at night, then running away. He was found next morning, shot dead. His front door was wide open – just as Sue Taylor had left it, hours earlier.'

'She murdered him?'

'It looks that way. And there's more – they were having an affair. Had been for some time, it seems.'

The weight of the revelations took a moment to rest on Cora.

'I know,' Minshull sympathised, watching her reaction. 'We strongly suspect Sue used her position and influence for Cuskie's benefit. I've just been going through his record with the Guv and it's damning. Only one conviction for a couple of years, then quick dismissals from every other case he was implicated in. He was an informer, always dancing between police and the criminal element in Felixstowe. We're only now scratching the surface of it, but I reckon we'll find much worse.'

'Wow, I had no idea...'

'Nobody does yet. So that has to stay within these walls, okay? We can't risk the media finding out until we know the extent of what we're dealing with.'

'Of course.' Was that a promise Cora could make? The question stung.

'Thanks.'

'Do you think DCI Taylor shot him?'

'Your guess is as good as mine. We've seized her car and there are some items inside it that we think were present on the night she visited Cuskie. Will you take a look at them when they're ready?'

'Happy to.' She offered Minshull a smile, despite the nerves biting the edges of her conscience. 'How are you doing with all of this?'

Minshull blew out a long breath. 'Where do you even start? Everyone's working their backsides off, staying late, getting in early. That would be more than enough on its own. But this Sue Taylor thing has knocked us all sideways. I mean, none of us were her greatest fans, as I'm sure you're aware. But this? It's beyond anything we can get our heads around. And when it's one of your own – it kicks like nothing else.'

'A betrayal.' The words burned as they left her.

'Yeah, that's it. Total betrayal. Trust is hard won in this place – hard won with me, even more so with Joel. Finding out someone's taken advantage of it, flaunted in your face like it had no worth – that hurts.'

It was too much. Cora averted her gaze, desperate to look at anything other than Minshull's expression.

Would he feel like this if he knew about Shona?

'I can't imagine what that's like.'

'We'll find a way through it. We have to – especially now it could be what links the two murders.'

Cora looked back. 'What? How?'

'Shona Pickton.' His eyes raised to the meeting room ceiling missed Cora's shock; by the time they returned to her she'd stuffed it away. 'Cuskie broke up with her on the night of Cassandra Norton's murder. Then, when she cited him as her alibi, he refused to comply. I can't prove it, but I think DCI Taylor might have framed Shona to get her out of the way.'

IF SHE SPEAKS... IT'S OVER.

The memory of the ghost-voice from the older messages returned. Could the notes Shona received in prison have come from DCI Sue Taylor?

'I can't prove it yet. And unless I can talk to Shona I won't know if it's even possible. But my gut tells me it's too convenient to be a coincidence. We found a witness statement misfiled that contradicted the one presented to the court placing Shona as the closest person to the murder scene. Had that been included in the evidence for the trial, it would have presented the jury with reasonable doubt. What if Sue deliberately hid it, to make sure Shona was convicted?'

They knew I was onto them. They were scared. But they're not scared now.

Cora baulked at the memory of Shona's words.

'Are you saying Sue Taylor killed Karl Cuskie because she thought he might change his mind and take Shona back?' she asked, already fearing the answer.

'See, *this* is why I wanted to talk to you.' Minshull's hand brushed Cora's where it rested on the meeting room table. 'I've been trying to tell myself I'm mistaken, that I'm reading stuff into it. But you see it too, don't you? The link.'

I'M WATCHING YOU. SAY NOTHING.
SPEAK AND SOMEONE DIES.

Was that why Karl Cuskie was murdered? And why Shona believed her life was in danger?

'I do,' Cora replied, her mind a mess of thoughts, theories and remembered voices. 'But how can you prove it?'

'I don't know. But together...' He glanced at his hand beside Cora's, pulling it back. 'If you can hear anything from the belongings in Taylor's car it could be a start. And then there's the clothing seized from Shona Pickton's home when she was arrested.'

'Clothing?' Cora's throat constricted.

'Officers found a black hooded sweatshirt and black leggings bundled together in Shona's closet when they searched her home. It proved inconclusive for forensic evidence but was kept along with everything else pertaining to the case. Joel found it this morning when we were sorting out Cassandra's belongings ready for you to see them. I just thought – if it's possible and the audible fingerprints have been preserved – you might hear something regarding Shona and Cuskie.'

Panic surged within Cora. She hadn't anticipated the possibility of hearing Shona's voice from the physical evidence she was here to inspect.

And now she'd heard Shona's voice for real, how could she confirm it without revealing to Minshull how she knew?

'It's a lot to take in, I know.' Minshull was watching her carefully. 'I'm just glad you're here now. You might just be the difference we need to untangle it all.'

'I'll do what I can,' Cora replied, willing away the wave of guilt that followed.

How was she going to do this?

FORTY-ONE

MINSHULL

She was quiet when they returned to the CID office.

Minshull couldn't blame her. He'd had the benefit of the revelations arriving one at a time. To be hit with all of them at once would be hard to take.

Cora had never met Sue Taylor, but she would be in no doubt of the DCI's dislike of her. Taylor's fury when an internal inquiry cleared Cora's involvement with the missing child case that began their association was well known. And Taylor had fought Anderson's invitation to Cora to join CID as a consultant expert all the way to the top. Might the knowledge of that be fuelling her trepidation now?

Or was his mistake in the meeting room to blame?

He hadn't meant to touch her hand. It had happened before he'd realised what he was doing. It was just such a relief to finally have her on the case; to be able to ask her opinion and hold nothing back. The blanket ban he'd imposed on outside communication for the CID team was borne out of necessity, but he'd hated the barrier it had placed between them.

He needed Cora, and valued her insight and company. The more they worked together, the more obvious it became. He was more than capable of doing his job, of that there was no doubt, but having Cora alongside him made it so much easier.

I think you *need Cora.* Anderson's wry observation had cut too close to the bone. Minshull had experienced the loneliness of heading the team and the long hours of work this case had necessitated only served to underline the fact. Now Cora was part of the investigation, he could lay that aloneness to rest and focus on the task.

She seemed preoccupied, though.

Perhaps it was the stress of the ongoing tension between certain councillors and her department over their continuation of the traveller outreach project. Or the emotional aftermath of the attacks she'd witnessed. Maybe, after losing her car to the St Columba Street site attack, and dealing with violent opposition at her workplace, the sudden deluge of information about the investigations was simply overwhelming.

Or maybe he was tired, over-protective of his friend and reading too much into it.

Anderson welcomed them both into his office, where a trestle table had been erected. Seven large evidence bags had been arranged along it, each one containing items collected during the first murder investigation. Beside him were DIs Tsang and Guthrie, invited in to observe.

Another thing Minshull should have told Cora.

He watched her quickly conceal her surprise as Anderson introduced them, her shoulders squaring against it.

'Dr Lael has a unique skillset,' Anderson beamed, as proud as if he were talking about the prowess of his child. 'She's able to sense audible fingerprints from objects, revealing details of the last person to handle them, together with peripheral sounds that can indicate the location of where the item was kept. We've worked on several cases now and each time Dr Lael's insight has been remarkable.'

'Pleasure to meet you,' Tsang smiled, as Guthrie shook Cora's hand. 'Please, proceed as you see best. Just forget we're here.'

Easier said than done, Minshull thought. He'd seen Cora working under the gaze of several different people and witnessed the focus it required for her to block them out. That, coupled with challenge of finding audible traces in nine-year-old evidence, must be daunting.

Tsang and Guthrie retreated to a respectful distance as Cora and Minshull moved to the table.

'Where should I start?' she asked.

'Wherever you feel drawn to,' Minshull replied. 'We can arrange them in any order that works for you.'

'Thanks.' She considered the line of evidence sacks, opting for the largest, two in from the right.

Shona Pickton's clothing. The set found during the search of her home, bundled together as if taken off in a hurry. The last person to open the bag had been the final forensic scientist who had examined the contents and found them inconclusive for traces of DNA.

Minshull recorded the evidence bag number in his notebook, his pen poised over the page as he awaited Cora's assessment.

Taking hold of the bag, Cora looked over her shoulder. 'Ready?'

'Ready.' Minshull joined her at the table.

Cora went through her preparation – now so familiar to Minshull. Pulling on blue medical gloves, checking for any rips or tears. Then a settling breath, a steadying stance, and a moment of stillness before she pulled open the evidence bag. When he'd first witnessed it, he'd dismissed her careful routine as theatre, performed to impress the onlooker rather than benefit Cora. But he knew better now. It was necessary for Cora to settle herself, preparing her mind and body for whatever might be heard within the evidence bags.

There was much about Cora that he understood now. He liked the change.

The moment the bag was opened, her shoulders stiffened. Minshull heard the catch of breath as she closed her eyes. She was still for a long time – searching, exploring, quantifying what she heard.

He'd hoped her ability might function beyond the time parameters she'd previously worked to, even though the idea of audible fingerprints still being present after nine years in a sealed bag seemed unlikely. What was she hearing now? And had it deteriorated over time?

'What can you hear, Dr Lael?' Anderson prompted, ignoring Minshull's pointed look.

'It's very faint…' she replied, her eyes still closed. 'More like a wrinkle where sound once was. I'm going to try pushing into it…' Another long pause, her breathing so light in the silent room that it was barely audible.

Anderson opened his mouth to launch another question, stopped mid-breath by Minshull's hastily lifted hand. Tsang and Guthrie leaned closer, fascinated by the sight of the young woman holding the room with her every breath. Did it unnerve them as it had Minshull, three years ago?

'*Need… to… get… away…*' She spoke the words in a flat monotone, reporting without emotion.

Minshull looked over at Anderson who was studying Cora, his hand curled around his chin.

'It's like a whisper rather than a shout. Or the shape around where a whisper would have once been.' She shook her head. 'It's so fragmented and delicate, like flaking paint.'

'Because of the age of it?'

'Yes, I think so.'

'Can you tell if it's a male or female voice?'

'Definitely female.' Her answer was so swift that it clashed with the end of Minshull's question. She flushed a little, her eyes remaining closed.

'Any idea of the location?' Anderson asked.

'No… No, sorry. It's too unstable to get a hold of the shape of the air. I'm trying to find a way in but…' She fell silent, the effort of her ability tensing every muscle.

'Take your time.' Minshull spoke softly, as if nobody else was in the room.

Cora slowly turned the evidence bag around in her hands.

'Wait… there's someone else.'

'Where? In the background?' Minshull asked.

Cora nodded. 'Another voice. Again, it's the sense of where a voice was rather than a clear sound.'

'Can you make out any words?'

'Hang on...' A frown knitted her brow. '*What... what he...* Sorry, it's so fractured...'

'There's no rush.'

Her eyes still closed, Cora changed her grip on the bag, placing one palm flat on the paper. It crumpled softly beneath the gentle pressure. '*What... he... wanted...* There's a sound like *sss* before it... No – *it's*, not *sss... It's what he wanted.*'

What who wanted? Minshull knew better than to ask for clues to identity now, while Cora was still investigating the unseen soundscape surrounding the clothing items. What Karl Cuskie had wanted? Could it have been a friend, consoling Shona Pickton, as Shona struggled out of the clothes she'd been wearing, desperate to leave?

'It's a strong delivery,' Cora concluded, her shoulders visibly relaxing. Minshull recognised the change in her position as she slowly retreated through the layers of sound towards the onlookers in Anderson's office. She'd described it once like backing out of rooms while taking care to close doors on the way out. If it was hurried, she told him, more damage could be done in the areas surrounding the voices, sounds becoming muddled beyond recognition and her own mind becoming a jumble of experienced sound and actual sound. *Housekeeping*, she'd called it, when Minshull had asked why a measured retreat was preferable. *Keeping everything in its place.*

Minshull waited for Cora's eyes to open, signalling her return to the room. When they did, he rushed to get his question in while Anderson was still considering what to ask.

'Was the second voice consoling the first?' he asked.

'Could be. Although it felt stronger even than somebody getting fired up on Shona's behalf.'

'Someone telling her off?'

Cora caught his stare. 'Or warning her.'

'About?'

'I'm not sure. I don't want to read anything into it that isn't there.'

'Theories, then?' Anderson had left the wall where he'd been leaning. 'Like we do in team briefings. Supposing it was a woman, could the second voice be someone telling her to lay low? Or might it infer the involvement of someone else?'

'If Cuskie had split with Shona because of his relationship with DCI Taylor, might it refer to that?' Minshull suggested. '*It's what he wanted*... to be with Sue and not with Shona?'

Cora wasn't convinced. 'It felt like more than that.'

They observed one another, a charged silence settling between them.

Minshull tried to make sense of what Cora had reported. He was elated that his theory about the sealed evidence bags had been proven – revealing a further layer to Cora's startling ability. But if what she'd heard was degraded to the point of hardly being audible, what practical use could it be to the investigation?

'We can work on theories later,' he said, as much to himself as to his colleagues. 'Are you okay to move to another evidence bag?'

'Absolutely.' She seemed relieved to be asked. Why was that?

'If you could move to the first bag on the left,' Anderson cut in. 'The items found around Cassandra Norton where her body was discovered. Might be best to dispense with this now.'

'Okay.'

While the clothes discovered at Shona's house had been of interest, this next evidence bag was the most critical to the investigation. Minshull had already noted the contents from the neat list pinned to the front of the bag, the items inside packaged separately but stored together for convenience. A cross-body style bag Cassandra had been wearing. A pair of sunglasses found on the pavement nearby where they'd landed when she fell. The mobile phone she'd been holding, the smears of her blood in the spider-cracks across its screen a stark reminder of her violent death. Her clothes were in a separate bag, further along the table, but it was her belongings Minshull was most interested in. Cassandra had likely touched all of them minutes before she was attacked – Minshull was banking on the items therefore being more likely to have retained sound.

The judder of Cora's shoulders when she opened the bag containing the three items was the confirmation he'd hoped for.

'Are you okay, Dr Lael?' Anderson rushed, an immediate response to Cora's pronounced reaction.

'Yes… Thank you,' she replied, her breath in short, sharp bursts, as if she had broken into a run. 'Her scream…'

As one, the gathered police officers dropped their heads.

It was one thing to see the grotesque aftermath of a violent assault. Bad enough, Minshull and his colleagues would agree, even though each one of them had been called upon to witness such scenes, many times. But it was rare to be present at the point of murder, when horrors and pain converged in the worst nightmare.

'Can you sense any words?' Minshull asked.

'One word,' Cora replied, wiping tears from her eyes. '*YOU.*'

'You?'

She nodded. 'There's a tremendous stab of pressure – here.' She placed her shaking hands flat against her collarbone, either side of her sternum. 'It's physical, like a push, but emotional, too.'

'Fear?'

'Yes… And realisation. I think…' she struggled against the shortness of breath, 'I think she knew her attacker. I think it was the last person she expected to hurt her.'

FORTY-TWO

CORA

She could still feel the bruises an hour later, as she sat with Anderson, Minshull, Tsang and Guthrie around Anderson's desk.

Bruises both physical and emotional.

Unlike all the other sounds she had encountered from the older evidence objects, Cassandra Norton's scream had pierced her sub-conscious as if it had just been released. She hadn't expected that. Encouraged by what she'd heard from Shona's letters before, she'd prepared herself for a similar level of sound, with its degraded and fractured nature. The scream had blown all of her careful preparation apart.

Cassandra Norton knew her attacker.

That in itself was more than the investigation had proved before. Shona had denied any knowledge of Cassandra during her first interview. But by the final interview – the details of which they were now poring over at Anderson's desk, her adamance had been broken down to an admission that she'd heard Cuskie mention the young woman's name, which had thrown her into a rage of jealousy.

'So she left Cuskie's apartment, upset and angry, and went looking for Cassandra?' Guthrie asked.

'That's what DCI Taylor implies in the transcript.' Anderson frowned at the text. 'Although we now suspect that *she* had been the reason Cuskie ended his relationship with Shona.'

'Was the only evidence Shona could have killed Cassandra the direction in which she was seen running?' Cora asked, her question a gut-kick to her police colleagues.

'Primarily.' Anderson gave a long shrug as if trying to shake off the mistake. 'But DCI Taylor was adamant that was the smoking gun in the case. Shona ran along Hamilton Road in the direction of Orwell Road, caught by a CCTV camera there around ten minutes before the taxi driver saw Cassandra on the ground and a figure dressed in black with white trainers standing over her.'

'It's hardly any distance between the two, especially if you're running, and a large window of time in which it happened. If she'd carried on running after the CCTV camera captured her, she could have been streets away when Cassandra was attacked.'

Minshull and Anderson sagged further at Cora's observation.

'Did Shona say she knew Cassandra at any point in the interviews?'

'She admitted to hearing the name towards the end of the final interview,' Anderson replied, turning the transcript pages until he found it. 'She said, "I might have seen her in town, I don't know. Or in the paper when she won that beauty contest." To which Taylor responds: "I think you knew her, Shona. I think you were jealous of her looks and popularity, and when you found out Karl was working with her, you couldn't handle it." Shona says, "No. That's not true!" and Taylor replies: "You attacked her because she was beautiful. Because she had everything you wanted."…'

'She was taunting her.' Tsang shook her head. 'And if what we now know about Taylor's relationship with Cuskie was her motive for framing Shona for Cassandra's murder – and Shona, as we suspect, knew about it – this questioning is especially cruel.'

Cora considered the strands of evidence they'd gathered, the weight of her own secret knowledge of Shona heavy on her conscience. Something didn't feel right about it all. Not the intention and the implied motive of DCI Taylor to rid herself of a love rival, which, while horrible, was easy to imagine.

There was something else. A disconnect. Two strands that didn't quite meet up as everyone around her appeared to be assuming.

Shona said she knew who killed Cassandra. And that she had tried to warn her about them. So, she had lied in her interview about knowing the former beauty queen. But was that in retaliation against DCI Taylor, a refusal to give her what she wanted, despite knowing she was likely to be accused of murder?

If Cora talked to Shona, how could she discover the truth about this without finding out who killed Cassandra Norton?

Was Shona protecting someone else? If she had lied about knowing Cassandra, had she also withheld the truth of Cassandra's real killer? And why, if it could have made the difference between prison and her freedom?

'Cora?'

Minshull and the others were watching her when Cora looked up.

'Sorry?'

'I said, what do you think?'

'I don't know,' she replied quickly, hoping it might kill the question in the room while so many other considerations beset her mind.

Minshull persisted. 'You don't seem convinced.'

'I'm not,' she admitted, her answer feeling scarily close to the edge. 'I heard Cassandra say, YOU. That to me implies someone she knew well, not someone she'd barely met. I heard the shock of betrayal in her voice, a sudden, world-altering revelation that hit her emotionally before her assailant attacked her. That level of betrayal isn't there when it's just an acquaintance.'

'Dr Lael has a good point,' Tsang agreed. 'If the pathologist's report is correct of bruising consistent with a violent shove, would Cassandra have known initially she was about to die?

Neither her nor her attacker would have known she would hit her head as she fell. So was the *YOU* an expression of anger at being betrayed, not fear that her life was in danger?'

The detectives considered this.

'It felt like anger,' Cora confirmed. 'Shock and hurt, too, but anger fuelling that single word.'

'It's frustrating we can't talk to Ms Pickton,' Guthrie said, looking at Minshull. 'Have you contacted her solicitor again, in light of the new information regarding Taylor and Cuskie?'

'I haven't, Guv, because we were trying to keep it in-house for now.'

'I see.' Guthrie rested his elbows on the desk. 'It might be worth pursuing once the news is out.'

Cora forced her dancing nerves to be calm as she listened. There were questions for Shona – but until Cora could persuade the terrified woman to talk to Minshull, she would have to be the one asking.

What was Shona concealing? What did she know about Cassandra's killer?

And would Minshull forgive Cora if he found out she was asking Shona the questions he couldn't?

'I think we share this with the rest of the team now. Get their perspective on it all,' Anderson said, checking his watch. 'We only have a few hours left to hold DCI Taylor until we charge or release. If there are avenues we've not yet considered, we need to identify them before we're called back in.'

–

There was a new energy in the CID office when the detectives, Cora and the observers returned. Cora sensed it as soon as they filed back into the room.

Bennett and Ellis raised their hands together, much to Minshull's amusement.

'You should be careful, Kate,' he said, clearly savouring the joke. 'Drew's influence is starting to rub off on you.'

'He wishes,' Evans muttered, receiving a well-aimed paper ball at his chest, lobbed by a mortified Ellis.

Bennett ignored them both. 'I've been doing some more digging into Jake Kilburn. I think he took Cassandra under his wing.'

Minshull frowned. 'What makes you think that?'

'I was looking at interviews the family gave during the seven days of the murder trial and later, when the first hint of an appeal was made public. In almost all the statements they thanked Jake in the list of supporters who were helping to keep the case in the public eye.'

'Which of the family members were interviewed?'

'None directly. Their solicitor read a statement on their behalf every time. But in the photos I've found, Jake is always standing alongside Cassandra's mother, brother and aunt.'

'Was he related?'

'I don't think so. He was included in a list of friends who had supported the family.'

'That is odd,' Anderson conceded. 'Kate, make a note to ask Ryan Norton about Kilburn when he comes in. There may be some familial link we're missing.'

'Imagine being related to that thug,' Evans said. 'No wonder they thanked him every chance they got. He'd probably threatened to break their knuckles if they didn't.'

'There's another link with Kilburn we need to look at, Guv,' Bennett said.

'Oh?'

'Nicholas Wright attended a private poker game hosted by Kilburn the night Cassandra was killed. He admitted it when he came in to reaffirm his statement.'

Anderson observed his DC. 'Is that so? Strange he should be mentioned twice.'

'I think it's more than a coincidence,' Bennett pushed. 'We know Kilburn knew Cassandra, but if he knew her boyfriend, too – so much so that he contracted Wright for work – that implies Kilburn was closer to them both than the first investigation ever realised.'

'Who's Jake Kilburn?' Cora asked.

'Upstanding local businessman officially,' Minshull replied. 'And – allegedly – kingpin of the local crime fraternity.'

'Weird that he was so visibly involved with the family. You'd think a man like that would be keen to stay out of the limelight,' Ellis observed.

Minshull gave a hollow laugh. 'Not as an upstanding businessman he wouldn't. One look at those clippings shows that. Kilburn has always believed he's above reproach – and no charge has ever been made to stick against him.'

'Was he interviewed with Cassandra's friends and family during the first murder investigation?' Cora asked.

Anderson stiffened. 'No. I don't believe he was.'

'We should put that right this time,' Ellis said, offering Anderson a look of apology when the sentiment spoken aloud sounded more condemnatory than he'd intended. 'Sorry, Guv, I didn't mean...'

'No, you're right, Drew. Dave, can you find a contact number for Mr Kilburn and see if we can talk to him at his earliest convenience?'

Wheeler paled. 'Me?'

'Problem?'

'Well, no, I – I just thought it might be better coming from you...'

Cora caught the shift in tension immediately. Every detective's head ducked, avoiding Anderson's incredulous stare. Was Jake Kilburn so terrifying to the detectives? And if so, why would Cassandra Norton's family be so close to him?

The question played on her mind as Minshull escorted her to the car park exit at the back of the building. A taxi rank was only a street away and it was easier to leave by the detectives' favoured exit than going back through the building to reception.

'Will you be okay to get back?' he asked, at the top of the ramp, his hands buried deep in his pockets against the prevailing wind.

'It's only a short taxi ride,' she replied with a smile, more than relieved to be out of the building.

'Must be annoying having no transport. What are you going to do about replacing your car?'

Annoying didn't begin to cover it. Having lifts from Tris and being taken to see Shona by Joss the other day had brought home to Cora just how much she needed her own vehicle. 'When all of this dies down, I'll start looking. I can't think about it now.'

'I get it,' Minshull said. 'Car shopping is the worst.'

'Mind your backs now, people, coming through!'

Cora turned at the sound of the voice to see PC Steph Lanehan heading towards them, a large cardboard box in her hands.

'You doing your weightlifting practice again, Steph?' Minshull called. 'You know, there are much nicer places to do it. They're called *gyms*...'

'Ha bloody ha, Sarge,' Lanehan replied. 'Remind me to give your next comedy night a miss.'

'Want a hand?'

'No. But thanks for asking.' She paused at the top of the ramp and nodded at the box. 'Donations from the lads for those kiddies on the St Columba Street site. Toys and books and craft stuff. Some of the younger ones got chatting to them when they were on patrol. Poor littlies scared to bits.'

'The kids or the cops?' Minshull asked, yelping when Cora's elbow met his ribs. 'I mean, that's a lovely gesture.'

'Well, you got to do something, haven't you? All that crap aimed at them – and police not exactly crowned in glory on that score, either. 'Bout time someone redressed the balance.'

'They'll be thrilled, Steph, thank you,' Cora replied. 'If you ask for Joss Lovell at the gate, he'll see it gets distributed.'

Steph grinned. 'The handsome chap with the beard? Happy to chat to him any day of the week. Although don't tell my Fred I said that.' She began to walk down the ramp to the patrol car.

'Actually, Steph,' Minshull called after her, 'you couldn't drop Cora back at the LEA buildings on the way, could you?'

The PC brightened. 'Course I could. Come on, Doc, let's get you back.'

—

Lanehan's happy chatter washed over Cora as she sat in the passenger seat, watching the frosted Ipswich streets pass by. Despite the optimistically placed air freshener on the dashboard, the car bore the unmistakable odour of use – stale breath, sharp disinfectant and the ghost of old snacks. Crumpled crisp and sandwich wrappers crammed into the side of the door grumbled of late shifts and relentless trouble, tinged with the kind of grim humour Cora now recognised as a binding characteristic of police officers of all ranks.

She'd done her best for Minshull, as she always wanted to do. Yet the mention of betrayal felt by the team about DCI Taylor – and Anderson's frustration that Shona wasn't part of the new investigation – pricked her conscience.

Was she betraying them, too? Working against the team she now felt fully accepted by?

'Traffic's a bit of an arse, sorry,' Lanehan said, stopping at the third set of temporary traffic lights they'd encountered in the last ten minutes. 'Bloody roadworks as always.'

Cora managed a smile in spite of the lingering guilt. 'It's fine, I appreciate the lift.'

As Lanehan concentrated on navigating a particularly twisty stretch of half-excavated road, Cora checked her phone for messages. Tris had been trying to arrange another session at St Columba Street and had promised to keep Cora in the loop.

There was a message waiting for her when her screen illuminated.

But it wasn't from Tris.

> Hi Cora. I'm ready. Can we talk?
> Shona

FORTY-THREE

News report

…And now to Felixstowe, and a significant development in the Karl Cuskie murder case. Matt Warwick has the latest.

'Thanks, Elodie. In the last half hour, a senior police spokesman has confirmed that an arrest has been made in the search for the killer of Karl Cuskie, whose murder shocked this popular seaside community yesterday. Speaking to waiting journalists at the Ipswich headquarters of South Suffolk Police, this is what Superintendent Ian Martlesham had to say…'

[camera cuts to video of the Superintendent on the steps of Police HQ]

'I know many people in Felixstowe have been concerned after the discovery of Mr Cuskie's body at his home in Maidstone Road, yesterday morning. As we promised, my colleagues and I have been working tirelessly to apprehend those responsible for Mr Cuskie's death. I can confirm that a fifty-four-year-old woman from Ipswich was arrested yesterday in connection with the case, and is currently assisting us with our inquiries. I must stress that no formal charges have been made at this point. We will give another statement if and when charges are made. I will be answering no further questions on the matter. Thank you.'

[camera returns to reporter in the street]

'While the police statement remains frustratingly vague, it offers the possibility of a swift conclusion to this murder investigation. South

Suffolk Police are infamous for withholding developments from the media until formal charges have been made, so this is an unprecedented move for sure. People here are hoping that's a good sign. Matt Warwick, BBC News, Felixstowe.'

FORTY-FOUR

MINSHULL

The afternoon wore on, an endless carousel of old evidence, delays and theories. After DCI Taylor's solicitor forced yet another delay, Anderson put in a call to CPS, requesting an extension to the initial twenty-four-hour custody allocation. With less than twenty minutes remaining, the call came back that a further sixteen hours had been granted.

It didn't feel like enough. But it would have to be.

While they awaited the collection of doorbell CCTV footage from six addresses in neighbouring King Street, there was little Minshull and the team could do regarding Taylor.

But there was one thing that needed to happen. And needed to happen soon…

Seizing the opportunity, Minshull ducked into Anderson's office.

'I think I should pay Jake Kilburn a visit.'

'Dave palmed the job off on you, has he?' Anderson asked wryly.

'No, Guv. He'd do it if we asked him. I just think a personal visit might be best. Kilburn was open in his support of Cassandra's family: perhaps us calling on his help regarding the reinvestigation might appeal to his *local standing*.'

'His filthy big, entitled ego, you mean?'

Minshull grinned. 'Exactly, that's what I said.'

Anderson dismissed him with a wave of his hand. 'Yes. Go. Do it now. Dave located his home address thanks to the local

Rotary Club secretary, who was very accommodating. Best to arrive there without warning, I reckon. I hear Mr Kilburn is a firm fan of surprises...'

–

For a man so fond of flaunting his own good fortune – and creative when it came to the alleged truth of his multifarious business interests – Jake Kilburn was depressingly unimaginative when it came to his home. It bore all the hallmarks of a moneyed criminal: the twenty-foot-high perimeter wall, the sophisticated video entry system by the imposing steel gates, even the pair of snapping, snarling Dobermans held on a short leash by a no-necked, many-muscled security guard.

Beyond that, the house was a parody of villainous lairs. A faux mansion with preposterous pillars and portico, a crude dolphin-and-nymph stone fountain in its foreground and terrifying bronze lions atop its roof. A covered pool stretched off to one side, while a selection of expensive cars lined the other.

All that was missing was a boardroom with its own under-floor shark tank.

Although, Minshull mused while waiting for the security guard to call through to the house, there was still time to discover that inside.

'Okay,' Mr No-Neck grunted at him, dragging the dogs aside as the gates opened.

Suppressing a grin, Minshull drove the pool car through the gateway, parking next to the grand pillared entrance. Part of him wished Wheeler could have accompanied him, just to see how ridiculous the home was of the man he clearly feared. Wheeler's reaction to the mention of Jake Kilburn's name had been surprising, especially for someone who'd seen so much during his police career. Had he encountered Kilburn before?

For now, it was better Minshull was here alone. He didn't intend on staying long.

A stern-faced woman met him at the door. 'Mrs Kilburn will see you in the drawing room,' she intoned, setting off at a pace across the marble floor without waiting for a reply.

'Mrs Kilburn?' Minshull replied, jogging after her. 'It's Mr Kilburn I'm here to see. It's important I speak with him.'

The housekeeper said nothing, heading along a corridor that ran from the opulent hall behind the grand staircase into the heart of the house.

Had she misheard his request? Or had the no-neck security guard relayed the wrong message?

Frustrated, he followed the housekeeper until she came to a large oak door at what Minshull guessed to be the back of the house.

'In here, please. You have ten minutes.'

'Thanks, I – sorry?'

Taken aback, Minshull watched the housekeeper stride away. That was it? No introduction? Reluctantly, he knocked on the door.

'Enter.'

In the large, brightly lit sitting room Minshull entered, a tall woman rose from a rose-patterned armchair by a blazing log-burner stove.

'DS Minshull. This is an unexpected pleasure.'

She said it as if she had known him for years, the warmth of her welcome not quite reflected in her expression.

'Good afternoon, Mrs Kilburn. I'm afraid there's been some confusion. It's your husband I'm here to see.'

'No confusion,' she replied, motioning for him to sit. 'I'm Joanna, Jake's wife.'

Still none the wiser, Minshull sat on the edge of a sofa covered in the same fabric as the chair. 'I don't understand.'

Joanna Kilburn reclaimed her seat and folded her hands in her lap. 'My husband is dead, Detective.'

How on earth had that happened? More to the point, how had the news not filtered through to the community?

For someone so officially important in the Suffolk business community – and unofficially huge in the criminal underworld – a secret end seemed unthinkable.

'I'm sorry, I didn't know,' he replied, remembering his manners.

'Nobody does. It was… what he wanted.'

Minshull thought he caught a flicker of disdain in Kilburn's widow's expression.

'Can I ask when he passed?'

'Two days ago. It was very sudden.'

'My condolences.'

'Thank you. He'd been under a lot of pressure with the businesses lately and his heart – well, it wasn't as strong as we all thought.'

Her impassive tone was oddly cold against the warm comfort of the room. Shock could do that to you, Minshull knew. He'd seen very personable, friendly people reduced to immovable, silent icebergs by grief before. And the loss of such a larger-than-life character as Jake Kilburn must have been a blow his wife never saw coming. Not least the logistical nightmare of suddenly inheriting his significant business interests. As for the rest, would that also fall to her now?

'Apologies for intruding… had I known I…'

'You couldn't have known. Nobody outside of the family and immediate circle of friends has been informed.' She smoothed the folds of her lavender velvet skirt with a hand that bore several gold and diamond rings. 'It's necessary. There are certain parties who would take great interest in my husband's business empire. We'd rather keep them out of the loop until his estate is settled.'

She spoke impassively, a sigh threading through her words.

Minshull couldn't imagine what it must be like to have to manage not only the news of a partner's passing, but also the estate they left behind. Joanna Kilburn sat straight-backed and proud in her armchair, but her skin was pale, deep purple shadows smudged beneath her carefully made-up eyes.

His heart went out to her – but the news did nothing for the investigation. Had Jake Kilburn taken details of his association with Cassandra Norton to his grave?

'But those are my problems, DS Minshull. How can I help you?'

Going for broke, Minshull replied. 'We've reopened the investigation into Cassandra Norton's murder in 2015, after the acquittal of Shona Pickton. Going through old press clippings between the time Ms Norton won her Miss Suffolk title and her murder, it's come to our attention that Mr Kilburn appeared to be close to her. I was wondering if you could shed any light on that?'

Joanna Kilburn gave a slow nod. 'I thought that might be why you'd come. My husband was very fond of Cassandra. The whole family, in fact. He saw himself as a father figure to her – her own father was estranged from the family. Not being blessed with children of our own, Jake felt particularly protective of Cassie. He helped her find work, once the beauty contest PR work dried up. She looked up to him, as did her younger brother.'

'Her death must have hit Mr Kilburn hard, then.'

Another sigh. 'It did. He'd imagined he would always be around for her. He was devastated.'

'Did Jake ever say who he thought might have killed her?'

'He had his theories.' Joanna gave a weary smile. 'As we all did.'

'Did he believe Shona Pickton was guilty?'

Kilburn's widow considered his question, her long fingers folding together as she did so. 'Yes, I think he did. But he never discussed it with me in any great detail. My husband always believed in actions, not words. It was why he did all he could for Cassie's family.'

'How did Ms Norton's family respond to your husband's interest in Cassandra?'

'Ah, now that was more complicated. They don't come from money, you see. They were suspicious of his intentions. Not so suspicious when he paid their legal bills, it had to be said...'

'Legal bills?' Minshull asked.

'They took one of the tabloid newspapers to court over a not-so-complimentary story they published after Cassie's death. Suggesting she'd been trading sexual favours for advancing her business interests. Nasty piece, I remember. Tabloids doing what they always do when a young woman dies – looking for the dirt, apportioning blame. I'd like to think they've learned from mistakes made over the years, but it seems to be getting worse.'

'So your husband paid for their civil action?'

Joanna nodded. 'He gave them money during the murder trial, too. That's why they were so thankful in the statements they gave to the press.'

It still felt an odd contradiction of everything else in Kilburn's life, but Minshull had to accept that the questionable businessman must have genuinely cared for Cassandra.

It was a revelation he could never have anticipated.

On the drive back to Police HQ, Minshull called Anderson.

'Well, I never had Jake Kilburn pegged as an emotion-driven philanthropist on my murder investigation bingo card,' the DI laughed. 'You live and learn, Rob.'

'Indeed. But it doesn't take us any further down the road for the investigation. Unless one of the *other parties* Mrs Kilburn mentioned wanting to keep the news of her husband's death from saw Cassandra as a weak spot in Jake's armour.'

'Jealousy?'

'Maybe?'

'Ryan Norton's due in soon,' Anderson replied. 'Kate's taking the lead on that, with Dave as second. I'll remind her to flag it.'

'Cheers, Guv.'

'Where are you now?'

'On my way back. Should be with you in twenty minutes.'

'Good. I've had word from Sue Taylor's solicitor – they'll be ready to go again in an hour.'

'Okay.' Minshull rolled his shoulders as he held the steering wheel, trying unsuccessfully to shift the knot that sat stubbornly there. Today, like every day during the double investigations, felt endless.

And a niggle remained beneath it all: why had someone wanted Cassandra Norton dead? And was her murder linked to Karl Cuskie's apparent execution?

Who stood to gain most from Shona Pickton's conviction and Cuskie's murder?

And did they have other targets in their sights?

FORTY-FIVE

BENNETT

Sitting opposite Ryan Norton in Interview Room 1 was an unnerving experience. Bennett had been on edge since the young man had arrived to revisit his statement. Now, she understood why.

He was the spitting image of his sister.

The team had become so accustomed to the sight of Cassandra Norton from the portrait photo Minshull had attached to the whiteboard – the one widely circulated at the time of her death – that Ryan instantly appeared familiar. Watching the way he moved, his expressions and his physical appearance, felt like seeing the photograph of his sister animated.

Wheeler, seated beside her, had noticed it, too. Bennett was aware of him frequently checking the blank page of his notebook to prevent himself staring.

The saddest part of this coincidence was that it inevitably led to thoughts of the life Cassandra Norton might have lived, had someone not stolen it. Her brother was a successful insurance broker, working for a well-known local firm. He had made something of himself, changed his prospects from those he'd been born into, and wanted the world to know it.

Had Cassandra been allowed to live, would she have been able to boast the same?

It hit Bennett again – the stark unfairness of murder. Those that took lives might lose their freedom if caught and convicted, but they still got to live. For the victim and their loved ones the sentence was far heavier, robbed not just of life but of everything that stolen life might have contained. Achievements never attained, significant life events never celebrated, birthdays and Christmases and anniversaries never observed. But more than that – perhaps the cruellest part – was the loss of the small things: the myriad everyday exchanges, smiles, tears and frustrations never experienced.

The blinks and the sighs…

Bennett remembered her grandma's lament when her grandad passed away. 'I'll never see another blink from him. Or hear him sigh. That's the worst. I think of all the ones I missed before, when I could always get more if I wanted them. But now they're gone – and I don't recognise life without them.'

'Will this take long?' Ryan Norton asked, looking at his watch to underline his point. 'I have a business networking event at seven.'

'Shouldn't take more than forty minutes or so.' Bennett took two copies of Norton's original statement from her folder, handing one to him and one to his solicitor. 'This is the statement you gave us in 2015. If you'd have a read of that now, please, to re-familiarise yourself with what you told us. Take as much time as you need.'

Norton and his brief began to read. Bennett poured two cups of water from a bottle she'd remembered to bring, handing one to Wheeler. It was as much a diversionary tactic to busy herself while Norton and his solicitor were reading as it was a supply of hydration.

Wheeler smiled his thanks and returned to his sparse note-taking.

After a few uncomfortable minutes, Norton looked up. 'Okay.'

'Thank you. I'd just like to clarify a couple of points, then ask you a few questions, and then we'll be done.'

'Questions? What kind of questions?'

'Some new information has come to light in the course of our investigation,' Bennett replied, as reassuringly as she could. 'We need to see if you can help us with any of it.'

Norton's solicitor offered his client a knowing nod, which appeared to appease the young man.

'Okay, let's make a start. In your statement you said that you spoke to Cassandra on the phone, shortly after she had argued with her then boyfriend, Nicholas Wright.'

'Correct.'

'How did she sound to you?'

'Angry. She thought Nick was lying to her.'

'What about?'

'He was gambling. I knew it, Cass knew it, even his mum had worked it out.'

'But he said he wasn't?'

'He made this big *why doesn't anyone believe me* speech whenever anyone called him out on it. But I knew what he was doing.'

'Okay, thanks.' Bennett moved to the next item on her list. 'So, that night, you spoke to Cassandra on the phone and then you say you went to the pub.'

'That's right.'

'Alone?'

'I went on my own, but my friends came along later.'

'How much later?'

'I got there around nine p.m., and they rocked up just before ten.'

'Did you walk?'

'Yes. It wasn't far.'

Beside Bennett, Wheeler gave his notepad a gentle tap. Bennett glanced down to read the note he'd written there for her.

Confirm friends' names

'And who were you meeting at the pub?' Bennett asked.

'Just some guys from college,' Ryan replied. 'Funny, I don't talk to any of them now. We all moved on – a few moved out of town, one guy emigrated to Canada and the others just drifted away.'

'It happens,' Wheeler observed.

'It does.'

Norton seemed to relax a little, much to Bennett's annoyance. What was it with male interviewees? It didn't matter how professional you were, how prepared, how well you conducted the interview – the moment a male colleague joined the conversation, the interview subject would respond better to them.

Of course, it helped that the male colleague in question today was Dave Wheeler. His ability to put people at ease was nigh on legendary – and Bennett had to admit that she'd asked him to join her for this interview precisely for moments like this. As with so many aspects of the job, sometimes it was best to roll with the things that most frustrated you, in order to get the results you wanted.

'We've been trying to contact the friends you were with at the pub who gave statements at the time. Do you have any addresses for them?'

'No, sorry. Like I said, we're all out of touch now.'

It was worth a shot. Moving on, Bennett asked the question she'd looked forward to least. 'When were you first aware that something had happened to Cassandra?'

It was impossible to predict how questions like these would be received, especially when asked several years after an incident, when time and grief had woven layers around guilt and regret. Bennett didn't have Ryan Norton down as someone likely to succumb to emotion, but you could never tell.

'Someone ran into the pub, yelling about coppers and a white tent by the church on Orwell Road. I called Cass' mobile – still to this day I don't know why. We aren't twins, but I always felt like we had a connection…' He took a sharp gulp of breath

– the first indication of any emotion Bennett had witnessed – and pressed on. 'I called and left a voicemail. That was it. The next I knew about it was much later, at home, when two officers came to the door.'

'Why do you think you called her?'

Norton's eyes grew wide. 'I wish I knew. It was just she said she was going out with friends because she'd sent Nick packing. They would have been meeting at Bailey's, the wine bar that used to be on Hamilton Road. She'd likely have passed the church on the way and… I don't know, I thought maybe she'd seen something. I don't think I thought it could be her.'

Bennett smiled and looked down at her notes. Why hadn't Ryan mentioned the phone call to his sister in his initial statement? It seemed a significant omission.

'Did Cassandra have any recent associations, any new friend groups, prior to this? Anyone she'd argued with, or anyone who might have wished her harm?'

'Not that I was aware of. I mean, Cass was Cass, you know. She took no prisoners. She said it like it was and if you didn't like that it was your problem. Anyone who knew her for any length of time had to accept that or move on.'

'Did you ever argue with her?'

Norton snorted. 'All the time. She was this gorgeous, confident beauty queen and I was, what? Nineteen years old? Baby of the family, a joke to most people. I kicked back against that because who wouldn't?'

'What did you argue about?'

'I don't see how that's relevant.' The sudden shut-down after Norton's openness was like a snap.

Bennett steadied her breath and pressed on. 'I'm just trying to put together a picture of your sister so we can better understand what motivations, frustrations and ideas shaped her life.'

'Cass wanted the best. She wanted full attention and got mad if it didn't happen.'

'Was that why she was angry with Nicholas Wright?'

'No. That was because he lied to her. Cass could cope with most of the crap people threw at her, but lying to her face was something she wouldn't tolerate. Nick promised her he wasn't gambling, but I saw him at a poker game. So I told her.'

'When did you tell her?' Bennett asked.

'The day before.' The confession seemed to dim him.

'Where did you see him playing poker?'

Norton shrugged. 'A private meet.'

Had Norton stumbled across the poker game attended by Jake Kilburn? Or had he been invited, too?

The suggestion was as good an invitation to ask about him.

'Okay. Tell me about Jake Kilburn.'

'What?' Norton's reaction was instantaneous.

'We saw some clippings following Cassandra's Miss Suffolk win showing her joining Mr Kilburn for charity events. And Mrs Kilburn told our colleague that Mr Kilburn was fond of you and Cassandra.'

'You talked to Joanna?'

'Our detective sergeant spoke to her earlier today.'

Norton appeared to be stung. Did he know Jake Kilburn had died? Was he part of the inner circle Joanna Kilburn was maintaining to protect her husband's estate from unwelcome parties?

'He's everything,' he said, his voice tight. 'Everything we have we owe to him.'

'Can you explain why?'

'He looked out for us. After Dad left, Cass and me didn't have anyone other than Mum. And she struggled. But meeting Jake changed it all. And Joanna. They helped Cass and they helped me, and then Jake helped Mum to fight a court case against *The Daily Call* for all the shit they printed about my sister.'

Bennett was genuinely touched by his words, by the honest transformation of the brisk young businessman into a grateful, humble human being.

'Do you think someone might have had an issue with how Mr Kilburn helped your sister? Could that be the connection to her murder?'

'There were plenty of people who were jealous, I mean, he treated Cass and me like we were his kids, his heirs. That's got to have put some backs up. But nobody would dare do anything to get at us. Jake and Joanna Kilburn were our allies. They weren't involved.'

Bennett noted down what Norton said, still reeling a little from his glowing tribute. 'I think that's everything from me. Do you have anything to add, DC Wheeler?'

'All good here.' Wheeler smiled at Ryan Norton. 'Is there anything else you'd like to tell us?'

Norton glanced at his solicitor. 'No, that's all. Except... I remember you. I gave you and the other guys a hard time, first time round. I was probably out of line, so I apologise for that. I just didn't like your DCI or the way she seemed to get off on the power of the case. Guess I was proved right, considering what happened with the woman she nicked for it.' He leaned a little towards Wheeler and Bennett. 'She couldn't solve it, so now it's your turn. Please don't let me or my family down.'

FORTY-SIX

CORA

Meeting at Cora's apartment had been her idea. Borne out of necessity, owing to her lack of transport and the willingness of Joss to drive over, together with Shona's insistence that she speak with Cora tonight.

It had to be at night, she'd urged. There would be less chance of being seen.

It was almost nine p.m. when they arrived, just as Cora was wishing she'd opted for a daytime meeting tomorrow instead. After inspecting the physical evidence at Police HQ – and all the conflicting emotions that brought with it – what Cora needed more than anything was an uneventful night, preferably alone.

But the moment Shona and Joss set foot in Cora's apartment, she knew she had to see this through. The intense whispers around Shona were louder than before, more tightly packed around her body as if attempting to squeeze the air from her lungs.

Cora ushered them over to her sofa near the window overlooking the sea. It was clear tonight, the moon full and unhurried in the sky, stars bright. A path of silver danced across the ink-black sea towards the shore, moonlight bathing the roofs of the beach huts in otherworldly light.

She thought of Minshull, and what he'd joked about his evening plans when they'd met earlier in the day: *It'll just be me, a large Chicken Jalfrezi with a Peshwari naan as big as my head and a whole night of crap telly I won't really be watching. I can see it now, a glittering reward I may never reach…*

Had he achieved his dream night-in, unlike Cora, who hadn't been able to stomach any food as she waited for this meeting? What would Minshull think if he knew who Cora's late-night houseguests were?

She kicked the thought away. She had suggested her home for the meeting; she had promised to hear what Shona had to say. Worrying about the consequences was of no use to her now.

'You have a nice home,' Shona began – as good a way into a conversation as any. Her voice betrayed a flutter of nerves, her body language screaming *protection*. Hands clasped to knees, elbows clamped to her sides, her shoulders drawn in, her head bowed. It was as if she were about to contract in on herself, slowly disappearing from view.

Minimising. That was how Tris termed it.

'A physical manifestation of an incorrect inner belief that the person has no right to exist. A drawing-in; a lessening. Shrinking in on themselves so as not to offend those they perceive to have the right to inhabit the space.'

Tris should have been here tonight. Cora wanted to call him, but the urgency of Shona's request to meet and the late hour changed her mind. He would be hurt, possibly angry, but he would understand eventually. Tris always did.

Besides, he had enough to deal with.

While Cora had been at Police HQ CID with Minshull and the team, rumours had begun swirling around the Local Education Authority offices that the four outspoken councillors were planning a public rally. Tris had dismissed it at first, but as the afternoon wore on, the gossip intensified. Several venues were mooted, including the gates of the St Columba Street gypsy and traveller site and the entrance to Felixstowe Pier.

By the time Cora had returned to work, the list of possible locations had grown to six and Tris was at his wits' end. He'd called a meeting for the morning with officials, some sympathetic councillors and community officers. Cora suspected he would get as little sleep tonight as she would.

She wouldn't tell Shona and Joss about it yet, she'd decided. Listening to Shona's story was of paramount importance. To do that, it was imperative that Shona felt as comfortable and safe as possible.

Cora had lit calming candles, placing them around her living room and open-plan kitchen area. Lamps and strings of warm white fairy lights offered soft illumination in favour of the main ceiling fittings, cushions and throws from the blanket box in Cora's bedroom had been added to those on the sofa and armchairs. A large pot of tea on a wooden tray, surrounded by three earthenware cups, had pride of place on the low coffee table around which the sofa and chairs were arranged.

The only concession to the task ahead of her was the lack of music, which she usually played at night to rest her mind. Tonight, Cora intended to be listening as much to the whispers surrounding Shona as to the words the young woman would share. Silence was necessary to frame the physical and emotional soundscapes that would be created here tonight.

Joss smiled his approval at the setting Cora had created, and this act of solidarity was the encouragement she needed to begin.

'Talk to me,' she invited. 'Take your time – we have all night if you need it. You're safe here, I promise.'

'Safe…' Shona closed her eyes. 'I haven't felt safe for nine years.'

'Then let it begin in this room.'

Joss reached across the sofa cushions to rest his hand on Shona's arm. 'Tell the Doc what you told me. All of it.'

'But the police…' Shona began.

'Leave that for now,' Cora said, wishing she could be certain that this approach was right. 'Talk to me.'

'What they told everyone about Cassandra – it's all lies.'

'Go on.'

'All the stories about her being sweet and innocent, all those newspapers calling her an *angel*. They had no idea. If she was

alive, she'd be laughing at them all. Cass liked to fool people –
that was her favourite game. Play the role they expected, take
the piss out of them behind their backs. She was a shapeshifter,
a chameleon. The moment you thought you knew her, she'd
flip and stab you in the back.'

'How did you know her?'

Shona's gaze dropped to the cup in her hands. 'Jake introduced us.'

'Jake?'

'Kilburn,' Shona replied, the name a bitter taste on her lips.
'He liked her because he's a shapeshifter, too. Wants everyone
to think he's an upstanding pillar of the community when he
and his associates have half of the businesses in Felixstowe in
their pockets.'

Jake Kilburn. Cora had a vague recollection of the name.
A feature of reports in the local paper, a name in a caption
under photos of tuxedo-clad, middle-aged men toasting their
own success. 'He runs a protection racket?'

'He calls it insurance. Operated through his company,
Hurren Associates. You'll have seen their posters up around
town. *For all your business needs…*' She gave a bitter laugh. 'That's
how entitled he is: advertising his so-called services when every
business owner in town knows full well what he is.'

'How do you know him?' Cora asked.

'He's blood.'

Confused, Cora looked at Joss.

'Related. Distant, but one of ours.'

'A traveller?'

'Yes. He keeps it quiet,' Shona explained. 'Him and his
family don't speak. Haven't for years. He had a fistfight with
his old man when he was still a kid and they sent him packing.
Sixteen, out on the streets.' She shook her head. 'It happens.
And his dad was a bastard. Probably did him a favour, chucking
Jake out like that.'

'So, if he doesn't talk to his family, how come you met him?'

'My ma knows him from way back. They were kids together. Close, like brother and sister. Ma taught him to read. They kept in touch after he left and he always said it was her faith in him that got him to where he is now. Not that he told any of his business associates where he'd come from. Hid his heritage from everyone outside the community, but exploited it with us when it suited him. He offered me work in one of his clubs. Private clubs, two here and one in Ipswich. Said it was the favour he owed my mum. I was seventeen and couldn't find a job. It seemed like the perfect deal.'

The air had stilled around Shona, the whispers dropped in volume. Cora noted it as she formed her next question. 'How long did you work for him?'

'Three years. It was a good job to begin with. Most of the guests were respectful, I made good tips and I learned a lot. Loved him, of course. He was like the dad my father couldn't be. Jake made things happen, not waving empty promises around when the beer was flowing, like Dad did. I was starry-eyed about Jake. Thought he could do no wrong. Excited for the future, thinking he was going to help me become as successful as he was. But then he started talking about his *heirs...*'

A swell of the shapeless whispers rose up from her feet, circling her body once more.

'Heirs?' Cora asked.

'His chosen ones. The people he was going to leave his empire to when he died. He doesn't have any children of his own, so he said he was going to recruit the best kids for the job. It started out as a joke – at least, that's what I thought it was. But then he started asking me to prove how loyal I was to him...' Tears welled in her eyes, sparkling in the lamp light surrounding her. '*Do this for me*, he'd say, *and I'll keep you on my list...* It was small stuff at first – stealing something from behind the club bar without his manager noticing, bringing him stuff I'd taken from Mum. Like a game. Little shiny things for Mr Magpie. But it didn't end there.'

'He made her steal money from the clients,' Joss growled, as Shona sagged beside him. 'And when she wouldn't do it, he'd blackmail her into offering "favours" instead. Bastard that he is. Bastard that he always was.'

The picture that emerged was of a cat-and-mouse game, the stakes ever higher, as Kilburn collected lists of Shona's supposed misdemeanours, only to use them to make her go further. A vicious circle of cause and effect.

'I was so ashamed. I couldn't tell Mum without admitting what I'd stolen from her, and Jake would come round to charm her any chance he got. She'd never hear a bad word said about him, not even when he sided with Cassandra's family to try to stop my appeal. If I tried to say I wanted to leave my job, she'd send me straight back. To thank him for his *generosity* to me.'

'I'm so sorry that happened to you.' Cora's heart went out to the young woman, aching for the years lost, the injustices served. But how did this link to Cassandra Norton?

'Thank you. I got away, eventually, when I was twenty-one. Found a job and told him I was leaving. He screamed blue murder, threatened to bring me down – everything I'd feared most. But then Joanna stepped in.'

'Joanna?'

'His wife,' Joss said. 'Poor woman. She must have known what he was doing, but she couldn't leave. Heaven only knows what kind of crap he was holding over her.'

'She was good to me,' Shona replied. 'Came and found me, promised that Jake wouldn't do any of the stuff he'd threatened. I never asked her how she bought my freedom. I don't want to think of what she had to do.'

'Did you know Cassandra through the club?' Cora asked, sensing the whispers spike at the mention of the murdered woman's name.

Shona nodded. 'But she didn't work there. She was doing her beauty contests and Jake sponsored some of her bathing suits and gowns. It was a thing back then – girls who wanted to enter the contests had to have business sponsors. I think it was to sell tickets to the crowning ceremonies and get them greater exposure in the press. Cass was nineteen when she won Miss Suffolk – and Jake loved it. Invited her to all his business events, posed for photos with her on his arm for the papers and magazines. I met her not long before I left the club. I wouldn't say we were friends, but two girls in a smoky room full of letchy old men tend to stick together. We swapped numbers and met up for drinks occasionally – at Bailey's, which used to be in Hamilton Road. That's where she first told me Jake wanted her as an heir.'

Cora could imagine the horror Shona had felt, knowing what Kilburn's twisted scheme might ultimately lead to for Cassandra. She saw it now, as Shona screwed her eyes tight against the memory of it.

'I tried to warn her. I said it was a ploy to get her to do whatever he wanted. But she said he was infatuated with her and would do anything she asked him to. I couldn't believe how sure of herself she was. She believed she was entitled to have whatever she wanted, and could wrap any man around her finger to make it happen. But then Joanna said Jake had started talking about Cassandra and her brother Ryan like they were his actual heirs. He was obsessed with his legacy, of leaving his businesses to someone who would run it in his name.'

'Did Cassandra believe she and her brother would inherit?'

Shona nodded, bringing her sleeve to her eyes. 'Yeah. Joanna said Jake was serious. He was ready to change his will.'

'Tell the Doc about the letter,' Joss urged.

Shona's body began to close in on itself again, the whispers pressing in. 'Cass started doing delivery jobs for Jake – part of proving herself as a worthy heir. She'd take threats to local businesses disguised as rent arrears letters, never staying to collect money, just being the face of Jake's racket. They knew not to mess with her because Jake saw her as a daughter. I told her it would end up the same way it had for me, but she insisted she was in control. Then, when she'd argued with him one day, she delivered a letter to the local paper – sent him a photo of her standing outside the newspaper office holding the envelope covered in his handwriting. She'd switched the contents, but he didn't know that. It was only when the paper ran a story thanking Jake for his generous donation to their charity appeal that he realised she'd been bluffing.'

Her voice cracked and she held her cup out to Joss for more tea. After a long, steady sip, the whispers ebbed a little.

'You can stop if you need to,' Cora said.

'No. You need to know this. That letter changed everything. How Jake talked about her, how much he paraded her around. Then Ryan started working for him, running errands, handling bits of business. Joanna said Jake felt like he'd met the son he'd never had. Cass did less, Ryan did more. That was about a month before she was killed.'

Cora's nerves began to play in her stomach. 'Do you think…?'

'You said I couldn't tell you that. Because of the other work you do.'

'I said I'd have to tell the police if you named a suspect. I think you should talk to my friend, Rob. He's a detective sergeant in CID…'

'No.'

'He could right the wrong that's been done to you.'

'*I* righted that wrong. With my KC and his legal team. The police would have been happy if I'd been locked up for life.'

'But he didn't work on the first investigation…' Cora began.

'Makes no difference,' Shona returned, her voice gaining in strength as the whispers began to surge. 'They're all the same.'

'He's a good man.'

'You said you'd help me! You *promised*…' She slammed her cup down and made to stand, stopped by Joss, who blocked her.

'You said you wanted the Doc to help you, Sho. She can't do that if you don't tell her what you know.'

'But she'll run straight to her copper!'

'And what if she does?' Joss folded his arms across his chest, rising to his full height. 'Maybe they owe you, have you thought of that? Maybe you helping them find Cassandra's killer will let them make amends for what they did to you.'

Shona faced him, her breathing hard, hands balled into fists beneath the frayed cuffs of her jumper sleeves.

'You know I'm right.' Joss stared her down. 'This is never going to go away unless you break the chain.'

'They hated me,' Shona hissed back, every syllable an accusation. 'Because I was one of *us*. And it doesn't matter what they say about working for our benefit, it always comes back to this: they hate us, and we don't trust them.'

'That woman was wrong.'

'That *bitch* judged me guilty before I even spoke a word.'

DCI Taylor. Should Cora tell Shona what she'd learned from Minshull?

'She's not part of this investigation,' she said.

'So they say...'

'She's been removed,' Cora rushed. 'The Superintendent saw to it himself.'

Shona's eyes narrowed. 'Then who's in charge?'

'Rob. And his detective inspector, Joel. They're good people, Shona. They want to find Cassandra's killer. But unless you tell them what you know, they might miss it.'

'Come on, Sho. You want this over, don't you? Why else are we here?'

Shona was quiet as she considered his words.

Cora waited, hardly daring to breathe.

'This Rob. Do you trust him?'

Cora didn't hesitate. 'I trust him with my life.'

Shona sat slowly back down. She picked up her cup and drank. Around her the tide of whispers rose and fell, their power diminishing with each wave.

'Jake Kilburn murdered Cass. I'm sure of it. He'd threatened her once before, when she said she'd reveal his protection racket for real. She didn't believe him and told one of his clients what Jake really did for a living. It lost him a huge account and he was furious. Joanna told me she was scared of what Jake would do. That was four days before Cass died.' She looked up at Cora. 'And now you have to tell your detective friend.'

'You'll talk to him?' Cora asked, her heart thumping.

'Tomorrow,' Shona replied. 'You, me and him. Set it up. I'll tell him everything I know.'

'Where? Here?'

Shona shook her head. 'Somewhere public. Somewhere I can walk away if I don't feel safe.'

'You're safe here…' Cora began.

'Outside,' Shona stated, her stare sharp. 'Or no deal.'

Cora thought on her feet. She had to make this happen. What Shona told Minshull could bring the answers he and the CID team desperately needed – and Jake Kilburn to justice.

'I know a place,' she stated. 'Outside, with a main road nearby. If you don't feel safe, you can just go. I'll make sure Minshull is there alone.'

Shona glanced up at Joss, whose tight smile willed her to comply. 'Okay. I'll meet your policeman and tell him what I know.'

It was enough.

FORTY-SEVEN

MINSHULL

Minshull's desk phone was ringing as he arrived in the office. He snatched up the receiver before its final ring.

'DS Minshull?'

'Hi Sarge, it's Lydia Cawley in Tech.'

'Blimey, Lyd, you're in earlier than me this morning.'

'Yeah, well, I wanted to sort the doorbell camera footage from King Street. I can concentrate better when it's quiet. Besides, Adam Orson's taken to bringing kippers in for his breakfast, some kind of odd diet he's doing. I thought I'd get the jump on the stink of fish.'

'Ah, good plan,' Minshull laughed. 'How's the footage looking?'

'I've sent you a clip and four stills. Open your email.'

Minshull did as he was told, willing the cranky old PC on his desk to fire into life. Cawley's email was at the top of his inbox. He clicked the first image open – and lost his breath.

'*Shit...*'

A black-clad figure was captured, entering the alleyway that led from King Street to the rear of the gardens in Maidstone Road. Their face was obscured by a hood, but as they paused beneath the streetlamp at the entrance to the alley, they pulled something angular and sleek from their pocket. It caught the light for a split second before it was placed in the back pocket of their dark trousers.

A gun?

'What's the timestamp on the first image?' Minshull asked, breathless from the revelation.

'Eleven forty-one p.m. It tallies with the window of time between Cuskie's phone call with DCI Taylor at eleven twenty-six p.m. and her arrival at eleven fifty-seven p.m.' Cawley's voice shook with adrenaline. 'Check the video clips.'

There were two attached to the email. Minshull opened the first to see the black hooded figure hurrying down the alleyway and out of view. The second made Minshull thump down heavily in his desk chair.

'What the hell?'

'It's what we needed, Sarge. Timestamp is 12:07a.m.'

'She was telling the truth…'

Minshull didn't know whether to punch the air or drop his head into his hands. The video suggested that the gun-carrying intruder had gained access to Cuskie's home via the rear of the property minutes before Taylor's arrival and had run back out of the alleyway into King Street shortly before the DCI was seen hurrying away from the house in Maidstone Road.

It could be unrelated. But given the timings was that even a consideration?

'This is a game-changer, Lyd,' he said, a little shaken by the sudden turn of events. 'Brilliant work.'

'You're going to let her go, aren't you?' The question had an edge Minshull recognised.

'I think we have to. The misconduct thing will still stand, but you know how those things drag out.'

'What about framing that poor woman for murder? Surely you've cause to charge Taylor for that? Especially with her shagging Cuskie?'

Minshull wished they had. 'Conjecture, for now. However much common sense says it's probable. CPS would never go for it. And while I'd love to see Sue face the music, she didn't kill Cuskie. Our priority must be finding who did.'

'So she walks?'

'Afraid so. Until the misconduct hearing.'

'Suspended on full pay, I imagine. Unless she jumps. Can't say I'll be at her leaving party.'

'Me either, Lyd,' Minshull agreed, the grim joke covering a multitude of grievances.

With only two hours left to charge or release Taylor, a decision had to be made. As Minshull waited for Anderson to arrive, the news sat heavy on him. He should inform Martlesham, too, but not until Anderson was told. Minshull owed him that much.

And what did it mean for the murder investigation?

Now they had proof of a second, earlier visitor to Cuskie's house – a visitor who was still there when Taylor arrived – but with no clear picture of the intruder's face, they were back to the beginning. The search would have to be widened, more CCTV and doorbell camera video studied, tracking the intruder's journey to and from Cuskie's home. Forensics had found no fingerprints apart from Taylor's and Cuskie's at the crime scene. Whoever had dispatched Cuskie knew what they were doing.

And what did it mean for the Cassandra Norton murder? Had the unknown intruder killed her, too? Was there any way of knowing?

It could take weeks, months even, to gather the information required, and even then there was no more guarantee of a result than they had today.

'What?'

Minshull's expression was clearly a beacon, honed in on by Anderson as he entered the CID office.

'Lydia Cawley found our intruder.'

'Who? Where?' Anderson dropped his bags in the middle of the floor and hurried over to Minshull's desk.

Minshull replayed the video, showing Anderson the stills Cawley had produced from it. 'This person pauses at the entrance to the alleyway between King Street and Maidstone

Road here – and that object they're carrying looks like it could be a gun. They don't appear in the Maidstone Road footage – we checked that before right through to nine a.m. next day. But then here, minutes before Taylor leaves, the figure returns to King Street via the alleyway.'

'Timestamps tally,' Anderson growled.

'It's too much of a coincidence for Taylor to have concocted her story so closely matching those times.' Minshull watched his superior carefully, knowing what this would be doing to him. 'We can't charge her for this.'

'She should have reported it.'

'Yes, she should. But we know why she didn't. And as for misconduct, the evidence is overwhelming.'

'So she's won.'

'You can't think like that, Guv.'

Anderson's explosive expletive temporarily turned the air blue. 'She conspires to frame her lover's ex-girlfriend for murder, absolves him of any chargeable offences from then on and seriously undermines the security of CID because she can't keep her knickers on – and we're the ones picking up the pieces? How the hell is that fair?'

'It isn't, Guv,' Minshull returned, trying to calm Anderson down. The observers would be in soon, along with the CID team. And nobody needed to see Anderson in a state like this. 'But even after all that, Sue Taylor isn't a murderer. If you tried to send her down for it, you'd be exactly like she was in charging Shona Pickton. And you're better than that.'

His words punctured the air, deflating Anderson's rage.

'It isn't fair,' he repeated, this time a cry of injustice rather than a roar of anger. 'I need to tell the Super. But if he suspends her on full pay, I'll not be responsible for my actions.'

'We have no control over that. But look at it this way, Guv, if she loses her job, she loses her power. That's the only thing she's wanted since she arrived. And what else does she have? Her lover is dead, her name is mud, Martlesham will make damn sure the press knows what the misconduct case against her will be about. Meanwhile you have your position, your lovely Ros and a settled home. And us lot in CID.'

'Not sure the last one is a particular blessing.' Anderson managed a wry grin.

Minshull mirrored it. 'Best we can offer you, sorry.'

'Guv, I need to say something…' Wheeler burst into the office, coming to a halt when he saw Minshull and Anderson. 'What?'

'We have Cuskie's intruder on film.' Anderson twisted Minshull's PC screen around to reveal the image.

'What? Then Sue was…?'

'Telling the truth? About that, if nothing else.'

Shocked and out of breath, Wheeler looked at the clock over the whiteboard. 'We only have an hour and a half to charge her.'

'Then we need to get a wriggle on,' Anderson replied, snapping back to his usual self. 'I'll call the Super, then inform CPS.'

'Before you do, I need to say something.' Wheeler was flush-faced, but his request was strong.

Surprised, Anderson gave Wheeler his full attention. 'Go ahead.'

'We need to be looking at Jake Kilburn.'

'Dave…' Minshull began, realisation dawning.

'No, Sarge, hear me out. I haven't slept all night going over it and I've debated it to death. Kilburn's behind it all. I know it now, and I think I always have. But I haven't said anything because…'

'Dave, wait…'

'For the love of all things holy, don't stop me, Joel! If I don't say this now, more people could die. And I couldn't bear that on my conscience. See, Kilburn damn well near destroyed a good friend of mine, years ago. And I was scared that if I spoke out about it he'd come after me and Sana and the kids, too. Because that's the sort of cold-blooded, scheming evil bastard he is…' He glared at Minshull's next attempt to get him to listen. '*No*, Minsh. It has to be said. Look at the evidence: he was close to Cassandra and her family, he was present at Shona Pickton's trial, he paid for the libel case on behalf of her family, he employed Karl Cuskie. Everywhere you look, his filthy paws are all over this case! He's the link we've missed. He's…'

'*Dead*.' Minshull stated.

Silenced mid-flow, Wheeler's mouth bobbed wordlessly.

'He died a few days ago.'

'Has it been corroborated? Do you have proof?'

'His widow Joanna told me when I went to visit yesterday. They're keeping the news quiet until his business affairs have been sorted out. Nothing official yet. I told the Guv when I got back, but you and Kate were in with Ryan Norton. I'm so sorry I didn't get to tell you.'

'He's dead.' Wheeler stated, flatly.

'Take a moment, Dave,' Anderson said, kindly. 'Rob, stick the kettle on. I'll call the Super and CPS.'

–

Nobody was surprised by the decision Martlesham and the CPS returned. The misconduct charges would stand and could be formalised, pending an internal inquiry. But there were no grounds for a murder charge. Minshull and Anderson dutifully went down to the custody suite to inform Taylor and her solicitor of the decision.

As expected, Taylor was triumphant.

'So this whole charade has been for nothing,' she crowed when the recording concluded, her solicitor not intervening to curb her celebrations. 'All that time wasted. And Karl and Cassandra's killers still at large. Good luck explaining that to the media. I'd love to help you, but unfortunately, I'm on suspension.'

It was a battle to bar any sign of emotion from his expression, but Minshull did it nevertheless, sheer bloody-mindedness winning over the wounds Taylor's words inflicted. She could rant all she wanted: her position and power were both gone, the driving force of her entire police career. And even if the independent police inquiry didn't uphold her misconduct charge, Martlesham had vowed to personally ensure Taylor was never allowed to work for South Suffolk Police again.

'A challenge we'll no doubt relish,' Anderson replied – and Minshull wondered if he, too, was biting down his anger. 'And I hope you can rest easy, what with Karl Cuskie's killer still at large.'

'A threat!' Taylor exclaimed to her solicitor. 'Did you hear that? He threatened me.'

'You really should get some rest, Sue.'

'It's DCI Taylor!'

'Not any more,' Anderson muttered as he and Minshull left the interview room.

FORTY-EIGHT

CORA

Cora called Minshull that night, after Joss and Shona left. Despite it being almost midnight, she couldn't afford to delay the call. She had kept far too much from him already. Now Shona had agreed to meet Minshull, it was time to put wheels into motion.

'I need to see you,' she said, careful to keep her tone as light as possible. 'I think I might have found some information that will help you.'

'Tell me now,' Minshull croaked, the shock of being awoken tempered by his desire to know more.

'It has to be done in person, sorry. Too much to explain over the phone.'

'Cora, what's going on?'

'I'll tell you tomorrow morning. It's good news, I promise. Trust me, okay?'

Trust me. She winced at the words. Would Minshull trust her again when he discovered who else would be at the meeting?

After the call ended, Cora headed to bed, her mind replaying their conversation as if checking for loose threads. He'd agreed, at least: that was a start. But it didn't make for an easy night of sleep.

Next morning she rose early, dressed and ate breakfast, watching the clock for a suitable time to leave. Her apartment still bore the ghost-scent of last night's candles, the furnishings bearing audible traces of the whispers Shona Pickton carried with her like a penance. Despite the frost etching its patterns across her windows and the stiff wind coming straight off the sea, Cora opened a window, thrilling in the rush of air that burst into her home.

It was a cleansing, a removal of all that had gone before. From today there would be no more secrets, nothing held back. Minshull would get the testimony he needed, Shona the right to have her voice heard. And Cora would be free of guilt for withholding information from the police team she loved feeling part of.

She had arranged to meet Minshull – and Shona – by a small mobile coffee shop housed in an old Airstream caravan that was permanently parked on the pavement overlooking the sea where Undercliff Road East met the gentle rise of Brook Lane. It was quieter there than further along the promenade where the Sea Front Gardens and Felixstowe Pier attracted visitors. It was also one of the few refreshment kiosks that remained open all year round, a firm favourite with dog walkers and brave open water swimmers who particularly loved the over-the-top hot chocolates the coffee shop served and the warm blankets provided by the owners on every blue plastic chair.

It was as open and non-threatening as possible, accommodating Shona's conditions for the meeting. If Shona needed to go quickly she wouldn't have to navigate crowds of visitors to make her escape through the town. And the sea would provide a constant soundtrack, filling unnerving gaps in conversation like the tide rushing back in to flood rockpools and abandoned sandcastle forts on the beach.

She checked her watch. Another half an hour and she would set off.

The shrill ring of her doorbell pulled her back from the open window. A parcel, maybe? She couldn't remember ordering anything, but that didn't mean much when it came to her online browsing habits. Heading to the door, she answered the intercom.

'Thank goodness you're in. Can I come up?'

'Tris? It's my day off – what are you doing here?'

'Let me up and I'll explain.'

A minute later, a windswept Tris blew into the apartment. His eyes were as wild as the wind-blown peaks in which his hair now stood.

'It's *today*,' he rushed.

'What is?'

'One of the secretaries in Roy Alsingham's office tipped me off this morning. I came straight over. They're bloody going ahead with it! When the Leader of the Council expressly forbade them…'

'Okay,' Cora interrupted him, not knowing what to make of Tris' sudden intrusion. 'Come and sit down and we can talk about it.'

'I have to… oh, okay…'

She led him over to the sofa, persuading him to relinquish his jacket as he sat. Then, perching beside him, she took his hands in hers.

'What's going on?'

Tris steadied his breath. 'The public protest – the one the Apocalypse Four have been threatening – it's happening today. In the middle of town.'

'Where?'

'I don't know, but my guess is wherever they can cause the most disruption, where the biggest crowds will be.'

'Hamilton Road.' The main shopping street in the town was Cora's first thought. In the summer, the promenade, the beach and the pier could vie for the busiest location. But this time of year, the busy shopping street with its shops sparkling with Christmas decorations was the obvious choice.

'Exactly.'

'What time?'

'One p.m. Busiest time, biggest impact.'

'And one of the councillors' secretaries told you this?'

Tris nodded. 'Cynthia works for Roy Alsingham. She over-heard a meeting with the four of them this morning, going over logistics. There was some talk of outside help...'

The chill that passed over Cora's skin had nothing to do with the still-open window.

Outside help meant coachloads of people, bussed in to swell the crowds. Sympathetic to far-right politics – or just out for a fight – they had been a problem across Suffolk during a spate of so-called 'freedom of speech' marches. Felixstowe hadn't seen one since before the coronavirus lockdowns, but many in the town would remember the disruption, the threat and the damage to shops and businesses caused by troublemaking thugs laying siege to the streets.

'They don't have permission – it was expressly denied by the Leader of the Council who threw out their request. They're just going to turn up and cause havoc.'

'Have you called the police?'

'I called them before I left. They're sending officers to the main shopping area and reinforcements to St Columba Street, in case the town centre protest is a decoy for another attack.'

Cora raced through contingencies in her mind. Provided the roads weren't blocked off, Joss, Shona and Minshull could still get there to meet as planned and be gone long before the protest.

Minshull...

'I need to send a message to Rob,' she said, jumping up. Finding her phone, she fired off a message to Minshull, then sent a text to Joss Lovell:

> Tris just told me about the protest march in Felixstowe.
> Are you still okay to meet me as planned?
> Let me know – and take care. Cx

Returning to Tris, she placed her phone on the arm of the chair and turned to face him.

'Shona Pickton is coming over to meet Rob.'

'What?' Tris stared back. 'You told him?'

'I'll tell him when they meet.'

'You should reschedule.'

'No – it has to happen today.'

'It's too dangerous to be in town…'

'We won't be. We're meeting at the coffee caravan opposite Brook Lane.'

'No!' Tris let out a frustrated groan. 'There'll be protestors all over town! They can't see her – think of how that would look for their cause if Shona Pickton was identified by the mob! She's the figurehead for their hate – she's been in hiding because of it.'

'She knows who killed Cassandra Norton. And she suspects they murdered Karl Cuskie, too. They're linked, and she can prove it.'

A gust of icy wind shook the window as it blasted into the room. Cora quickly slammed the window shut, looking back at a visibly stunned Tris.

'You're sure?'

'As sure as I can be. So far, Shona's resolutely refused to have anything to do with the reopened murder investigation. But I heard her story last night – all of it – and it could help put Jake Kilburn away for life.'

'When are you meeting?'

'At eleven. I've asked Rob to meet us there. I *have* to be there, Tris. Shona might retreat if this meeting doesn't happen. She might change her mind.'

Tris shook his head. 'Then I'm coming with you.'

'No, you can't! Shona's only agreed to this if it's me, her and Rob. She doesn't know you – she'll think she's been set up and then we might lose her for good.'

'Then I'll follow you and sit on one of the benches nearby. Or on the beach. So you have backup if you need it.'

Cora hadn't banked on a non-dissuadable hanger-on today. She couldn't risk scaring Shona away – she had put everything on the line to make it happen, including deliberately withholding what could prove to be vital evidence from Minshull, Anderson and the team.

'Fine,' she bit back. 'But you stay out of sight. Understood?'

Tris held up his hands. 'You won't know I'm there, I promise. But if anyone tries to cause you trouble, I'll be there for you. For all of you.'

FORTY-NINE

MINSHULL

The walk back from the custody suite made Minshull feel like he had rocks in his boots. Defeat dragged his steps, weariness sneaking in where he'd held it at bay. They had seemed so close to a solution for Karl Cuskie's murder. Now they were back in the dark.

'I don't want to tell them,' Anderson admitted, pausing on the second-floor landing, his hand on the double doors. 'Poor sods have worked their asses off and for what? So Sue Taylor can live it up on fully paid suspension while she waits for a misconduct hearing that could take years to happen?'

'She's out of here, though,' Minshull repeated, his counter-argument wearing as thin as the faded carpet of the CID office. Taylor might never be seen within Police HQ again, but what kind of total nightmare would they get in her place? The position of DCI had hardly been a fertile ground for driven, honest officers in recent years: his own father squatting jealously in dubious power in the role for twenty-two years, swiftly followed by the cheating, self-serving Sue Taylor as his successor.

'Aye, she is. But I know people like her. They'll find a way to worm back in.' He pushed open the door and the two men stared helplessly down the corridor.

'I'll tell them, Guv,' Minshull offered, surprising himself.

'No, you won't. My circus, my shit.'

'You've dealt with enough,' Minshull replied. 'And not just with this investigation.'

Side by side, Anderson and Minshull observed each other. And more was said there than either would ever confess.

'Your gig it is.' Anderson gave a weary grin. 'Best to get it over with, eh?'

News would have spread to the team by now, every detective learning of Taylor's unavoidable release. Minshull braced himself for sullen faces, angry questions and more.

Which was why the sight of the CID team, joined by Tsang and Guthrie, gathered around a large paper delivery bag and a small tower of takeout coffee cups shocked him and Anderson into silence.

'We figured a celebration was in order,' Wheeler beamed, recovered now from his earlier confession. 'So we had a whip-round.'

'A celebration?' Anderson repeated. 'For what?'

'For uncovering corruption.' Superintendent Martlesham emerged from Anderson's office, causing Minshull and Anderson to snap to attention. 'Oh for goodness' sake, Joel and Rob, relax.'

'But we had to release DCI Taylor,' Minshull said.

'You did. But you prevented us from repeating history at a time when we are expected to fail. For that, you have my sincere thanks.'

'There's so much still to do,' replied Anderson. 'Starting the search for the hooded figure at Cuskie's house, continuing the search for Cassandra Norton's killer.'

'And I have every faith in you all to achieve both things,' Martlesham smiled. 'But please, give yourselves twenty minutes to enjoy this. It's been a hell of a morning.'

'Sir.'

'Yes, Sir.'

'Excellent. Now, the pressing question we all must answer is: ketchup or brown sauce on your bacon roll?'

As the team converged on the breakfast treats, Wheeler made his way over to Minshull.

'Bet you a tenner you never saw that coming.'

'You sound like Les,' Minshull chuckled.

'I'm training him well, Sarge,' Evans called, as he passed them with two bacon rolls.

'Here's to a return to normality.' Wheeler handed Minshull a coffee cup, clinking – or, more precisely *clunking* – his cup against it in a toast.

The coffee was hot and smoky, and Wheeler appeared to have stirred several spoonfuls of sugar into it. Minshull grimaced at the sweet hit, even if today it was probably needed.

'I'm sorry about first thing, Minsh,' Wheeler said quietly, keeping his eyes on the smiling, jovial detectives.

'You were right to mention it. You always should.'

'I was so convinced Kilburn was responsible.'

Minshull put his cup down on the nearest desk. 'There were links. It's easy to see how they joined together.'

'But now we'll never know. Without Shona's help.'

'We have to put that to rest,' Minshull replied. 'It's only one testimony. There'll be others. They'll just take some finding, that's all.'

Wheeler appeared pacified by this, a sight that Minshull was glad to see. The DC wandered off to chat with Tsang and Guthrie, with whom he had already managed to strike up a firm friendship.

Minshull smiled to himself.

Dave Wheeler – meeter, greeter and all-round legend of South Suffolk CID…

A buzz from his mobile sounded, just as every desk phone in the office began ringing. The gathered detectives scattered back to their desks, Ellis winning the race to answer the call.

'Guv – we just got word of a potential hate march, happening today.'

'What?' Anderson spluttered, discarding his coffee cup. 'Where?'

'Felixstowe.'

Minshull looked up from his phone as he was about to check his message. 'Felixstowe? Are they sure?'

Is that what Cora wanted to see him about? Had she uncovered plans for the protest rally?

'Yes, Sarge. It's been arranged by four councillors – the same four that have been mouthing off about gypsies and travellers in the papers this week. There's a strong possibility they've called in reinforcements from out of town.'

Minshull's heart sank. They'd largely escaped the kind of protest-tourists the county had seen pre-Covid, but the prospect of coaches of troublemakers bussed into the busy seaside town was unthinkable.

And Cora was in Felixstowe. It was her day off today, she'd told him. After their arranged meeting at the coffee caravan, she said she was going to start her Christmas shopping, maybe treat herself to lunch in the town. If busloads of far-right thugs descended on Felixstowe, where would they likely head?

Hamilton Road. Where she might be among the crowds...

'What's happening with Response?' Anderson barked from his office doorway, Martlesham at his shoulder.

'Two Support Unit vans and three patrols heading there now. They'll monitor arrivals and secure a route away from the town centre,' Ellis replied. 'Two patrols are headed over to the St Columba Street site, too.'

'Okay, good.' Anderson turned to Martlesham. 'What do you want us to do, Sir?'

'Stand by,' Martlesham decided. 'Wait for the reports from the initial response teams. But be ready to go if they need backup.'

Gone was the light joviality of minutes before. The team hunkered down behind the stacks of evidence files, casting concerned glances at each other.

Minshull carried the remains of his unexpected breakfast over to his desk, only then remembering to check his phone.

> Rob,
> It won't just be me seeing you at Gertie's this morning.
> Shona Pickton wants to see you.
> We know who killed Cassandra.
> Meet us both at 11 a.m., please. I'll explain everything.
> C x

'Guv! We have Shona!' he yelled, raising his phone in the air.

'What? How?'

'She's with Cora and she wants to meet me.' He glanced at his watch. 'In an hour.'

'Where?'

'In Felixstowe.'

Anderson swore. 'Go! Kate, go with him.'

Minshull dropped his bacon roll and ran, Bennett racing out after him.

FIFTY

SHONA

I'm terrified. But Joss says I'm doing the right thing.

It goes against everything I said, breaks every rule I set for myself. I have no guarantee they'll be able to stop Jake. Or if they'll even believe me.

But I have to try.

Cass was adamant I was wrong when I tried to warn her. She said Jake liked to throw his toys out of the pram, but it meant nothing. She believed she was above his threats, that he wouldn't touch her. She honestly thought he'd come running back to her, his tail between his legs. But I saw the signs: the arguments when a new favourite arrived on the scene, a slow withdrawal of favour, increased threats to keep her in line. It's what happened to me when Cass arrived on the scene.

Why didn't she listen to me?

I've asked myself that question so many times over the last nine years. How her life might have turned out, if she'd lived. How different my life would have been. Almost a decade of my life lost because of Jake Kilburn. More, if you count the dignity and pride he took from me during the years I worked for him.

Cass believed the shapeshifter Kilburn was, refusing to see his true form. She lost her life because she trusted a shadow that was never real.

I said nothing about this in prison because the letters told me they were watching. I couldn't risk Kilburn getting to anyone I loved to make good his threat. I know the letters came from him. Deep down, I think I've known it all along. I'd hoped Karl would stand up to Kilburn for me, but when he didn't – when he chose that Taylor bitch over me – I knew I was alone.

I said nothing because I had no choice.

But I have a choice today.

I'm just thankful for Joanna. The things that man put her through over the years I daren't even imagine. I'm so glad she decided to confide in me, all those years ago. She gave me the gift of the truth when I was surrounded by lies. Joanna was an ally to me when I was working at Jake's club, and when Karl threw me over in favour of that copper.

She was there the night Cass died. I called her as soon as I got home, and she came round straight away. She said Karl was like Jake – that when they decided what they wanted nothing could stop them.

I was going to run away that night, but Joanna calmed me down. She said that was what Karl wanted, for me to disappear, and that I shouldn't give him the benefit of the doubt. And she was right.

I know what she's had to put up with for years. The decisions her husband has made for her, the times she's had to bite her tongue. And I know that she's been there for me, secretly, under his radar.

So when she called this morning, asking if we could meet, I didn't hesitate to accept. I feel like I finally have a chance to get my power back. I can't put into words what that means to me. Telling Dr Cora was the first move towards reclaiming my life. Telling her detective friend will be next. But first, I'm going to tell Joanna. I know she's thinking of leaving Jake. I think Karl's murder has finally scared her into action.

Joss can't come with me after all. There's a rumour of some trouble at St Columba Street and he has to be there. Lucky for me, then, that Joanna said she didn't mind giving me a lift to Felixstowe. She says we can talk on the way over.

I'm watching for her green Jaguar from my window, now. And I've decided: I'm going to persuade her to come with me to meet Rob Minshull and Cora. She's suffered enough in Jake's name. It's time her voice is heard.

What is it they call it? *Poetic justice.* If the women Jake Kilburn thought he could control end up sending him down, it will be the best revenge I could hope for.

FIFTY-ONE

CORA

'He's still coming,' Cora said, relief flooding through her limbs as she jogged down the hill from her apartment building.

'Well, that's something,' Tris puffed, several yards behind. 'But we still have fifteen minutes – can't we slow down?'

'I want to get a seat where we can watch the road,' Cora called back, wishing Tris hadn't insisted on accompanying her. She needed to focus on the challenge ahead and his relentless chatter was distracting. 'And I want to make sure you're out of sight for when they arrive.'

'Charming,' he returned, attempting a joke.

Cora kicked pace into her steps, kicking her irritation away with it. 'We have one shot to get Shona and Rob talking. We can't afford to lose it.'

'I won't cause a problem,' Tris repeated, as he had several times since leaving Cora's apartment.

You already have, Cora grumbled.

Gertie's was a restored 1950s Airstream trailer, converted into a mobile coffee shop. It had been granted its pitch not long after Cora moved into her apartment in Felixstowe and was one of her favourite haunts. Minshull knew it well, too, having been

336

introduced to its excellent coffee by Cora during their many weekend runs.

The wooden chairs and bistro tables were quiet today, as Cora had hoped, the biting winter wind and thick cloud cover keeping people away from the seafront. Several tables were available, so Cora chose one that had a good view of both the promenade stretching away alongside Undercliff Road East and the intersection with Brook Lane.

It was as good a vantage point as they could get, meaning Cora could be watching out for potential trouble while Shona and Rob talked.

She blessed Tris with a coffee as thanks for agreeing to keep out of the way, then directed him to a set of benches over where the beach met the promenade. He could see them from there without being noticed by her guests.

Then, cradling her own drink, she took a seat at her chosen table and waited.

FIFTY-TWO

SHONA

Joanna is quiet in the car. I don't try to make conversation, just let her drive.

I wonder what she told Jake this morning to get out of the house. Ordinarily he sends one of his simpering minions out with her. Like Ryan Norton used to be. That's how it started off for him: accompanying Joanna on shopping trips and days out, reporting back to Jake, as they all have to do. I guess that's why he stood out to Jake. Spending so much time with Joanna, doing what he was told, never questioning anything.

I hope that kid got away. We never saw eye to eye – what with him being so blinded by Jake's glory and all – but I wouldn't wish a lifetime tethered to that bastard on anyone. Ryan always struck me as too bright to be wrapped up with the likes of Kilburn and his associates.

'How are we doing for time?' I ask Joanna.

'Relax, we'll make it.'

'We won't be long, will we? My meeting is important.'

'Who are you meeting again?' she asks. 'I was so busy talking to that lovely young man of yours that it passed me by.'

I giggle. Joss Lovell is handsome and will no doubt be some woman's dream come true one day, but he's basically a brother to me. 'I'll tell him you thought he was lovely.'

She gives a sly grin – the kind I've only ever seen her wear when she's escaped Jake for a few hours. 'No harm in looking, is there? Always was a fan of window-shopping. So, who are you meeting? Boyfriend?'

'No fear,' I laugh. 'I've sworn off men since Karl.'

'I don't blame you.'

'She's a therapist,' I lie, because any other explanation feels wrong to share. 'I've just started seeing her, but she's helping me work through stuff and it's making a real difference. We have a session on the seafront at eleven.' I glance at her, take the risk. 'You can just drop me in town, if you like. I can walk to my meeting from there.'

Will she take the bait? Beneath the cuffs of my too-long jumper sleeves, I cross my fingers on both hands.

If Joanna talks to Cora's detective, we can nail Jake Kilburn once and for all.

But I need to get her there first.

'No need to walk, I can drive you,' she offers.

It's all I can do not to squeal out loud.

FIFTY-THREE

BENNETT

'It's probably bollocks,' Bennett offered as the CID pool car sped towards Felixstowe. 'Remember that English Patriots League march that was meant to happen a couple of years ago? They promised coaches from all over the UK descending on Ipswich and we prepared all the streets for thousands of protestors. Shops boarded up, Uniform bods brought in from Essex and Norfolk, the lot. And then one half-empty mini-coach turned up.' Her laughter felt forced, quickly ebbing away as she glanced at Minshull's grave expression.

'They're organised,' he replied, glaring at the road ahead as if it might pick up its skirts and carry them to Felixstowe. 'You saw what they did to the St Columba Street site. And what they did to the LEA offices.'

'But we're meeting Shona long before it's due to begin,' Bennett countered, wishing Anderson had picked anyone else but her for this job. Hard to believe that less than twenty minutes ago, Minshull had been enjoying breakfast and laughter with the team.

She recognised the look he wore now – the one she imagined could cut through steel if it were focused on it for long enough. When the DS got the bit between his teeth it was as if a suit of Rob Minshull-shaped armour replaced his exterior.

And when Dr Cora Lael was involved, it was worse.

She and Ellis had discussed the strange tension between Minshull and Cora at length when Minshull was out of the office.

'I reckon he's crazy about her,' Ellis had insisted, after Cora's visit yesterday. 'Total unrequited love stuff. Only he can't admit it to himself because he's scared of letting anyone in.'

It never ceased to amaze Bennett that out of the two of them, Ellis was the hopeless romantic. Maybe she had been one, once. But the rawness of her almost-granted divorce had robbed her of it. Would she ever feel hopeful about love again?

One thing was certain: Minshull's instinct to protect Cora was strong.

So strong, in fact, that he almost missed a corner, grazing one wheel against the kerb as he swung the car around at the last second.

'Watch out, Sarge!' she yelled.

'Sorry.'

'We've still got ten minutes. Hang in there.'

His shoulders dropped a little. 'Yeah, sorry Kate.'

'Just get us there in one piece, okay? You'll be no use to Cora in a body bag.'

The glimpse of a smile Bennett received in return was worth challenging him for.

FIFTY-FOUR

SHONA

We're taking a route through the back streets. I should recognise these roads, but so much has changed in Felixstowe while I was inside.

In prison you see the same routes, over and over again. You don't travel far, but every brick, every path, every window measures your journey. To the exercise yard, to the kitchen, to the library if you're lucky. To the meeting room where for years Mum was waiting, growing paler and smaller by the visit. She seemed to shrink, like the plants that regularly perished on the kitchen windowsill of our tiny two-bed terrace before I was sent down.

I never had this trouble in the van, she'd say about the wilted leaves and browning stems, over and over, as if it was a new revelation every time. *I had orchids there as old as you.*

I used to ask her if she missed the travelling, the vans, the community and the ever-changing scenery. The freedom. But she'd never give me a straight answer. She seemed content enough being settled within four walls. But every now and again I'd catch her gazing out at the moon, or sitting on our back step, ciggie in hand, muttering to the birds.

I thought about freedom a lot while I was inside, too. Odd thing is, it quickly becomes something *other*, something *out there*. Like, you know waterfalls exist, but if you don't see them day to day, you only have the image of them in your head to go by. Something removed from where you are. I wanted freedom, more than anything. I dreamed of it. But I wasn't sure it would ever come.

I sit up a little in my seat.

None of these streets look familiar.

'Which way are we going?' I ask Joanna.

'Just my little back route,' she smiles. 'Jake will only ever take the main roads, the fastest route. When I'm away from him, I like to kick back.'

Freedom. It's different things to different people, I guess.

All the same, we're cutting it fine. I can't look at my watch without making it obvious I'm checking. My phone is in my bag at my feet. If I reach down to the footwell to retrieve it, she'll guess why. Besides, she's braking so sharply at the end of the narrow backstreets that she'd probably send my head smashing back through my spine with the dashboard if I leant down to the footwell now.

She's good for driving me. I can't be rude.

All the same, I wish I knew where this route was going to come out. I can't see the sea yet, or any landmarks I recognise.

I hunker back down in my seat, squashing my nerves down with it.

It's kind of Joanna to drive me, I remind myself again. I don't know the roads like I used to. And my nerves are just there because I'm going to talk to Dr Cora's detective friend. Or boyfriend? I can't remember. It doesn't matter. We'll arrive soon, and when we do…

Oh.

We've stopped.

There's a row of large wheelie bins and cracked yellow paint on the broken tarmac that spell the words LOADING BAY.

'We're here,' Joanna smiles, getting out of the car. 'Come on.'

I pick up my bag and open my door. The air smells of garlic and ashes and old rubbish sacks.

I can't smell the sea. Or hear it. Just the hum of an industrial heating unit and those damned gulls eyeing us from the roof.

'Where are we?' I ask, a slight tremor in my voice now.

'It's just this way,' Joanna says, flicking her oversized scarf over her shoulder. 'I told you, I have my own little routes.'

I hesitate, just for a moment.

Then I follow her towards a brick archway at the edge of the building.

Just her little route. Her small rebellion against Jake Kilburn. Every step a kick in his face. When she meets Cora and Rob, she'll look back on this journey as the one that led to her ultimate revenge: gaining her freedom while he loses his.

Pushing my fear aside, I follow her.

FIFTY-FIVE

CORA

> Hi Cora
> Running late – argh! Just arrived in Felixstowe,
> but my friend got us lost. On our way now, tho.
> See you soon, Shona x

'Sorry, sorry,' Minshull rushed, reaching the table with a red-faced Bennett beside him. 'We got here as soon as we could.'

'It's okay, she's running late,' Cora said, turning her mobile towards them to reveal Shona's message. 'Hi, Kate.'

'Hey, Cora. I'll make myself scarce for when Shona arrives. I just came to make sure this one didn't drive himself off the road.'

'It was *fine*, it was just one kerb,' Minshull protested.

'Only the one? Oh, that's all right, then,' Cora returned with a grin. 'You should let Kate drive. I've been in the passenger seat when you've been doing your police driving and it's scary.'

Outnumbered, Minshull surrendered. 'Yeah, okay, laugh it up, both.'

'Tris is over on the bench near the rocks, if you want to join him,' Cora said to Bennett.

'Ace. I'll grab a coffee and sit with him,' Bennett replied, leaning a little towards Minshull, 'where I'm *wanted*.'

Rolling his eyes, Minshull took a seat opposite Cora. 'Tris is here?'

Cora gave a rueful smile. 'You're not the only one in protective mode today. He was the one who called the police about the protest.'

'Tris called it in?'

'He had a tip-off from the secretary of one of the ringleaders – Roy Alsingham?'

'I know of him. Who else do you think is behind it?'

'The usual suspects. Roy, Julianne Gilbert, Stephen Moss and Imogen De la Hay. They're using Shona's acquittal and the press obsession with attacking gypsy and traveller communities to stir up hate. I'm pretty sure they orchestrated the attack on our offices, although I can't prove it, of course.'

'We're aware of them. Some of the think-pieces they've published in local papers lately are tantamount to incitement.'

'I just hope people aren't listening to them. I don't want to think how horrible it could get if they gain more support.' Cora winced. 'How bad is it in town?'

'Sounds like there's nothing yet, from what came over the radio on the way here.'

'Let's hope it stays that way. Maybe the threat and the disruption it causes you guys is what they're after,' Cora suggested. 'Shaking confidence in everything with the promise of trouble. It's all about power and control.'

Minshull leaned back to look at her. 'I hadn't thought of it like that.'

'It's what I do.'

They exchanged smiles. As they did, Cora's eyes strayed to the yellow neon-circled clock mounted on the open door of the coffee trailer. Almost ten minutes late, now. How lost could Shona's friend be in Felixstowe?

Where were they?

FIFTY-SIX

SHONA

I thought the brick archway led to the street. An alleyway between the buildings.

Another of Joanna's short-cuts.

But there's just a door here.

A dirty yellow door, with a key code box beside it and a padlock hanging limply from the handle.

'I think we took a wrong turn,' I say, my voice shrill now. Too bright. Too loud. 'Maybe we should go back to the car...'

'Stop worrying, Shona. We're exactly where we need to be.'

She knocks on the door, the expensive gold chains at her wrist jerking violently with each strike.

Then, she looks back at me.

And I don't recognise Joanna any more.

She looks pinched, her smile too tight, her skin too taut. Then her lips part, her too-white teeth appearing.

It isn't a smile. It's a sneer.

I want to back away, run out into the light, as far as I can get from this gurning mannequin of a woman where my friend was moments ago.

But there's someone behind me.

'You can't go that way, Shona,' Ryan Norton says.

I start to scream, but his hand catches the sound in his palm as it clamps across my open mouth.

Then the dirty yellow door creaks open and I'm shoved inside...

FIFTY-SEVEN

MINSHULL

She wasn't coming, was she?

Minshull didn't want to be the one to call it. Not with Cora determinedly scouring the road for Shona and her friend. She was so certain, so firm in her conviction that the meeting would go ahead, that anything other than that eventuality wasn't even in her sphere of thinking.

When she was sure of something, she *shone*.

Had it not been for the lack of time available to him, and the pressures of the cases awaiting his attention back at Police HQ, Minshull would have been content to sit here, by the side of the shiny chrome coffee trailer, and watch Cora Lael at her most determined.

But time was not on his side.

Over by the beach, Kate Bennett and Tris Noakes kept stealing not-so-subtle glances back at Minshull. It was clear they were thinking the same thing. How long would they all wait before someone asked the question?

And none of this solved the mystery of how Cora had managed to get in contact with Shona Pickton, let alone persuade her to meet with Minshull, when nobody, not even her solicitor, had been able to track her down for days. How long had she been in touch with Cora? Had Cora known yesterday, when she came to inspect the belongings held as evidence?

'How did we get here?' he asked, at last, preferring this conversation to the one that would shatter Cora's hope.

'Here? Well, Tris and I walked from my place and you and Kate came by car...'

He stepped lightly over the joke. 'You know what I'm asking.'

Cora's smile vanished. 'I can explain...'

'So *explain* it to me. Because yesterday, when you were with us inspecting Shona's clothing from the evidence files, I said how much we needed her input – and you said nothing.'

It was only when he gave voice to the conflicted feelings he'd had since Cora's text that anger began to seep around him.

'I'm so sorry. I didn't plan it...'

'And when I said betrayal was the worst thing about discovering the truth about Sue Taylor, you still said nothing.'

Her smile was gone now; so too her light. Minshull might as well have told her this meeting was futile. He kicked himself for putting her on the spot, but his anger was building, refusing to be pacified.

'I didn't know she wanted to meet with you until she and Joss Lovell came to see me last night.'

'How long have you been in contact with her?'

Cora avoided his stare. 'A few days. Joss asked me to help his friend. I didn't know it was Shona until I got there.'

'Help her how?'

'With some letters. She had letters that had been sent to her, some from her time in prison and some pushed through the letterbox of the flat she's renting now...'

'Threats?' He waited for a reply, but Cora fixed her gaze resolutely on the grey horizon beyond the rolling sea. It was the worst thing she could have done. 'Threats, Cora? For how long?'

'It's for her to tell you, not me.'

'She isn't here. You are.'

'It was in confidence. I promised...'

'Wait – you promised Shona Pickton confidentiality over something pertaining to the investigation we're working on?'

'Keep your voice down,' she hissed, casting a glance in the direction of an older couple, two tables away.

'Tell me,' he whispered back.

'Shona's going to tell you. Because I persuaded her last night, along with Joss. Which is the only reason I agreed to talk to her in the first place.'

'You should have told me.' The crack at the end of his words was telling, giving her too much power.

'I'm telling you now. Without me, Shona wouldn't be talking to you at all.'

'Well, forgive me for not recognising your brilliance,' Minshull shot back, hating his response. 'Tell me, what magic words did you incant to get her to change her mind?'

Hurt, Cora lifted her chin. 'I told her I trusted you with my life.'

The volley hit him like a thunderbolt.

'I—'

'But that's immaterial now, isn't it? Because she isn't coming.'

Cora kicked back her chair and stalked away along the promenade.

Helpless to change what just happened, Minshull watched her leave.

FIFTY-EIGHT

SHONA

My arm hurts when I try to move it. I think it might be broken.

I'm in a bright office, on the floor, with my back against a tall grey filing cabinet. And Ryan Norton is sitting in a chair opposite, a black handgun trained on me.

It's the last place I expected to be.

When he shoved me through the yellow door, I thought I'd be in a dark, dank cellar, or a locked outbuilding. But instead, there was a stairwell. Joanna dragged me up to the first floor, to an office that I recognised. Not from the interior, but from the name picked out in gold letters across the window – in reverse from this side:

S E T A I C O S S A N E R R U H

I can't see out of the window from where Ryan threw me. But I know exactly what's outside.

Hamilton Road. The main shopping street. The place where Cassandra was supposedly heading the night she was murdered.

Why have they brought me here?

If I can sneak my hand into my bag that's lying beside me, when they aren't watching me so closely, I can try to get word to Cora. She must be wondering where I am.

But I can't do it yet. They're watching me.

'I need to see my therapist,' I say. 'She'll be worried about me.'

Ryan gives a shrug.

I look to Joanna instead. 'You were taking me to meet her.'

'No, I don't think I was,' she says.

'Why is Ryan here?'

'I work here,' he replies.

Hurren Associates. Jake Kilburn's insurance company. Since when has Ryan Norton worked here? The last I heard, Kilburn was training him as a runner, someone who could take messages and do odd jobs for him. Only the top dogs work at Hurren Associates.

But I've been away for almost a decade, haven't I? Anything could have changed in that time. Ryan is no longer the short, skinny little blond kid who was as tall as me. He's taller now. And strong. The kind of qualities Jake Kilburn wants for his so-called insurance brokers.

He's moulded himself into the perfect heir. Jake must be thrilled.

Another idea occurs to me. 'Where's Jake?' I ask. 'Is this his idea of a sick joke?'

They don't reply. Their silence is taut, like the air before a thunderstorm.

Why won't they say anything?

'What's going on?' I ask, keeping my eyes on the gun in Ryan's hands. I think I have a right to know, even though I'll never trust anything Joanna Kilburn says ever again. 'I don't understand. Please, Joanna. Tell me why I'm here.'

'Because you got out,' she says, like it's the most rational reason.

'Got out of where?'

'You could have just stayed there. Twenty-two years, less with a bit of good luck and a sympathetic probation hearing, out in fifteen if you were really lucky. You're a young woman. You could have afforded the time.'

'I didn't kill Cassandra.' I'm appealing directly to her brother now. 'You know I didn't, Ryan.'

He says nothing.

'Of course you didn't,' Joanna states. 'You weren't anywhere near where she died.'

Finally, the truth!

'You know exactly where I was, Joanna. You came to see me, the night I broke up with Karl. The night Cass died. You said I was better off without him, that Jake would be pleased we weren't together any more. That it was what he wanted...'

'What he wanted.' Joanna gives a bitter laugh. The sound grates when I hear it. 'It was always what Jake wanted. It was all about being the heir, wasn't it? The lengths you'd all go to win the prize. To be his heir, his kid. It was too bloody easy because of how greedy you all were. Vicious, grabby little shits who'd stop at nothing to get what you wanted. Just like him.'

Ryan says nothing, but indignance swells inside me. 'I wasn't anything like him! I tried to warn Cass of the fire she was playing with. I could see it coming. Because I knew what a bastard Jake is.'

'*Was*.' Ryan says, quietly.

My heart slams in my chest. 'What?'

'Jake's dead,' Joanna states. 'Just like Cass and Karl. So now it's down to us three.'

FIFTY-NINE

CORA

The wind was strengthening now, whipping spray from the peaks of white waves that relentlessly pummelled the shoreline. Even the hardiest customers at Gertie's were admitting defeat, scurrying away to their cars parked on the seafront or the warmth of their hotels.

Cora felt she should be hurrying away, too, beating a retreat to her apartment. But remain she must, in case Shona found her way here. An hour since her last message, Cora's replies to her had gone unanswered, her calls straight to voicemail.

Something was wrong. She knew it. Shona had every intention of being here.

Minshull was still sitting at the table, refusing to look at her. She'd expected as much, but seeing his reaction was the worst. She went against her better judgement because she believed she could bring Shona into the case. But all that happened was that she'd damaged his trust, risking her place on the CID team into the bargain, all with nothing to show for it.

Except she couldn't shake the feeling that this wasn't what Shona wanted.

Finding Joss Lovell's number in her phone, she placed a call, turning her back to the approaching storm to have a hope of hearing him.

'Hi Doc. Did it go okay?' Hope filled his words; nerves, too.

'She never arrived,' she replied, hating the bad news as she delivered it.

'No, that's not possible. She was heading straight for you.'

'The last I heard was a text message an hour ago, saying her friend had got a little lost in Felixstowe, but they were on their way.'

Joss didn't reply immediately, the sound of loud conversation swelling in place of his voice. 'Hang on, let me just move...' The sound ebbed away, replaced by the thud of footsteps and the stabs of focused breath. 'Have you tried calling her?'

'I've left messages. I just wondered if you might have had more luck than me.'

'I haven't heard anything since she left with Joanna.'

'Joanna?'

'Her friend, the one who offered to drive her over when I couldn't.' Another pause. 'Wait – how do you get lost in Felixstowe?'

'I don't know, it feels wrong. I'm worried something's happened, Joss.'

'Is your detective still with you?'

Cora looked back to Minshull, who had his back to her, his shoulders hunched against the elements. 'Yes. But he can't stay long. And the protest is due to start soon.'

'Tell him we need his help. I saw the woman Shona went off with. She looked like she knew *exactly* where she was going.'

Minshull looked up in surprise when Cora raced back to their table. 'Joss doesn't know where she is. He said the woman who was giving Shona a lift here looked like she knew where she was going.'

'Did he catch her name?'

'Joanna. No surname, but he said she was an old friend from years ago.'

She saw the click of Minshull's mind register in his expression, the sudden setting of his jaw. 'Joanna Kilburn.'

'I don't know. Wait – Jake Kilburn's wife?'

Jake Kilburn murdered Cass. I'm sure of it...

355

Suddenly, Cora understood. 'Shona was going to tell you she believes Jake Kilburn killed Cassandra Norton. He had some twisted scheme where he promised young people the chance to inherit his empire, playing them off against one another. Shona was part of it for a while – the chosen one to lead Kilburn's empire. But she fell out of favour when Cassandra arrived. On the night Cassandra died, Shona tried to warn her what was coming. She could see Kilburn's favour passing to her brother, Ryan, but Cassandra was convinced she had Kilburn under control. She believes Kilburn ordered the hit on Karl Cuskie, too. Because he knew too much… What is it? What's the matter?'

Minshull wore a look of pure horror. 'Jake Kilburn is dead.'

'What?'

'He died a few days ago. But his wife is very much alive. If she thinks Shona knows too much that would give her a strong motive for taking her out of the picture. She told me she'd kept news of Jake's death quiet to stop certain parties from claiming a stake in her husband's business empire… And Ryan Norton works for Kilburn's company as an insurance broker.'

'Hurren Associates,' Cora confirmed, the threads beginning to meet. 'Shona said it was a front for a protection racket. She'd hoped that Ryan was no longer involved…'

Minshull was standing now, phone in hand. 'We need to call it in. Kate!'

Over on the bench by the shore, Bennett stood, Tris following suit. Seeing Minshull's signal, both began to race over.

'Why?' Cora asked, her own gut confirming danger was approaching.

'Because if Cuskie is dead and Jake Kilburn is dead, it can only mean one thing: Shona is next.'

Fear and dread engulfed Cora as she watched Minshull call Anderson.

'Guv,' he barked into the phone. 'We need everyone you can send down here. Shona Pickton has disappeared with Joanna Kilburn in Felixstowe. We believe her life is in danger.'

SIXTY

BENNETT

They piled into the pool car and drove as far as they could. When traffic began to slow to a crawl in front of them, Bennett parked the car and they ran. The four of them, tearing along the road, heading for the centre of town. The gathering storm was at their backs – and Bennett prayed it would give them an advantage.

Dr Tris Noakes was at her heels, Minshull and Cora out in front. None of them knew where they would start looking once they reached the town centre, only that it made sense to run that way.

Bennett couldn't work out what Minshull had said to make Cora storm off earlier. One minute they had been chatting at the table, the next Cora was staring out at the sea with Minshull glaring after her.

Tris Noakes had been worried about Cora, too, but Bennett knew he was very protective of her. What was the deal there, she wondered, as they ran. Did Tris even like Minshull? He'd been watching them like hawks the whole time he and Bennett were sitting together on the bench. She could have been telling him the location of the Holy Grail and he wouldn't have heard it.

Must be nice to have two people looking out for you, Bennett thought.

She'd be happy with just one.

As they neared the junction of Gainsborough Road with Hamilton Road, the noise began. Thudding dance music, shouts, jeers.

The protest.

Bennett caught sight of a patrol car parked across the junction, four uniformed officers in fluorescent jackets and thick stab vests standing shoulder to shoulder, blocking the entrance of the road from passing protestors. PC Steph Lanehan raised her hand as Bennett, Minshull, Tris and Cora headed for them.

'Bloody nightmare this is,' she grimaced.

Minshull came to a halt beside her, placing his hands on his knees as he regained his breath. 'How many are there?'

'Not as many as those cocky bastards told everyone there'd be,' Lanehan replied. 'Probably saw the weather forecast and decided to give it a miss. Proper cry-babies in winter rain, I heard.'

'Better than we'd hoped, then.'

'I'd say that, but the idiots that did turn up are taking over the street.'

Bennett followed Lanehan's pointing finger. Sure enough, one end of Hamilton Road was gridlocked with rowdy, placard-toting protestors, the local shoppers scurrying quickly out of their way. Someone with a loudhailer was trying to direct the crowd in shouting derogatory chants, while others blew whistles and kicked at anything in their path.

Bennett watched Cora, who was staring blankly into the crowd. What could she hear behind the sound and fury?

'Where to now, Sarge?' she asked Minshull, who was scanning the street.

'We could split up and search the backstreets off this road,' he suggested. 'The Guv, Drew and Dave are heading here now, Steph. When they arrive, can you let them know Shona Pickton has been abducted and we need to find her?'

'No problem, Sarge.'

Minshull glanced at his phone. 'Okay, this in from the vehicle team: Joanna Kilburn drives a custom British Racing Green Jaguar E-Pace. That's the vehicle we're looking for.'

Bennett and the others nodded together.

'Sarge.'

'Rob'.

'Kate, you and Tris take the right side of the street; Cora, we'll take the left.'

Bennett watched for any hint of protest from Cora, but there was none. Sharing a fist-bump with Tris, they split from the other two and set off down the street.

SIXTY-ONE

SHONA

'I don't believe you.' My voice is a mouse cry, a butterfly lament.

'Believe what you like. Jake is dead and now I decide his heir.'

The *heir*. The hook Jake used to coerce us into acting out any whim of his.

'It's all about loyalty, isn't it? He had you fighting over each other to become the chosen one. You remember those trials, don't you, Shona? Tell me, what did you do to be Jake's heir?'

I don't want to remember what I did. Images of it haunt me every single day. I don't want to think of his clients' grabbing hands, their filthy mouths. The pain…

'How did Jake die?' I ask, still not believing it.

'He died as a test, didn't he, Ryan?' Joanna smiles. 'The ultimate sacrifice: killing your idols.'

Ryan glares at her. Says nothing. The gun dips in his hands.

Suddenly, it becomes horrifically clear. 'You killed him, Joanna.'

'Not me. I didn't have to prove anything to anyone. Unlike *some* people.'

Ryan shifts.

'His first attempt wasn't impressive, but he's learning. That was always the difference between the two of you: Ryan never gave up.'

Cassandra's brother. The new favoured one I warned her about. The one now promoted to work for Jake Kilburn's flagship business.

'You killed Cass first,' I breathe, pain in my heart like I've never felt.

Because it all makes sense. Ryan was my height when Cass died. Blond hair like mine. Some of the clients mistook us for brother and sister. When I went to warn Cass, earlier that day, she told me that she wasn't worried about Ryan. They were going to meet soon and clear the air between them, like they always had since they were kids.

I didn't think she meant the day she died.

Why am I only remembering this now?

'I told Cass to get out,' I spit back at him, ignoring Joanna. Whatever lies she spun around him to get him to hate his sister, he needs to know the truth. 'I went to her house, that morning, and begged her to leave Jake and all of his HEIR programme shit. I told her she was in danger. That she could die.'

The smallest crease appears in Ryan's brow. 'You're lying.'

'It's the truth.'

'Ignore her,' Joanna growls, but I'm not about to listen to her.

'We might never have been friends, but I cared what happened to her. I didn't want her life ruined. I never wanted her dead.' I seek out his expression, willing him to listen to me. Even though he's a killer. Even though he murdered Cass. 'You know I didn't.'

'Liability,' Joanna hisses. I have never seen so much hate in that woman's face. Why did I ever think she was a friend? 'That's all you ever were, Shona, and that's all you'll ever be.'

'And Karl? Was he a liability, too?' I'm terrified, but I have to know.

'He knew too much. Him and his filthy copper lover. Thought it kept him safe from us. Insurance against the consequences. Karl should have known better. You should all have known better.'

You.

Not a slip of the tongue. Deliberate, targeted, inescapable…

It begins as a single stab of pain. Then it builds, block by block, cords of burning rage tacking onto the central source. With it comes a swell of hopelessness, stronger than I felt in my earliest days in prison.

I know why they brought me here.

Why Ryan has a gun aimed at me.

Why Joanna is watching.

I'm here for the same reason, aren't I?

'Murderer,' I say, my voice low.

'What did you say?'

I fix my stare on his. Send every last syllable straight into his brain. I stare at Ryan Norton and aim nine years of injustice and hate at the man who plans to kill me. Jake Kilburn's heir. Joanna's chosen one.

'Murderer... Murderer... *Murderer.*'

One for each life he's stolen. Cassandra Norton. Karl Cuskie. Jake Kilburn.

And one for me:

'*MURDERER.*'

'Shut up! Just shut up!' he yells, pointing the gun at my head.

I close my eyes.

SIXTY-TWO

CORA

Sound beset her on all sides. Dizzying, disorientating waves of thick physical and emotional noise that punched the air from Cora's lungs.

She and Minshull hurried through the crowd of Christmas shoppers and protestors, curious onlookers and worried visitors. Cora pushed at the constant jostle of shouts, grievances, frustrations and seething hate. Ahead, shaven-headed marchers elbowed people out of their way, the atmosphere around them charged with electricity. One of them jabbed an elbow into her side and she staggered – the street spinning as her balance faltered.

'Cora...'

Warmth cocooned her left hand – and when she looked down she saw Minshull's fingers closed around hers. Letting herself be led, they pressed on together.

She had been in crowds before, at gigs and festivals in her teenage years and football matches with her late father, Bill. In all of those, the soundscapes had been lineal, clear lines of audible connection between the audience and what they were watching. Sound lines like those were easier to control, Cora simply reducing the level of sound like moving volume sliders down on a sound desk.

Here, so many conflicting factors were at work that finding strands of sound to mute was like trying to pull loose threads from a tangled ball of wool. It was an overwhelming, all-encompassing onslaught, and for the first time in years she found herself utterly lost in it.

It was only when Minshull ducked down a side alley and Cora followed that the power of Hamilton Road's sound realm began to lessen.

'There's a narrow road leading to the back of the shop units here,' he said. 'We can get a good look at any vehicles parked along it, too.' He squeezed her fingers, still connected to his. 'Are you okay?'

'The noise...' Cora replied. 'I can sort it, though. Let's keep going.'

She let her hand fall away, the rush of cold air stark where their skin had been touching.

They sprinted down the back street, running parallel with the pedestrianised section of Hamilton Road, noting any vehicles parked on the kerb or in one of the small loading bays beside large, industrial wheelie bins, many of which bore the bumps, dents and scratches of years of use.

The noise from Hamilton Road was blocked a little by the row of buildings, but punctuated by bursts of sound from each of the properties, much like the patchwork of sound that would come from walking along the shopfronts. Grumbles from the industrial bins, fragments of conversation from the scraps blowing in tiny hurricanes around the cracked concrete parking places.

But no sense of Shona Pickton.

'Wait,' she said, slowing to a walk, as Minshull turned back to meet her. 'If we keep doing this we could miss her. There are too many possibilities – and that's considering we're starting in the right area. We've no guarantee she's even on this road.'

'Hang on...' Sudden revelation illuminated Minshull's features. 'That's it!'

'Sorry?'

'*On this road...* We know there's a link to Jake Kilburn *on Hamilton Road*. I can't believe I didn't think of it first.'

'Rob, what are you…?' Cora began, confused.

But Minshull was no longer listening. Pressing his phone to his ear, he paced in circles until the call connected. 'Kate, what number on Hamilton Road is Jake Kilburn's insurance company's office?' He waited a moment more. 'Brilliant. Head there. And tell Dave, Drew and the Guv that's where we're going. Fast as you can.' Ending the call, he faced Cora. 'Unit 48A. That's where we start looking.'

Realisation dawned on Cora as they began to run. The centre of Jake Kilburn's legitimate business empire was above a shop in Hamilton Road. It had an unusual name, the kind that catches your eye as you're walking through town, one of countless tiny signposts your mind subconsciously maps to confirm where in the world you are.

Hurren Associates.

It had first caught Cora's eye because one of the children she was working with who had been bullied at school had that name. His teacher told her that Hurren was an old Suffolk nickname, meaning someone with messy or shaggy hair – a source of great amusement to her because the Hurren in Cora's professional care loved his sharp grade-one buzzcut.

Emerging back onto the pedestrianised area of Hamilton Road, Cora braced her body against the blows of sound. A group of counter-protestors had arrived now – greater in number than the original protestors, it had to be said – engaged in heated chants calling for tolerance and justice.

As they reached the address with the brightly decorated gift shop beneath, Cora and Minshull stopped. A light was on in the window directly over the shop, the hand-painted letters of the business glowing across its glass.

'That's it,' Minshull said. 'And it looks like it's accessed by that door to the right of the shop window.'

Sure enough, a narrow, yellow door was situated in the wall between the gift shop and the menswear retailer next door. Mounted on the dusty yellow paintwork was a faded black cast-iron handle; above it a tarnished brass number set, reading *48A*.

Minshull made his way to it, as Ellis, Wheeler, Bennett and Tris Noakes emerged from the crowd.

'Careful, Guv,' Wheeler warned. 'You don't want to spook them if they're inside.'

'Noted,' Minshull said, taking hold of the handle. Slowly, tiny movement by tiny movement, breath held, he began to depress the handle, which stuck at first, then started to move…

…just as a loud gunshot and an explosion of glass erupted from the first-floor window…

SIXTY-THREE

SHONA

There are screams outside the window. Loud wails and sobs. Panic, pain and fear.

But inside the brightly lit office, it's surprisingly calm.

I feel like I'm floating above my body, scanning the lines of the blue carpet tiles towards the shattered glass. I watch a thick stream of dark blood meeting crystal clear shards across the blue, rivulets of life ebbing away.

It wasn't how I thought it might be.

I'm not scared. Not at all. And at the centre of my being there's a lightness I've never felt before.

Right until Ryan pulled the trigger, I feared the worst. I knew I was going to die – and I prayed it would be quick. Over in a heartbeat. Done.

Was it like that for Karl? Or Cass? Or Jake?

Now, time is blooming, expanding, like the gentle opening of a delicate flower. I relax into it, let it carry me wherever it wants.

Freedom.

It's in my blood.

From my mum to my baba before her.

But I never understood how it really felt – not until now.

All my life, I've been surrounded by the opinions of others. Whispers, pervading and insidious, snaking around me like a boa constrictor, tightening and squeezing and misshaping me until I don't recognise what remains. Expectations, but never of anything good. Ambitions, but never mine. Plans to control and shape, alter and move me against my will. Squeeze me tighter. Twist me until I break.

They wanted me to contort myself into a killer's form. They forced me into the mould, and the media joined the sport. They never wanted me to get out, to demand justice or seek answers.

It's over.

Finally.

I'm free.

Somewhere in this space, somebody is crying. And far in the distance – though I can't tell where – there's the sound of approaching thunder...

SIXTY-FOUR

CORA

The door from the street shattered inwards, throwing splinters of old yellow painted wood across the stairwell. Ellis and Minshull were first in – followed by Cora, with Wheeler and Tris bringing up the rear.

The stairs were cramped and narrow, hardly accommodating five grown adults. The loud drumming of their boots on the stairs must have sounded like an army approaching at pace.

Not waiting for any kind of conversation, Minshull shouldered the door to the first-floor office, the nameplate upon it half slipping off its fixings.

RYAN NORTON – Broker of Insurance

Bursting into the office, Minshull, Ellis and Cora stopped dead.

The scene that met them was carnage.

Shattered glass everywhere. Blood in pools and spattered across the white paint of the large bay window. Ryan Norton curled in a ball, sobbing. Shona Pickton lying on her back, one arm thrown over her eyes.

And Joanna Kilburn, a single gunshot wound to her forehead, crumpled in a sitting position, surrounded by dark blood and glass shards that shone like diamonds.

A black handgun lay on its side, not far from Norton. Ellis kicked it out of reach, sending it skidding beneath an office desk. As Tris watched helplessly from the doorway, Wheeler approached Norton with Bennett. Cora and Minshull hurried to Shona's side.

The image of the woman who, hours ago, had trusted Cora to set up a meeting with the police, swam now in Cora's sight as hot tears flooded her eyes. Minshull knelt beside her, searching for a pulse in Shona's wrist.

The chaos of the scene outside in Hamilton Road still raged beyond the window. But it was the sound inside the office that stopped Cora's breath.

The whispers were gone.

Shona's body lay in perfect stillness, both physical and audible. And in the shadow cast by the crook of her arm, her lips were smiling.

More footsteps on the stairs heralded the arrival of Anderson, closely followed by a paramedic first responder.

The team stepped back respectfully as their paramedic colleague knelt by Shona.

Heart shattered like the splintered glass beneath her feet, Cora turned into Minshull's open arms and buried her face against his chest.

It was so unjust, so unfair. Shona had dared to tell the truth, refusing to accept the wrongful conviction that could have stolen twenty-two years of her life. But for what?

What had all her bravery won her, in the end?

Minshull's arms surrounded her, his heartbeat insistent beneath his coat. Cora filled her mind with the sound, feeling its warmth and strength soothing her, pushing every other thought aside.

'There's a pulse.'

Startled, Cora pulled back, Minshull's arm remaining around one shoulder.

'It's there but it's very weak. We need an ambulance,' the paramedic ordered. 'Now!'

SIXTY-FIVE

ANDERSON

'My client would like to read a prepared statement,' the grave-faced solicitor said, as soon as the recording began.

'Go ahead, please,' Anderson agreed, wishing he'd trusted his damn instincts this time. That was another tenner he owed Evans. Would he never learn?

The solicitor fixed a pair of reading glasses on the bridge of his nose and began to read.

'*…Nine years ago, I was responsible for the death of my sister, Cassandra Lucy Norton, in Orwell Road, Felixstowe. It was not my intention to kill her. I had been asked by my friend and mentor, Jake Kilburn, to warn Cassandra about the increasingly dangerous demands she was making of him. He told me to scare her – and that if I succeeded, I would be rewarded.*

'*I met her on the way to meet friends in Bailey's wine bar, formerly of Hamilton Road. I walked with her for a while, and when we reached Trinity Methodist Church in Orwell Road we started rowing. Cass was getting hysterical, calling me all the names under the sun, saying she was going to demand Jake drop me from the HEIR programme – his fast-track programme for young people to progress within his companies. Furious with her, I shoved her away. But she lost her balance and fell, hitting her head on the edge of a concrete planter.*

'*I'll never forget the sound it made. Or the blood. The memory continues to haunt me. At first, I thought she was okay. But then I saw the blood at the back of her head. A taxi driver pulled up and asked me if Cass needed help. I panicked and ran.*

371

'Later, Joanna Kilburn told me that another of Jake's mentees on the HEIR programme had been nearby, wearing clothes that were really similar to mine. She said she thought this woman was having an affair with Jake and was out to extort money from him. She said if I helped her, she would make sure I won the top position in the HEIR programme. She said Jake would reward me for helping.

'So I said nothing when Shona Pickton was convicted of murdering Cass. I was promoted within one of Jake's companies immediately.

'But then Shona Pickton was acquitted, and Joanna Kilburn said Jake's empire would be threatened if Shona's ex-boyfriend, Karl Cuskie, was allowed to talk to police. He was once one of Jake's favourites but he fell out with him when Shona went to jail.

'Joanna said she thought Karl would try to frame Jake for Cassandra's death. She gave me Karl's address and a handgun. I was terrified, but I wanted to prove to Jake that I was the best choice to lead the HEIR programme. So I went to Karl's house and shot him...

'Excuse me,' the solicitor said, taking a long sip of water. 'Apologies. The rest of the statement reads: ...Jake Kilburn said nothing about me killing Karl Cuskie, but Joanna said he was very happy with what I'd done. But then she met me in Sea View Gardens in Felixstowe and told me she wanted Jake dead. She said she'd put up with his affairs over the years and had been forced to stay silent. And then she told me that Jake had been lying to me all along — that she was the power behind the business empire, doing it all while he took the credit and made us do all of those terrible things...'

Ryan Norton sat hunched beside his solicitor, refusing to make eye contact. The solicitor continued.

'...She told me I would become Jake's heir, inheriting his business empire, if I could prove that I cared more about the HEIR programme than anything else. She said it was time to kill my idol and take everything that was owed to me. Including her...'

Anderson could barely contain his surprise. Wheeler, seated beside him, paled and fixed his eyes on his notebook.

'...Three days ago, I shot and killed Jake Kilburn in the bath at his home. Joanna and I removed the body. Joanna arranged for it to be *sent to a private mortuary, paying them to hold fire on registering the death until the business could be legally made ours.*

'*I have provided my solicitor with details of the private mortuary, so that my testimony can be verified.*'

The solicitor handed a single sheet of paper to Anderson. Ryan stared resolutely at the half-empty plastic water cup on the table in front of him. His solicitor pressed on.

'*Joanna carried on operating as if Jake was still the head of the organisation. But yesterday, Joanna said that Shona had contacted her unexpectedly, saying she was going to talk to a detective from South Suffolk Police. She invited Joanna to come to the meeting, too. So Joanna arranged to give Shona a lift to Felixstowe, while I prepared the office to receive them.*

'*…Joanna abducted Shona and brought her to Hurren Associates. She wanted me to murder Shona like I murdered Karl and Jake. But I heard how Joanna spoke to Shona, like she was filth and worthless. She hated Shona because her family were from the gypsy and traveller community, and she hated them because Jake's father was a traveller, and had thrown him out as a kid. And when I had to pull the trigger, I couldn't do it. Joanna was yelling at me, calling me a piece of shit, saying I was no better than Jake had been. So I turned the gun on Joanna instead…*'

'I don't know whether to feel sorry for the boy, or glad he's been charged with murder,' Wheeler admitted later, when the team gathered in the CID office for a debrief.

'I don't get it, Guv,' Bennett said. 'Ryan murdered all those people just to win a competition?'

Anderson shook his head. 'It was more than that. Jake Kilburn groomed so many young people by promising them they'd become his legal heirs. He used that to demand whatever he wanted in return. Do whatever thing he asked, be rewarded with money, status, gifts and the ultimate prize: to become his son, with all the power and money that entailed.'

'What happens now?' Bennett asked.

'He's been charged with three counts of murder for Karl, Jake and Joanna, plus one of manslaughter for Cassandra Norton. He'll go into custody to await trial, with no provision for bail.' Minshull observed his team. 'Fantastic work, everybody. The Super has confirmed both investigations are now closed.'

'On that note…' DI Guthrie raised a hand.

Anderson smiled. 'Go ahead, Boyd.'

'On behalf of DI Tsang and I, we'd like to congratulate you on operating two excellent murder investigations. Everything we've observed here has been exemplary. I know certain factions of the media would like it to be believed that the detectives in this CID team are sub-par,' he gave a wry smile, 'but we've seen a fantastic, highly skilled and dedicated team, pulling together despite considerable challenges, and still managing to find humour in the midst of it all.'

'Although we maybe won't mention DC Evans' questionable gambling activities,' DI Tsang added, laughing when she saw Evans wiping imaginary sweat from his brow in relief. 'Joel, you should be very proud of your team.'

Anderson's chest swelled with deep pride as his team grinned back at him. 'I am, Joy. I think you're all incredible. But repeat that outside of this office and I'll deny every word.'

He waited until the celebrations were underway – a pizza delivery courtesy of Martlesham to express his thanks – before he sneaked away.

A thin layer of snow had settled across the car park during the afternoon's debrief. It sparkled now in the mid-afternoon sunshine. *Like magic*, he thought. It covered every imperfection, every rust spot. It softened the onlooker's gaze, allowing them to ignore what lay beneath.

A blank page turned. A fresh start.

Sue Taylor would not be returning to her post, no matter what the misconduct hearings found. She had tendered her resignation that morning, settling into early retirement with the twin blessings of a full pension and a clever escape.

It left an opening for a new DCI to take her place.

Interviews would start next week, with the aim of installing her successor within the month.

Standing at the top of the fire escape ramp, overlooking the snow-covered vehicles, Anderson pulled a white envelope from the inside pocket of his jacket. Held against the backdrop of white, it was almost invisible.

White swirls of his breath in the iced air drifted into the marshmallow white sky, as he turned the letter over in his hands.

Not the application for the DCI post that Ros had urged him to submit.

But a resignation.

Anderson was tired. The past few months had been brutal – he didn't know if he had another major investigation in him.

He'd been kicked from pillar to post by this force. Overlooked, overworked, blamed and sidelined, made to doubt everything he loved about the job. He'd served under two DCIs, neither of them worthy of even being in the same space as the uniform. Did he trust his superiors to get it right this time?

'You'll catch your death out here, you daft beggar.'

Wheeler was standing in the doorway, an extra scarf in one hand and a mug in the other.

'How long have you been standing there?'

'Long enough.'

'You shouldn't sneak up on old fellas like me. I could have had a coronary.'

'You're not that old. And I can't help it if I'm a ninja.'

Anderson gave a loud snort. 'A ninja is it, now?'

'Yeah. A bloody freezing one.' Wheeler chucked the scarf at Anderson, waiting for his colleague and best friend to wrap it around his neck, before handing him the steaming mug.

God Bless Dave Wheeler and his relentless friendship…

'Cheers, Dave.'

Wheeler joined Anderson at the top of the ramp, leaning against the handrail. 'So, you want to talk about it?'

'Nothing much to say.'

'Plenty to say, Joel, actually. *Bollocks*, for one.'

'Really, I'm fine.'

'You're talking to me, remember? Not Rob or one of the whippersnappers. They might buy your unflappable, Captain Aloof act, but it won't work on me.'

'I need a break, that's all.'

'Probably. But if you think that white envelope you just stuffed into your pocket is going to bring it, you're wrong.'

Anderson groaned. 'You didn't see that.'

'And you didn't submit it. Right?'

'I need to think about it.'

'So think. But don't go looking for escape routes, Joel, because you're meant to be here.'

The DC and the DI shared a long look.

Wheeler turned his face back to the freshly fallen snow. 'Now shut up and drink your coffee.'

'Coffee?' Anderson exclaimed. 'Is that what it is?'

'You can go off people, you know.'

Anderson grinned into his mug, glad of his friend's wisdom. Whether he'd listen to it, only time would tell.

SIXTY-SIX

CORA

Whoever said Christmas was just for kids had obviously never met a volunteer team at a festive crafts session.

Glitter covered the tables and floor as far as the eye could see, every available surface draped with tinsel, red and green foil, ribbons and cotton wool. Around the tables in The HappyKid Project classroom, children and adults from the St Columba Street site joined volunteers making tree decorations, pop-up cards, T-shirts disguised as gaudy Christmas jumpers and more, the room filled with laughter and activity and hope.

Cora cut another long length of red string and handed it to Trinity. 'There you go.'

'Cheers, Doc!' she beamed back. 'Do you have any gold? My ma loves it best.'

'Did someone say *gold*?' Tris boomed, arriving beside them. He carried a plastic stack box filled with sequins, ribbons and stick-on-gems, a ridiculously shiny gold foil crown balanced precariously on his head.

'Someone call the Nativity,' Cora laughed, 'one of their Three Kings is missing!'

'Hey, I make this look good,' Tris protested, throwing a length of gold ribbon at her.

You're just jealous – it said in his voice.

Cora accepted his favourite trick with a grin. 'Probably.'

'Do I have a bit of glitter in my beard?' Joss asked, striding into the classroom, eliciting cheers and raucous laughter from the children. His dark beard was drenched in green and pink glitter – a shock to see it sported by the usually serious project officer.

But it was a development Cora would be happy to live with.

In the three weeks since the events in Hamilton Road, The HappyKid Project had regained much ground. Sitting councillors, horrified by the actions of the Apocalypse Four, voted new policies into place protecting the right of the gypsy and traveller communities to access council services and be recognised as equal alongside house-dwelling South Suffolk residents. It was a start, rather than a result, but Joss, Tris, Cora and the HappyKid teams viewed it as a win.

It wouldn't stop the voices of dissent around the settled sites, but it would go a long way to make the communities feel accepted here.

'Looks amazing, Cora,' Joss remarked, brushing clouds of glitter from his very festive beard.

'Speak for yourself,' she smiled. 'How long did that take you?'

'I can't remember. But I reckon I'll be picking the stuff out of my beard for months to come.' He nudged his arm against hers. 'This is good, though. It's healing.'

'I hope so. How's Shona?'

Joss shrugged, dislodging another sparkling shower from his beard. 'That healing will take a bit longer, I reckon. I don't know if she'll stay. She's seen a job advertised up in Scotland – a hotel resort in the Highlands. There's accommodation too, if she gets it.'

'Wish her the best from me.'

'I will. I reckon seeing a bit more of the world might be what she needs.' He cast a glance at Cora before looking back at the festive crafts. 'I wanted to thank you, Doc, for what you did for her. For listening.'

'It was my pleasure. I hope she finds a way forward.'

Joss nodded. 'And thank your copper friend, too, would you? I'd thank him myself, but I reckon he's a bit busy at the moment.'

Cora looked across the busy craft tables to the story corner, where a tall, curly brown furred reindeer was sitting on a red velvet stool, reading Christmas books to a small group of rather puzzled children.

As apologies went, it was novel.

Minshull reached the end of his story and closed the book, an action met by pleas from his audience for an encore. Picking up another picture book from the large pile beside his brown furry feet, he looked over to Cora, the tinsel wrapped around his antlers dancing as he wiggled them at her.

He hadn't always understood why this project mattered. But it meant the world that he was here now.

'Doc! We need four more bits. Long ones this time!'

Returning to her string-distributing duties, Cora smiled.

A letter from MJ White

Dear Reader

Welcome to the fifth case for Dr Cora Lael, DS Rob Minshull and the CID team from South Suffolk Police!

This story is about injustice – who deals it, who is hurt by it and how it can be tackled. I wanted to write about someone who was failed, not just by the justice system, but also the increasingly polarised views of the media. But it's also about redemption and the power that change can make.

While I was writing *The Unspoken Truth*, I witnessed the sudden rise in accusatory, twisted news reports, pandering to prejudice to gain attention. The search for a missing woman became a vicious dissection of her character when her body was found in a river. Another woman and her daughter, murdered by her husband, was painted as selfish for accepting a job more senior to his – and that was offered as justification for his actions. And manufactured ire over displaced people arriving in small boats from France reached fever pitch, with immigrants being blamed for seemingly every ill in the country.

I wanted to write about the impact that such hate-filled, twisted narratives can have on individuals and communities – and how the opinion of a certain section of the media can negatively affect lives. I hope this story resonates with everyone who has felt sidelined, misjudged and unworthy. Everyone deserves the right to be heard, to be seen and to be believed.

Thank you for reading *The Unspoken Truth*! I would love to know what you think of it. You can find me on the links below.

Brightest wishes,

MJ White

LINKS:
Website: www.miranda-dickinson.com
Twitter: @wurdsmyth
Instagram: @wurdsmyth
Facebook: MirandaDickinsonAuthor
YouTube: youtube.com/mirandawurdy
Mastodon: @Wurdsmyth@mastodon.social
Threads: @wurdsmyth
Bluesky: @wurdsmyth.bsky.social

Acknowledgements

Firstly, I want to thank my wonderful readers for their continued support of Cora. Five books is beyond anything I'd dared imagine for her and your love, encouragement and enthusiasm for Cora, Minshull and the detectives of South Suffolk CID has made it possible.

Thanks to my wonderful editor, Keshini Naidoo, whose passion for this series has been a huge driving force. Thank you for your wisdom, your insight and your excellent manuscript comments! Thanks also to the team at Hera and Canelo – Thanhmai Bui-Van, Iain Millar, Jennie Ayres, Kate Shepherd, Lindsey Harrad and Vicki Vrint. And thanks to the brilliant designers at Head Design for creating the stunning book covers for the Cora Lael series.

As always, thanks to my agent, Hannah Ferguson, for her continued faith in my writing and for always being in my corner.

My sincere thanks to PC Steve Franklin for his expert advice and insight into police life. Any mistakes in police procedure are mine alone.

Gypsy, Roma and Traveller communities continue to face barriers, prejudice and injustice. **Friends, Families and Travellers** is a brilliant organisation fighting for a fair deal for Gypsy, Roma and Traveller people. Find out more about their vital work at **www.gypsy-traveller.org**

Thanks to fab author chums for supporting me and my Cora Lael series – Craig Hallam, A. G. Smith, Kim Curran, C. L. Taylor, Rob Parker, Neil Lancaster, Steve Cavanagh, Luca

Veste, Chris Callaghan, Adam Simcox, Mari Hannah, D. V. Bishop, Ian Wilfred and Mick Arnold.

Thanks to the amazing booksellers who have championed Cora on their shelves, especially William and Katy at Tea Leaves & Reads, Alex and team at Bert's Books and John, Mark and the team at Waterstones Wolverhampton. You're all superstars and the reason more readers are discovering Cora. I hope you know how much you're appreciated!

Huge love to my followers on social media, and the gorgeous community of viewers who watch my weekly Facebook Live show, Fab Night In Chatty Thing, for rooting for Cora and the South Suffolk CID team. I have so many more adventures for these characters and I can't wait to share them with you!

A special mention for Alan Gilles, whose name I have respectfully commandeered to star as Shona Pickton's KC in this story. Thank you to you and Sandra for your support of me and my books, and for being wonderful friends to Mum.

Love as ever to my fabulous family, especially my lovely Bob and gorgeous Flo. I love you to the moon and back and twice around the stars.

This book is about injustice and those who fight against hate. I hope you enjoy it.

Brightest wishes
MJ White

Book playlist

For every novel I write, I compile a soundtrack playlist that captures the emotion and atmosphere of the story I want to create. Here are the songs and pieces of music that inspired *The Unspoken Truth*. Happy listening!

MAIN THEME of *The Unspoken Truth*: SOLAS – Valtos – *Valtos*

THIS IS THE BEGINNING – Ely Eira – *This is the Beginning – Single*

ALL THAT REALLY MATTERS – ILLENIUM & Teddy Swims – *All That Really Matters*

TARANSAY – Elephant Sessions – *For the Night*

NÍU – SKÁLD – *Vikings Chant (Alfar Fagrahvél Edition)*

NOT HOLDING BACK – HAEVN – *Holy Ground – EP*

TINY RIOT – Sam Ryder – *The Sun's Gonna Rise*

EDGE OF MIDNIGHT (MIDNIGHT SKY REMIX) – Miley Cyrus feat. Stevie Nicks – *Plastic Hearts*

CHARLIE'S ON THE RUN – Valtos – *Valtos*

PLAY DEAD – Björk & David Arnold – *Greatest Hits*

CHASING THE SUN – Sara Bareilles – *The Blessed Unrest*